THE STONE CHAMBER

On a summer's evening, Robert and Greta Gerdner are shot dead at their isolated home in the Devon countryside. DI Wesley Peterson suspects the execution-style murders might be linked to Robert's past career in the police — until Robert's name is found on a list of people who've been sent tickets anonymously for a tour of Darkhole Grange, a former asylum on Dartmoor.

When his friend, archaeologist Neil Watson, finds the skeleton of a woman buried in a sealed chamber dating back to the 15th century at his nearby dig, Wesley wonders whether there might be a connection between the mysterious stone cell and the tragic events at Darkhole Grange. With the clock ticking, Wesley must solve the puzzle before the next person on the list meets a terrible end . . .

SPECIA

THE ULV
(registere
was established
diagnosis and t
major projects

- The Child
Hospital, Lo
- The Ulvers
Ormond Str
- Funding r
treatment at
Ophthalmolo
- The Ulver
Institute of C
- Twin opera
Ophthalmic
- The Chair
Australian C

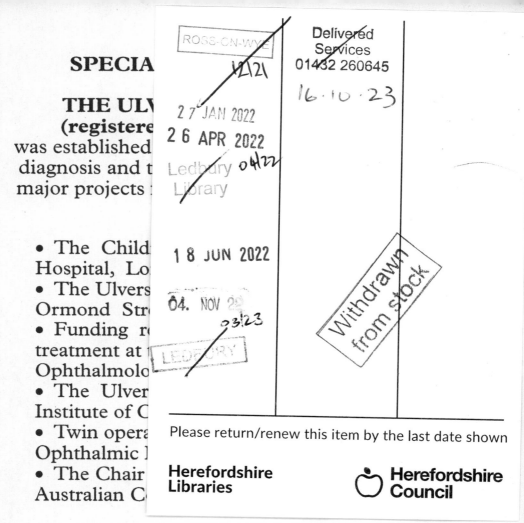

You can help further the work of the Foundation
by making a donation or leaving a legacy. Every
contribution is gratefully received. If you would like
to help support the Foundation or require further
information, please contact:

THE ULVERSCROFT FOUNDATION
The Green, Bradgate Road, Anstey
Leicester LE7 7FU, England
Tel: (0116) 236 4325

website: www.ulverscroft-foundation.org.uk

KATE ELLIS

◆

THE STONE CHAMBER

Complete and Unabridged

CHARNWOOD
Leicester

First published in Great Britain in 2021 by
Piatkus
An imprint of
Little, Brown Book Group
London

First Charnwood Edition
published 2021
by arrangement with
Little, Brown Book Group
An Hachette UK Company
London

A catalogue record for this book is available
from the British Library.

ISBN 978–1–4448–4767–3

Published by
Ulverscroft Limited
Anstey, Leicestershire

Printed and bound in Great Britain by
TJ Books Ltd., Padstow, Cornwall

This book is printed on acid-free paper

For Orla Grace,
welcome to the family.

1

The Pharaoh's Tomb needed tidying. The hen party had had far too much to drink before they'd even set foot in the place, and they'd left it in a terrible state.

Charlie Maddox keyed in the code and pushed the door open. As it swung shut behind him, he heard the lock engage. He would be trapped in there until he entered the override code, which he knew off by heart.

He pressed the switch concealed behind the painted panel in the wall, and the hidden lighting flickered on, casting shadows on walls decorated with hieroglyphics and images of animal-headed gods. The statues stationed in each corner stood tall as a man, the painted eyes of the jackal heads focused on the massive sarcophagus in the centre of the room. The stone finish looked convincing, but the lid was made of fibreglass, light as air and easy for the punters to shift to get at the clues hidden inside. The lid was lying askew, revealing the mummy, its bandages half unwrapped and draped over the side of the tomb like the entrails of some long-dead creature. The hen party had really gone for it.

The models arranged around the room had been lovingly copied by an artist friend from examples in the British Museum. But now they lay scattered, and there was an empty Prosecco bottle balanced on a replica boat as though it was about to be ferried down the Nile by the wooden oarsmen.

Charlie secretly enjoyed this time on his own at the

end of the day, when he'd sent the others home and he could gather his thoughts, taking his time before the homeward journey. And since his visit to Darkhole Grange, he'd had a lot to think about. The memory of what he'd seen there made him uncomfortable. But was he really responsible for the sins of his forefathers?

He pushed the thought from his mind and made a start. Another group was booked in the following morning, so the clues had to be laid again. His head throbbed as he went round dropping the litter into a bin bag, silently cursing the giggling hens who'd wreaked so much havoc. Stag and hen parties, he'd found, were always the worst.

As he lifted the mummy from the sarcophagus and began rewrapping the grey bandages around its plastic torso, the thing slipped from his grasp and he clutched the side of the tomb. His head was swimming and he was hit by a wave of nausea, and as the strength left his body, he slumped to the floor, struggling for breath. This wasn't right. He must have eaten something that disagreed with him. That pasty he'd had at lunchtime perhaps.

He fumbled for the phone in the back pocket of his jeans before remembering that there was no signal in the Tomb. He needed to get out, but the room around him was turning black. He was vaguely aware of vomiting as he crawled towards the door. At least he thought it was the door.

The paintings and cartouches swam in and out of focus until he collapsed at the fibreglass feet of Anubis, the god of the dead. The last thing Charlie Maddox saw was the god's dog face smiling at yet another triumph.

2

2

A week later

The doorbell rang. A cheerful bing-bong.

'Expecting anyone?'

Greta Gerdner had been engrossed in a wildlife programme on the small TV next to the wood-burning stove. She looked at her husband and rolled her eyes, irritated at the interruption. It was a stupid question. They rarely communicated with anyone in the immediate area. Why would they? They'd moved into Hawthorn Barn less than a year ago and had made no attempt to get to know anyone who lived nearby. Not that they had many neighbours, because they were a mile from the nearest village and as isolated as you could get. That had been the appeal after the milling crowds of London. Peace and quiet in the Devon countryside. Away from noise. Away from the constant threat of the kind of crime Robert had dealt with all his working life. They'd kept a pied-à-terre in the capital, of course, somewhere to stay when they went up to visit the galleries and theatres Greta loved so much.

Robert Gerdner grabbed the remote and lowered the volume on the TV before rising slowly from his seat, holding onto the arm of the chair. Greta thought he'd gained a new zest for life since his retirement from the Metropolitan Police, probably because of his new project.

She'd allowed him to hang onto one fragment of

3

his old life, although she refused to have any reminder of it in the house, insisting that he rent an office so it wouldn't taint her new existence. Before Greta's own retirement she'd held a responsible and well paid post in the Civil Service, earning considerably more than her husband. But that old life was behind her now and she was determined that these were going to be her golden years.

In spite of Robert's little business, the thing she knew he'd always dreamed of undertaking, she insisted that they were there to enjoy the best the stunning Devon countryside had to offer. But so far the dream hadn't worked out quite as she'd imagined. The neighbouring farmer's vehicles always churned up mud in the lane. Then there was the noise of the animals. And the terrible smells that drifted their way if the wind was in a certain direction. Things would have to change. She would insist on it.

'It might be that farmer,' Robert said, glancing at Greta nervously. 'You were very abrupt with him yesterday.'

'Well you'd better go and see. And if it is him, make sure you don't stand for any nonsense.' She pressed her lips together in annoyance. When she'd planned her retirement down to the last detail, she'd forgotten to take into consideration the hell that was other people.

She heard Robert opening the door, followed by the sound of muffled voices. Then a shout, 'What the hell — ' suddenly cut off by a sharp explosion, like the crack of a whip, followed by a whimper; the desperate, puzzled sound of a wounded animal. She didn't trust the locals, but she'd never expected them to turn violent. She stood up, ready to confront the visitor

4

and put him or her in their place.

She marched into the entrance hall, adrenaline coursing through her body, ready for a fight. But the sight that greeted her made her freeze.

Robert was lying on the flagstone floor with an expression of mild surprise in his staring eyes and a neat black hole in his forehead.

Her limbs paralysed by shock, she was unable to move from the spot as the dark, hooded figure in the open doorway began to glide slowly and silently towards her. She could see something in its black-gloved hand. Something the shape of a gun. And it was pointing straight at her.

3

Detective Inspector Wesley Peterson snatched a surreptitious glance at his watch, wondering if he should have postponed meeting his old university friend for a lunchtime drink in the Tradmouth Arms — soda water in his case, because he was still on duty. But it was May, the start of the tourist season, so things were likely to become a lot busier in the foreseeable future as the local villains emerged from their winter hibernation in the hope of rich pickings from the newly occupied holiday cottages.

'Drones,' said Neil Watson. He took a bite from his tuna sandwich, and a thin slice of escaped cucumber tumbled down onto the plate. 'They're wonderful things, you know. A few years ago we would have had the expense of getting hold of a light aircraft and a photographer. We've had a lidar survey of the area too.'

'That's progress for you.'

Neil leaned forward, his eyes glowing with untold news. With his ancient combat jacket and long fair hair, thinning a little now, his sartorial style hadn't altered since he and Wesley had studied archaeology together at Exeter University. Wesley, in contrast, was black, good-looking, and neatly dressed in a jacket and open-necked shirt. Neil often teased him for looking like a chartered accountant.

'I've been interested in the site since last summer's drought revealed crop marks. We knew right away we'd found the lost village of Long Bartonford, because of old records and an entry in Domesday Book. The uni's using the site as a training dig and we're planning to get the community involved too at some point. It's a big site, so we'll be there for a few seasons. You'll have to pay us a visit.'

'Certainly . . . if I've got time.' Wesley might not have pursued a career in archaeology as Neil had, but he still maintained a keen interest in the subject that had enthralled him for three happy student years. He checked his watch again, knowing he needed to return to the station in twenty minutes.

'Make time. It's not often you find a deserted medieval village clustered around the ruins of a church dating back to the twelfth century. Annabel's looking for material in the archives. Am I tempting you, Wes?' Neil's grin widened.

'Yes, but it's a temptation I'll have to resist for the moment.'

'We've got a couple of your old customers helping out.'

'What old customers?'

'A couple of ex-offenders from a hostel in Morbay. It's part of an initiative. The powers-that-be think a spot of archaeology is going to keep them on the straight and narrow.'

'What powers-that-be are these?' Wesley asked, curious.

'It was all arranged by a charity for ex-prisoners — I spoke to a woman with purple hair who goes by the name of Pixie.' Wesley raised his eyebrows. 'Hopefully it'll stop them troubling us for a while. How are they getting on?'

'They keep their heads down and don't say much. To give them their due, so far they've been doing what's asked of them — when they haven't been taking cigarette breaks,' Neil added with a knowing look. 'Someone picks them up in a van at the end of the working day, so they don't get a chance to socialise in the pub. We're told not to ask them what they were inside for. Hope it was nothing violent.'

'They wouldn't have released them if they posed a danger to the public — or at least that's the theory.' Wesley took a sip of his soda water, wishing it was the best bitter advertised on the pump clips ranged along the bar. 'Who knows, the dig might give them a whole new purpose in life.'

'Let's hope so,' Neil said as though the subject was closed. Wesley guessed his mind was more on his dig than the principle of rehabilitation. 'There's not much information about the site at the moment apart from some old maps and a few mentions of the manor house nearby. I contacted an antiquarian bookseller who wrote a local history booklet about Long Bartonford a while ago, and he promised to dig out his notes for me. I'll pay him a visit when I find a moment.' Neil took a leisurely sip of shandy. 'Hey, I never told you about Chris's stag do the Saturday before last, did I?' he said as he put his glass down.

The sudden change of subject took Wesley by surprise. He'd met Neil's fellow archaeologist a couple of times; an earnest young man who hid his prematurely balding pate beneath an Indiana Jones hat, trying to look the part.

'You mentioned you were going. How was it?' Wesley took out his phone and scrolled through the messages, hoping nothing urgent had come in while he'd been away from the station.

'It was cancelled. Someone died.'

8

'Not one of your team?'

'Fortunately not.'

'What happened?'

'We were booked into an escape room in Morbay. Escape from the Pharaoh's Tomb, which seemed appropriate as most of us are archaeologists. We thought it'd be a bit of fun before we went off for a few drinks, but as it turned out, the Tomb was occupied by a fresh dead body rather than a mummified pharaoh. Not that we ever set foot inside the place. As soon as we got there, they told us the whole thing was off.'

'Who was it who died?' Wesley asked. The incident hadn't come to the attention of Tradmouth CID; it was something he would have remembered. Which meant the death must have been natural or accidental, probably dealt with by uniform or Morbay's local station.

'It was the guy who owned the place — name of Charlie Maddox. Someone said he was checking the escape room at the end of the day when he collapsed. Most likely a heart attack or something. He was locked in there alone and wasn't found until the next morning. It put a bit of a dampener on the stag do, I can tell you. We'd been looking forward to the Pharaoh's Tomb and nobody felt much like going on the pub crawl we'd planned for afterwards.'

'I bet.'

Wesley's phone began to ring and Neil slumped back in his seat, resigned to the interruption. Police business came first.

After a brief conversation, Wesley killed the call. 'Got to go, I'm afraid.'

'What's up?'

'Couple of suspicious deaths near Chabliton. Gerry's already set off. I'd better join him.'

Neil finished his sandwich and drained what remained of his pint of shandy. He was driving too. 'I'm going that way. Want a lift? I'd better get back to the dig — check how it's going.'

'If you could drop me off, it'll save me going back to the station to pick up the car. Thanks.'

As they walked out of the Tradmouth Arms, Wesley fell silent, thinking of the call he'd just received. A double shooting — and it looked like murder.

21 August 1956

They've shut me in and I'm bored. I want to get out to the village and see human faces. My family are human — sort of — but they don't count.

We live in the manor house, which means my father's the lord of the manor. That's still an important thing in Chabliton, even though things have changed a lot since the war. The most interesting thing about our house is the old legend about a girl being walled up somewhere for sleeping with her brother. My parents say the story's rubbish, but I wonder if it might be true. If it is, she was even worse than me. I used to tell them at school that I lived in a haunted house, and some people believed it. I enjoyed the looks on their faces. Priceless.

People in the village hang on Father's every word and nod to him respectfully in church on Sunday, but the truth is, my mother controls everything he says and does. She's in charge and she's the one who really cares what the world thinks. And she knows the world doesn't think much of me. The names she calls me make me smile: little whore; trollop; a disgrace to the family name. But I don't care what anyone thinks, because I know everything will be all right in the end.

Then there's my mealy-mouthed sister. The golden girl; the Oxford undergraduate. My mother thinks she's still a virgin, and she might be for all I know. Ursula never does anything wrong. Ursula's a saint. Wasn't St Ursula a virgin martyr? But my name means 'lost'.

I'm not allowed to go into the village any more, but I still have the freedom of the house for the moment. Mother says she'll lock me in my room when I begin to show, because she wouldn't want the housekeeper and the cleaners to find out. She says it's for my own good, because gossip spreads like a disease around here.

So while I have this small slice of freedom, I'll do my best to keep my mind occupied. There's a room off the kitchen corridor that is always kept locked, and I've often wondered what was in there. I think I'll try and find the key. When you're a prisoner, the smallest things can be diverting.

4

DCI Gerry Heffernan was waiting for Wesley beside the wooden garden gate. He was a big man, carrying too much weight according to the posters on display in most doctors' surgeries. His excuse, pronounced with relish in the Liverpool accent he'd never lost in spite of living in Devon for over twenty years, was that he was 'a growing lad'. As soon as he saw Wesley emerging from Neil's car, a cheerful smile lit up his face.

'Wes. What kept you?'

'Sorry,' Wesley said, offering no explanation. A lunchtime drink with an old friend was no excuse for lateness, and he felt a nag of guilt that he'd been so readily distracted from his duty. His strict but loving upbringing by parents from the Caribbean had endowed him with a strong sense of right and wrong — something his wife, Pam, brought up by a feckless New Age mother, found quaint and faintly amusing.

'What have we got?' he asked, trying to focus on the new case.

'Two bodies. Man and woman in their late fifties. Both shot in the head.' Gerry looked round. The pristine barn conversion stood beside a copse of trees, well away from the road and accessible only by a narrow track. 'Nearest house is a farm a quarter of a mile away. We need to speak to whoever lives there.'

'Who found them?'

'Postman noticed the front door ajar, so he pushed

13

it open and saw the man's body lying in the hall. He's been interviewed and sent on his way. Poor man was in shock, so I don't think the old theory that whoever finds the body is the killer applies in this case.'

'Do we have an ID for the victims?'

'According to the postman and the electoral register, they were a Mr and Mrs Gerdner — Greta and Robert. Moved here last year.'

Wesley sighed. 'I suppose we'd better have a look.'

'Colin Bowman should be here any minute to give his verdict, but from what I've heard from the CSIs, the cause of death is pretty obvious. Shot in the head at close range. Neat job.'

Wesley took a deep breath. His parents had come to London from their native Trinidad in the 1970s to attend medical school; once qualified, they'd stayed in their adopted country and carved out successful careers. His sister too was a GP, so, being squeamish by nature, he'd always felt like the odd one out in his high-flying family. During his archaeological training, all the dead bodies he'd encountered had been reduced to dry bones, but unfortunately this hadn't always been the case over his police career.

After reporting to the plump uniformed crime-scene manager and donning the white paper overalls Gerry always referred to as 'snowman suits', they made for the front door, solid oak with frosted glass panels either side.

It stood open, and Wesley could see the CSIs milling about inside, working in silence as they recorded the scene with cameras, dusted for fingerprints and took samples.

He heard a cheerful greeting, and when he turned his head, he saw Dr Colin Bowman, the pathologist, approaching down the garden path with a genial smile on his face. After exchanging the customary pleasantries, he let Colin enter the house first, and watched the doctor's expression switch from amiable to deadly serious.

Wesley and Gerry stood together in the doorway as Colin squatted down next to the body on the floor. The dead man's eyes were wide open and his expression was one of astonishment. Wesley could see a neat hole in the forehead, and blood and brain from the wound left by the bullet's exit stained the flagstones beneath the head.

'Someone mentioned there were two,' he said to a CSI who was doing something mysterious with tape on a nearby door frame.

'Through there,' the young woman said, nodding towards an open door to Wesley's right.

Wesley caught Gerry's eye. 'Better see what we've got.'

The two men gave the man's body a wide berth, keeping to the stepping plates placed on the floor to protect any evidence the perpetrator might have left behind on the stone flags. Beyond the door was a large living room with exposed pine ceiling rafters, a remnant of its days as a working farm building. The room was tastefully decorated, with two large white leather sofas arranged around a wood-burning stove at the far end of the room. The floor was stone-flagged like the hallway, and a gallery ran around the top of it, accessed by a wide wooden staircase at one side. Wesley could see doors at the far end of the gallery, presumably leading to the bedrooms. It was a desirable residence; the sort of place Pam dreamed of owning — if their salaries as a police officer and a teacher could ever stretch that far.

The second body lay in a far corner, half concealed by a sofa and the living bodies of the CSIs working around it. A portable TV chattered away next to the stove. Nobody had bothered to switch it off.

When Wesley edged closer to get a better view, glad of Gerry's comforting presence close behind, he saw that the second victim was a woman, tall in life with well-cut steel-grey hair. She was wearing trousers and a Breton top, and again there was a neat hole in the centre of her forehead. The attack on both these people had been clinical, almost professional. And Wesley couldn't help wondering what had led up to it.

'A burglar high on drugs? Someone they'd annoyed who lost control?' Gerry mumbled as though he was thinking aloud.

'Any sign of a break-in?' Wesley asked the CSIs.

'Nothing obvious,' was the reply from a young man who was busy taking samples from the nearby sofa. 'The killer didn't force entry, so they must have let him in. Probably someone they knew,' he added with satisfaction.

'Any valuables missing?'

'Her purse is still in the bedroom full of cash and credit cards.'

'Not a burglary gone wrong then,' Gerry muttered as they picked their way back over the stepping plates to the hallway, where Colin was still conducting his examination of the man's body.

'What can you tell us, Colin?'

'Shot at close range. No other injuries that I can see. At a guess he answered the door and his attacker shot him right away. Took him by surprise. I understand there's another one.'

16

'A woman in the living room,' said Gerry. 'Probably shot once her husband was dead or dying. Can you give us a time of death?'

Colin wagged his finger. 'You should know better than to ask that. Have all my years of training you been in vain?' he added with a grin.

'A rough estimate?' Wesley tried.

'Some time over the weekend. Possibly Saturday afternoon or evening. But that's just a guess. I'll do the post-mortem in Tradmouth at nine thirty tomorrow if that suits you, gentlemen.'

'Looking forward to it,' said Gerry with inappropriate enthusiasm. 'But anything you're able to tell us now will be useful.'

Colin thought for a few moments, staring down at the body as though he was willing it to give up its secrets. 'There seems to be something . . .' he searched for the right word, 'controlled about this, don't you think? Looks almost like an assassination.'

Wesley nodded. Colin was right. There appeared to be a cold-blooded calculation behind the double killing.

'We need to nail this bastard before he decides to kill again,' said Gerry as they walked slowly back to the car.

'Do you think that's likely?'

'Don't you?'

'I'm not sure,' said Wesley. 'This smells personal to me. Whoever did it wanted these particular people wiped from the face of the earth.'

'We need to speak to the neighbours,' said Gerry. 'I saw a farm sign on the lane we came up. Farmers are out and about at all sorts of weird times when the rest of us are tucked up in our beds, so someone

17

might have seen something or heard shots. Shall we pay them a call?'

Wesley looked at his watch. 'I'd like to ask Rachel to come with me. She might get more out of them — one farmer to another.'

'Good thinking, Wes.' Gerry looked round, frowning. 'I'll get a patrol car to take me back while you wait here for Rach.'

As Wesley watched the patrol car drive off with Gerry in the passenger seat, he took his phone from his pocket to call DS Rachel Tracey. He felt a little nervous. Rachel had been unusually quiet in recent months — ever since she'd discovered she was pregnant with her first child. She and Wesley had been so close at one time, but now he sensed that an invisible barrier had developed between them. Although it was possible he was imagining things.

He waited for her outside, making conversation with the crime-scene manager, who seemed to assume the murders were drugs-related. Rival gangs, he reckoned. Wesley said nothing. He was keeping an open mind.

5

As Rachel drove down the narrow, high-hedged lane, Wesley spotted a swinging sign beside the metal gate boasting of Lower Kington Farm's prize-winning herd of Friesians. The evidence of their presence was all around, and he suddenly regretted not bringing his own car, because he kept a pair of wellingtons in the boot — something he'd learned to do when he'd first transferred from London to rural Devon. It had only taken one pair of ruined shoes to teach him that particular lesson.

Rachel, however, daughter to one local farmer and now wife to another, had come fully prepared, and she waited impatiently for Wesley to pick his way gingerly across the farmyard, avoiding the cowpats and muddy puddles. As soon as he'd caught up with her, she raised the door knocker and let it fall three times, setting the dogs barking inside the farmhouse. Then she waited, resting her hand on her swelling abdomen, avoiding Wesley's eyes.

The door was opened by a woman in her mid to late thirties, around Rachel's own age, with tousled ginger hair and freckles. She wore jeans, a baggy blue T-shirt and a harassed look on her round face. Her expression changed to a worried frown when Wesley and Rachel introduced themselves and showed their ID.

'What is it? What's wrong?'

Wesley broke the news that there had been an incident at Hawthorn Barn, down the lane. He didn't elaborate on the bare statement and asked if they could come in and have a word.

The woman, who introduced herself as Claire Fulford, looked uneasy as she led the way into a large, shabby living room where a toddler was playing with a set of plastic bricks, engrossed by the colourful tower he'd created. When Rachel said she was sure they'd met before, at a farmers' social, Claire relaxed a little, and once Rachel's credentials as part of the local farming community had been established, she offered tea and home-made flapjacks. Because of this rapport, Wesley decided to leave the talking to Rachel, who swiftly discovered that Claire lived there with her husband, Andy, who had recently taken over the farm from his parents. Claire's in-laws now lived in the newly converted stables on the other side of the farmyard, and her two elder children were out at an after-school club. Wesley saw Rachel's eyes straying to the toddler, and he wondered whether she was thinking of her own impending motherhood.

'So what's happened at Hawthorn Barn?' Claire asked. She sounded anxious.

Wesley joined the conversation. 'How well do you know the people who live there?'

Claire glanced at her son, who'd just demolished his tower. 'We don't know them at all really,' she answered quickly.

'They're your nearest neighbours.'

'The barn's on the edge of our land, but it hadn't been used for years, so Andy's dad decided to do what a lot of farmers round here do and convert it and sell it.' She gave Rachel a meaningful look. 'You've got to get extra income where you can in our business, as you'll know.'

20

'Very true,' Rachel said sympathetically. 'Some of my parents' outbuildings have been made into holiday lets.' She paused. 'You must know something about the people in Hawthorn Barn. Where they came from, for instance?'

'They're from London.' The last words were loaded with meaning. 'And they don't think much of our country ways. Always moaning to Andy about the smells and the mud on the lane.' Claire rolled her eyes and Rachel gave an understanding nod.

Claire suddenly frowned. 'Has something happened to them?'

'There have been two fatalities at Hawthorn Barn. We're treating them as suspicious.'

A look of horror appeared on her face. A shock that surely couldn't have been feigned.

'What else do you know about the people who live there?' Rachel asked.

It took Claire a few moments to compose herself. 'Not much. I only know that their name's Gerdner and they decided to retire here.'

'But you have spoken to them?'

'A couple of times.'

From the look of embarrassment on Claire's face, Wesley guessed that her encounters with the Gerdners hadn't been pleasant neighbourly chats. He caught Rachel's eye and they waited for Claire to continue. There was a long, awkward silence, but eventually their patience was rewarded.

'To tell the truth, they've been an absolute nightmare since they moved in. Especially her. She had our phone number and she started calling us at all hours, moaning about something or other. First it was the state of the lane. We're mainly dairy, but we have

21

some crops, and when Andy started muck-spreading it didn't go down well. They complained about the mud the vehicles left behind, and the smell. We have to move the cows from the fields on the opposite side of the lane to the milking parlour twice a day. A couple of times that held the Gerdners up for ten minutes when they were coming home in their Range Rover Discovery, and she was furious. It was one thing after another. The cockerel crowing early in the morning. The noise of the farm vehicles. Even the cows mooing.'

Wesley could sense Rachel's irritation. He'd been brought up in the city himself, but he hoped that when he'd first moved to Devon, he'd had more empathy with the rural way of life than the Gerdners had shown. And working closely with Rachel for a few years had taught him a lot; if he'd made any faux pas, she would have been sure to put him right.

'When did you last see them?' Rachel asked.

'Robert Gerdner turned up here on Friday afternoon, throwing his weight around, saying he used to be a policeman and we were causing a public nuisance . . . ' She hesitated. 'Well, things got heated. This is a working farm, but they seemed to think that the countryside is some sort of theme park. They didn't understand.'

'We'll need to speak to your husband.'

A wary look appeared in Claire's eyes. 'He's out visiting one of our feed suppliers in Newton Abbot.'

'Can you tell him we want a word as soon as he gets back?'

She nodded.

Wesley cleared his throat. 'Where were you both on Saturday?'

'Where we always are. Here. And before you ask, we didn't go out. I tell a lie: Andy went over to see his parents for half an hour at around seven. Then he came back and we had an early night as usual. You don't stay up beyond nine when you have to be up for the morning milking.' She looked at Rachel, who nodded in support.

'Did you see or hear anything out of the ordinary over the weekend?' Wesley asked. 'Did you hear any shots, for instance?'

Claire's eyes widened. 'Not that I remember. But we wouldn't necessarily have noticed. A lot of people have shotguns around here and go out after rabbits or whatever. You tend to ignore the sound of shots if you're used to it.'

Rachel nodded again. She understood. But the Gerdners hadn't been killed with a shotgun, that much was certain.

'Is that what happened? Were they shot?'

Wesley didn't answer the question. 'Does anyone else live nearby — apart from your parents-in-law?'

'No. We're pretty isolated here. The nearest village is Chabliton, and that's a mile away. Sorry, that's all I'm able to tell you.'

She turned her attention to her son, who was about to throw a brick in Rachel's direction. She took it from him gently and tried to distract him by building another tower. 'You'll have this soon,' she said, looking Rachel in the eye. 'When's yours due?'

'I've got just over three months to go.'

'First?'

'Yes.'

'Do you know what it is yet?'

Rachel shook her head. 'I want it to be a surprise.'

'It always comes as a surprise — the sleepless nights and all the other delights of motherhood. Wouldn't swap it, though.'

Wesley saw a sceptical look pass across Rachel's face, swiftly hidden. She'd hardly mentioned her coming baby since she'd announced the news, as though it was something she was trying to forget. When Pam had been pregnant with Michael and Amelia, it was something she'd lived and breathed with excited anticipation. But instead of continuing the baby talk, Rachel stood up. 'Thanks, Claire. We'll have a quick word with your in-laws. And if you can tell Andy we'd like to speak to him . . .'

Claire scooped her son up in her arms and carried him to the front door, where she pointed out the converted stable block across the cobbled farmyard.

'I think she's hiding something,' Wesley whispered to Rachel once Claire had shut the front door.

'Why?'

'Just a feeling,' he replied as they headed for the stable block's tasteful heritage-green front door. There was little evidence now of its former function. Instead it had gleaming windows and neat pots of colourful bedding plants lined up against the front wall. When he saw a curtain twitch at one of the windows, he suspected that Claire had telephoned to warn of their visit.

'I need to call the Met,' he said, taking his phone from his pocket.

'That's fine. My parents know the Fulfords, so . . .'

She didn't have to go on. With Rachel's family connection, he knew that the older generation of Fulfords were more likely to be open with her if he wasn't there. She was part of their world, something he never could be. He left her to it and returned to the car to make his call, hoping it wouldn't be long before he had an answer to his query.

As Rachel was leaving the Fulfords' home, his phone rang. It was the news he'd been waiting for. Robert Gerdner had indeed been a police officer in the Met, reaching the rank of sergeant.

6

Keep calm. Don't panic. Take deep breaths. Try again.

Arthur Penhalligan's palms were moist with sweat as he tried to grasp the tarnished brass doorknob of his tiny stockroom. When his fingers slid off the metal once more, he wiped them on the worn corduroy trousers he always wore to work. Another try might do the trick.

Still no luck. His fingers failed to get a grip on the slippery surface and he could feel his heart beating against his ribs like the wings of a trapped bird as a wave of heat engulfed him. He'd left his mobile beside the till in the shop, so there was no way of getting help. A stupid thing to do. He should have kept it in his pocket, but when he'd last used it, he'd put it on the counter without thinking.

Keep calm. There was a way out of this. Mouth dry, he ran his tongue around his lips. They felt dry. Cracked. Why hadn't he had that catch seen to? Why had he gone into the stockroom and shut the door? He looked around in despair and saw a sliver of light creeping in from the tiny window near the ceiling. No means of escape there. He began to breathe faster, shallow breaths, panting for the air that seemed to be vanishing from the enclosed space.

His bladder felt uncomfortably full, but there was no way he was going to relieve himself near the precious books crowding in around him; some rare, some very old. They were his babies, and harming any of them was out of the question.

He felt cold now, and near to tears. He heard someone calling for help, and it took him a few seconds to realise that the voice was his own, echoing around the cramped room stacked high with books. But even if a customer were to come into the shop — a rare occurrence — he was unlikely to be heard. And with the shop door unlocked, anyone could walk in and help themselves to the money he'd taken in the till that day — such as it was.

He closed his eyes tightly. Focus on something else. Picture a tranquil scene; somewhere you feel relaxed and happy. That was what Rosemary had taught him to do, and she was an expert in treating irrational fears. For a brief moment, her wise words drowned out his rising panic, until thoughts of Elena de Judhael began to flood into his aching head, his mind conjuring the noise of stones being mortared into place, trapping Elena in that tiny chamber, while the people on the other side of the wall, the side of freedom, chanted their prayers. Prayers for the living dead.

The stockroom was eight feet square. A prison cell. As he struggled for breath, he summoned the strength to wipe the sweat off his palms again, opening his eyes as he grasped the smooth handle once more. If he failed this time, he knew he'd die.

7

When Neil checked the time, he found it was four o'clock already, which left him an hour to get from the dig to Neston before the bookshop shut.

As he carried the plastic trays containing that afternoon's finds to the wooden garden shed they'd erected to serve as the site hut, his thoughts strayed to Wesley's double murder. The fact that he had dropped Wesley off near the scene made him feel that he had a special interest in the investigation, even though officially it was none of his business. His job was to solve puzzles from the past. Dealing with present day mysteries was Wesley's chosen path, not his.

So far his team had only tackled one section of the extensive Long Bartonford site, but even so, they'd already found a good haul of medieval pottery and the bone handle of a knife that had long since rusted away in the soil. They'd also found stone — lots of it — including the foundations of two longhouses, with accommodation for a family at one end and their livestock at the other. The geophysics results suggested that Long Bartonford had once been a thriving community, and the excavation would last all season. Because of this, a Portaloo had been brought in, which in the archaeological world counted as every modern convenience.

Neil planned to sink some trenches nearer to the church the following day, but his main worry was the human remains they were bound to find in the overgrown churchyard. The church itself had been

28

abandoned in the sixteenth century, when a new one had been built in the nearby thriving village of Chabliton, and had fallen into picturesque ruin, standing alone in a field full of intriguing lumps and bumps — the only evidence of the old settlement still visible above the ground.

When the inevitable skeletons were uncovered in the old churchyard, he'd need to inform the police and the coroner, which always caused delays. He was trying not to think about the problem as he kicked the shed door open with his foot, balancing the finds tray carefully in his arms. The unexpected sound of a man's voice behind him almost made him drop his precious burden. He turned his head and saw Nathan Hardy standing there.

Nathan was in his twenties, short and wiry, with a tattooed snake slithering across his shaved head. It seemed to be winking, and Neil found it hard not to stare. Nathan's eyes were the palest blue he had ever seen, the pupils almost invisible, which gave him the sinister look of a Bond villain.

'Dave said to tell you he's making a start on trench three like you said,' he muttered without looking Neil in the eye.

'Great. Thanks, Nathan.' Neil could tell Nathan would rather be somewhere else, but as long as he didn't make trouble, he'd do his best to keep him busy — and, if possible, interested. 'I expect you'll be off soon.'

As soon as he'd asked the question, he knew it was a silly one. The hostel van was due to come for Nathan and his mate Tel any moment.

'Someone said you're starting on the churchyard tomorrow. Said there might be skeletons. Can I help?'

This was the first glimmer of enthusiasm Nathan had shown in the month since the dig had begun, but his question sounded warning bells, even though Neil told himself he was reading too much into it — or worse still, showing prejudice. 'I'll think about it,' he said. 'Although it might need someone with more experience.'

Nathan looked disappointed, and Neil was relieved to see the van drawing up at the edge of the site — not a prison van as such, but a plain navy blue Transit used by the Morbay hostel where the two ex-offenders had been staying since their release.

After Nathan and Tel had driven off, Neil left the team to carry on and headed for his car. He wanted to see whether Arthur Penhalligan had anything for him. The man's shop was crammed with esoteric treasures: musty manuscripts, rare histories and ancient volumes on Devon folklore. Penhalligan's particular enthusiasm was local history, and he'd written a booklet about historical Chabliton that featured a section on the lost village of Long Bartonford. He'd indicated that he was happy to share his research if Neil returned when his shop was less busy. It hadn't seemed busy at the time, but Neil hadn't argued.

Annabel, Neil's contact at the Exeter archives, had been searching for material about the village, but so far she hadn't found much. The medieval court rolls recording the crimes and misdemeanours of the inhabitants around that time appeared to be missing, but she'd promised to keep looking. Things dating back that far, she'd explained, were often filed away in the wrong place.

When Neil reached Neston, he parked behind the council offices, a modern building that was the sole

30

blight on the pretty Elizabethan main street of the New Age town. As he walked towards Arthur's shop, passing crystal healing centres and vegan cafés, he was serenaded by a busker playing a didgeridoo while his dog looked slightly embarrassed.

Arthur Penhalligan's bookshop was down a side alley, and when Neil opened the door, it set a bell jangling. He shut the door behind him, surprised that there was no sign of the proprietor. On his previous visit Penhalligan had bustled into the shop to greet him, and his absence made Neil uneasy.

He called Arthur's name, and when there was no answer, he wondered whether he'd nipped out for a few moments. But he thought this unlikely, because the shop was unlocked, with the till standing on the little counter to tempt the light-fingered. Perhaps a call of nature, he thought, edging behind the counter, where the door leading to the back of the shop stood slightly ajar. A mobile phone lay on the counter; wherever Arthur had gone, he hadn't taken it with him.

When he opened the door, he saw a tiny kitchen, and beyond that, a narrow corridor leading to the back door. He suddenly heard a scrabbling noise and a muffled voice, so he made for the source of the sound, calling out a nervous hello.

He caught the word 'help', weak but urgent, which seemed to come from an old wooden door at the end of the gloomy corridor. He tried the tarnished brass knob, but it wouldn't budge, so he put his shoulder to the door. It was something he'd seen done in TV dramas, but he'd never tried it before himself and he was surprised at the pain he felt when his body hit the wood.

On his third attempt, the door burst open to reveal

31

Arthur Penhalligan cowering on the floor like a terrified child, with tears running down his thin cheeks.

'What happened?' Neil asked, crouching beside him.

It took Penhalligan a few moments to compose himself enough to get the answer out. 'The door locked itself. I was trapped.' He took a deep breath and pulled a handkerchief from his trouser pocket to wipe his eyes. 'I suffer from claustrophobia, you see; a terror of confined spaces. I've been seeing someone about it, but . . . '

Neil knew what claustrophobia was. During a distant evening of drink and confidences in their student days, Wesley had confessed to a fear of being trapped in a small space with no means of escape. Neil's response had been to joke about him joining the university potholing society, but Wesley hadn't laughed as he'd expected; instead he'd looked embarrassed and swiftly changed the subject.

Neil took Penhalligan by the elbow and guided him to freedom before suggesting that he make them both a cup of tea. The shop owner nodded gratefully, and Neil filled the kettle in the tiny kitchen behind the shop.

'You'll find the tea bags on the shelf up there,' said Penhalligan, sounding more like his old self. 'That catch has been playing up for a while and the wind must have blown the door shut behind me.'

'Are you sure it wasn't locked on purpose so someone could steal from the shop? Is anything missing?'

The man hurried into the shop to check the shelves and the till. Once he'd finished, he shouted through to the kitchen. As far as he could see, nothing had been touched.

'Must have been an accident like you said,' Neil called out, dipping the tea bag into the mugs of boiling water before fishing them out with a teaspoon he'd found on the draining board.

When he brought the mugs through to the shop, Penhalligan took his with a grateful nod. 'How is your dig progressing?' he asked, as though he was anxious to forget about what had happened.

'It's a fantastic site. The parch marks left by the dry weather last summer revealed the exact layout of the village. You promised to find a copy of your local history booklet for me,' Neil said hopefully.

Without a word, Penhalligan returned to the stockroom, coming back a couple of minutes later with a thin volume that he handed to Neil as though it was a delicate treasure. Neil flicked through the pages.

'I've mentioned Elena de Judhael in the Long Bartonford section, although I couldn't find any new material about her. All I could do was repeat the old legend that she was walled up in the manor house as a punishment for becoming pregnant by her brother. These stories become embellished over the centuries, so I don't know how true that is.'

'A friend's been looking for any reference to her in the archives in Exeter, but so far she hasn't found anything.'

Arthur Penhalligan thought for a few moments. 'There might have been people at the time who did their best to hush up the affair.' He took a sip of tea before putting his mug down on the counter. 'There are always those with power who will be keen to cover up murder when it suits them. I expect it even happens today.'

'Murder?'

'Legends invariably contain a grain of truth. If Elena de Judhael was walled up alive, it means she was murdered. Don't you agree?'

8

Rachel drove back to Tradmouth; because of her local upbringing, she was far more confident than Wesley was on the winding single-track lanes flanked by tall hedge.rows that crowded in like prison walls. The journey was filled with speculation about the case. Had Claire Fulford and her parents-in-law been telling the whole truth, or was there something they'd neglected to say about their troublesome neighbours?

When Wesley enquired after Rachel's health and asked how her pregnancy was going, she told him she was fine. She had three months to go and everything was OK as far as they could tell. Her reply was almost dismissive, and when he advised her to take it easy, she shot him a killing look and said, 'Fat chance.'

It was almost six o'clock when they arrived in Tradmouth, and as soon as Wesley reached the incident room, he called Pam, the call he'd made so often before. There's been a murder. Sorry, I'll be late.

He heard her give a weary sigh. 'It's been on local radio. Double shooting near Chabliton. Is that the one?'

'Word gets round fast when people hear sirens. See you when I see you then.'

'Your mum called.'

'What did she say?' Wesley's parents lived in the Dulwich area of south London, in a large Georgian property purchased before house prices went sky high. Although they'd retired recently, Dr Cecilia Peterson from her GP practice and Mr Joshua Peterson from his work as a consultant surgeon, they still sat on numerous boards and committees, so their retirements were hardly leisurely.

'Nothing important. She just wanted a chat.' There was a short silence before Pam spoke again. 'I'm a bit worried about Michael. He's been closeted in his room since he came home from school.'

'He's thirteen,' said Wesley. His son was a teenager, so choosing to be shut in his room seemed like perfectly normal behaviour.

'I know, but . . . he's not looking well. I think something's wrong.'

'I'll have a word.'

'When?'

'As soon as I can,' he said, fearing he was being a neglectful father and hating the thought. 'I'll try not to be too late,' he promised, before ending the call.

Pam's words kept echoing through his mind. If something was bothering Michael, he needed to know. But murder would keep him from home for the foreseeable future, unless the Gerdners' killer was caught quickly.

★ ★ ★

DCI Gerry Heffernan settled back into his seat, thinking about the murdered couple at Hawthorn Barn. The chair creaked under his weight, reminding him that he'd promised his partner, Joyce, that he'd try to eat more healthily. It sounded easy in theory, until he became involved in a case and the takeaways were delivered to the incident room. There was nothing like police work for giving a man an appetite, he always claimed.

Since Joyce had turned down his proposal of marriage over Christmas, he'd feared she was having misgivings about their relationship. She'd claimed that her job as a registrar of births, marriages and deaths made her cautious about commitment, explaining that whenever she joined a couple in matrimony, she couldn't help wondering if it would last. But Gerry suspected that her reluctance had more to do with her first husband walking out on her for another woman. He himself was a widower who'd been devoted to his late wife, Kathy, and he'd assured Joyce that he wasn't the type to abandon her, but this had made no difference. Her fears were too deep-rooted, she said. Commitment had become a phobia, like the fear of heights or spiders.

Gerry, normally quick-thinking, hadn't been able to think of an appropriate answer. For the time being, though, he was quite happy with the status quo. At least it meant that his daughter, Rosie — who considered her father's involvement with any other woman to be a slur on her late mother's memory — wouldn't make waves.

His thoughts were interrupted by Wesley opening his office door without knocking.

'Every household within a mile radius of the murder scene has been visited and nobody admits to seeing anything suspicious. I've asked for all the CCTV and dash-cam footage in the area, but I'm not holding my breath.'

'Those murders weren't committed by a ghost, so we might find something,' said Gerry optimistically. Then he looked up and frowned, as though an unpleasant possibility had just occurred to him. 'You don't think it was some sort of gangland thing? It bears all the hallmarks of a professional hit, and Robert Gerdner served in the Met, didn't he? Nobody's managed to trace any relatives yet, but it shouldn't be difficult to find out about his working life.'

'I'm waiting for the Met to send details,' said Wesley. 'I've asked for a list of all the cases he worked on — and whether he made any enemies in the course of his career.'

'Didn't the nearest neighbours, the Fulfords, say the Gerdners were reclusive? Maybe they were keeping their heads down for a reason.'

'They didn't mix, but they weren't slow to make complaints, so they were hardly hiding away. Hopefully we'll have a fuller picture soon.'

As soon as Wesley left the office, the phone on Gerry's cluttered desk began to ring, and he picked up the receiver hoping it would be good news. Perhaps they'd found clear fingerprints at Hawthorn Barn, or the killer had conveniently dropped his driving licence, and once he'd been apprehended, they could all go home. Instead he heard a man's voice. Local and vaguely familiar, although he couldn't quite place it.

'Mr Heffernan?' the voice said.

'Yeah. Who's that?'

'Steve.'

'Steve who?'

'Steve Masters. I put a new boiler in for you eighteen months ago.'

Gerry scratched his head with his free hand. In his experience plumbers didn't usually make unsolicited phone calls. Normally you had the devil's own job getting hold of them. 'What can I do for you, Steve? The boiler's fine, so I don't see — '

'It's not about work, Mr Heffernan. It's . . . '

'What?' Gerry wished he'd get on with whatever he

38

was about to say. The Steve Masters he remembered had been a cheerful soul, singing as he worked. Now he sounded frightened.

'Can I come and see you, Mr Heffernan? I think I'm in serious trouble.'

30 August 1956

Father gave me the key to the room quite happily, as though he was pleased I was keeping myself busy. He's a man who likes a peaceful life. I've heard a lot of men are like that. Trouble is, I've never met one — and I don't particularly want to. To live like that is hardly being alive.

The door lies off the corridor leading to the kitchen, and I waited until nobody was around before trying the key in the lock. According to Father, it hasn't been opened for years, and at first the key wouldn't turn, but I persisted and eventually the door opened. Father calls it the muniment room; somewhere old documents are kept. One day, he said, he'd get somebody in to look through them, to see if there's anything important, but it's hardly been a priority. He said some of them might date to when the house was built in the fifteenth century, but he didn't seem very interested. History doesn't excite my father; he prefers shooting things and catching helpless fish.

Sometimes I wish I had a gun. It would have made everything so much easier. If there's one thing I've found out, it's that having power over life and death is exciting.

9

Gerry had wondered whether the church hall in the village of Chabliton, a mile from the murder scene, would have made a more suitable incident room. However, the upheaval of getting all the equipment and staff up there — not to mention the disruption to the life of a village that used its hall for a variety of things, from pensioners' lunches to playgroups and Pilates classes — hardly seemed to be justified, especially when it wasn't too far from Tradmouth.

In the end, he agreed to the compromise of parking a mobile incident room on the green outside Chabliton church in case any local residents had information they wanted to share. Yet as the Gerdners had never joined in with the life of their nearest community, he feared such information might be in short supply, especially as the initial house-to-house enquiries had yielded nothing.

The team's first job was to discover everything they could about the victims. All they had so far was that the Gerdners were London people who had chosen to spend their retirement in Devon. There had, as yet, been no suggestion that their roots in the West Country went any deeper than a liking for the area. But that was something they had to find out.

The victims had moved into the converted barn ten months ago — not a particularly happy ten months, according to their neighbours the Fulfords. However, Gerry wondered whether the motive for the murders lay in their London past, in particular Robert

41

Gerdner's police career.

Wesley agreed that the nature of the crime added weight to Gerry's theory. The victims had hardly gone out of their way to make themselves popular with their farming neighbours during the short time they'd lived in the area, but they hadn't been killed with a shotgun, the weapon so common and available in the countryside. According to Colin, a handgun had been used, probably a revolver, which narrowed the field. The bullets had been retrieved and sent off to ballistics for examination; now it was a matter of finding the gun that had fired them.

Wesley was awaiting the detailed forensic reports and the CCTV and traffic camera footage he'd asked for; the killer had to have reached the house somehow, and he doubted whether they'd travelled on foot. Then there were the Gerdners' phone and bank records, although he knew from experience that these might take longer to arrive.

Like Robert Gerdner, Wesley had served in the Met before transferring to Devon, and he rang a former colleague, DI Sam Piper, to ask for any inside information he could find about the victim. Sam promised to make enquiries, and Wesley was pleased when he rang back a couple of hours later.

It turned out that Robert Gerdner had spent most of his career in the traffic division, so he was unlikely to have come into contact with any hardened criminals, unless he'd arrested them for a motoring offence. He'd never pitted his wits against gangsters in the interview room, given evidence in court or made enemies amongst the criminal fraternity in the course of his work. He was regarded by his colleagues as a plodding and unambitious officer, the type who went through the motions and counted the days until he could draw his pension. He hadn't been particularly popular or gregarious, but he was certainly an unlikely target for organised criminals.

As for his wife, Greta, she had recently retired from the Civil Service, where she'd held a very senior post. The couple had no children or close family, and Wesley was surprised to hear that when they'd moved to Devon they'd kept on a property in London — a small flat in Maida Vale purchased when they'd sold their house in the same district, probably to serve as a base whenever they visited the capital from their new country retreat. Nothing else was known about them. As far as the authorities were concerned, the Gerdners were a pair of unremarkable, law-abiding citizens.

In spite of living in London all their lives, their retirement and departure had left little impression on the community they'd left behind, Sam said. Word had it from Gerdner's station that even his customary retirement do had been a dull affair. Wesley was beginning to form a picture of Robert Gerdner in his mind. He was grateful when Sam offered to send someone over to the Gerdners' flat to see whether anything relevant could be found there. John Donne had said that no man is an island — the Gerdners must have had friends and relatives. And once these people were found, Wesley wanted to speak to them.

It was seven o'clock when Gerry sent the youngest uniformed constable out for takeaway, announcing cheerfully that it was fish-and-chips day. It was only DC Trish Walton who raised any misgivings. She was on a diet, she said, but she'd donate her chips to DC Paul Johnson. Wesley suspected that Trish and Paul had rekindled their former romantic attachment. Almost as soon as Rachel had moved out of the house she and Trish had shared, Paul had moved in, allegedly just as a housemate, although Wesley suspected he was now something more. Once Gerry got wind of it there were bound to be jokes at their expense, so no wonder they were erring on the side of discretion.

At ten o'clock, Gerry told everyone to go home, because they needed to make an early start in the morning. The incident room was up and running and there was little more they could do that day. Wesley seized on the invitation; Pam's concern about Michael was nagging at the back of his mind. But as soon as he reached the office door, Gerry called him back.

'I've had a call from my plumber. He wants to come round.'

Wesley raised his eyebrows. 'Boiler on the blink?'

'No. He sounded worried. Said he was in serious trouble.'

Wesley sat down by Gerry's desk. 'Any idea what sort of trouble?'

'No, but he's dropping in tonight, so I'll find out then. Why don't you get off home.'

Wesley didn't have to be told twice, and soon he was walking back to his house on the hill above the town. It was a steep walk but it did more for his fitness level than any daily visit to the gym. He remembered a time when his legs used to ache on the uphill journey, but over the years it had ceased to be much of an effort.

As he walked, he paused to turn round and enjoy the vista of the port laid out before him, the lights of the town reflected on the river and the boats lit up as they bobbed at anchor. He took a deep breath, thinking how thankful he was that Pam put up with his antisocial hours during a major inquiry without much complaint. But she was a busy woman herself, with her teaching job at a local primary school — not to mention her wayward mother, Della, who at times seemed to fill the role of an extra child.

When he reached his front door, he put his key in the lock but didn't call out a greeting as he stepped into the hall. It was after ten, and with any luck, Michael and Amelia would be asleep. He could hear the murmur of the TV from the living room, and as he pushed the door open, Pam stood up to face him.

Wesley was shaken by the worried look on her face. A few years before, she'd been diagnosed with breast cancer. After treatment, she'd been given the all-clear, but the threat of it returning was always there, lurking at the back of his mind like a shadow that could never quite be dispelled. Whenever she didn't appear to be her usual self, it was the first thought that popped up, like a malevolent jack-in-the-box.

'What's the matter?' he asked.

She took his hand and led him to the sofa, glancing at the door before she sat down.

'It's Michael,' she said.

'You said he wasn't well. What's the matter with him?' he said, trying his best to stay calm.

'He won't come out of his room. Says he doesn't want to go to school because he's too tired. He went in today and fell asleep as soon as he got home. He won't eat either. I told him I'd make an appointment at the doctor's, but he says he doesn't want to go.'

'He's thirteen. He hasn't any say in the matter.'

'I'll make an appointment tomorrow. I rang Maritia and she said it's probably nothing. A virus.'

'She could be right, but it needs checking out.'

'How's your murder case?'

Wesley didn't feel inclined to talk about it, but he gave her the bare facts.

'So either the farmer finally lost his patience or they made some dangerous enemies in London.' She frowned. 'He was in the Met, you say?'

'Traffic. Can't really see him getting on the wrong side of the sort of people who'd do something like this.'

'What about his wife?'

'Civil servant. Department of Energy. Hardly MI5.'

'Unless that was her cover story,' said Pam, letting her imagination wander. 'Could it have been a random attack — some madman on the loose?'

He'd been trying not to think about this particular pos.sibility, but now that Pam had put it into words, he knew it was something they had to consider. 'I don't know.'

As he said the words, a shudder ran through his body.

10

It was ten thirty by the time Steve Masters arrived on Gerry's doorstep. He was wearing a woolly hat and a thick puffa jacket. His hands were thrust into his pockets and he appeared to be shivering in spite of the mild May evening.

'Come in, Steve. What can I do for you?'

The plumber turned his head as though he was checking that he hadn't been followed. Gerry's house stood on the cobbled quayside, with the inky churning river only a few yards away. The old-fashioned lamp posts on the water's edge cast splashes of light onto the water, and Gerry could hear the chatter of voices drifting from the pub on the corner.

'Come in,' he repeated, taking pity on the young man. 'You look cold.'

Steve stepped inside the tiny hallway, his hands still in his pockets. Gerry ushered him into the living room, where Joyce was sitting watching TV — a detective series she loved in spite of Gerry telling her it reminded him too much of work.

'Come through into the kitchen,' said Gerry. He knew better than to disturb Joyce while she was engrossed in the plot. 'I'll make us a brew. Unless you fancy something stronger. I've got some beer in.'

'Not for me, thanks. I'm driving,' Steve said quickly, as though he was afraid the chief inspector was trying to catch him out.

Once Steve was sitting comfortably at the breakfast table, Gerry made the tea and brought the mugs over, then sat down opposite him.

'So what's this about you being in trouble? What have you been up to?' He had always believed in coming straight to the point.

'Nothing, I swear. But the police in Morbay think otherwise.'

He was impatient to learn the reason for this strange visit, but he waited for his visitor to continue.

'It was the week before last,' Steve said eventually. 'I know I never did anything wrong, but now I'm getting the blame. They're saying I missed something when I was servicing it, but it was fine when I left.'

'You'd better start at the beginning,' said Gerry, taking a sip of tea.

'I mended an old boiler a week last Friday. Routine job. I know what I'm doing.'

'I'm sure you do.' The job Steve had done for him had gone smoothly. No complaints whatsoever.

'It was an escape room in Morbay. Their boiler was ancient so I told the bloke in charge he should really get a new one fitted, and he said he'd think about it. I got it going and gave it a service. It was a museum piece but I was sure it was safe or I would have disconnected it there and then.'

'So what happened?'

'The guy I dealt with was found dead the next morning. Carbon monoxide poisoning. They're blaming the boiler, but I know I did a proper job.'

'You're bound to be cleared of blame if it turns out it wasn't the boiler.'

'But it must have been because it was the only appliance in the room.'

Gerry waited for him to continue.

'I think someone tampered with the flue. I went

48

back to take another look and found some threads caught up in the vent at the back of the building — as though someone had stuffed a cloth into it so the fumes would seep back into the room.' He paused. 'It could have been an accident or it might have been done deliberately, but whatever it was, I swear on my baby's life I had nothing to do with it.'

'What did the Morbay police say?'

'That it was an accident caused by my negligence. They said I could be prosecuted for manslaughter.'

'Were you interviewed by anyone from CID?'

'A detective from Morbay spoke to me at first, but once they'd decided it was an accident, they left it to a couple of constables in uniform. When I went to the police station, I told them about the threads, but they didn't want to know — said it wasn't important. They probably thought I was trying to wriggle out of it, but if you could have a word . . .'

Gerry stood up. 'Leave it with me, Steve. I'll make enquiries.' He looked down at the young man and saw tears welling in his eyes. 'If you've done nothing wrong, we'll get it sorted.'

As he showed Steve out, he wondered how he was going to deal with the matter. He knew nothing about boilers, and the last thing they needed at that moment was another death to investigate.

11

Neil Watson's official job title was Heritage Manager — Archaeology and Historic Environments, which in his opinion sounded far too grand. On this occasion, however, he was acting as site director in charge of the Long Bartonford excavation, something he was quite comfortable with when it came to his fellow archaeologists, students and community volunteers. However, he was a little vague about his responsibilities towards Nathan and Tel. Was he supposed to be keeping an eye on them? And if they decided to wander off, what, if anything, was he supposed to do about it? He'd never seen himself as an authority figure. Although when they'd been students together he would have said the same about Wesley Peterson, and now he was a detective inspector.

So far the two ex-offenders had given him no real cause for concern, and Neil felt a little ashamed of the prejudiced assumptions he'd never thought were part of his nature. They were both working in trench four helping to uncover a midden behind one of the long-houses, and he watched as they trudged to and fro carrying buckets of soil to deposit on the spoil heap nearby. They looked bored, and he hoped boredom wouldn't lead to trouble.

From the historical records he'd seen, he knew that Long Bartonford had been a village of some hundred or so souls back in the sixteenth century before the settlement had dwindled and died, probably because of something as undramatic as a change in farming practices. It had been the former lords of the manor, the de Judhael family, who'd built the church, and their old home, Bartonford Manor, was the scene of the unsubstantiated legend about a woman being walled up somewhere in the building. The manor house had survived when the village was abandoned and was now in private hands.

Arthur Penhalligan had dropped vague hints that he might be able to lay his hands on an exciting document connected with the village, although Neil hadn't taken this too seriously. There was something of the obsessive about Penhalligan. But he was a lover of old books and manuscripts, so perhaps obsession went with the territory.

From where Neil was standing, he could see a couple of second-year students clearing undergrowth next to the north wall of the church, some way from the trenches they'd already opened up. He took a sheet of paper from the cardboard folder he was holding, a copy of an eighteenth-century sketch of the church that Penhalligan had used in his booklet. The building in the black-and-white sketch, drawn with a draughtsman's attention to detail, was a lot more intact than the roofless ruin it later became. The tower, now reduced to a stump, stood proudly, and the Gothic tracery of the windows was clearly visible. Long Bartonford church had been dedicated to St Leonard, who, according to the website Neil had consulted, was the patron saint of prisoners, something that, if his suspicions about what lay beneath the earth were correct, might prove very appropriate.

When he'd studied the sketch closely, he'd spotted something interesting: a small rectangular addition to the building protruding from the north wall; the devil's

51

side of the churchyard according to popular belief at the time. He needed to see whether the foundations of this small extension still existed beneath the tangle of undergrowth that had encroached on the building over the centuries like the briars surrounding Sleeping Beauty's castle. Because he had spotted faint words inscribed on the sketch: *anker cell.*

Ever since he'd discovered those small and almost indecipherable words, he'd been trying to discover more about the anchorites and anchoresses who were part of the spiritual landscape back in the Middle Ages. More women than men followed the vocation, and they hadn't necessarily been living as nuns and monks when they vowed to live a life of contemplation and prayer in complete solitude, confined in a small cell that was often attached to a parish church. The most famous of these women was St Julian of Norwich, who'd been born in the late fourteenth century and had been the first woman known to have written a book. Others had followed the same path, choosing to live lives of isolated prayer rather than join a religious community. There was no suggestion in any of the websites he'd consulted that the decision to become an anchoress was anything other than freely chosen, and whatever people today might think of the choice, there had been no shortage of willing volunteers.

It was impossible for Neil's twenty-first-century mind to comprehend, but it seemed that those who chose this life were regarded as living saints at a time when saints were guaranteed a place in heaven, although the price they paid in this life must have been a heavy one. If St Leonard's Church, Long Bartonford, had indeed been home to one of these holy people, he held out little hope of finding any archae-ological evidence of his or her presence so many centuries later. But the possibility still intrigued him.

He walked over to the place where he estimated the cell on the drawing must have been and watched as the students gallantly wrestled with the weeds around the church wall.

'After you've got this area cleared, I need a geophys-ics survey of this side of the church,' he said. 'There's a drawing that shows a structure around here, so we'll open another trench. I'd like to know what's down there.'

'Right you are, boss,' said one of the students before hurrying off towards the site hut where the equipment was stored.

Neil seized the opportunity to do the rounds of the site and came across Tel and Nathan taking a break on the grass at the side of their trench, rolling ciga-rettes with an intense concentration that made him wonder whether the thin white tubes contained some-thing more illegal than tobacco. He hesitated for a few moments before making a decision.

'Nathan, Tel, I've got a job for you,' he said, trying to sound cheerful, as though what he had in store for them was a treat. 'Can you help Emma and Ollie clear the undergrowth from the north side of the church? We're going to do some geophysics over there.' He pointed to the area he wanted cleared and smiled hopefully. 'Can't see any brambles or tree roots, so it shouldn't take too long.'

The two former prisoners exchanged glances and put their newly created cigarettes away slowly.

'When you've done that, you can watch while Dave and I go over the area with the geophys equipment.

It's quite interesting.'

They looked unconvinced.

'Have you heard about that murder?' It was Nathan who spoke. 'It wasn't far from here.' The question was asked with what Neil thought was unseemly relish, as though the idea of murder excited him. He found himself wondering once more what the pair had done to be put in prison in the first place.

'Yes, it was on the news.' He decided not to mention his friendship with Wesley, suspecting that any connection with the police might not go down too well.

'Someone said it was two old dears who got themselves shot. Don't know who'd do a thing like that, do you, Tel?'

Tel looked away, and Neil was sure he wasn't imagining the sudden flash of panic that passed across his pinched features, there for a second then gone.

'Better make a start on those weeds,' Tel muttered, his eyes lowered to avoid Neil's gaze.

'Do you know anything about the murders?' Neil regretted the question as soon as it had left his lips.

'No. Why should we?' There was a challenge in Nathan's reply.

Neil thought he was lying, but he didn't dare say so.

12

When Gerry Heffernan arrived the following morning, he marched straight to his office and shut the door. Wesley waited a few minutes before following him. Gerry usually took the briefing as soon as he got in, and Wesley wondered whether something was wrong.

He gave a token knock on the door of Gerry's glass-fronted office, and when he entered without bothering to wait for a response, he found Gerry sitting at his desk with the telephone receiver in his hand. He looked angry.

Wesley sat down and waited for him to finish his call.

'Thanks for nothing,' Gerry growled into the receiver before slamming it down.

'What's up?'

'Like getting blood out of a stone.'

'What is?'

'Morbay nick. I wanted to speak to someone about a case, but nobody's available.'

'Which case is this?'

'You remember I had a call from Steve, my plumber, yesterday? Well, he paid me a visit last night.'

Wesley waited for him to continue.

'He thinks he's going to be accused of killing someone in Morbay.'

Wesley frowned. 'We haven't been told about this.'

'According to Steve, Morbay have been dealing with it.'

'Surely if it's a murder case it should have come to us. What's Steve supposed to have done?'

'His job, according to him. And it's manslaughter, not murder. The lad's done work for me and he's a perfectionist, so I'm inclined to believe him. I promised I'd look into it.'

Gerry's phone rang again and Wesley watched as he answered. After a brief monosyllabic conversation, his face clouded.

'That was Auntie Noreen,' he said once he'd replaced the receiver. Auntie Noreen was Gerry's nickname for their boss, Chief Superintendent Noreen Fitton, as though the cosy title would render her less formidable. 'She wants to see me later for an update on our progress. Trouble is, I've got nothing to tell her.'

Wesley looked at his watch. 'Want to do the morning briefing, or shall I take over?'

'Would you, Wes? And remember, Colin's doing the Gerdners' post-mortems at half nine.'

'How could I forget?' said Wesley with a sigh.

★　★　★

Once Wesley had allocated the tasks for the day, Gerry emerged from his office to have a word with Rachel Tracey.

Wesley thought she looked tired, but he knew it was tricky combining her duties on the farm with her pregnancy and a major murder inquiry that kept her from home till all hours. Some years ago they had experienced a moment of temptation in a Manchester hotel while they were up there on a case. Their mutual attraction had come to nothing, but ever since then Wesley had felt awkward about showing too much

56

concern. Although once you cared about somebody, it was hard to stop, even though he now regarded her as a friend and nothing more.

His thoughts were interrupted by Gerry, who was approaching his desk, hands in pockets. 'Better set off, Wes. Colin'll be waiting for us. Rach'll let us know if there are any developments.'

The mortuary at Tradmouth Hospital was within walking distance of the police station, and Wesley was glad of the chance to stroll along the embankment next to the river in the weak sunshine. It was a fine, if cloudy, spring day, and a lot of boats had ventured out onto the water. He could see the steam train sitting at the station on the opposite bank, a heritage railway popular with tourists throughout the season. As the engine set off with smoke pouring from its chimney, the sound of its laboured chugging carried across the sparkling water.

When they arrived at the mortuary, Colin was waiting for them, a solemn look on his normally cheerful face. He had two post-mortems to perform, one after the other, and he dealt with Robert Gerdner first, keeping up a running commentary into the microphone dangling above the stainless-steel table. Wesley stood at the side of the tiled room, as far as he could get from the action, and averted his eyes as he waited for the pathologist to deliver his verdict.

'Well, gentlemen,' Colin said as his assistant finished off. 'I can confirm that the victim died as a result of a gunshot wound to the head, and the tattooing to the skin around the wound suggests that he was shot at close range. If it wasn't for the lack of weapon and the position of the body, I would have suspected a case of murder-suicide — that he killed his wife before turning the gun on himself — but I think we can rule that out. Anything from forensics yet?'

Gerry shook his head. 'Still waiting. The bullets retrieved by the CSIs have been sent off to ballistics. Once we get the results back, we'll know more about the weapon our man used. If the killer was a man.'

'Can you really see a woman doing it?'

'Not like you to be sexist, Colin,' said Gerry with a smile.

'When you put it like that, Gerry, I admit I am making assumptions.'

Greta Gerdner's post-mortem didn't tell them anything new, apart from the fact that she showed signs of early liver disease — she liked a drink, as Colin put it. She too had been shot in the forehead at close range, and from the position of her body, it looked as though the killer had backed her into a corner. Trapped like an animal.

13

Once the post-mortems were over, they refused Colin's offer of tea and biscuits in his office and made their way back to the station. But instead of entering the building by the main door, Gerry took Wesley's arm and steered him towards the car park.

'I want to go to Morbay to speak to Geoff Weston. But as far as anyone knows, we're still at the hospital. Right?' he said, tapping the side of his nose.

'Do you need me, or . . . ?'

'I need you to drive. And I'd value a second opinion.'

Since Wesley's arrival in Tradmouth, he'd never known Gerry drive. Rumour had it that he could, although this was something he'd always denied. He'd never given any explanation, but Wesley suspected it had something to do with his late wife, Kathy, who'd been killed in a hit-and-run accident.

Nothing much was said during the journey over the river on the car ferry. The sun had emerged from the thin layer of cloud, and Wesley was enjoying the trip across the sparkling water as the hills rose up on each bank. The oak trees fringing the water were in full fresh leaf and the fields above were a startling green.

The beauty of the south Devon landscape still stunned him at times.

Once he'd driven off the ferry, he navigated the country roads until he came to the outskirts of the seaside resort of Morbay. Decades ago, Morbay had been one of the country's most fashionable resorts, a Riviera on English shores. But now the proud old lady looked decidedly shabby, with pound shops, fast food outlets and amusement arcades taking the place of smart emporia and genteel tea rooms.

Morbay police station stood in the middle of the town, away from the seafront and hidden from the well-heeled visitors of yesteryear in case its presence suggested that their holiday haven was plagued by the criminal classes.

Gerry burst through the double doors and marched to the front desk, demanding to see Inspector Weston, the man in charge. The civilian manning the desk looked alarmed when he produced his ID, and made a swift phone call, which produced immediate results.

Weston was a small, bald man with a stomach to rival Gerry's own, and he greeted the DCI with a wary smile, shaking hands with him and then with Wesley. He invited them to come to his office and tapped out the code that would let them through to the business end of the building.

'Sorry I was out when you called, Gerry,' he said once they were settled in his office with tea in china cups. 'I've been dealing with an arson case — a tattoo parlour near the town centre was torched on Sunday. Whole building destroyed, including the office above the shop. I was getting the report from the fire investigator.'

Gerry leaned forward. 'That's not our problem, Geoff. I understand you've got an unexplained death on your books that we haven't been told about. And Steve Masters, plumber of this parish, is in the frame.'

Weston seemed to relax. 'The charge'll be manslaughter if we can get the CPS to buy it. There's no question of a murder charge, so I didn't think it was worth bothering your major incident team at Trad-mouth.'

'Why don't you let me be the judge of that? I've had a visit from Steve Masters. He came to me for advice.'

Weston leaned back in his chair and steepled his fingers, his lips fixed in a rictus smile. 'The experts say the boiler was the only way carbon monoxide could have got into that room. And Steve Masters had just serviced it.'

'He says it was fine when he left it. He reckons the flue was tampered with. It's on an outside wall and he thinks someone blocked it up on purpose so the fumes would seep into the room.'

'Well he would say that, wouldn't he? It's a case of negligence on his part. Manslaughter at worst, like I said.'

'Nothing for me to worry my pretty little head about.' There was a note of threat in Gerry's words. 'I know Steve Masters. He's done work at my house. He's pernickety. A perfectionist. I can't imagine he'd make a schoolboy error like that. He swears he left the installation perfectly safe, and I believe him.'

'With respect, Gerry, you're not an expert.'

'But I know when someone's telling me pork-ies — pride myself on it.' Gerry leaned forward and treated Weston to a mirthless smile. Wesley knew that when the DCI smiled like that, it heralded danger for the recipient. 'You do realise that if Steve Masters is telling the truth, you really could have a murder on your hands.'

Weston shifted nervously in his seat. 'I don't think — '

'But why make work for yourself, eh? I'll need the address of that escape room.'

61

Weston consulted one of the files piled on his desk and wrote the address on a slip of paper, which he handed to Gerry. With a quick nod to Wesley, the DCI stood up.

'I'll be in touch,' he said, making it sound like a threat.

Wesley, feeling a little sorry for Weston, thanked him and followed the boss out of the office.

'Did you say escape room?'

'That's right. In Morbay.'

'Neil was going to a stag do there, but it was cancelled because of the death.'

'He had a narrow escape then,' said Gerry quickly. Wesley wasn't sure whether this was a joke in bad taste.

'We've already got a double murder on our hands, Gerry. Is this really necessary?' he asked after checking his phone for incoming messages. There weren't any, which suggested that Rachel was coping perfectly well in their absence.

'Something about it doesn't smell right,' Gerry said.

Wesley didn't reply. From what he'd heard about Steve Masters, Gerry might have a point. But if the scene hadn't been sealed off, evidence might be hard to find. Any number of people could have trampled over the site since the tragedy happened.

'We should get back, Gerry. If I were you, I'd look for a second opinion to back up Steve's story. Know any other good plumbers?'

'I'll ask around amongst our technical people. Get someone to visit the scene. I know we've got our hands full with the Gerdner murders, but Steve could end up with a custodial sentence.'

Wesley knew that the chief superintendent would

probably say that Gerry was letting his sympathies get in the way of common sense. He also knew that if he found himself in the DCI's place, he might well be tempted to do exactly the same.

31 August 1956

Mother doesn't mind me spending time in the muniment room. As far as she's concerned, even I can't get into mischief among the old documents stacked up in there. Some of them go back centuries: letters, contracts, indentures; the fragile remnants of everyday life. A year ago I would have sneered at such a tedious pastime, but now, taking a peek into other people's lives relieves the boredom.

I spent all morning in there searching through the old boxes. Most of them contained old ledgers full of estate business: the rents paid by tenant farmers; correspondence about building works and demands for payment. It was disappointing, because I thought their lives would be more exciting — like my life with Rupert was before all this happened.

Then I came across something more interesting. It turns out that one of the Judhael family, who built the house centuries ago, was a very naughty boy. I found threats from banks to foreclose because of his gambling debts. This was in the reign of Queen Victoria, the time my I-don't-know-how-many-greats-grandfather bought the house, so I guess that when the last of the Judhaels gambled all his money away, my ancestor took advantage of the situation, probably getting the manor house at a knock-down price. Desperation makes people careless.

I don't know how long I can stand this. I still feel sick every morning. I thought it would get better, but it hasn't, and now Ursula won't even look at me. I told Mother I hated her, but she said I was wicked for saying that, because she's my sister, the only one I've got. She uses the word 'wicked' a lot.

In the meantime, I shut myself away in the muniment room, trying to find something to distract me from my predicament. Father says decisions have to be made. And that I won't have a say in what happens to me.

I used to be defiant, but now I just want to cry.

14

Once they were back in the incident room, Wesley asked whether the Gerdners' bank and phone records had come in yet. The answer was a disappointing no.

He had a sudden desire to revisit the crime scene, and he decided to go alone, because that would enable him to call in at Neil's dig afterwards. He needed something to take his mind off the case in the hope that when he started thinking about it again, he'd come up with some fresh ideas. That was the excuse he made to himself anyway.

At three thirty, he brought the car to a halt outside Hawthorn Barn. Last time he'd been there, the place had been alive with activity, but now there was a heavy silence, punctuated only by the cackling of crows in the trees nearby. He'd obtained the key before setting off, and when he opened the door, he had the uncomfortable feeling that he was intruding on the Gerdners' privacy; the couple's moment of death.

He could see the bloodstain marking the place where Robert Gerdner's head had lain. Soon a team of specialist cleaners would be sent in to eliminate every sign of what had happened there, but now death seemed to hang in the silent air, as though the ghosts of the Gerdners hadn't yet departed.

The house still bore the telltale signs of the CSIs' recent activity: fingerprint powder, arrows to pinpoint blood splashes and other potential evidence. He wandered around, noting the small things; the personal relics of the victims' lives. His attention was drawn to the bookcase, where several shelves were occupied by a collection of classic American private eye novels, including Raymond Chandler and Dashiell Hammett. Someone, probably Robert Gerdner, must have been a huge fan.

On the upper floor, the drawers and wardrobes had already been searched for clues as to why the victims had met such an unhappy end. He knew that nothing had been found. The Gerdners hadn't been involved in anything illicit. The only shadow on their apparently blameless lives was the disputes they'd had with the farmer next door — a simple clash of cultures.

He'd hoped the visit to Hawthorn Barn would somehow be enlightening, but instead it left him feeling frustrated that he was no nearer solving the puzzle of the brutal double murder. He closed the front door with the sense that his visit had been a waste of time. On the other hand, it had given him a chance to think.

He was walking to the car when he caught a movement out of the corner of his eye. A tall, fair-haired man in a waxed jacket was disappearing round the side of the house, and there was something furtive about his movements. Wesley knew that whoever he was he shouldn't have been there, so he began to follow, speeding up as the man started to hurry down the Gerdners' garden, heading for a gap in the hedge.

'Police,' Wesley called out. 'Can I have a word?'

The man spun round, shocked, as Wesley held out his ID.

'We've had rubberneckers. I was checking the place was secure.'

'And you are?'

'Andy Fulford. I own the farm. The barn's on my land . . . or it used to be before we had to sell it.'

67

His explanation sounded reasonable. It wouldn't be easy having a brutal murder happen so close to home.

'You were interviewed after the Gerdners were found.'

Fulford nodded. 'I was in Newton Abbot when the police spoke to my wife and parents, but someone came to see me when I got back. Couldn't tell them anything. Didn't see a thing.'

'You didn't hear the shots?'

'Lots of guns round here. You don't notice after a while.'

Beads of sweat glistened on the man's forehead, and it was obvious he couldn't wait to escape.

'I understand you didn't get on with the Gerdners.'

Fulford opened and closed his mouth, frantically trying to come up with an answer. 'We . . . er . . . They were townies, weren't used to our ways, but that doesn't mean . . . Look, I told that other policeman everything I know, which is nothing. Can I go now? I've got things to do.'

Wesley saw no reason to detain him, but he could tell the farmer was uneasy about something.

* * *

Wesley drove on to Neil's dig, which was just a mile away, telling himself that, given the short distance from Hawthorn Barn, someone working there might have seen something they hadn't considered important enough to share with the police at the time. Yet however hard he tried to convince himself that this was his motive, he had to acknowledge the truth: he wanted to find out how the excavation was going.

He parked the car near the temporary fencing erected to protect the site from intruders; according to Neil, there were some ruthless metal detectorists about who thought nothing of sweeping the dig for valuables before the archaeologists had a chance to complete their painstaking work. He could see Neil in the distance, standing near the ruins of a church talking to one of his colleagues while the other diggers worked in hushed concentration. Wesley let himself in through a gap in the fence and picked his way across the site.

Neil's look of surprise when he spotted his friend turned into a welcoming grin.

'How's it going?' Wesley asked, looking around.

'I'd better warn you now that we'll probably find burials, but if we do, they'll be old. Nothing sinister,' Neil added with confidence.

'Unless they have modern dental work,' Wesley teased.

Neil pulled a face at the mention of every archaeologist's nightmare. He pointed to the ground a few feet away. 'I've got an old sketch showing what could be a small room jutting out from the north wall of the church. The geophys seems to confirm it.'

'A vestry?'

'There's writing on the sketch that looks like 'anker cell'. It's hard to decipher, but it's possible the church had a resident anchorite — a sort of solitary monk or nun — which is quite exciting. The lord of the manor had the church built in the fourteenth century, earning brownie points to get to heaven, no doubt.' He rolled his eyes. 'The manor house is still occupied.'

'Who by?' Wesley asked. As the manor house stood so close to the Gerdners' place, the present occupants must have been interviewed about the killings as a matter of routine. But unless they'd had something interesting to report, it wouldn't necessarily have been brought to his attention.

'A rapper. Made his pile in the music industry and bought a little place in the country. He's been down here to look at the dig. Wouldn't have guessed what he did for a living, but I suppose we all have our public persona, don't we?'

'Speak for yourself. How are your ex-cons getting on?'

Neil looked round, shielding his eyes from the sun that had just emerged from the clouds. 'The foundations of a nice longhouse over there are keeping them busy.' He paused, scanning the dig area. 'Or it's keeping one of them busy. No sign of Nathan. Maybe he's answering a call of nature in our luxury Portaloo.' He hesitated. 'Chris heard that someone's been questioned about the man who died in that escape room. The girl there told him when he rang up to get our deposit back. Know anything about it?'

Wesley didn't answer.

'I met the guy who died when I went there with Chris to make the booking.' He shuddered. 'Awful to think that a couple of weeks later he'd be dead.'

'What was he like?'

'Seemed a decent bloke.'

'You didn't see anything suspicious — or overhear anything?'

'No. We booked the room and that was it.'

Wesley decided that was probably all Neil could tell him about Charlie Maddox. He and Chris had been punters, not friends of the man.

'I take it someone's been here asking whether anyone saw anything around the time that couple were killed at Hawthorn Barn? Colin thinks the murder took place sometime on Saturday — afternoon or evening.'

'A constable came round but nobody could tell him anything. We were working here most of Saturday, but we'd all gone home by the evening. Besides, it's about a mile away so . . . I can ask around again if you like. Someone might have remembered something since then — perhaps they passed Hawthorn Barn on their way home and saw a car or something.'

Wesley thanked him, although he knew the likelihood was flimsy to say the least. 'Look, I'd better be off. Time and Gerry Heffernan wait for no man.'

By the time he'd said his goodbyes to Neil, there was still no sign of Nathan — and he noticed that the toilet door was standing ajar.

★ ★ ★

The hotel wasn't far from the dig. Posh place with a sea view. Not the sort of establishment Nathan Hardy was accustomed to — although he had once done two shifts washing dishes at a hotel in Morbay for a pittance until he'd discovered that crime paid a lot better.

This one called itself a country house hotel and spa. Nathan had seen the swanky olive-green sign as he came in, keeping to the rhododendrons lining the drive so he wouldn't be caught on the CCTV that was sure to be recording everyone's comings and goings. He'd left the car on the road outside the gates. The last thing he wanted was to draw attention to himself, and that rusty Fiat he'd bought for a hundred quid from a bloke in a pub would stand out like a sore

71

thumb beside the BMWs, Mercs and Audis.

He knew Teresa Nilsen was staying there and he knew it wouldn't be wise to venture too near the entrance. He would watch to see if she emerged. Surveillance, they called it. Just like the spy Nathan had always dreamed of being. The new James Bond.

15

When Wesley returned to the incident room, he found Gerry in his office, holding his telephone receiver to his ear, rolling his eyes in frustration. After a few moments, he slammed the instrument down.

'What's it got to do with me?' he asked. Wesley, being the only person in the room, assumed the question was addressed to him.

'What is it?'

'Geoff Weston at Morbay. There's been an outbreak of graffiti.'

'He's not blaming you, is he?' Wesley struggled to keep his face straight as a picture flashed through his mind of the DCI daubing obscenities on walls.

'He knows who did the dirty deed. It was Steve Masters' girlfriend. She was caught red-handed — or rather yellow-handed, because she was holding a spray can of yellow paint at the time. Weston blames me for interfering.'

'It's hardly your fault if the woman got a bit carried away.'

Gerry sighed and ran his fingers through his grizzled hair. 'I shouldn't say this, but if it encourages Morbay to look at the case more closely, it might not be a bad thing.

If Charlie Maddox's death had nothing to do with Steve, I don't see why it should ruin his life and his livelihood.'

'Have you done anything about getting a second opinion on that boiler yet?'

'I've asked someone from forensics if they know anyone who can check it out. That's another thing, Wes. I haven't mentioned Steve Masters to Auntie Noreen, and if she finds out I've asked a favour from forensics, she'll be giving me a hundred lines. *I must not waste the police budget.*' He gave another heavy sigh. 'The good news is that we've got the Gerdners' bank records at last. They had separate accounts and they were more or less what you'd expect apart from a regular payment from Robert's account to a company called Wyvern Properties. Judging from their website, they rent out commercial property — office space and that sort of thing. Paul's tried ringing them to find out what the payment's for, but he hasn't managed to get an answer yet. And Trish has been trying to trace the victims' relatives, but she hasn't had any luck either.'

'Happy families, eh,' said Wesley, sinking into the chair by Gerry's desk. 'I took another look at Hawthorn Barn and bumped into Andy Fulford. He said there'd been rubberneckers snooping around.' He glanced towards the main office, where Rachel was working at her desk.

'Believe him?'

'Didn't see any reason not to.' He thought for a moment. 'We really need to find out more about the Gerdners' background. From their dealings with the Fulfords, I wouldn't be surprised if they'd made a few enemies over the years.'

'You could be right.'

Wesley hesitated before speaking again. 'I'm happy to go to London if you want. The local police visited their London flat and didn't find anything relevant. But it might help if I spoke to the neighbours and Robert's former colleagues at the Met . . . get the

74

unauthorised version.'

'You mean you fancy some of your mum's cooking?' Gerry gave a wide grin that showed the gap between his front teeth, something he'd always claimed was a sign of good luck.

'My mum was a GP. She never had much time for fancy cooking. Mind you, if I'm in London, I'll probably pay my parents a call.'

'Quite right too.'

Wesley smiled. 'I've already had a quick word with Sam Piper, an old colleague who started at Hendon at the same time as I did. He's an inspector at Scotland Yard now. He's happy for me to go down and conduct some informal interviews.'

'Good to have friends in high places,' said Gerry, lean.ing back in his chair, which creaked dangerously under his weight.

As Wesley returned to his desk, he suddenly remembered Pam's concerns about Michael. Perhaps this was the wrong time to be away from home. But it couldn't be helped. He picked up his phone and called Sam Piper to tell him he was on his way.

* * *

One stone is a stone, two is a wall, three is a dwelling and four is a high-status building. Neil Watson was reminded of the old archaeological joke as he studied the row of stones emerging from the earth. They had been lying a few inches below the surface, all in perfect alignment, so he was confident that he'd found what he was looking for. It matched the eighteenth-century sketch exactly, and it always gave him a tingle of satisfaction when the archaeology fitted the records.

From what he could make out, it appeared to be a later addition to the original building, but this came as no surprise. In the Middle Ages, villagers were always keen to enlarge and embellish the church that was the community's pride and joy. However, there was something about the room that left him puzzled.

'What do you reckon?' Dave, the only colleague Neil had trusted to help with this part of the excavation, was standing behind him, shovel in hand, wearing a T-shirt with the slogan *Keep on Digging and Never Throw in the Trowel* emblazoned on the front.

Neil pointed to the church wall. 'It looks as though the entrance from the main church was blocked off at some point. It might have been used as a charnel house, where they stored bones from old graves when they dug new ones, but there's no evidence of a door to the churchyard, so that theory's out. Once the entrance from the church was blocked up, the room would have been sealed off completely.'

'Why would they block off a perfectly usable space?' Dave picked up a nearby finds tray and pointed to a coin, as yet uncleaned and caked with soil. 'I found this embedded in the mortar of the sealed entrance in the church wall. Henry the Sixth — 1457,' he said as he replaced it carefully in the tray.

As Dave returned to his own part of the trench, Neil adjusted the position of his kneeling mat and began to scrape away at the newly uncovered section of wall. After half an hour, he spotted something on the inside of the mysterious chamber that made him stop what he was doing and sit back on his heels.

Graffiti, religious or otherwise, was common in medieval buildings; the people of the past had often expressed their devotion or superstition by incising symbols into the stones. Only to Neil this didn't look like the kind of pious carvings normally found in a medieval church. Once he'd brushed the clinging soil away, it became clear that the letters had been roughly and deeply carved.

He squatted down and trowelled more soil away until he'd revealed the entire inscription. It was in English rather than Latin, and its position suggested that it had been done when the writer was supposed to be at prayer.

He brushed away the last powdery soil and began to read, tracing the letters with dirt-caked fingers. At first the words were hard to make out, but eventually he was able to decipher what was written.

Oh Lord, have mercy upon me. By thy great goodness save me from this place.

16

To Pam Peterson's surprise, her husband arrived home just after eight o'clock. With a double murder to investigate, she'd expected him later.

'You haven't cleared up the case already?' she said as soon as he set foot in the hallway.

Wesley gave her an absent-minded kiss of greeting. 'Not yet. How's Michael?'

'It was my day off, so I took him to the doctor's this morning — managed to get an emergency appointment. She sent some blood off to be tested and said it probably wasn't anything to worry about — but they always say that, don't they.'

'Hopefully we'll get to the bottom of it,' he said, trying to conceal his worry. He had a lot to occupy him at work, but in his rare idle moments his imagination had begun to plague him. What if Michael was suffering from something serious, something incurable? The terrible possibilities lingered at the back of his mind, painful and stubborn, like a piece of grit caught in a shoe.

It hardly seemed an appropriate moment to break the news that he had to go to London the next day, but it was something he couldn't avoid.

When he'd blurted out the words, Pam said nothing for a few seconds before assuring him that it was fine. But he could tell she was putting on a brave face to stop him feeling bad.

Before eating, he went up to Michael's room and tapped on the door, suddenly nervous. When he

78

opened the door, he saw his son lying on his bed, scrolling through the smartphone that Wesley had been so reluctant to let him have, only yielding when Pam persuaded him that all his friends at school had them and without one he'd be socially isolated.

'How are you feeling?' he asked as he sat down on the edge of the bed. The room was hung with model aeroplanes, and there were dinosaur posters on the walls. Relics of the childhood its occupant was rapidly leaving behind.

When Michael looked up from his phone, Wesley was shocked by how ill he looked. 'Mum's been asking me that all day. I wish she'd get off my case.'

'She's worried, that's all. Feeling any better?'

'I just want to sleep.'

'Not up to going to school?'

'I want to, but . . . '

'Nothing's wrong at school? Nobody's giving you any trouble?' Wesley had always feared that being a mixed-race boy in a predominantly white school might pose a problem, but so far there'd been no hint of bullying. On the contrary, Michael seemed to be popular with his classmates.

'No. It's fine. I'd like to go. I didn't want to miss double science tomorrow, but . . . '

'I'm going to London in the morning. Might be away a couple of days.'

Michael's bloodshot eyes lit up with sudden interest. 'On a case?'

'That murder case near Chabliton.'

'Know who did it yet?'

'I'm working on it. You get some rest, eh.'

'The doctor thinks it's a virus. So does Auntie Maritia.'

79

'Well she's a doctor too, so she knows what she's talking about. Viruses can be very nasty.'

The teenager permitted his father to give him a goodnight kiss without complaining that he was far too old for that sort of thing.

★ ★ ★

London was as crowded as ever. As Wesley walked to keep his appointment with DI Sam Piper, he felt hemmed in by people and traffic in a sea of pollution and tall buildings. He'd become too used to Devon. Gone native. All of a sudden, he knew he could never resume his old life and live in the capital again.

As he walked up to reception, he saw the civilian behind the desk give him a wary look, as though he was wondering what a smartly dressed black man was doing there. Wesley had come across racism, subtle and otherwise, many times and he knew the signs. However, the man's attitude softened a little when he produced his ID and introduced himself. After a couple of minutes, Sam Piper came down to greet him with a hearty handshake and took him up to his office. For the past few years they'd only communicated via scribbled notes on Christmas cards, updating each other on the major milestones of their lives. They had a lot to talk about, but after ten minutes, they got down to business.

'I've been making some enquiries about Robert Gerdner for you,' Sam began.

'What have you found out?'

'According to the people who worked with him, he was a miserable bugger who never mixed with his colleagues outside working hours. His wife was a high-flyer in the Civil Service and the consensus was that she ruled the roost — maybe that accounted for his grumpiness. Because of her job, they didn't seem short of a bob or two.'

'Anything else?'

'One of the blokes Gerdner worked with said he'd often talked about setting up a private detective agency when he retired. It was something he'd always dreamed of apparently.' Sam snorted. 'Though I can't see why. I mean, he wasn't even in CID. Spent some time in uniform and then traffic,' he added, shaking his head with disbelief. 'What would he know about detection?'

Wesley recalled the PI novels on the bookshelves at Hawthorn Barn. Robert Gerdner had obviously yearned for something more glamorous than the traffic division. His phone began to ring and he apologised to Sam for the interruption. It was the incident room, so he knew it was important.

He heard DC Paul Johnson's voice on the other end of the line. 'I've been in touch with Wyvern Properties, sir. Turns out Robert Gerdner rented an office from them under the name RG Investigations.'

'A private detective agency?'

He heard Paul gasp. 'How did you know?'

'I'm clairvoyant.' Wesley couldn't resist the joke. He'd just experienced one of those satisfying moments when another line of enquiry opened up like a new branch in a road.

'There's something else,' Paul continued. 'The office Gerdner rented was over a tattoo parlour, and the whole place was burned down last Sunday — the day after the shooting.' There was a dramatic pause. 'It was arson.'

17

The words Neil had found inscribed on the stones suggested despair — a plea for help — and he'd lain in bed in his Exeter flat thinking about them, unable to sleep. *By thy great goodness save me from this place.*

His partner, Lucy, was working in the Orkneys, a place filled with fascinating archaeology that she'd come to regard as her second home. She was up there so often, taking part in excavations, that he'd become quite used to being on his own. Self-sufficient so long as he had his colleagues at the dig for company — and Wesley, of course, as often as his friend's working life allowed.

His head was aching as he hauled himself out of bed that morning, throwing his duvet over the rumpled sheets to give the bedroom at least an appearance of order. He took a couple of painkillers before climbing into the shower, letting the hot water run over his body as the words of the inscription continued to echo through his mind.

Half an hour later, he was in his car driving to the dig when his phone rang. He pulled in to take the call and saw Arthur Penhalligan's name on the display.

'Hi, Arthur. Got something for me?' he asked hopefully.

'Yes.' There was a long pause. 'A manuscript came into my possession a couple of days ago and I think you might find it interesting. Would you like to see it?'

'Yes please,' said Neil, unable to keep the excitement out of his voice.

'I'll expect you later then.'

When Neil set off again, he was tempted to change direction and make for Neston. But his treat would have to wait. He was the site director. He had responsibilities. Especially since Nathan and Tel had become part of the team.

* * *

Wesley had spent the night at his parents' house in Dulwich, sleeping in his old bedroom. It had been tastefully redecorated since he'd left home for good, transformed into a pleasant, if bland, guest room, leaving few childhood memories behind. But lying there trying to get to sleep, he recalled the years he'd spent in there with his shelf filled with Sherlock Holmes stories and books about archaeology, reading detective stories under the bedclothes by torchlight. He was glad he had been born before the days of social media, as it might have robbed him of the innocent pleasure of books. His parents had tried to steer him gently towards science and medicine, but Wesley's curiosity had always been focused in a different direction.

When he came downstairs for breakfast, his mother was pouring coffee. She greeted him with a maternal smile. Dr Cecilia Peterson had been beautiful in her youth, and even though she'd put on some weight with the passing years, she was still a good-looking woman.

'How did you sleep, son?' she asked in the warm Caribbean accent she'd never lost.

'Fine,' said Wesley before asking his father politely if he would pass the toast. His devout, churchgoing parents had instilled good manners into their children. Even though they'd both come from well-to-do

83

families in Trinidad, they'd known that succeeding in their adopted country would take hard work and ambition, and they'd sent their children to the best schools. Wesley and Maritia's upbringing had been strict but it had also been loving, and Wesley counted himself lucky.

Mr Joshua Peterson FRCS looked up from his toast and smiled at his son. He was tall and distinguished, with greying hair and a small beard, and in spite of his recent retirement, he was still in the habit of wearing the bow ties he'd sported all his working life: the badge of the top consultant surgeon.

'Mind if I ask you something medical?' Wesley said once he'd buttered his toast.

'Mind?' his father said with a chuckle. 'We'd be offended if you didn't. What's up?'

Wesley outlined Michael's symptoms and saw his parents exchange a nervous glance. They had decades of medical experience between them, so that look concerned him. His mother told him it could be any number of things, most of them fairly trivial, but that split second glance between her and her husband had done nothing to allay his fears.

'I'm sure it's nothing to worry about, but let me know how he's doing, won't you, honey.'

'Course I will.' Wesley stood up. 'I'm sorry. I need to go.'

When his father gave him a farewell hug and his mother flung her arms around him and kissed his cheek, he suddenly felt reluctant to leave.

'Take care of yourself, son. I worry about you in that job.'

'I will. Promise. See you tonight.'

He gave his mother's hand a squeeze. He'd never

told her about the dangerous situations he'd found himself in over the years, but he knew she had enough imagination to realise the potential hazards of a murder detective's work.

At nine o'clock, he set out for the London pied-à-terre the Gerdners had kept on in Maida Vale. It turned out to be a second-floor mansion flat, and as he walked into the entrance lobby, he saw that the staircase was covered with sheets and paint pots and blocked by a couple of decorators who were painting the walls magnolia.

He was wondering whether he could negotiate his way past the obstacles when one of the painters looked up. 'You'll have to take the lift, mate.'

He took a deep breath and hesitated before stepping inside. After he'd pressed the button for the second floor, the doors swished shut and he closed his eyes. He forced himself to use lifts when no alternative was available, but he'd never been keen, whenever possible using the excuse that taking the stairs was healthier. He felt the lift gliding upwards, and when it came to a shuddering halt, the possibility that he was stuck between floors flashed through his mind.

To his relief, the doors opened smoothly, and he rushed out onto the landing. The victims' flat had already been visited and nothing useful had been found, but he wanted to find out what the Gerdners' neighbours had to say about the couple, although their attitude towards the Fulfords in Devon suggested that they weren't the type who socialised with the people around them.

Most of the block's residents were already at work, but he found the Gerdners' next-door neighbour in and more than happy to talk. The young man was an

IT professional who worked from home. He had a shaved head and a Yorkshire accent and offered coffee as though Wesley was a long-lost friend, showing no curiosity about the reason for his visit.

'What do you know about the people in the flat next door — the Gerdners at number fifteen?' Wesley began once they were sitting down. The coffee was in a large mug; just how he liked it.

'Only that they sold a big house nearby and bought the flat here about a year ago. I've heard they've got a place in Devon, but they stay here whenever they come to London. All right for some, having two homes,' he added. Wesley recognised the envy of the struggling mortgage payer. 'I thought you were here about the burglaries. Two flats done now,' he said with a sad shake of the head.

'It's not about that, I'm afraid.' Wesley paused for a moment. 'I'm sorry to have to tell you the Gerdners were murdered at their house in Devon last weekend. I'm on the investigation team.'

For a few moments the man looked stunned at the news. 'Wow. That's a lot to take in. I wouldn't say I know anything about them really. I said hello to them a couple of times, but they blanked me. I went round to their flat once to see if they were interested in setting up a home-watch group, but they shut the door in my face.' He sounded as though the rejection had hurt him.

His words reminded Wesley of Claire and Andy Fulford at Lower Kington Farm. Perhaps the Gerdners' antisocial attitude had somehow led to their deaths. He'd liked Claire Fulford, so he was reluctant to consider any of her family as suspects. But he'd been wrong about people before.

'I found out about the house they used to own here from Danuta. It was her who told me about the place in Devon too.'

'Who's Danuta?' he asked.

'She cleans for a few people round here and she used to work for the Gerdners when they had their big place down the road. She pops in for a cup of tea from time to time,' he added cheerfully.

The young IT worker clearly craved company, and Wesley hoped his unexpected revelation about Danuta might provide the breakthrough he'd been waiting for. Few people could hide things from their cleaners, so he'd been told.

'Do you know where I can find Danuta?'

'I don't know where she lives, but it's her day to do a couple of the flats on the floor above. She always makes a prompt start, so she should be there now. I'll go and tell her you want a word if you like.'

This was working out better than Wesley had expected, and the grin spreading across his companion's face suggested that he would positively welcome any distraction from his computer screen.

18

Fifteen minutes later, Wesley had another cup of coffee in front of him, and this time Danuta was there too, sitting on the edge of her seat. She was a pretty young woman with delicate features, and she spoke good, if heavily accented, English. She seemed wary at first, until Wesley reassured her that his sole interest lay in any gossip she could provide about the Gerdners.

'I did not like them,' she began, a spark of anger in her eyes. 'I do not care if I speak ill of the dead; they were not nice people.' She glanced at their host as though she needed his approval for what she was about to say. Then she focused her intense gaze on Wesley. 'He was policeman but not like you, I think. The wife treat me like dirt, as though I'm nothing. No please and thank you. Do this, do that. This is not cleaned well enough. I was happy when they left. The new people in their old house are a lot nicer, I think.'

'Do you clean their flat here?'

She shook her head. 'They say they move to the country. They are not here often so they do not need me.'

'What can you tell me about them? Did they have friends? Relatives?'

She considered the question for a few moments. 'I see no friends, but there is a cousin. She stay with them twice in the old house. She talk to me like I'm a person. Her name is Sandra.' She wrinkled her face as though she was making a great effort to remember. 'Sandra Wilson. She lived in Sussex but now she has moved to Pimlico. She ask me if I will clean for her and I put her on my waiting list. She is a nice lady, I think. Nicer than her cousin.'

'Do you have her address?' Wesley asked.

Danuta took a black notebook from the pocket of her overall, found the correct page and passed it to Wesley. The gesture was businesslike. The young woman was sharp, and probably made a good living from cleaning up other people's mess. He made a note of the address and thanked her. Danuta looked as though he'd put any misgivings she might have had about the British police to rest.

To Wesley's relief, his progress down the stairs was unimpeded by the decorators, who'd knocked off for a break. In celebration, he took a taxi to Pimlico, where, to his relief, he found Sandra Wilson at home in her new flat.

After introducing himself, he revealed the reason for his visit as gently as he could. Although Sandra was shocked at the nature of her relatives' deaths, she didn't seem unduly upset.

'I hadn't heard,' she said after a long pause while she took the information in. 'I never bother reading the newspapers, and the police obviously haven't been in touch . . . until now.'

'I'm sorry about that. We have been trying to trace relatives, but these things can take time. You're Mrs Gerdner's cousin?'

'No, it's Robert who's my first cousin, and as far as I know, I'm his nearest relative.' She hesitated. 'It's terrible, of course . . . really shocking . . . but Robert and I weren't close.' She hesitated. 'You shouldn't speak ill of the dead, should you?'

'That's what they say,' said Wesley quietly. 'But if

we want to find whoever killed them, the truth will be more helpful than convention.'

She gave him an understanding smile. 'Very well, if it's the truth you want, Robert and Greta made a good pair. Both of them liked to keep themselves to themselves. When I used to live in Sussex, I stayed with them at their old house in Maida Vale whenever I came up to London — that was before my husband passed away and I sold up to move to this flat. At my age it's so much more convenient being in town than being out in the sticks, especially now I'm on my own. I can't understand why Greta and Robert wanted to move to the middle of nowhere. But some people have this dream about a rural idyll, don't they?'

'Very true. Can you think of anyone who bore a grudge against your cousin and his wife?'

She considered the question for a while. 'Funny you should ask that. We hadn't been in regular touch since they moved, but I had an email from Greta a couple of months ago moaning about a *terrible* farmer who was making their lives a misery. Although I suspect it was more likely the other way round.' There was another pause. Then she smiled. 'I know I shouldn't say this in front of a policeman, but there were times when I was tempted to lace their wine with arsenic myself. Or should I say their tea — Greta and Robert didn't drink. At least that's what they said.'

She gave Wesley a knowing look and he recalled Colin's verdict about the state of Greta's liver.

'Robert was a police sergeant,' she continued. 'But I suppose you already know that. I wouldn't have liked to get on the wrong side of him. He was a miserable sod.'

She began to laugh. She must have been a similar

age to the Gerdners but as different in nature as it was possible to be considering she and Robert came from the same gene pool. Sandra was one of those people who twinkled with good humour, and Wesley guessed that although she'd never clicked with her cousin, she'd felt it her duty to keep in touch, blood being thicker than water.

'My aunt Gladys, Robert's mother, was exactly the same, you know. I used to dread going there on visits. My mother was her sister but she used to call Gladys a poisonous old bitch, and Mum never usually swore. Auntie Gladys used to be a nurse, would you believe, although I'm sure she didn't work in a hospital. I think it was some kind of institution, but wherever it was, I pity her poor patients.'

'Some people are like that, I suppose,' said Wesley. 'The Ebenezer Scrooges of this world.'

'Scrooge reformed. Auntie Gladys and Robert didn't.' She laughed again, then her smile suddenly vanished. 'Have you any idea who might have done it?'

'That's what we're trying to find out. What about Greta? Did she have any family?'

'Not that I know of. I believe her parents were quite old when she was born, and they passed away years ago. Even though Greta was a cow and Robert was hardly a ray of sunshine, they were still family, so I'll attend the funeral. When is it?'

'We won't be able to release the bodies for a while, I'm afraid. I take it they had no children?'

Sandra shook her head. 'Some people shouldn't have children, should they? Not temperamentally suited.' She glanced at the row of photographs on her mantelpiece: children and, presumably, grandchildren. She saw Wesley following her gaze. 'I've got two, and three grandkids. But my daughter's in Australia and my son's in Germany.'

Wesley nodded, understanding why she'd felt the need to keep in touch with her cousin even though they'd had little in common.

'Do you know anything about Robert setting up as a private detective?'

'Oh yes. It was something he'd often talked about doing in retirement because of his experience in the police force. I did point out that he'd been in traffic, but he said that didn't matter. Last I heard, he'd found suitable premises and he said it was going very well, but they hadn't been in touch since the email complaining about the farmer.'

After Wesley had thanked Sandra for her help, he stood up to leave and she spoke again.

'Robert's mum, my auntie Gladys, was a cruel woman, you know,' she said softly. 'My mum used to say that if someone had murdered her, it wouldn't have surprised her at all.'

3 September 1956

At last I've found something exciting in the muniment room. At the back of a cupboard I came across an old tin box containing a pile of letters written on yellowed parchment.

The writing is hard to read and the language is old-fashioned, like the Chaucer we were forced to read at school. I never liked those stories, apart from the rude one about the miller that made us giggle. I knew I'd never make head nor tail of the letters, so I took them up to my sister's room. She was reading — she's always reading — but when I told her about the box, she seemed quite interested. Nothing I've ever done has interested her before. She started to read the letters and said they were about someone called Elena, who was one of the de Judhaels — the family that built this house centuries ago.

She seemed excited and said it could be the same Elena who was supposed to have been walled up somewhere in the house. Not that we've ever been able to find out where she is, however hard we used to try when we were younger. Ursula said the story probably wasn't true. Just a legend people liked to believe.

According to the letters, Elena was causing problems and her father was asking the priest's advice about what he should do. The priest was called Sir Nicholas, and Ursula got the impression he didn't want to offend the lord of the manor. She said he was trying to hedge his bets.

I watched Ursula as she read, wondering if Elena was like me: the troublesome daughter who had to be dealt with. Ursula said the letters were written by men; that it was men who decided Elena's future and that she wished Elena had written her own version of what happened. Perhaps nothing much has changed in five hundred years.

I left the box with Ursula. She said translating the documents into readable English would be an interesting exercise.

19

'Are you sure you can manage?'

Normally Neil would have had no qualms about leaving Dave in charge while he drove to Neston to see what Arthur Penhalligan had found for him. Dave was perfectly capable of dealing with any archaeological problems that might arise in his absence, but the presence of Tel and Nathan made Neil uneasy. He could see them standing outside the fenced-off area smoking roll-ups again with the shifty look of a pair of loiterers on the lookout for a criminal opportunity.

He experienced a feeling of deep shame that he was judging these men when it wasn't his place to do so. How could he, a man who'd long claimed to hate prejudice in all its forms, be so prejudiced against a pair who'd already paid their debt to society? He was letting his baser instincts override his principles and he wondered what Wesley would say. Although he suspected that his friend's years in the police force had made him more cynical than he'd been in their student days.

Nathan had only just returned to the site after a short but mysterious absence. He'd told one of the postgrad students working in his trench that he had something to do before driving off in the battered old Fiat they'd arrived in for the past few days instead of the hostel van. When someone asked Tel where his mate had got to, Tel had just given a theatrical shrug and said he didn't know, Nathan never told him, but he was sure he'd be back.

Neil took a deep breath and walked over to the pair. When they spotted him approaching, they threw the cigarette stubs to the ground and stamped them out.

'They could do with some help in trench two, lads,' he said with a fixed smile on his face.

'Right you are, Dr Watson,' said Tel, making a move towards the gap in the fencing that provided access to the site. When Nathan lagged behind, Neil couldn't resist asking the question.

'You went out earlier. Something important, was it?'

Nathan turned and gave him a look that most would describe as hostile, although in Neil's opinion it was his default expression. 'Had some business to do.'

Neil was about to ask him to inform either him or Dave of his absence in future; to point out that it wasn't fair to leave a postgrad student to manage the large trench on her own with a couple of first-year students to keep an eye on and only Tel to do the heavy work. But the words stuck in his throat and in the end he said nothing.

He left Dave excavating the trench on the north side of the church, where the mysterious room was being uncovered. They'd just found what appeared to be the remains of a step at the base of the blocked-up doorway leading down from the church level into the room. It was still a mystery why the entrance had been sealed. Then there was the graffiti carved into the wall. He needed to find out more about those desperate words, and in the absence of anything new from Annabel, who was still searching the archives for information, he hoped Penhalligan would provide a clue.

There wasn't much traffic on the road as he drove to

Neston, and he found an empty parking space, which he took as a good omen. He hurried down the gloomy alleyway to the strange little bookshop, remembering how on his last visit he'd rescued Arthur from the stockroom. This time, however, he found him stationed behind his counter, scribbling on a clipboard. He looked up when Neil entered, setting the bell jingling on the door.

'I believe you've got something for me,' Neil said as soon as he was inside the shop.

Arthur nodded but didn't move from the spot. 'It was in a folder with various other old manuscripts from a house clearance. Property of a retired academic. I'm not sure where he obtained it, but . . . '

He emerged from behind the counter and put the catch on the door before turning the sign to *Closed* and leading the way into the stockroom. Neil noticed that the door was now wedged firmly open.

On a table in the corner lay a folder, the kind used to transport small works of art. Arthur undid the tapes that held it closed and opened it with great care. 'Parchment,' he said. 'In remarkable condition considering the age. It's in Latin. Perhaps you . . . '

'Speak it like a native,' Neil joked as he descended on the document like a miser who'd just acquired some priceless new treasure. He took out his phone and took a photo. His Latin wasn't bad, but he'd prefer to translate it in the comfort of his own flat.

But he couldn't resist having a preliminary look at the words written in faded ink on the single sheet of parchment, well preserved in spite of its obvious age.

'It looks like a fragment from a fuller manuscript, and as far as I can see, it's a ceremony.' He fell silent as he studied the words, slowly realising that it described a rite transferring a woman from the land of the living to the realm of the dead. He saw the names St Leonard and Long Bartonford. And there was another name: Elena de Judhael, the woman who, according to legend, had been walled up inside the manor house.

By thy great goodness save me from this place.

A shudder ran through Neil's body as he wondered whether the manuscript was linked to those desperate words carved into the stone. And if there was a connection, what was their meaning?

20

Rachel Tracey hovered by Gerry's open office door. She could see his desk was piled with reports and statements and that he was talking to someone on the phone.

'Can't you hurry it up?' she heard him say almost in a growl, and she guessed that he was giving the person on the other end of the line a hard time.

At last he slammed the receiver down, muttering, 'And have a nice day to you and all,' then looked up and saw Rachel hovering there. 'Come in, Rach. What can I do you for?'

She forced herself to smile at his weak joke as she lowered herself into the DCI's visitors' chair. She felt fat and ungainly and she could feel her baby fluttering inside her. 'What was that call about, sir?'

'The Gerdners' phone records and the contents of their laptop. It would have been quicker if I'd given the job to the kids at the local primary school.' He looked her up and down, a frown of concern on his chubby face. 'You all right, Rach? Sure you don't want to be put on light duties?'

He sounded anxious. Rachel knew that underneath his bluster he was a softie. It would have been easy for her to take advantage of her condition, but that was the last thing she wanted. She had enough fussing from Nigel and her mother. She didn't need it at work too. She didn't want anything to change.

'I'm fine,' she said, and the determination in her voice prevented Gerry from pursuing the matter.

'There's been a call from a hotel on the coast near Chabliton. Uniform attended and informed us because it's not far from the Gerdner place.'

'What is it?'

'A guest has gone missing and they're worried she might have come to some harm. Have you heard anything from Wesley, sir?'

'He visited the Gerdners' London address this morning to see what he could find out, and he's spoken to Robert's cousin, who claims she's his only relative.'

'Paul told me the office Gerdner rented was burned down. Arson, according to the fire investigator.' Rachel hesitated before asking her next question. 'Are we assuming it's connected to the murders?'

Gerry frowned. 'Seems likely. Although Morbay have been working on the assumption that the tattoo parlour below was the target. According to DI Weston, the owner's a shady customer with some very dodgy associates. But now we know about the Gerdner connection, it changes things a bit.'

Rachel gave an earnest nod. 'When's Wesley coming back?'

'He's staying with his folks tonight, back first thing tomorrow. This missing person at the hotel — what do we know about it?'

'Only that it looks suspicious and they've called in the crime-scene team.'

'In that case we'd better get over there and see what's going on. Fancy coming with me?'

'If you want.' She favoured the boss with a grin, glad he'd decided not to treat her like an invalid.

★ ★ ★

Gerry decided not to involve any other members of his team until they knew exactly what they were dealing with. But the fact that the hotel wasn't far from the scene of the Gerdner murders meant he needed to establish that it wasn't related in any way.

Rachel drove while he relaxed in the passenger seat, stretching out his legs and keeping up a running commentary on any subject from the passing landscape to his plans to go up to his native Liverpool once the case was over to visit his daughter, Alison, whose existence he had only discovered a couple of years previously. He asked Rachel about her husband, Nigel, and how the farm was doing. Rachel said everything was fine. That was what she always said.

The hotel stood a few hundred yards inland from the cliffs on the coast between Bereton and Dukesbridge. The building was Georgian; a former gentleman's residence with an elegant portico and a gleaming orangery tacked onto one side. It had the pristine look of a luxury spa hotel, with manicured lawns, gleaming windows and a glass door at the entrance that glided open whenever anybody emerged from the building. A sign in black letters against tasteful sage green announced that this was the Cliffpiper's Rest Country House Hotel and Spa.

'Nice,' said Rachel with a hint of envy. To a woman who'd chosen to become a farmer's wife, up at four for the morning milking while holding down a job as a detective sergeant, a week in such surroundings probably seemed like an unachievable dream.

'If you like that sort of thing,' said Gerry, who couldn't imagine anything worse than being pummelled, massaged and bored stiff.

The impression of understated luxury was spoiled

by a pair of police cars parked haphazardly in front of the entrance as uniformed officers traipsed in and out of the building, setting the glass doors swishing open and shut. As soon as Gerry got out of the car, he hurried round to open Rachel's door and help her out. He'd been brought up to regard helping a pregnant woman out of a low car seat as a common courtesy, but Rachel waved his offered hand away and struggled out, slamming the door behind her and ignoring the puzzled look on Gerry's face.

'What's happened here?' Gerry asked the constable who was hovering inside the entrance. 'I've heard it's a missing person case, but what haven't I been told?' He glowered, and the officer took a step back.

'Sorry, sir, but it looks as if it could be an abduction. There are signs of a struggle. And an ashtray in the room has blood on it.'

'Ashtray? I thought this was supposed to be a health spa.'

'It is, sir. That's why I noticed it, because it seemed out of place. The chambermaid who came in to do the room said the hotel don't usually supply ashtrays, for obvious reasons. When I spotted the blood, I called the CSIs. It's not far from that double shooting, so . . .'

'Well done,' said Gerry, who believed in giving praise where it was due. 'Very observant.'

The young man's cheeks reddened.

'Does the missing woman have a name?'

'It's a Ms Teresa Nilsen. An American lady, according to the staff. Checked in three weeks ago saying she was visiting a relative in the area. Her hire car is still in the car park, and her things are in her room, including her handbag.'

'I suppose we'd better take a look. When was she last seen?'

'At dinner last night. She was alone as usual. Her absence wasn't discovered until the chambermaid went in this morning and found that her bed hadn't been slept in.'

The officer passed them their crime-scene suits and they retreated to the empty lounge to struggle into them. Rachel's stretched over her baby bump and Gerry's over his expanding stomach, which he kept resolving to do something about but never got round to.

The missing woman's room was on the ground floor, and they were directed past the grand central staircase to a corridor on their left. They'd been told that the room had French windows that led outside, so the hotel's other residents wouldn't have to be inconvenienced in any way by the presence of so many police officers and CSIs. Apart from the vehicles outside and the crime-scene tape blocking off the end of the corridor, there was remarkably little sign of disruption. Gerry had to give uniform their due; they'd organised things pretty well.

When the constable guarding the door of Room 111 opened it to admit them, he could see that the CSIs were already at work. He recognised some of them from the Gerdners' place.

'What have we got?' he asked nobody in particular.

'Looks like there's been a struggle,' a young woman said, nodding towards an overturned chair near the bathroom door.

As they walked into the room, his thoughts were interrupted by Rachel's voice. 'The constable at the door mentioned an ashtray.'

The CSI dusting for fingerprints nearby looked round. 'It's been bagged up. Over there if you want to take a look.'

'What about those French windows?' said Gerry. The voile curtains covering them had been pushed to one side to make access easier, and the doors stood open. 'Were they found locked?'

'No. They were open, with the curtain drawn across. We found traces of blood on the material,' the CSI said helpfully.

'So if it does turn out to be suspicious, that'll be how the abductor got in.'

'Silly thing to do, leaving the French windows unlocked on the ground floor,' said Rachel.

'Unless she thought this part of Devon would be a lot safer than where she's come from,' the CSI suggested.

'In which case,' said Gerry, 'she got that wrong.'

Before Rachel could reply, Gerry heard a voice calling his name. It was one of the uniformed constables from Dukesbridge, a young man he had never come across before, and he sounded excited.

'There's no sign of her phone, sir, but this was on her bedside table.'

Gerry fumbled inside his crime-scene suit for his reading glasses, and the constable passed him a business card. He recognised the name at once: RG Investigations, with *Bob Gerdner* scrawled on the reverse.

He took out his phone and called Wesley. He needed him back in Devon as soon as possible. If not sooner.

21

After Wesley's visits that day, he was looking forward to another quiet evening back in the cocoon of his childhood home in Dulwich. But things didn't work out as he'd planned.

Just as he was leaving Sandra Wilson's flat, he received Gerry's call summoning him back to Devon.

He took a taxi from Pimlico to his parents' house to pick up his things, and as he made his explanations, he saw a fleeting look of disappointment cross his mother's face.

'I'm sorry,' he said.

'Me too, honey,' she said before giving him a farewell hug. She too had been looking forward to another evening with her only son. But, as a doctor, she knew only too well how work could get in the way of family life. 'Your dad's at a hospital board meeting, giving them the benefit of his wisdom,' she added with a knowing smile. 'He'll be sorry he didn't get a chance to say goodbye, but we'll be in Devon soon, so we'll see you then.'

Wesley had almost forgotten that they'd arranged to stay with Maritia and Mark at the vicarage in a few weeks' time. Wesley's sister, married to a vicar who was responsible for several rural parishes, lived in a large, draughty Victorian vicarage with many spare bedrooms, so when their parents visited, they always stayed there rather than at Wesley's smaller house in Tradmouth.

'Yes. See you then.'

'Let me know about Michael, won't you.'

'Of course.'

It was half past four by the time Wesley caught the train from Paddington, calling Pam when he was half an hour into the journey to tell her he was coming home. He asked how Michael was, and she said he hadn't felt up to going to school that day. She'd contacted his head of year, who'd promised to arrange some work to be sent to him if the situation continued. When the call ended, Wesley's imagination began to conjure all sorts of distressing scenarios. Maybe it was a good thing he had the investigation to distract him.

Although it was early evening when he arrived back in Tradmouth, he knew Gerry needed him at the station as soon as possible. However, he called in at home first and Pam greeted him with a welcoming kiss. She'd been expecting to spend another night on her own, but now she'd have him back at ten — or whenever Gerry judged that they'd done all they could that day. He greeted his daughter, Amelia, with a hug and listened patiently as she chatted about her day, then the cat, Moriarty, rubbed up against his legs in the hope of more food. He ignored the animal's display of cupboard love and crept upstairs to Michael's room. The boy was fast asleep, curled up in his bed. He looked so young and vulnerable; a beautiful child with golden-brown skin and a fine down of adolescent hair on his face. At thirteen, he wouldn't have called himself a child, but to his father, that was what he'd always be. Wesley needed to be outdoors, where he could banish the fume-filled air of the capital from his lungs, so he decided to walk down the hill to the police station. When he reached the incident room,

Gerry greeted him like a shipwrecked man who'd just spotted a friendly lifeboat crew.

'Thank God you're back,' he said, ushering Wesley into his office and shutting the door behind them. 'What have you got to tell me about your jaunt to London?'

'All I found out at the Met was that Gerdner was very unlikely to be targeted by anyone in the criminal underworld. His cousin, Sandra Wilson, knew about him setting himself up as a private investigator, and she also mentioned the arguments they'd had with the Fulfords. She did say something I thought was strange.'

'What was that?'

'According to Sandra, Robert Gerdner inherited his anti-social tendencies from his mother. She said her aunt was a nurse in some institution — described her as a cruel woman.'

Gerry raised his eyebrows. 'Odd thing to say about your own aunt.' He thought for a few moments. 'So as far as the Fulfords were concerned, the Gerdners were the neighbours from hell. Is that enough to get them shot?'

'People have been killed for less.'

Gerry began to rummage through the papers on his desk. 'I've got Andy Fulford's statement here somewhere.' He pulled out a statement form, a look of triumph on his face. 'Here it is.'

'What does it say?'

Gerry scanned the sheet. 'He was at home with his wife. Saw nothing. Heard nothing. It was Paul who spoke to him.' He craned his neck to see into the outer office. 'He's at his desk. Tell him to come in, will you.'

Wesley went to the door, caught Paul Johnson's eye

and signalled to him to join them. The tall detective constable, a keen runner, stood up and hurried to the boss's office.

'Sit down, Paul,' said Gerry. 'You took Andy Fulford's statement.'

'It pretty much agreed with his wife's, sir.'

Wesley saw a look of uncertainty pass across Paul's open features. 'Is there anything the statement doesn't say?'

Paul shot him a grateful look, as though he was glad to unburden himself of a nagging suspicion. 'It's nothing I could put my finger on, but I had the impression he was nervous about something. But as I said, his statement agreed with his wife's and his parents', so I had no reason to take it any further.'

After Paul had returned to his desk, Wesley waited a few moments before he spoke. 'Perhaps we should take a closer look at Fulford, but we need to be discreet. I don't want Rachel getting wind of it. The farming community all know each other.'

Gerry nodded. He understood.

'What's this about a missing person?' Wesley asked.

'It looks like an abduction. Signs of a struggle and traces of blood. Her name's Teresa Nilsen and she's an American tourist; over here for a month to see a relative, apparently.'

'But not staying with family?'

'I thought that was a bit odd. If you come over here to see relations, why not stay with them and save yourself the expense of a hotel?'

'Perhaps money's no object — or she's doing the rounds of different relatives. Maybe she's here to trace her family tree.'

'It's a possibility. She left all her stuff in her room.'

Gerry leaned forward. 'And there was a business card on her bedside table. RG Investigations, with Robert Gerdner's name written on the back, which suggests she'd been in touch with him. Pity his office is a burned-out shell so we can't search his records. He certainly didn't keep any business stuff at home, which makes things more difficult.'

'So there might be an association between the missing woman and the Gerdner shootings?'

'I think we should be working on that assumption. With this new development, we could do with more help, so I've drafted in some officers from Dukesbridge. I'll contact Neston and all.'

At that moment, Rachel knocked on the door. She was holding a sheet of paper, grasping it as though it was something precious. When she spotted Wesley, she looked surprised.

'Thought you were in London till tomorrow.'

'Gerry said he needed me back here,' he said.

She handed the paper to Gerry. 'Someone's been looking at the computer from the Gerdners' house. They spent a lot of time on websites mentioning a place called Darkhole Grange. I looked it up, sir. It was a hospital. Or rather an asylum. Had a bad reputation, as far as I can tell. There's a lot on the internet about it being haunted. It's a ghost tour venue nowadays.'

'So the Gerdners were planning to go on a ghost hunt?' Gerry said.

Wesley glanced at Rachel who was listening with interest. He supposed it was one explanation.

22

When Neil woke up the next morning, the light was seeping through his thin bedroom curtains. He fumbled for his phone on the bedside table to check the time. It was still early, so he stretched out in the king-sized bed, which had felt too large since Lucy went off to Orkney. He missed her and wondered whether to tell her so when she called him that evening. Should he say he was shorthanded at the Long Bartonford dig? Should he ask her to come back and help? Or would such a request betray his feelings, something he'd never been in the habit of doing? As he lay there, he suddenly felt vulnerable. For years, archaeology and the camaraderie of the dig had been all he needed. But recently he'd found himself thinking of Wesley and his growing family and wondering whether the commitment he'd avoided for so long was such a bad thing after all.

He'd lain awake half the night, turning this way and that, adjusting his pillows. First too hot, then too cold. After a while he'd put the light on to read a book about Roman villas, and eventually he'd fallen into a fitful sleep and dreamed of Elena de Judhael. At first she'd had no face, and then she was transformed into Lucy, trapped inside an Orkney chamber tomb screaming his name. He couldn't reach her, and each time he tried, his limbs refused to move. He'd woken up covered in sweat, his heart pounding in panic until he realised it had just been a dream.

He knew he wouldn't feel fully awake until he'd

emerged from the shower and dressed, but when he looked out of the window, he saw that it was drizzling and the sky was grey. It was probably set in for the day, but that wasn't going to stop the work of the dig.

As he drove out of Exeter towards Long Barton-ford, he kept thinking about the document Arthur Penhalligan had found. He'd put his rusty Latin to use and discovered that a parish priest called Sir Nicholas de Moor had agreed in principle to accept a woman called Elena de Judhael as an anchoress at St Leonard's Church in the village of Long Bartonford. This seemed to disprove the old legend that Elena had been walled up in her family's manor house. The incarceration, if it had indeed taken place, had been within the church. The document outlined the ritual required to make this a reality, although Sir Nicholas hadn't seemed altogether happy with the arrangement, suggesting that he speak to the woman before any decision about her future was made. The priest's misgivings weren't expressed very forcefully, which made Neil wonder whether Elena's family were the sort of people a humble parish priest wouldn't want to offend. He thought of the words carved on the stones, and nebulous ideas started to form in his mind.

When he reached the dig, he parked the car, resolving to give Annabel a call later to see whether she'd managed to find anything about Elena in the Exeter archives. It was an ecclesiastical matter, and the Church at that time had kept good records. It was just a matter of knowing where to look.

He helped his colleagues remove the tarpaulins from the trenches, ready to start work, and after a word with Dave about the plans for the day, he made an enthusiastic start on what he'd begun to think of as the anker cell trench. He'd had a similar feeling before — that one particular trench might contain something remarkable — and, selfishly, he wanted to keep it to himself.

He began to scrape away at the soil, revealing more of the stones that formed the wall of the chamber. Last night's exploration of the World Wide Web had given him more clues about what he was excavating. All he needed was definite proof.

He looked up and saw Nathan standing on the edge of the trench staring down at him. If anybody knew about incarceration, it was their two latest helpers.

⋆ ⋆ ⋆

Wesley arrived at the incident room that morning to find a pile of messages waiting for him. But as he went through them one by one, he found nothing that might move the investigation forward. Next he scanned the huge white-board that took up the far wall of the room. There were pictures of the Gerdners along with shots of the neighbouring farmers, Claire and Andy Fulford. Teresa Nilsen's photograph, taken from the passport she'd left behind in her hotel room, had joined them, even though no firm connection had yet been established.

Gerry was at his desk, talking on the phone with an exasperated expression on his face, and Wesley strolled into his office to join him, taking a seat quietly and waiting until he'd finished his conversation.

'Any word from forensics about that ashtray yet? Is it blood?' he asked.

'Still waiting for confirmation,' Gerry said. 'The management told us the only ashtrays on the premises were the ones they put outside on the patio for people who can't kick the habit. The banished smokers of this world. You see them outside every pub and office block. Poor sods.'

'Any cigarettes amongst the victim's things?'

'None, so if it does turn out to be blood, that means it could have been brought in as a makeshift weapon. Although of course Teresa Nilsen could have taken it into the room herself for some reason.'

'A crafty smoke?' said Wesley, unconvinced. 'Do we know who she was over here to see yet?'

'We're working on it.'

'What about the Gerdner connection? Why did she have Robert's business card? Was it to do with his detective agency, or was it personal?'

'Who knows? I'm becoming more and more convinced that the tattoo parlour wasn't the target. I think it was Robert's office.'

'What if Teresa Nilsen consulted him about something that meant they both needed to be silenced?'

'That's exactly what I'm thinking, Wes. But what could she have consulted him about that warranted murder?'

'Do you think she's still alive?'

'I don't know. If the Gerdners' killer and Teresa's abductor are the same person, why wasn't she shot with the gun he used at Hawthorn Barn?'

'Perhaps he thought the sound of a gunshot in the hotel would be a giveaway,' said Wesley.

Gerry's eyes lit up. 'Or so we wouldn't connect it to the Gerdner murders.' He suddenly looked solemn. 'Teresa's phone's missing and it's switched off so we can't track it. But we're pulling out all the stops: questioning everyone at the hotel and going through all the available CCTV footage. Unfortunately there are no cameras on the side of the building where her room is.'

They were interrupted by Rachel, who appeared at the office door. From the expression on her face, Wesley knew she had news.

'There's been a call from one of the uniforms we left at the hotel to conduct the routine interviews. The hotel deputy manager showed her all the CCTV footage for the appropriate time, and there's something interesting. A camera at the entrance caught a battered old car turning round by the gate. A few minutes later, a man walked past the camera and was caught again outside the main building looking very shifty: hood up and head bowed. He hurried past the main entrance but he didn't appear again, suggesting he went out another way.'

'The abductor?' Wesley fought to keep the excitement out of his voice.

'Afraid not — this was Tuesday, and she was last seen at the hotel safe and well on Wednesday evening — but he might have been assessing the possibilities. He might have noted the cameras and learned what places to avoid.' A smile of satisfaction appeared on her face. 'The good news is that when the car turned at the entrance, the camera picked up the registration number.'

'And?' said Gerry, who was hovering expectantly. 'Don't keep us in suspense.'

'It belongs to a Nathan Hardy. An old customer of ours — or rather Morbay nick. Convictions for burglary and ABH.'

'Know where we can find him?'

She turned to Wesley. 'This might be right up your

street. His probation officer says he's taking part in an archaeological dig.'

23

Neil had mentioned the two ex-offenders at his dig and Wesley thought it highly likely that Nathan Hardy was one of them. Gerry gave him a knowing look.

'Go on. You'd better get down to that dig and see if Hardy's there — and if he is, I want a word with him sooner rather than later.'

Wesley didn't need telling twice. He plucked his coat off the stand in the corner of the incident room and headed for the door.

'Don't you want to take some backup?' Gerry called out after him.

Wesley stopped. He'd become so carried away by the thought of another visit to Neil's excavation that he'd almost forgotten the reason he was going. If Nathan Hardy was indeed responsible for Teresa Nilsen's abduction — and possibly the Gerdner shootings — it probably wouldn't be wise to tackle him on his own.

Gerry scanned the large room for a likely candidate. 'Rob Carter looks bored,' he said after a while. 'Why don't you give him a treat and let him drive you?'

Wesley looked across the room at DC Rob Carter. He was young and keen and preferred the more exciting aspects of police work to the routine stuff. Gerry was right: he did look bored as he stared blankly at his computer screen.

Rob had been stuck in the incident room for the past few days dealing with calls from the public and collating statements, so he greeted Wesley's offer of a trip to

Long Bartonford enthusiastically. As Wesley shared the latest developments with the young DC, he realised how little they actually had. Robert Gerdner was an ex-Met sergeant who'd set up as a private detective in his retirement. But his business premises — where presumably he'd kept his work records, because none had been found at his home — had been destroyed in an arson attack. The missing Teresa Nilsen had his business card, but they had no way of discovering whether she'd consulted him. Then there was the personal angle: the Gerdners had had disagreements with the Fulfords, but had the feud escalated with tragic results? There still wasn't enough to justify bringing Andy Fulford in for questioning. As for Teresa Nilsen, the case was too fresh for speculation.

'What was Nathan Hardy inside for?' Rob asked.

'Aggravated burglary, robbery, ABH. Someone hopes that taking part in an archaeological dig will make him a reformed character.'

Wesley saw a look of disbelief pass across Rob's face, and he shared his scepticism. As far as they could tell, no valuables were missing from Teresa Nilsen's hotel room, but if Nathan Hardy had gone there and found the French window open, it wasn't beyond the bounds of possibility that he'd sneaked in to see what he could find. If Teresa had disturbed him, he might have panicked and lashed out at her on impulse. But would a casual thief go to the trouble of removing the dead or injured victim from the scene?

Gerry had ordered a search of the shoreline below the nearby cliffs, and alerted the coastguard. Although if the missing woman had been pushed or thrown over, it might be hard to prove she hadn't fallen by accident. According to his record, Nathan had never killed before, so the first time might have affected him in a way he hadn't expected. The second time, Wesley thought pessimistically, would probably be easier — if he was allowed to get that far.

He let Rob drive, but after a while he started to regret the decision. The younger man tended to take the narrow lanes too fast, and Wesley gripped the sides of his seat, fearing that a slow-moving tractor would loom around a blind bend at any moment. By some miracle, however, they reached their destination unscathed, although Wesley felt his legs shaking slightly as he emerged from the passenger seat. Rob, however, was looking pleased with himself.

They'd parked beside the wire fence separating the dig from the outside world. Wesley squeezed through a gap in the fence and Rob followed, hands in pockets, trying to look as cool as his TV cop heroes.

'Where is he, then?' Rob asked, shielding his eyes from the sun that had just emerged from behind the clouds. Wesley knew he'd have to dampen his hunger for action if they wanted to bring the suspect in without unnecessary fuss.

Instead of answering the question, he made his way to the trench beside the church wall, where Neil was gazing downwards at the soil, deep in thought. Rob followed, looking around in the hope of picking out their suspect amongst the archaeologists and students. Wesley knew his way would be quicker.

Neil gave him a wave of greeting, trowel in hand, showing no curiosity about Rob's presence.

'You mentioned you had a couple of ex-cons here,' Wesley began. 'Is Nathan Hardy one of them?'

'He is, but he's not here today. His mate Tel turned up, but Nathan didn't. Tel doesn't know where he is — hasn't seen him since yesterday.'

'Do they live at the same hostel in Morbay?'

'So I believe.' He'd never taken much interest in what the pair did when they weren't at the dig. 'If you want a word with Tel, he's over there in trench two.' He pointed at a small man with longish blonde hair wearing a faded T-shirt.

Before Wesley could step away, Neil spoke again. 'Come and see what we've found. Tel won't be going anywhere except to dump that bucket of soil on the spoil heap. I promised to let him go over it with a metal detector later. Thought he deserved a treat, seeing as he's been working hard.'

'What about Nathan?'

'Let's just say I wouldn't trust him around the site hut if we'd found anything of value.'

Wesley stole a glance at Rob, who was shifting from foot to foot, eager to haul Tel out of his trench for questioning.

'Let's see what you've found, then.'

'Hadn't we better speak to this Tel?' Rob's question sounded peevish, a child asking whether they were nearly there yet.

'Yes, of course.' Wesley tried his best to sound patient, wondering if Rob's words could be reflecting the voice of his conscience. Duty versus self-indulgence. He chose the first option and gave Neil an apologetic look. His discoveries would have to wait.

They picked their way over the uneven ground, Rob swearing from time to time when he encountered some hidden hazard.

Although Tel looked young, he had the start of an impressive beer belly and the sort of physique achieved by the enthusiastic consumption of burgers

119

and kebabs. His moon-like face bore the traces of prison pallor, although a few weeks of working in the open air was bound to cure that. When Wesley approached the trench and asked if he could have a word, a flash of alarm appeared in his grey eyes.

'Nothing to worry about,' Wesley said, like a doctor reassuring a patient that it wasn't going to hurt a bit. 'We're looking for Nathan Hardy.'

'Don't know where he is.' Tel's brow furrowed with worry. 'You don't think anything's happened to him?'

'Good mate, is he?' Rob Carter chipped in. There was a hint of aggression in his voice, as though he was trying to catch out a master criminal who was telling him porkies. Wesley turned and gave him a look that said *leave this to me*.

'He's all right.'

'Do you know where he goes? Who he sees?'

Tel shook his head.

'Have you ever heard Nathan mention a place called the Cliffpiper's Rest Hotel? It's on the coast not far from here.'

'No. Why?'

Wesley didn't answer. Instead he handed Tel his card. 'If you see him, will you call me? We need to speak to him.'

'What's in it for me?'

'The satisfaction of knowing you're on the way to becoming a good and law-abiding citizen.'

Tel's expression was blank as he turned away.

'Do you think you were right to give him such an easy time, guv?' said Rob sulkily as they walked back towards the car.

'Sometimes it's best to take things gently, Rob. Gaining his trust might produce better results in the

120

long run.'

Rob said nothing, but one look at his face suggested that he had his doubts.

Wesley heard his name being called, and when he turned his head, he saw Neil standing in his trench waving at him energetically. He made his way back over, ignoring Rob's heavy sigh behind him.

'You shot off before I had a chance to show you,' Neil said accusingly, his eyes lighting up, eager to share his precious discovery with his friend. 'There's a weird inscription carved on the stones down there. 'Oh Lord, have mercy upon me. By thy great goodness save me from this place.' What do you think it means?'

Wesley craned his neck to see where Neil was pointing. 'I suspect you're going to tell me.'

'I've got an idea of who might have written it,' said Neil. 'There's an old sketch of the church and you can just make out the words 'anker cell'; very faint but just legible.'

'What's an anker cell?' Rob sounded as though he was losing his patience.

'In the Middle Ages, people used to shut themselves away from the world to spend time praying,' said Neil.

'Why?' Rob asked, as though he thought Neil was talking nonsense.

'They thought it brought them closer to God and that their prayers helped other people,' Wesley explained patiently. 'They were a bit like monks or nuns but they lived on their own.'

'More than that,' said Neil. 'They isolated themselves from the world, and I think that's what we've got here.' He pointed to the remains of the doorway.

'This was a room off the church, and I've got a horrible feeling it was sealed up so that whoever was in here could never get out.'

'Bloody hell,' said Rob. 'You mean they left them to starve to death?'

Neil caught Wesley's eye. 'From what I've read on the subject, there was always someone to leave food and take away their . . . waste products through a hatch in the wall, but strictly no human contact. Just imagine what that would do to someone psychologically.'

'I'd rather not,' said Wesley quietly, staring at the remains of the small sealed doorway in what remained of the church wall. The thought of what it represented made his heart beat faster as a faint memory flashed through his head. The scent of cedarwood. The heat and darkness. His screams drowning out faint laughter outside. The memory lasted a moment, then receded, hidden away, crushed as Neil's voice dragged him back to the present.

'I've got a copy of a document that might be relevant. It dates from the fifteenth century and mentions this church. I was thinking of bringing it round for you to have a look at. It's about a woman called Elena de Judhael, who according to legend was walled up in the local manor house. But it looks like she was walled up here instead — became an anchoress. It's in Latin, and I know Pam enjoys a bit of translation.'

'You think she has nothing better to do?'

Neil took a step back, and Wesley realised that he'd snapped at his friend. He was quick to smooth things over. 'Sorry. It's just that she's got her hands full at the moment.'

Neil's expression softened. 'It's not . . .'

'No.' He glanced in Rob's direction. He didn't want the DC knowing his personal business. Luckily Rob had wandered out of earshot, restless and longing for an arrest to brighten his day. 'No, her last mammogram was clear. It's just that Michael's not been well and we're a bit worried. Sorry,' Wesley repeated. 'I'm sure Pam would welcome the distraction. Come round any time.'

'What's up with Michael?' For a moment Neil sounded as worried as Wesley felt.

'We're waiting for some blood test results.'

'What does Maritia say?'

'You know doctors. They won't commit themselves.' Wesley thought of his parents' reaction. Talking about his worries had only made them loom larger. 'Found anything else in this trench?' he asked, trying to find a distraction from his dark thoughts.

'Yes. Look at this.' Neil squatted down and scraped some earth away from the stone floor. 'Some flags are missing.'

'So?' Wesley felt disappointed, suspecting Neil had called him over for nothing.

But Dave who was working with his trowel a few feet away, looked up and nodded. 'You're right, Neil. It does extend this way.'

'What does?'

'We've uncovered the floor level in the anker cell,' Neil said. 'Apart from one section in the middle. It's a rectangular gap two feet by six feet.'

Rob Carter had made his way back to the trench and to everyone's surprise, it was him who spoke first. 'It's just the right size for a grave.'

6 September 1956

I lie awake thinking about how I got into this situation. It was a wonderful adventure at first. Rupert was so different from the boys I know. He didn't make clumsy grabs for me like they did. He told me I was beautiful and that's why I thought it was different between me and him. The boys never said that; all they wanted was to get into my knickers.

Rupert's fifteen years older than me, but fifteen years is nothing in the great scheme of things. Lots of couples have a similar gap in their ages. According to my sister, his family are filthy rich — or rather his wife's are. Her father owned a factory and they say he made a fortune in the war. Ursula mumbled the word 'profiteer', which means he was a bad man — not like my Rupert.

Rupert says his wife's a bitch and they lead separate lives. But when I asked him when he was going to divorce her so we could be together for ever, he said it wasn't that easy because she's a Roman Catholic and she doesn't believe in divorce. And besides, she controls the money.

I smile whenever I remember the time Rupert took me to London. I'd lied to my parents and told them I was going on holiday with a girl I'd met at my last school; a vicar's daughter. They had no idea it wasn't true and they said they were pleased I'd made a sensible friend at last. I had to stop myself from laughing. I packed my bag and waited for Rupert at the railway station, and my heart leapt when I saw his car. I didn't care about anything or anyone else. It was to be my new beginning. We stayed in a swanky hotel with thick carpet and a four-poster bed, and ate at the best restaurants. I'd never been to a restaurant before. He had steak and I had fish cooked with grapes. The food was beautiful and the waiters called me madam.

How could I have known it would end like this? How could I have known I'd be locked up here with only the story of a five-hundred-year-old girl for solace? Did Elena feel the same as me? I wonder.

My brilliant sister says that what I found in the muniment room is a treasure trove, and for once, she's taking some interest in what I'm doing, although she still treats me like dirt. She's always taken my parents' side — it's three against one in this house.

Ursula has been transcribing Elena's story, saying it's going to keep her entertained until she goes back up to Oxford. Father's always saying how clever she is, and I'm glad of her translations, because reading the originals is far too hard. But I still hate her for the way she told Father about me and Rupert — the way she betrayed me.

24

The phone on Gerry Heffernan's desk was ringing when he returned from his meeting with CS Noreen Fitton. The meeting, in his opinion, had been a waste of time. While he'd been discussing budgets and overtime he could have been out with Wesley asking questions. But that was life in the modern police service.

He picked up the receiver, hoping to hear some news that would move his investigation forward, and heard a tentative voice asking if he was the detective in charge. When he answered in the affirmative, there was a short silence before the caller spoke again.

'We didn't meet when the police came to investigate the recent incident. My name's Mark Unsworth. I'm the general manager of the Cliffpiper's Rest Country House Hotel and Spa. I'm afraid I was away in London when the American lady went missing, but my staff have brought me up to speed. We at the Cliffpiper's Rest would be pleased to offer the relatives of the . . . missing lady accommodation — free of charge, of course — if they have to come over from the States to — '

'That's very good of you, Mr Unsworth. Is that all you called to tell me?'

Unsworth didn't answer for a few seconds, as though he was choosing his next words carefully. 'There's a rumour going round amongst the staff that an intruder got in through the French window.'

The upward inflection of his voice suggested this

was a question. In spite of the evidence, they hadn't yet changed the official line that it was an unexplained disappearance, and they were keeping an open mind. The words 'potential murder' hadn't yet escaped from the confines of the incident room, even though with each passing hour the likelihood of finding Teresa Nilsen alive seemed to be diminishing.

Gerry couldn't lie. 'Yes. We're treating Ms Nilsen's disappearance as suspicious, and we're grateful for the co-operation we've had from your staff. But the inquiry is still at an early stage.' He knew he sounded exactly like the bland statement they'd thrown to the press in the hope it would keep them off their backs for a few days until they were willing and able to release more details. An appeal had been put out in the media asking anybody who'd seen Teresa to come forward, but so far there'd been nothing useful. The nearby coastline had been searched and they'd even had the police helicopter out. But as yet, there was no evidence of what had happened to Teresa Nilsen.

'I'm told you asked for CCTV footage, and I see the area around the room's still sealed off.' Mark Unsworth clearly wasn't a man who could be fobbed off with official excuses. He was in management, so he'd probably used a few of them himself in his time.

'OK, Mr Unsworth, between you and me, we're hoping to find Ms Nilsen alive. But certain aspects of her disappearance — '

'You mean the blood in her room? You think she's been murdered?'

'We can't possibly know that yet. And I'd be grateful for your discretion. There are some things we're keeping from the media until we know more.'

'I quite understand, Chief Inspector.'

'Good. I'm afraid it might be a few days before we get out of your hair.'

'Of course.' Unsworth hesitated. 'There's something you need to know.'

Gerry sat forward in his seat. 'What's that?'

'If it was an intruder who abducted that poor woman . . . We've been having trouble at the hotel for a while now.'

He picked up a pen and pulled a budget report towards him, upsetting a pile of papers on his desk. 'Go on.'

'The caravan park next door to the hotel grounds . . . we've had people wandering around the hotel building. We wondered whether to tell our guests in the ground-floor rooms to make sure their French windows were always kept securely locked, but . . . well, we decided that in a luxury establishment like ours, that didn't fit with the sort of atmosphere we try to create.'

'You don't want them to get the idea that the area's so rough you can't leave your doors and windows open, you mean?'

'Something like that, Chief Inspector. I really would suggest that you visit the caravan park and ask some pertinent questions.'

'We've already had officers there making enquiries, but nobody had any relevant information.'

'They would say that, wouldn't they. I've heard that some of the people who stay there are . . . '

'Are what?' Gerry couldn't decide whether the man was just a prejudiced snob or whether he had genuine cause for concern. At that moment, his money was on the former.

'There have been other incidents. Tyres let down in

the car park. Scratches on high-end cars. A smashed window. Petty theft from vehicles and ground-floor rooms. We reported it to the local police station, but nothing was done.'

'And you never thought to warn your guests. I suppose you have a notice up saying you can't be held responsible for any loss or damage.'

'You'll find that's standard in most hotels.'

'And you're sure that whoever's been making a nuisance of themselves came from the caravan park?'

'Absolutely. When I went to speak to the person in charge of the place, he was most abusive. Are you going to send someone round to have a word?'

Gerry pondered the question for a moment before he answered, 'Yes.'

25

'As far as the press office are concerned, it's a simple missing persons case until we know otherwise,' said Gerry.

'The media have their uses,' Wesley pointed out.

'True, but once they get a whiff that it could be an abduction, all hell's going to break loose — especially after the Gerdner shooting. We'll have every nutcase and weirdo in the country saying they've seen her working in their local chippy along with Elvis, Shergar and Lord Lucan.' Gerry sounded despondent and Wesley felt his pain.

'All patrols are on the lookout for Nathan Hardy, so hopefully it'll only be a matter of time before he turns up.'

'We could try putting some pressure on your new friend Tel. He might know more than he's letting on.'

'According to his record, Tel's not in the same league crime-wise as Nathan. In fact I had the impression he's a bit scared of him.'

'What does Neil say about the odd couple who've been foisted on him?'

'Only that he wouldn't trust Nathan with any valuable finds — if they were lucky enough to discover any. He reckons Tel's OK, though. Just gets on with what he's asked to do.'

'We need to find Nathan Hardy.'

'He wasn't seen on the hotel CCTV around the time Teresa disappeared.'

'That doesn't mean much. When he was spotted

the day before, he was probably doing a recce — getting the lie of the land and noting the locations of the cameras so he could avoid them on his next visit. But we won't know until we ask him.' Gerry took a deep breath. 'By the way, I had a call while you were out. Mark Unsworth, the general manager of the hotel. He's just back from a few days in London and he told me something interesting. Something nobody else at the Cliffpiper's Rest has thought to share with us.'

'What's that?'

'There's a caravan park next door — bit downmarket according to the World Wide Web. Mr Unsworth says the park's residents have been coming onto his premises and making a nuisance of themselves. Criminal damage, theft, spot of vandalism. Uniform's already been there and they were greeted by the usual three monkeys act — saw nothing, heard nothing, saying nothing. I think someone should go over and have another word.'

Before Wesley could reply, there was a knock on Gerry's office door and it swung open to reveal Trish Walton standing there holding a clear plastic folder, her face aglow. It had been a while since Wesley had seen her looking so excited.

'The team's been going through Teresa Nilsen's belongings. They found this in her suitcase. It's the place the Gerdners were looking up on their computer.'

She handed Wesley a leaflet decorated with skulls and misty figures. When he opened it, he saw that it was advertising a place called Darkhole Grange on Dartmoor.

Devon's foremost spooky attraction. He took out his phone and found the website.

There were plenty of reviews. It seemed popular, although a couple said it was far too frightening for anybody under the age of sixteen.

From what they'd already managed to glean about Teresa Nilsen, it didn't seem to be the sort of place that would interest her — or the Gerdners for that matter. Unless there were things about them they had yet to discover.

★ ★ ★

Rachel had said she didn't mind visiting the Chabliton View Caravan Park on her own, claiming she wanted a bit of fresh air after being stuck in the incident room. She drove past the entrance of the Cliffpiper's Rest with its tasteful sign and manicured grass verge and continued on a quarter of a mile until she reached another entrance. This one couldn't have been more different.

The pair of rusty wrought-iron gates stood wide open, and they looked as though they might fall off their hinges if anyone attempted to close them. The sign, in contrast to the neighbour's, looked home-made, the name of the place painted inexpertly in black paint on a flaking white background. Some wit had converted the work 'park' to 'fart'. They had probably considered the alteration hilarious, but humour was a very individual thing, Rachel thought as she drove through the entrance.

Static caravans lined the pitted driveway, only these weren't the latest luxury sort. She guessed they dated from the later years of the twentieth century; desirable holiday accommodation in their day, but that day had long passed. Water-stained brown and orange curtains drooped at their windows, and only about a third had vehicles parked outside. It looked as though business was slow even though the weather was picking up.

Outside one of the caravans further up the drive, a toddler was hitting an upturned plastic box with a stick. The child looked fed up, and Rachel sympathised.

The reception building resembled a concrete bunker, with an aluminium double-glazed door of roughly the same vintage as the caravans. It was plastered with hand-written signs, mostly terse instructions to the guests, hardly suggesting a warm welcome.

Rachel parked outside reception in an area marked *Reserved*. She was there on police business, so she assumed it didn't apply to her.

When she pushed the door open, the man behind the counter looked up. He had closely cropped hair and heavily tattooed arms. She had expected at least an attempt at a pleasant greeting, but his expression didn't change when she introduced herself and showed her ID, which made her wonder whether he regarded a visit from the police as a routine part of his day.

'You've heard about the incident at the Cliffpiper's Rest Hotel?'

'We've had your lot round already.' He sniffed. 'One of the punters said he'd seen lots of cop cars speeding around. Bloody dangerous seeing as we've got kiddies here. Surprised no one's been run over.' He stared at her as though he held her personally responsible for the police drivers' thoughtlessness.

'I understand you don't get on with your neighbours at the hotel.'

'Too bloody right. Always moaning about something. That manager accused my punters of vandalism. Said they'd been trespassing. I told him they wouldn't go anywhere near his overpriced snob-hole if he paid them. I know for a fact that someone got food poisoning after having afternoon tea there. All fur coat and no knickers, that place.'

'So you haven't visited the hotel recently?'

The answer was a snort. 'Do me a favour, love. I've got my hands full here. Why would I go there to get ripped off?'

'What happened when the complaints were made?'

'That twat Unsworth came storming onto my site shouting the odds. I told him to piss off. Said he was trespassing. He didn't like that,' he added with a satisfied smile.

'You didn't return his visit? You didn't venture onto the hotel's property?'

There was a moment of hesitation. 'Well, er . . . Why would I?'

'They've got CCTV.'

'So they have.'

He sounded confident, and Rachel suspected that he knew exactly where the cameras were and how to avoid them.

'Thank you, Mr . . . ?'

'Smith. Paddy Smith. Is that all, love, 'cause I've got work to do.'

The open copy of the *Sun* on the counter in front of him told Rachel this was a lie.

'Have any of your . . . guests mentioned the hotel to you?'

He shook his head. 'No one's said nothing to me.' He avoided her eyes. Probably another lie.

134

'I take it you have a list of the people staying here?'

'It's on the computer, like everything these days,' he said grudgingly.

'Someone'll be round to speak to them then.' She paused, the ghost of a smile on her face. 'And we might want another word with you, so don't leave town, will you.'

She marched out, ignoring the comment Smith muttered under his breath. He was hiding something all right.

26

Wesley felt uncomfortable about allowing Rachel to go to the caravan park alone. Not that she would have considered herself at all vulnerable. In fact he knew she'd be offended by the suggestion.

He was deep in thought when Tom, the head of forensics' tech team, strolled into the incident room. Tom was a tall, good-looking young man whose wife had recently given birth to their second child. Wesley thought he could detect dark circles beneath his eyes — but then a new baby in the family had that effect on people. After a few moments, he spotted Wesley and marched over to his desk.

'Got something for us?' Wesley asked hopefully.

'I have. Teresa Nilsen's phone is missing, but her laptop was found locked in her hotel room safe.'

Wesley leaned forward, suddenly hopeful. 'And?'

'Most of her emails seem pretty routine. There was a lot of work stuff. She has a job in real estate and it looks like she took a long leave to come over here. No partner or family mentioned, so I assume . . . '

'You should have my job,' said Wesley.

Tom ignored the remark. 'She spent some time on a site called 'Trace Your Roots'. Her father's side of the family came from Connecticut.'

'What about her mother?'

'Seems her mother's from around these parts. She's called Ursula and she married an American citizen. They lived in this country until the 1970s, when they moved to the States. Ursula was a successful academic and on the board of some large companies, and her late husband, Dwight Nilsen, was in the same line of business. Teresa was born in 1964 in Morbay Hospital. There's no mention of Ursula's death.'

'So Teresa has Devon roots, though presumably Ursula's still in the States.' He thought for a moment. 'Someone at the hotel said Teresa was over here to see a relative. Does her family tree research tell us who that might be?'

'Funny you should ask that.'

Wesley sensed Tom was about to reveal some useful information.

'There's a draft family tree on her laptop and it seems Ursula had a sister, but I can't find any other information about her.'

'That would be Teresa's aunt. It might be her she's come over to see.'

'It's possible. According to the family tree, Ursula's maiden name was Crane, and she was born in 1938. Her sister's name was Perdita; born in 1940. It's an unusual name, so she shouldn't be hard to find.'

'Anything else?'

Tom hesitated. 'Teresa paid a lot of visits to one particular website: a house called Bartonford Manor, near Chabliton. House and gardens open to the public on bank holidays and weekends if you're interested.'

'Teresa Nilsen obviously was.' Wesley typed the name into his own computer and a picture of an ancient stone house popped up. For a manor house, it was on the small side. Built of mellow stone, its central great hall had tall windows and its symmetrical wings protruded either side around a central cobbled courtyard. There were few details about its history apart from the fact that it dated from the fifteenth century and had been built by the de Judhael family. The same name as Neil's Elena.

Tom spoke again. 'She also showed a lot of interest in a place called Darkhole Grange on Dartmoor. It's a former asylum they've turned into some sort of ghost-hunting venue.'

'There was leaflet about it amongst her possessions. Don't suppose you know anyone who's been there?' Wesley asked, more in hope than expectation.

Tom shook his head. 'Not really my scene. But I'll ask around. Better get back.'

Wesley watched him rush off, consulting his phone as though he was expecting an urgent message.

It was possible that Teresa had simply wanted to visit a picturesque and quintessentially English manor house. Wesley suddenly recalled that Neil had mentioned there was a manor house near his dig; a place that now belonged to a rapper. From the pictures on the website, Bartonford Manor hardly looked like a pop star's country retreat — and if it was, he was surprised that its famous owner opened the property to the public.

But it was Darkhole Grange rather than the manor house that occupied Wesley's thoughts as he ate his lunch at his desk — a tuna sandwich brought in by one of the young officers Gerry had sent out to fetch sustenance for the team. There were cakes, too, and Wesley succumbed to temptation, telling himself he'd need the sugar for energy if it was going to be another late night.

Both Teresa and the Gerdners had shown an interest in Darkhole Grange, which made him want to learn more about the place. From its elaborate website, he discovered that the Gothic monstrosity had been built as an asylum in the latter years of the nineteenth century. In the twentieth century it had continued to be used for the same purpose, although the patients it took in had been private rather than National Health. Reading between the lines, he guessed it was somewhere the wealthy had used to put away family members who'd become an embarrassment, and he was surprised to see that it hadn't closed until as late as 1998. What had become of the patients, the website didn't say. Darkhole Grange was isolated, a mile from the nearest small village, with spectacular views of Dartmoor. Even though the drive out there would be lengthy, Wesley was eager to see the place for himself.

As soon as he'd finished lunch, he strolled into Gerry's office, hands in pockets, trying to look casual. He leaned against the door jamb and waited until Gerry had finished his own sandwich before speaking. He knew the DCI hated being interrupted while he was eating.

'Wes, what's new?' Gerry said with his mouth full after taking the final bite.

'Darkhole Grange — the ghost-hunt place. I want to know what the Gerdners and Teresa Nilsen found so interesting about it. Fancy coming with me?'

Gerry looked at his watch. 'Why not? If Auntie Noreen wants me, someone can tell her I'm out pursuing enquiries.'

'Which will be true.'

Their eyes met in a moment of understanding. Both men were sick of the hothouse atmosphere of the incident room, supervising the sifting of information, sorting the gold from the dross. And both knew they needed some gold if they were to make any progress.

Fifteen minutes later, they were driving out of Trad-mouth towards Dartmoor.

'Are we going on the ghost tour, or what?' said Gerry as he slumped in the passenger seat looking comfortable while Wesley sat upright, concentrating on the road ahead.

'We'll have to see when we get there. Apart from the fact that Teresa Nilsen had an RG Investigations business card, it's the only link we have between the murders and her abduction.'

'We haven't heard from the police in the States yet. They're supposed to be tracing her mother. Surely it can't be that difficult.' Gerry sighed. 'She must be quite elderly, so I'm glad it's not up to us to break the bad news.'

'Perhaps she's away and they can't get in touch with her. I'll ask Trish to give them another call; find out what's going on.'

'Teresa isn't married. No partner or kids as far as we can tell. We need to find out more about her life over in the States. And why she decided to take time off work to visit Devon.'

'It might have something to do with her family tree research. I think we should concentrate on that angle. Nobody's found any trace of her mother's sister, Perdita, yet.'

'She might have gone to live abroad like Ursula.' Gerry thought for a moment. 'What if Teresa was over here tracing her relatives and she stumbled on one who turned out to be a serial killer.'

'It's not impossible.'

He grunted. 'They say that where there's a will there's relations. Perhaps Teresa turned up out of the blue and deprived someone of their expected inheritance.'

140

That theory seemed as far-fetched as the serial killer relative, but Wesley said nothing. 'We're waiting to hear from her lawyer in the States. With any luck we might learn more when we do.'

The rest of the journey passed in amicable silence as Gerry gazed out of the window at the Dartmoor landscape. The rolling fields and green hills dotted with granite tors flashed by as Wesley tried his best to avoid the suicidal sheep who kept wandering into his path. There were ponies, too, who roamed about as if they owned the place, which they had every right to do, he thought.

The fact that Darkhole Grange was well signposted suggested that it attracted a lot of visitors; people who were happy to pay good money to be scared out of their wits. When they reached their destination, the entrance looked forbidding, with a wrought-iron archway over the open gates. Beside the new-looking sign bearing the words *Welcome to Darkhole Grange, the West Country's Premier Ghost-Hunt Venue*, there was another one, smaller and much older, set on a rotting wooden post. The words were barely legible on the flaking, faded surface, but Wesley could just about make out the warning: *Strictly Private. Keep Out. Trespassers Will Be Prosecuted*. The sight of those inhospitable words made him shudder as he navigated up the long tarmac drive to the car park. The place was isolated; somewhere a person could easily be forgotten.

'Looks like something out of a bad horror movie,' Gerry said as Wesley parked at the end of a row of cars in front of the hideous building.

The boss was right, and as they walked towards the entrance, Wesley couldn't help wondering how many unhappy patients had been cowed and intimidated

141

by the very look of the place. If you were in a vulnerable state, the last thing you'd need was to be hauled inside its forbidding portals.

27

Gerry took his ID from his jacket pocket and Wesley did likewise. A queue of punters snaked up to the ticket desk, mainly people in their twenties along with a few in early middle age, all casually dressed, all in a cheerful mood. Up for a laugh and not a nervous expression between them. They reminded Wesley of a theatre queue, eager to be amused. If there were indeed unquiet spirits in the building, they'd embarked on a new afterlife career in the entertainment industry.

Gerry pushed his way to the front of the line, earning himself mutters and hostile looks. But when he showed the young man on the desk his ID, everyone fell silent, anticipating excitement.

They were swiftly shown into an office behind the desk, where a middle-aged woman sat at a computer. She was plump, with a neat helmet of dark brown hair, and she finished typing on her keyboard before she looked up.

'Yes?'

'We'd like to ask you a few questions,' said Gerry once they'd showed their ID. There was just the hint of menace in his voice. 'Ms . . . er . . . ?'

'Mrs Anstice. Jane. My son, Kerry, runs Darkhole Grange. Please sit down.' There was an air of efficiency about her that reminded Wesley of the long-vanished breed of hospital matron he'd only seen in black-and-white films.

'How did your son come to own the premises?' he asked, always intrigued by people's life choices.

'It used to be an asylum. A lunatic asylum they would have called it in the old days. Of course we live in much more enlightened times, thank goodness.'

'Thank goodness,' Wesley echoed.

'It lay empty for years after it closed and Kerry saw it was up for sale. Had to borrow a lot from the bank to set up the business, of course, but at least he was able to leave the place more or less as he found it — with a few safety alterations, of course. We had to be inspected before we allowed the public in,' she added quickly, as though she feared they might report any breaches of health-and-safety regulations to the relevant authorities.

'What do you know about the history of the place?' Wesley asked, earning himself a look from Gerry that suggested he thought the question was a waste of their valuable time.

'It was built in the 1880s as an asylum catering for members of wealthy families who were suffering with mental health problems.' Mrs Anstice pressed her lips together in disapproval. 'From what I gather, the majority of them were women who were catego-rised as 'hysterical', but I suspect most of them were suffering from depression. Then there were probably others who were merely eccentric or an inconvenience to their families. Either that or they were just plain bolshie and their husbands were more than happy to pay to have them put away,' she added with a bit-ter smile. 'I confess I don't altogether agree with the way my son exploits those poor people's unhappiness, but . . .'

Her sensitivity to Darkhole Grange's tragic past caused her to rise in Wesley's estimation.

'I know a bit about the subject because I once

144

trained as a psychiatric nurse,' she continued. 'Not that I ever had anything to do with Darkhole Grange. I told Kerry to be respectful of the people who must have suffered here, but I don't think my words had much effect. The young think they know it all, don't they,' she said with a hint of sadness. 'In my opinion, some of the theatrical effects go way over the top, but Kerry's my son so I feel I have to support him.'

'What's your role here?'

'I'm in charge of the admin. Strictly back office. I take the bookings, pay the actors and do the accounts.'

'You use actors?'

'You'd be amazed at the number of resting actors who leap at the chance to take on the job. When people pay good money, they expect to see ghosts, and we make sure they do. But I'm sure you haven't come to ask about our ghost tours. What can I do for you?'

'We're investigating the murders of Greta and Robert Gerdner. You might have heard about it on the news.'

'Yes. It was terrible. People assume the countryside is safe, but — '

Wesley interrupted before she could say any more about rural crime, a subject with which he was only too familiar. 'We're linking the Gerdners' murders to an abduction in the area. Does the name Teresa Nilsen mean anything to you?'

She said nothing for a few moments. 'I need to check something, if you'll excuse me.'

She walked over to the bank of filing cabinets and hunted through the drawers. After a few minutes, she returned to her desk holding a sheet of paper. Wesley donned the crime scene gloves he always kept in his pocket and took it from her.

145

'I thought I'd heard her name before,' she said. 'The name Gerdner's on it too.'

'Where did you get this?'

'It came in the post about three weeks ago — a list of names and addresses and a covering letter asking me to send them tickets for the ghost tour. I remembered the name Nilsen particularly because the address was care of a hotel. The sender enclosed cash, which is most unusual these days. I'd forgotten all about it until you reminded me, or I would have contacted the police. Is it important?'

Wesley felt a thrill of excitement as he scanned the list, conscious of Gerry reading over his shoulder.

The first address was Robert Gerdner's office above the tattoo parlour. Teresa Nilsen was there too, her address given as the hotel. There was also a Susan Elwood, not a name they'd come across before. Everyone on the list was to be sent tickets anonymously, because it was intended to be a surprise.

The final name, followed by an address in the village of Belsham, was Charlie Maddox. It took Wesley a few seconds to make the connection, but as soon as he did, he passed the folder to Gerry.

'Isn't that your plumber's alleged victim?' he said.

'That's right. He owns — or should I say owned — that escape room place. But what the hell has he got to do with the others?' Gerry replied with a puzzled frown on his face.

Mrs Anstice handed Wesley the covering letter — printed, like the list. He held it up for Gerry to read.

'Signed J. Jones. Morbay postmark, but no sender's address,' said Gerry, disappointed.

Wesley was trying hard to contain his excitement as

he turned to Mrs Anstice. 'Did you see these people when they arrived?'

She shook her head. 'Sorry, I'm stuck in here so I don't see the visitors.'

'Is there any way of finding out whether they actually came for their visit?'

Wesley and Gerry waited in silence while she typed something into her computer. Eventually she looked up and smiled. 'You're in luck. We keep a record of visitors who've bought tickets in advance, and mark their names when they arrive to prevent them using the ticket twice. It has been known. According to this, Susan Elwood, Teresa Nilsen and Charles Maddox turned up, but Robert Gerdner didn't. This Mr Jones had already paid, so I presume they couldn't resist a freebie. I'll make a copy of the list for you if you want.'

She held out her hand for it, but Wesley shook his head. 'We need to keep the original, I'm afraid. And we'll arrange for your fingerprints to be taken for elimination purposes.'

'No problem. Would you like to take the ghost tour? Complimentary, of course. Another group's due to start in ten minutes.'

'That's very kind of you, Mrs Anstice, but . . .' Wesley looked at Gerry, wondering if he'd want to accept the invitation or get back to the incident room to follow up their new lead. Wesley himself had been inclined to turn down the offer because of the possibility that Susan Elwood, the only person on the list who wasn't already dead or missing, might be in imminent danger. However, from the look on Gerry's face, he realised that he was looking forward to seeing the inner workings of Darkhole Grange.

And perhaps Gerry's approach was the right one.

Perhaps the tour would provide a lead. There must have been a reason why the killer — they were presuming J. Jones was the killer — wanted to get the victims there.

'Thanks very much, love,' Gerry said. 'It would be rude not to take you up on your kind offer, eh, Inspector Peterson?'

Mrs Anstice smiled. 'If you'd like to follow me . . .'

She swept from the room and they followed her into the entrance hall, where a group of people was waiting for the guide. Some of them gave Wesley and Gerry curious looks. In their working clothes, they probably didn't look like your average punter.

While Gerry joined the waiting group, Wesley found a quiet corner and made a call, asking for Susan Elwood to be traced and contacted as a matter of urgency.

The arrival of the guide just as he rejoined the group almost made him jump. A man wearing a tail coat and top hat burst out of a door to their left and looked around. His face was deathly pale and he carried an old-fashioned leather doctor's bag, the type Wesley had only seen before in period dramas.

'Are you here to be admitted?' he asked in sepulchral tones. 'Of course you are. Come with me. Anybody who doesn't obey my orders to the letter will be dealt with.'

There was a genuine hint of threat behind his words as he towered in front of them, his hostile eyes assessing each person and finally alighting on Gerry. 'You, man. Come to the front.'

Gerry smirked, treating the whole thing as a great joke. But the smirk vanished when he saw what the man had whipped from his bag. It was a straitjacket.

148

Wesley touched the boss's sleeve, wondering whether to intervene, to identify them both as police officers, but Gerry nudged his hand away. Whatever was about to happen, he was willing to go along with it for the sake of the investigation.

In a trice, he was trussed into the straitjacket — a stained white garment that didn't look overly hygienic — and the cadaverous doctor addressed the rest of the group. 'Do I need to restrain anybody else?'

There was no answer, only a nervous silence. Some people took a step back, unwilling to draw attention to themselves.

'In that case, it's time we kept our appointment on the wards.'

As he led the way into the gloomy depths of the building, Wesley noticed that a few people were looking at Gerry, no doubt hoping they wouldn't receive the same treatment. The doctor opened a pair of swing doors with a violent kick and they found themselves in a darkened space. As Wesley's eyes adjusted, he saw that it was a dilapidated hospital ward furnished with iron bedsteads. There was a dreadful smell of decay — and something white moving at the far end of the long room. The thing was floating noiselessly towards them, and as it came closer, he could see that it was a corpse-like woman in a long Victorian nightgown. She let out a piercing scream and promptly vanished.

'That was Alice,' the doctor said in a stage whisper. 'She killed her entire family with an axe, so beware. If she takes a fancy to you, I can't answer for the consequences.'

As they were led onwards into an adjoining ward, Gerry, his arms still trapped, whispered to Wesley to scratch his nose. He had a terrible itch.

'Do you want me to help you out of that thing?' Wesley asked as he did as the DCI had requested.

'No. Let's play along with it,' was the hushed reply.

They followed their guide through the hospital, meeting various ghosts on the way. The operation was slick and the actors professional. But once they reached the basement, Wesley began to feel really uneasy. Here there were baths arranged in a row, where, it was explained, the patients were immersed in icy water as part of their cure. In the adjoining room, which was as airless and dank as a castle dungeon, was a line of beds with straps attached. They looked like instruments of torture or punishment — and what was more, they looked like the original fixtures and fittings from the old asylum. As they walked back up the cold stone steps to the first-floor operating theatre and the isolation cells, Wesley felt he couldn't bear it any longer. Making the past misfortunes and mistreatment of others into cheap entertainment didn't seem right. Without being asked, he tugged at the straps of Gerry's straitjacket and released him.

'We need to go.'

Gerry raised no objection. Like Wesley, he'd had enough.

Once they'd emerged into the daylight, Gerry turned to him. 'Were you OK in there, Wes? Only I got the impression it was bothering you.'

'I didn't like the idea of treating something like that as fun. It's only one step removed from people in the eighteenth century mocking the lunatics in Bedlam.'

'I think you're reading too much into it. People love a good spooky experience.'

'It obviously means more than that to whoever sent

150

that list. I want Kerry Anstice spoken to, and I need all those actors interviewed as soon as possible. One of them might know something — particularly our creepy doctor friend.'

'He was good. Very convincing. But I can't think why he picked on me.'

Wesley took his phone from his pocket. 'I'll see whether they've managed to locate Susan Elwood yet, and I'll ask Rach to arrange those interviews. In the meantime, we have the list. We need to find this Jones character, although I suspect that's not his real name. And we need to speak to Susan Elwood as soon as possible.'

'Too right, Wes. We need to find her before it's too late.'

8 September 1956

My sister has finished transcribing some of the letters for me. I don't know whether she did it out of kindness or whether she just found them interesting. She came to my room last night and handed them to me, but she said nothing.

As soon as I started to read them, they seemed to speak directly to me. Elena fell in love with the wrong man too. She and her brother's tutor were discovered in bed together, and her father told Sir Nicholas, the priest, that 'She beseeched me to allow them to marry, but he is far below her in station and she is promised to another.' Sir Nicholas replied that 'Although fornication is a grave sin, I am certain the matter will be resolved to the satisfaction of all.' Sir Nicholas sounds as though he was trying to keep in everyone's good books.

I wonder whether Elena truly loved her man like I love Rupert. I wonder whether she chose to defy those who imagined they had power over her and convinced herself that her dream would come true — until she was forced to face reality. I wonder if the story about her being walled up in this house is true. At least they can't do that to me. Not in this day and age.

I understand now that my passion for Rupert has been the cause of all my troubles. I was overcome with love when he drove me to London in that sports car of his. When he put the top down, I was wearing the silk Hermès scarf he'd given me and I leaned back in the passenger seat feeling like a film star. He said

I needed new clothes, so he took me shopping; if I'd been Grace Kelly herself I couldn't have felt more glamorous.

I thought my dream life with him would last for ever and that we'd be together always once Rupert had left his dowdy bitch of a wife. We'd go to all the places I'd ever dreamed about: the South of France; the Italian Riviera instead of the English version.

I was sixteen with all my life before me. Perhaps my mother was right when she told me I was fooling myself.

28

Gerry sent a team over to interview everyone who worked at Darkhole Grange, whether in an administrative or a supernatural capacity. Kerry Anstice's burgeoning enterprise might suffer some disruption, but the murder inquiry took priority over economic concerns.

The clock on the office wall told Wesley it was five o'clock already. The list and the letter Mrs Anstice had given him had been sent off to forensics for testing, but he knew the chance of finding any identifiable prints that could lead to an arrest were thin. Their main priority, however, was finding Susan Elwood and, if necessary, giving her some protection against the faceless killer whose motive remained a complete mystery. There'd been nobody at home when officers from Plymouth had called at her address, and Wesley prayed they'd contact her soon — and that it wouldn't be too late.

It wasn't until nine o'clock that evening that Trish received a call from Susan Elwood, who'd been out all day and had only just arrived home, surprised and curious about the messages left on her doormat and answerphone. Susan, who lived in Plympton, had been baffled by the arrival of the ghost tour tickets out of the blue and had taken it for a marketing ploy, but she'd gone there with her partner and enjoyed the experience. Trish told her someone would be round to speak to her, and advised her to take precautions with her safety in the meantime, but Susan sounded puzzled and didn't appear to be taking the matter very seriously.

'We still don't know for sure that it's a hit list,' said Wesley as he put on his coat. It had started to drizzle, and from the office window he could see the mist descending on the river like an army of ghosts.

'What else could it be? I knew Steve Masters was telling the truth. Someone sabotaged that boiler, and that list proves it. I bet it was the killer who set fire to Gerdner's PI office to destroy evidence of whatever's going on.'

Wesley thought for a moment. 'OK, Robert Gerdner and Teresa Nilsen might have had dealings with each other, possibly connected with tracing Teresa's relatives, but what's the connection between them and the other two people on the list? Susan Elwood told Trish she'd never heard of any of the others.'

'Why don't you get home, Wes. Remind your Pam what you look like. Early start tomorrow.'

Wesley didn't need telling twice.

When he arrived at his house, Pam came out to greet him and Amelia appeared at the top of the stairs wearing her pyjamas and gave him a wave before returning to her room. Pam looked worried and Wesley's first question was about Michael. How was he? Had the test results come back yet?

'He's much the same,' she said, her eyes flickering over to the staircase. 'Didn't go into school today and spent most of the time asleep. Your sister's promised to have a word with our GP — see if she can hurry things up.'

'Good,' he said. Pam's worry was infectious, and for a moment he forgot all about the case he'd been working on and took her in his arms. Their son's health was the only thing that truly mattered.

She broke away. 'What have you been up to?'

'Gerry and I went on a ghost tour. Former asylum on Dartmoor.'

'All right for some. My mother was going on about that place a while ago. One of the men she met on the internet told her it was really frightening. He wanted to take her there.'

'How romantic,' Wesley said, rolling his eyes. His mother-in-law, Della, was one of those people who'd never quite seemed to attain adulthood, emotionally at least. Even in her late sixties she behaved like the sillier sort of teenager. 'Did she go?'

'No. She said she'd heard all sorts of things about the place when it was a hospital. And they weren't nice.'

'What sort of things?' Wesley asked, suddenly interested.

'It was private, and if people had the money to send their unwanted relatives there, no questions were asked. There were rumours of abuse and . . . Anyway, she didn't fancy it. Not like her to be so picky or to pass up the chance of an evening out with a new bloke. Whatever she'd heard must have been bad.'

She took Wesley's hand and led him into the living room, where the TV chattered in the corner and a bottle of red wine was waiting on the coffee table.

'She was going to go to that escape room with this new man, but then the owner died and — '

'I think we'll be treating that as murder now.'

The news left Pam speechless for a few seconds. 'It hasn't been on the news.'

'We're not making a song-and-dance about it, not until we know more. If our suspicions are correct, we've got three victims now and they might be linked. The Gerdners and the owner of the escape room, Charlie Maddox. There's still no sign of the American woman who went missing from that hotel near Chabliton, and with every hour that passes . . .'

'The local news just said she was missing and the police were concerned for her safety.'

'We're trying to contact her relatives, so we've been liaising with the authorities in the States.' He paused. 'The strange thing is, we think her disappearance and the murders could be linked too. We've found a list.'

Her eyebrows shot up. 'A hit list? What are these people supposed to have done?'

'To be honest, there's no obvious connection between them — apart from the fact that they were all sent free tickets anonymously for the ghost tour at Darkhole Grange.' Wesley suddenly felt despondent. 'In the meantime, we've contacted the only other person on the list, but she hasn't a clue why anyone would want to target her.'

'I hope she's getting twenty-four-hour police protection.'

'Our budget won't run to that, but we've told her not to take any risks.'

Realising he was starting to sound defensive, he stood up. It was time he faced his fears and went upstairs to see Michael.

When he knocked on his son's bedroom door, there was no answer, so he pushed the door open. Michael was lying in bed, and his eyes flicked open when he heard his father come in.

'How are you feeling?' Wesley asked, perching on the bed.

'Everyone keeps asking me that. I wish they'd stop.'

Michael turned over.

'Sorry. Hey, I went somewhere exciting today. A haunted hospital.'

This seemed to grab his attention. He raised himself up on his pillows and Wesley could see his eyes were glazed and tired. 'The one on Dartmoor — something Grange. One of the boys from school went there. Said it was lame.'

'Lame?'

'Stupid. Pathetic,' Michael translated for his father's benefit.

Wesley didn't contradict the teenage verdict. Perhaps it had been overly theatrical, but he hadn't been able to forget about the real stories, the real events that must have happened in that place.

'Think you'll be up to school tomorrow?'

Michael shrugged. 'Hope so. I'm fed up of feeling like this.'

Wesley put his hand on the boy's and squeezed it. 'I know. Hopefully when the doc has the results . . . '

Michael suddenly grasped his hand. 'Dad. Is it something . . . serious?'

Wesley felt as though he'd been punched, but he had to put on a cheerful face. The last thing they needed was to give in to worry. 'I'm sure it isn't. They'll get you sorted out. Promise,' he said, hoping it would be a promise he'd be able to keep.

★ ★ ★

With all the excitement generated by the Gerdner murders and Teresa Nilsen's disappearance, Gerry had been tempted to put Steve Masters' little problem to one side. Being accused of negligence would

158

cast a huge shadow over the unfortunate plumber's life, but murder took priority, and besides, the matter was being dealt with by Inspector Weston from Morbay. If it wasn't for his personal connection with Masters and the fact that the man had begged for his help, Gerry wouldn't have considered it was any of his business. But since he'd seen Charlie Maddox's name on the Darkhole Grange list, the situation had changed.

As soon as he arrived at work on Saturday morning, he contacted the expert who'd promised to re-examine the boiler. The man told him that a report had been prepared and would be with him at the start of the following week. But Gerry didn't have time to wait.

'Just tell me. Did Steve Masters leave that boiler in a dangerous condition? Yes or no.'

'In a word, no. The boiler needs replacing, but it was safe enough. Probably would have plodded on for years; these old boilers were built to last.' There was a long pause. 'In my opinion, something probably blocked up the outside flue which sent fumes back into the room. But strangely, no obstruction was found after the incident.'

'So someone removed whatever it was before it could be examined?'

'That's not for me to say. I was just asked to report on the boiler.'

Gerry knew there was probably little more to say. Steve Masters was in the clear, but Charlie Maddox had died in that room and the supposed accident had acquired a sinister twist.

His hand hovered over the phone as he wondered whether to put Masters out of his misery. After a while, he decided the good news should wait until he'd sorted things with Morbay, so instead of calling the plumber, he punched out Inspector Weston's number. It was something he needed to be told right away, before the case against Masters proceeded any further.

'Interesting,' was Weston's first reaction. 'Send me the report and I'll sort things with the CPS from this end. Looks like your friend could be out of the woods.'

Gerry thought he heard a note of disappointment in the inspector's voice, but he might have been imagining it.

'I want to have a look at the scene,' he said. 'There's been a new development and we've reason to believe Charlie Maddox's death could be linked to the two murders we're investigating, as well as a possible abduction.'

'Looks like you've got your hands full.' Weston paused. 'How could Maddox's death be linked?'

'His name was on a list along with Robert Gerdner's. And if my expert's right and that boiler flue could have been blocked up deliberately . . . '

'I see,' said Weston after a few moments. 'If you want any extra officers from Morbay . . . '

'I may take you up on that. I'll let you know.'

Once he'd finished the call, Gerry sat for a few moments, deep in thought. Steve Masters had mentioned seeing threads on the flue, but nobody had taken any notice. It was time he had a look for himself.

He walked to his office door and saw Wesley at his desk. He was talking on the phone, writing on a notepad with his free hand. Once he'd put the receiver down, Gerry made straight for him.

'We're going to Morbay,' he said.

Wesley stood up and reached for his coat.

29

The escape room was housed in a converted warehouse on a run-down back street behind Morbay's main shopping drag. It was accessed through a pair of dusty glass doors; the plaque beside them bore the words *Charlie's Great Escape* in bold letters. The first thing Gerry did when they arrived was ring his boiler expert on his mobile and ask what he should be looking for. The conversation didn't last long, and when the call ended, Gerry looked serious.

'He said that if there's any evidence it'll be outside, but not to hold out too much hope because it happened a while ago. The flue's in the alley round the back, so let's take a look.'

Gerry marched ahead with a look of determination on his chubby face, and the two men arrived in a dank and mossy alley that ran between two rows of tall buildings of indeterminate age. It wasn't a place anyone would choose to spend much time. And judging by the amount of litter — fast food containers and drinks cans mainly — it was a place where the council's street cleaners rarely ventured.

The flue was easy to locate: it was the only one protruding from the back wall of the escape room building, and it was large, square and corroded with age. Gerry reached up to examine it. He had suspected that Steve Masters had been so keen to clear his name that he'd imagined evidence where none existed, but sure enough, several threads had snagged and caught on the rough rusted surface. The plumber had been right.

Gerry turned to Wesley. 'Got an evidence bag?'

Wesley, ever efficient, produced one from his pocket and watched Gerry pick off the threads carefully and drop them in.

'Can you see anything these threads might have come from?'

Wesley looked round and spotted a large piece of cloth a few yards away. Filthy and trodden into the dirt of the alley, it looked like an old towel. He produced a second evidence bag, picked the tattered cloth up with gloved fingers and dropped it inside.

'Think this might be a wild goose chase, Wes?'

Wesley shook his head. 'At one time I would have said yes, but now that it looks more like a case of murder, we need to check it out. I think we should have a look at this escape room while we're here.'

'Wasn't your mate Neil booked in to come as part of a stag weekend?'

'Charles Maddox's death put a stop to that.'

'At least you'll be able to let him know what he missed.'

Gerry led the way round to the front of the building and found a bored-looking girl sitting behind the reception desk. She was a goth, with jet-black hair and clothes to match. Her face was porcelain pale, like a Victorian china doll. As soon as she saw their ID, her look of studied ennui vanished.

'We've had the police round already. They came when Charlie was found. They said it was an accident.'

'I know, love,' said Gerry. 'But things have changed since then.'

'Changed? How?'

Gerry glanced at Wesley, who knew the DCI was

leaving the rest of the talking to him. The boss subscribed to the theory that Wesley would be more of a hit with younger members of the opposite sex.

'We're treating the death of Charles Maddox as suspicious.'

The girl's hand went up to her mouth. 'Nobody would want to harm Charlie,' she said with disbelief. 'Everyone liked him. He was a great bloke.'

'What's your name, love?' said Gerry.

'Grace.'

'Well, Grace, did you ever hear Charlie mention the name Gerdner? Or Teresa Nilsen?'

'Gerdner. Isn't that the name of those people who got shot? And that missing American woman — she's been on the news.'

'Did he ever mention any of those names?

She shook her head.

'Did he seem worried about anything in the weeks before his death? Did he have any arguments with anyone, or were there any unfamiliar visitors? Anything you can remember might be helpful.' Wesley gave her an encouraging smile, but the answer was still a shake of the head.

'Can we see where Charlie died?'

The girl glanced at the clock on the wall. 'No problem. Our first group's not due for an hour,' she said before leaving her post to lead them down a long, dingy corridor. At the end was a wooden door decorated with padlocks and chains. 'That's the Dungeon of Doom,' she said matter-of-factly. 'The Pharaoh's Tomb's through here. It hasn't been used since . . .'

They followed her down another corridor that led to a door decorated with Egyptian hieroglyphics, mainly the jackal-headed god Anubis. God of the dead. She took a key from the pocket of her long skirt and opened the door.

'You lock people in here?' Wesley asked.

'The door's locked but the players can override the locking mechanism if they work out the code from the clues provided. The clues are placed all around the room, one leading to the next, and they have an hour to discover the code.'

'What happens if they don't find it?' Wesley asked.

'If they can't solve all the puzzles they can knock on the door to be let out, but that means they've lost the game.'

They entered the room and Wesley heard the door click shut behind them. They were locked in. It was dimly lit, but as his eyes adjusted, he saw that the walls were painted with Egyptian gods and cartouches containing pictograms that he guessed formed part of the code. There was a large sarcophagus in the centre, with statues and coffers dotted around. The room wasn't large — around thirteen feet square — and the thought of being locked in there with several other people made him uncomfortable.

Until the girl released them, they were trapped, and he felt a sudden flutter of panic. Gerry, however, seemed perfectly calm as he looked round, picking up the fake artefacts and asking the girl about the heating arrangements.

'The boiler for the whole floor's in there,' she said, pointing to a cupboard with a discreet lock, painted in common with the rest of the room and barely notice-able. 'The plumber said we needed a new one, but he serviced it and said it was safe for the time being. Charlie said he'd replace it one day. He was always putting off things he considered boring. Turned out to be the death of him in the end,' she added gloomily. 'After he died, they came along and disconnected it and put stickers all over it saying it was dangerous. The police said the plumber didn't do the proper checks. Said he might be prosecuted — or struck off or whatever it is they do to plumbers.'

'We don't think it was the plumber's fault.' Wesley took a calming breath as he tried to focus on what he was there to do. 'We think the system was tampered with deliberately. Can you tell us exactly what happened on the evening Charlie died?' He could have found out from Morbay, but he wanted to hear her version of the story.

'Charlie's always the last to leave. He liked to check the place himself before he went home. A couple of the punters got trapped in the Dungeon last year and he didn't want that to happen again.'

'Who knew his routine?'

She shrugged her shoulders. 'He never made a secret of it. All the clues have to be put back for the next party, which can take some time. Some of the punters leave the place in a terrible mess; they rip everything apart trying to find the clues and they take in bottles, crisps — all sorts of rubbish. I kept telling Charlie he should have been stricter with people, but that wasn't his way. Too laid-back for his own good,' she added fondly, as though she'd had a soft spot for her late boss.

'How many people work here?'

'It was just me and Charlie that day. The police said he'd come in here and been overcome by the fumes. I'd gone home by then, of course. It was me who found him the next morning.'

'But the fumes hadn't affected the party who were

165

in here last.'

She shrugged. 'The police said they must have been lucky, that the boiler must have failed after they'd left.'

'It must have been a terrible shock for you,' said Wesley, loosening his collar. He was getting hotter. If he didn't get out of there soon, he feared he'd faint. 'Look, can we . . . Do you have the key to get out of here?'

'It's a code. Hang on.' She uncovered a keypad concealed beneath a large scarab and punched in a set of numbers. The lock clicked, and when she pushed the door open, Wesley dashed out after her, stopping to catch his breath.

'You OK, Wes?' He felt Gerry's hand on his shoulder.

'It was stuffy in there, that's all.' It was a lie, and the truth was he felt like an idiot. He was a detective inspector, a man who had come face to face with vicious criminals. He told himself that the fear he'd had since childhood was irrational. And yet it was something he found hard to control.

Before they left, they asked the girl more questions about Charlie Maddox. Did he have any enemies? Had he fallen out with anyone? Once more the answer was no. Charlie was a great guy; an ex-surfer who was liked by everyone. He was married to a woman called Angie, and Wesley asked for her address. They needed to speak to her, but in the meantime they had to send the threads and the cloth to the lab.

Wesley said nothing to Gerry, but the feeling he'd experienced in the escape room lingered in his mind. He'd always hated confined spaces, although it had never presented much of a problem during his police career. But he dreaded finding himself in a situation one day where it would prove a serious disadvantage. Even though his phobia was relatively mild, he knew he ought to seek help. There were lots of people around who claimed to be able to cure irrational fears — if he ever had the time to arrange a consultation.

Gerry's phone rang as they were driving off the car ferry, and after a short conversation he turned to Wesley, who had his eyes fixed on the road ahead.

'Bit of news, Wes. Forensics say that letter and list of names from Darkhole Grange were printed on a laser printer, but the address on the envelope was written in neat capitals to disguise the handwriting. They're examining it for DNA and prints, but they're not holding out much hope.'

'Pity,' said Wesley. 'We need to know who sent it. And why.'

30

'There was a small diary in Teresa Nilsen's handbag,' said Rachel when they returned to the station. She was standing uncomfortably, with her hand pressed to the small of her back. Wesley had already invited her to use the seat on the other side of his desk, but she'd taken no notice.

'Anything interesting?'

'Not really. Routine stuff back in the States mainly. Dentist appointments, things like that. But she'd scribbled some notes in the back. Details of more genealogy websites, and another website about the way some women were treated in the 1950s for the 'crime' of having a baby out of wedlock.' Her hand strayed to her own baby bump and rested there protectively. 'I had a look at it. I knew that sort of thing went on in Victorian times, but in the 1950s and '60s . . . '

'Different times,' said Wesley with a sigh. 'Anything else?'

'I'm worried about Susan Elwood. In my opinion she should be given proper twenty-four-hour protection. She says she doesn't want it because she can't think of anyone who'd want to do her any harm, but I think she's being naïve. If she's on that list, she's a potential target.'

'What do we know about her?'

'Only that she's a retired teacher who lives with her husband, John, in a bungalow in Plympton. She's promised to be cautious, but . . . '

'That might not be good enough.'

Wesley knew they could hardly force the woman to go into hiding. But the last thing they wanted was another fatality on their hands.

* * *

Wesley got up early on Sunday morning, leaving Pam in bed. He looked in on Michael before going downstairs to make himself some breakfast — and the coffee he would take up to Pam, a small offering to apologise for leaving her alone. Amelia and Michael were both fast asleep, and Wesley hovered by his son's door for a few moments, listening to his breathing. Pam had been told that the results of the blood test wouldn't be available until the following week. Perhaps the waiting — the not knowing what they were dealing with — was the hardest part, he thought as he shut the door quietly.

It was a pleasant morning, and from time to time the sun peeped shyly from the covering of white cloud. As he walked down the hill to the town, he could see the sparkling river below, dotted with more craft than there'd been a few weeks earlier. Ferries, tourist boats and yachts, large and small. He carried on until he reached the level ground of the town centre and made for the police station that stood next to the arts centre, overlooking the green expanse of the Memorial Gardens, with the river beyond.

Most of the team had arrived before him, and he felt a twinge of guilt as he walked into Gerry's office, the list preying on his mind. Gerry was slumped at his desk with the phone receiver clamped to his ear, but once the call was over, he gave Wesley a wide grin of greeting. 'Sit down, Wes. Take the weight off your feet.' He looked at the watch Wesley knew had been an anniversary present from his late wife, Kathy; a precious memento.

'I've just been speaking to the man in charge of the hostel in Morbay. There's still no sign of Nathan Hardy. He's gone to ground.'

'Think it's suspicious?'

'Too right I do. He was at that hotel the day before Teresa Nilsen went missing, so we need to speak to him sooner rather than later. His mate Tel has no idea where he is.'

'I got the impression they weren't exactly bosom buddies.'

Gerry picked up a pen and turned it over and over in his fingers. 'I took a look through Nathan's record. He's used violence, but nothing on the scale of the Gerdners' murders. And would he be familiar enough with boilers to know that if you block an outside flue, it sends carbon monoxide into a room?'

'Unless he was taught a bit of plumbing during his time inside.'

'Good thinking, Wes. Get someone to check it out, will you. And we need to have a word with Charlie Maddox's wife. She might know of someone who had a grudge against him.'

Gerry gathered some papers from his cluttered desk and strode out into the main office with Wesley following. In complex cases like this, he always appreciated Wesley's input into the briefing he jokingly referred to as his 'morning sermon'.

The investigation team had grown considerably in recent days as officers had been brought in from Dukesbridge and Neston, and the large incident room was starting to look crowded. As soon as the briefing was over, they set off.

Belsham, the small village where Angie Maddox lived, lay between Morbay and Neston. It was also where Wesley's sister, Maritia, lived with her husband Mark. Charlie Maddox had been one of Mark's parishioners, although whether he'd ever darkened the door of the church was something yet to be discovered. Perhaps his widow would be able to tell them.

When Wesley parked the car on the road outside the church, he could hear the bells ringing, fast and joyous. He stole a glance at the vicarage. His sister and brother-in-law would be in there with their toddler, Dominic, preparing for the morning service. Maritia would hardly have time for a visit from her brother wanting to pick her medical brains about Michael's symptoms face to face rather than over the phone.

Gerry strode ahead, looking for the right address. Wesley followed and quickly caught up.

'The house is called Surf's Up,' he said, trying to be helpful.

'Not much surf around here,' Gerry muttered. 'Belsham's not exactly famous for its rolling waves.'

At first, Wesley feared they'd come to the wrong place. They found themselves in a cul-de-sac of new-looking bungalows with gleaming UPVC double-glazed windows and neat front gardens. It didn't look much like a surfer's retreat; more somewhere to spend your retirement.

'Well it's the right road,' said Gerry, as though his thoughts matched Wesley's own.

Without another word, the two men walked slowly around the cul-de-sac, with its central circular patch of freshly mown grass. At the far end, they spotted the sign beside the glazed front door. The plaque depicted

171

a vintage VW camper van with surfboards on the roof, with the words *Surf's Up* scrawled beneath. There was no sign of a similar van on the drive; just a five-year-old Toyota with a child seat in the back.

'The dreams of youth,' Gerry muttered to nobody in particular as he pressed the plastic doorbell.

The woman who answered the door was wearing pyjamas — or leisure wear, depending on how you saw it. When they introduced themselves, she invited them into a lounge filled with toys, where a toddler — a girl — was playing happily with brightly coloured interlocking bricks, chattering away to herself, unaware of the newcomers.

'She's very good,' said Wesley once they were settled on the saggy velvet sofa. 'What's her name?'

'Ophelia,' said Angie. 'Charlie was a great fan of Shakespeare.'

'I've got a nephew around the same age. Lives at the vicarage down the road. My sister's kid.'

Angie's brown eyes lit up with recognition. 'Dominic. I take Ophelia to the church playgroup,' she said by way of explanation. 'Is she your sister — the vicar's wife? Maritia, isn't it?'

'That's right.'

Gerry caught his eye. Now that Wesley had established a rapport with Angie Maddox, he'd leave him to do the talking.

'We're very sorry for your loss, Mrs Maddox,' said Wesley.

'Thanks. But . . . well, you have to carry on, don't you. For her sake if nothing else,' she added, looking at the child, who was now dismantling her handiwork.

Wesley knew the news he was about to deliver would come as a shock, but it had to be done. 'I don't know whether anyone from Morbay police station has been in touch to tell you that we're now treating your husband's death as suspicious.' He spoke as gently as he could, his eyes fixed on Angie's face.

She shook her head. 'That can't be right. Who'd want to kill Charlie? Everyone loved him. He didn't have an enemy in the world. I was told he was killed by a faulty boiler. How can it have been murder?'

'We think the boiler was tampered with, and if that's the case, his murder might have been premeditated. I'm sorry, but it's really important that we learn more about anyone he had dealings with.'

She took a tissue from her pocket and blew her nose. Then she straightened her back and stared ahead. 'Like I said, everyone liked Charlie. I can't think of anyone who'd want him dead.'

'Business contacts?'

'He bought the escape room premises outright with money he inherited when his father died. He started it eighteen months ago and there's been no trouble in all the time it's been open. People go there to have a good time.'

Being locked in a room was hardly Wesley's idea of a good time, but he let it pass. 'Employees?'

'There's Grace on reception, and Stanislaus, but they all got on really well. A few students help out when things get busy in the holidays, but that's all.'

'One big happy family,' said Gerry. Wesley shot him a glance, wishing he'd kept his thoughts to himself.

'Yes. It is, I suppose. Charlie was great at jollying the punters along — even the stag parties — and Stanislaus is a gentle soul. Popular. Wouldn't hurt a fly and neither would Grace. If you're looking for a killer, it wasn't either of them.'

173

'No arguments with customers, then? Nobody who demanded their money back?'

'Not that Charlie mentioned to me. He kept saying how well things were going. The escape room was really popular.'

'Any disgruntled ex-employees?' Wesley guessed that the person responsible for Charlie's death had known the victim's habits and the layout of the place, so it seemed the obvious question to ask.

'There were a few temps who worked on reception before Charlie gave Grace the job permanently, but they all got on fine with him as far as I know.'

'Names?'

Angie shook her head. 'Sorry, can't remember. None of them were there very long. In fact I don't think I even met any of them.'

'Did Charlie have debts?'

'Like I said, he inherited a lot of money from his father, so he didn't need to borrow. We were lucky that way.'

'What did he do before he opened the escape room?'

'He managed a surf shop in Newquay. Gave him a chance to pursue his passion. Then his dad passed away and I got pregnant. Major change of lifestyle.'

'Have you ever heard the name Teresa Nilsen?' Wesley asked.

'Isn't that the woman who's missing?'

'That's right.'

'I'd never heard of her before it was on the local news.'

'What about Susan Elwood?'

'No. Sorry.'

'Robert and Greta Gerdner?'

A flicker of alarm passed across her face. 'They're

the couple who were murdered, aren't they?'

'Had you ever heard their names before their deaths were reported?'

'Never. Why?'

Wesley cleared his throat. 'Your husband's name appeared on a list along with the others I've mentioned.' Angie Maddox was an intelligent woman and he saw no point in keeping the information from her. 'Have you any idea why that would be?'

'Absolutely none.'

'You don't recall him mentioning any of those people to you?'

She shook her head, puzzled.

'What about Nathan Hardy?'

'Never heard of him.'

'He's an ex-offender. Is it possible Charlie took pity on him and gave him a job at some stage?'

'He never said anything to me about employing an ex-offender. I'm sure I would have remembered something like that. He preferred to employ students for casual work. Reckoned it was easier.'

'Did he receive a complimentary ticket for a place called Darkhole Grange?'

'Funny you should mention that. A ticket turned up out of the blue. Charlie thought it was a marketing thing. He went along out of curiosity and to see if he could get any new ideas for the escape room, but he didn't say much about it when he got back. Seemed a bit subdued, actually.'

'Tell me about Charlie's family.'

'His dad died of a heart attack a couple of years ago. He was a lot older than his mum. They got married when he was fifty and she was in her twenties — twice her age. He'd been married before, but Charlie was his only child.' She smiled sadly. 'Charlie used to say his dad couldn't keep his trousers on. Randy old goat, he called him. I only met him a couple of times, and the second time he made a pass at me — his own son's wife. Disgusting.' She shuddered. 'I'm glad Charlie never wanted much to do with him.'

'But he left Charlie all his money.'

'Like I said, only child. Only one he knew about, anyway. He had a number of affairs while he was married, I believe. Priapic was the word Charlie used.' Her expression softened. 'Charlie wasn't a bit like him. He was a good man, Inspector. That's why I can't believe anyone would want to kill him.'

'Is his mum still alive?'

Angie bowed her head. 'No. She died in a hospice last year. Cancer. She was a nice woman and she'd had a lot to put up with.'

There was a long pause before she spoke again.

'Charlie was kind,' she said softly. 'They say people inherit bad blood, don't they. The sins of the fathers and all that. But thankfully he took after his mum.' She hesitated. 'If it had been his dad who'd been murdered, I wouldn't have been at all surprised.'

'But he's dead.'

'That's right,' said Angie. 'He's dead and buried.'

10 September 1956

When I lie awake at night, I keep thinking of Elena. I wonder if I feel close to her because her story is so like mine — like an echo over five hundred years.

Sometimes I wish I'd never found out about her. Sometimes I think she's driving me mad; that she's become an obsession I can't shake off. If she is walled up somewhere in this house, I'm scared that she might be haunting me. Perhaps I should try and find her. Perhaps that's what she wants.

They say I'm mad. They call me 'morally degenerate' — not strong like my sister, the golden girl, the chosen one. Ursula would never have done what I did, not in a million years. I can still imagine her smug smile when Father found out the extent of my wickedness.

Everyone says my sister has a bright future — unlike me. I'm the one who was always in trouble at school. I'm the one who smoked and hung round with the boys from the village. I'm the one who liked going on the back of motorbikes and meeting lads behind the village hall. I was no better than I should be. A little tart. But when I met Rupert, all that changed. He opened my eyes to a new world. I fell in love.

They probably said Elena was a tart too, although they didn't have fags and motorbikes in her day, and they probably had another word for girls like her. She must have done something really bad to be punished like that.

Bad girls never prosper.

I continued my search of the muniment room and made another discovery. Hidden behind a pile of old deeds, I found a wooden box full of more letters. Only these hadn't been sent. Someone, her brothers or her parents, had intercepted Elena's letters and hidden them away.

I won't give these ones to Ursula. Even if it takes me a long time, I'll unravel the strange language on my own.

31

It was Monday morning and Nathan Hardy still hadn't turned up at the dig. Neil felt uneasy as he watched Tel labouring away with what appeared to be enthusiasm. Perhaps he'd turn out to be one of the hostel's success stories. Neil found the thought rather gratifying.

He strolled over to trench four, and as soon as Tel saw him approaching, he struggled off his kneeling mat and stood upright, a nervous smile playing on his lips. 'Everything OK, Dr Watson?'

'Fine, Tel. Any news of Nathan?'

A frown passed across Tel's face. 'He hasn't been at the hostel for a few days, but his stuff's still in his room. A couple of cops came to have a look, but they never said nothing to me.'

'Any idea where he might be?'

'I told the cops he'd mentioned a cousin in Manchester he hadn't seen for a while, so he might have gone up north.'

'He should have told me if he wasn't going to be here. I could have given someone else a chance to take his place.'

Tel looked as though he was deciding whether to say something, so Neil waited and eventually the words came out in a rush. 'Nathan had cash and I don't know where he got it from. Said it was easy money.' There was a long pause, as though he was gathering his thoughts. 'And last time I saw him, he seemed a bit scared.'

'What of?'

'Dunno. You don't think something's happened to him?'

Neil didn't answer the question. 'Look, I could speak to that mate of mine in the police if you're worried.'

'The black one who came here before?'

'He's one of the good guys. He'll get it sorted if anyone can. If you haven't heard from Nathan by tomorrow, I'll give him a call.'

Tel raised no further objections, so Neil reckoned his concern was genuine.

* * *

After Gerry's Monday morning briefing, Wesley sat at his desk turning over all the possibilities in his mind. But he was still as puzzled as he had been a few days ago. Charlie Maddox, the ex-surfer who, according to his wife, was everybody's friend, and the antisocial Gerdners, who'd found the rural idyll didn't live up to their dreams, appeared to have little in common.

No trace had been found of Teresa Nilsen, and with every day that passed, Wesley felt pessimistic about the possibility she'd be found alive. They were still waiting for more information from the States. He wondered whether the cops there had broken the news of her disappearance to her elderly mother — and whether she would make the journey over the Atlantic. There was no clue about the relative she'd mentioned at the hotel either.

During the briefing, Gerry had announced that their appeal for anyone who'd used RG Investigations to come forward in confidence had produced a few responses. But these had all concerned trivial matters — mostly missing dogs and errant husbands — and Wesley felt a profound disappointment that so far every line of enquiry had led them nowhere.

His phone rang, and when he picked it up, he heard a woman's voice. It sounded familiar, although he couldn't quite place it; then, to his relief, she said her name and he cursed himself for not recognising it right away, especially as he'd only seen Angie Maddox, the widow of Charlie, the previous day.

'Mrs Maddox, what can I do for you?'

'You asked me to let you know if I thought of anything. Well, I've just had a call from an old surfing mate of Charlie's.'

Wesley waited, sensing there'd been more to the call than an old friend passing on his condolences.

'I've always thought this bloke was bad news. I never felt comfortable when Charlie went out with him.'

'Why was that?'

'Charlie used to smoke a bit of weed when he was younger. He gave all that up when we got together, but Paddy went on to bigger things, if you get my meaning.'

'You suspect this man might have had something to do with Charlie's death?'

'It's possible. He tried to muscle in on the escape room about six months ago, but Charlie was having none of it. Paddy's own business wasn't doing well, and when he saw the escape room was a success, he pulled the old mates act; wanted part of the action. I told Charlie not to touch him with a bargepole.'

'And Charlie agreed?'

'Absolutely. He'd started the business with his father's money and he didn't want to give Paddy a slice. Would you?'

'Definitely not.'

'I've been looking at Charlie's phone, and Paddy called him a lot over the past month or so. Charlie said he was getting fed up of it. The last time was the day before he died.'

'They argued?'

'I don't know.'

'Do you know where we can find Paddy? We'd like to have a word with him.'

'He runs a caravan site on the coast between Bereton and Dukesbridge. Chabliton View, it's called.'

'Paddy Smith?'

'That's right.' He could hear the surprise in her voice.

Wesley hesitated, wondering how much to tell her. 'We've already spoken to him about another matter, but thanks for the information. If you think of anything else — or if you need anything . . .'

He heard a child crying in the background. Ophelia.

'I'd better go,' she said, leaving him listening to the dialling tone.

Gerry was out of the incident room, reporting the latest developments to Noreen Fitton in her well-appointed office on the top floor, but he felt the need to share Angie's revelation with someone, so he made for Rachel's desk.

'Fancy another visit to the Chabliton View Caravan Park?' he said, trying to sound cheerful about the prospect.

'I'd rather do a stretch in Holloway than spend a

week at that place,' she said with a grin. 'As a matter of fact, I'm just going through their list of customers. No familiar names, but I'll ask uniform to contact everyone who was there when Teresa Nilsen went missing.'

'I've just had an interesting conversation with Charlie Maddox's widow. Turns out Paddy Smith was an old surfing pal of Charlie's.'

'Small world.'

'Smith tried to muscle in on Charlie's business, and according to Angie, he was becoming very persistent. It looks like Charlie was trying to distance himself from his old mate, but Paddy wasn't having any of it.'

'If Charlie kept saying no, that probably created a lot of bad feeling.'

'Charlie's name was on Darkhole Grange's list.'

'So is Susan Elwood's and Trish says she's fine — no hint of anything unusual. What if we're letting that list distract us from other possibilities?'

Wesley shook his head. Robert Gerdner's name was on it, and Teresa Nilsen's. It was relevant all right.

'Want me to drive to Chabliton View?'

Wesley nodded gratefully and Rachel smiled with a slight roll of the eyes. She'd always found Wesley's nervousness about driving on Devon's narrow country lanes mildly amusing.

'Everything OK?' Wesley asked as they turned onto the Dukesbridge road.

'Nigel's nagging me to take it easy.'

'He could be right.'

'Don't you start. I was brought up on a farm, so I've had dealings with plenty of pregnant livestock in my time. It brings everything into perspective.'

'You're not a sheep or a cow.'

'Principle's the same,' she said with a smile.

Wesley was glad to see her cheerful again. He'd been worried about her over the past few months, but now the shadow that had been looming over her seemed to have lifted. He hoped it would stay that way.

When she steered the car through the gates of Chabliton View Caravan Park, she stole a glance at Wesley in the passenger seat. 'Not your dream holiday destination, is it?'

'Bit of a contrast to the hotel next door. You can understand why Mark Unsworth thinks it lowers the tone.'

'Riff-raff was the term he used to one of the DCs.'

She brought the car to a sudden halt outside one of the static caravans that lined the rough single-track road to the reception area.

'That's Paddy Smith.'

Sure enough, a man was emerging from the caravan door carrying a Calor gas cylinder. He stared at the car for a moment, and when he recognised Rachel, his belligerent expression became wary, as though another visit from the police was as welcome as a plague of rats.

'Can we have a word?' said Wesley as he emerged from the car.

The man focused on Rachel. 'See you've brought a little friend this time.' He rolled his eyes, showing the bloodshot whites. 'A black and a pregnant mum. Couldn't they find any proper cops?' His lips twitched into a self-satisfied grin.

'Just watch what you're saying.' Rachel sounded indignant, but Wesley caught her eye and gave a tiny shake of his head.

'Look, love, I've told you everything I know. You're wasting your bloody time.'

For a moment he looked as though he was about to retreat into the caravan and shut the door in their faces, but instead he told them to drive up to reception. He'd meet them there, although he didn't sound too happy about the prospect.

'Charming man,' said Wesley.

'We shouldn't have to put up with that sort of thing.'

'I couldn't agree more. But in this case I suspect that if we made an issue of it, he'd just clam up altogether.'

'Even so . . .'

'Teresa Nilsen's still missing. We need him to talk.'

Rachel scowled and said nothing.

Ten minutes later, they were sitting in the office where Rachel had last spoken to Smith. The newspaper was open at the sports pages, and a tall pile of clean bedding took up half the desk.

'We haven't come about the incident at the hotel this time,' Wesley began after introducing himself and showing his ID, which Smith examined closely, as though he suspected he was an imposter. 'You know Charlie Maddox.'

Smith said nothing for a few seconds, and Wesley suspected that he was toying with the idea of denying it. But in the end he said yes, he did know Charlie. He was an old surfing mate from his Newquay days.

'Charlie's wife says you were hassling him — wanting a share of his escape room business.'

'Silly cow's got the wrong end of the stick.' He glanced at Rachel. 'Women have a habit of doing that.'

Wesley knew that Rachel wouldn't want to let this comment pass, but he got in first. 'You deny you've

185

been pressuring him to give you an interest in his business.'

'Why shouldn't I want a share of Charlie's good fortune? We were mates until that bitch came along.'

Wesley had liked Angie Maddox and he felt a little offended on her behalf. 'Mrs Maddox had every right to defend her husband's business interests. When did you last speak to Charlie?'

He shrugged. 'Must have been a couple of weeks ago. Why?'

'You haven't tried to call him since?'

'I have, but I got a voice saying the number wasn't available. He must have changed it and forgot to let me know.' He sounded a little hurt.

'You haven't heard about his death?'

Smith's mouth fell open and he sat in shocked silence. Then the words came out in a rush. 'No. Nobody's bothered to tell me.'

'It was on the local news. He died in a suspected accident at work.'

'Never listen to the news — only the football. When was this?'

His reaction seemed genuine. But Wesley had known a lot of killers who were excellent actors.

'It happened at the beginning of the month. He died in the escape room of carbon monoxide poisoning.'

'You said it was an accident. What's it got to do with me?'

'We now know that the central heating boiler was tampered with. There are heaters in your caravans. You know how they work.'

There was a look of injured innocence on Smith's face. 'That's a load of crap. I'd never want to do away with Charlie. Nobody would. He was a good bloke. The best.'

'We're working on the assumption that he was murdered.'

'Well don't look at me. Over the past few weeks I've been here getting ready for the start of the season. It's the same every year. Busy time. Anyone'll tell you.'

'Nobody's accusing you,' said Wesley, surprised at how quickly the man assumed he'd need an alibi.

'I wouldn't hurt a hair of Charlie's head, and that's the truth.'

As they left, Wesley told him that someone would be round to take another statement. And when he turned his head to look back, he saw that the look of shock had vanished, replaced by a smirk of satisfaction.

32

Neil had left the dig early on Monday afternoon to catch Arthur Penhalligan before he shut up shop. When he'd arrived, Arthur's eagerness to talk made Neil suspect he was lonely. He'd already mentioned that he was divorced and lived alone in a new apartment overlooking the river in Neston. Neil had seen the inflated prices of similar apartments and wondered fleetingly how he could afford it. Arthur had admitted that most days the shop had very few customers, and Neil suspected it was more of a passion than a commercial enterprise.

Arthur's main topic of conversation, however, was the therapist he'd consulted about his claustrophobia. She was wonderful, he said, and he couldn't recommend her too highly. Neil didn't suffer from any phobias, apart from a terrible fear of not being able to work in archaeology, but he said that if he knew anyone who needed help, he'd be sure to tell them. He thought of Wesley, but his friend's dislike of confined spaces wasn't something he felt inclined to share with Arthur Penhalligan. That was Wesley's business and his alone. Neil knew that his friend had never allowed it to interfere too much with his life but he'd still mention it if he called Wesley that evening for a chat.

Before he'd left the shop, Arthur had lent him a local history book featuring a section on Long Bartonford, and that night he'd fallen asleep while he was reading it. The day's digging tired him out more than it used to. With that and the pains in his knees, he feared age was catching up with him.

When he reached the dig the following morning, he found that Chris and Dave had arrived before him, along with Tel, who was drifting about near the site hut with a worried look on his face.

'Any news of Nathan yet?' Neil asked.

Tel shook his head. 'He still hasn't turned up at the hostel, Dr Watson.' He always addressed Neil by his official title. 'The police are after him, aren't they?'

'I think they want to speak to him, yes.'

'I thought that was why he was lying low. But now I'm getting a bit worried,' said Tel, shuffling his feet awkwardly.

Neil told him he'd call Wesley once the tarpaulins had been taken off the trenches.

★   ★   ★

Wesley was halfway down the stairs, making for the kitchen, when his phone rang. When he looked at the caller's number, he saw it was the station.

A body had been found by bin men in a Morbay alley. A young man who'd probably been dead a few days.

'It's a male, so at least it's not Teresa Nilsen,' Gerry said as soon as Wesley arrived in the incident room.

'Have we got an ID yet?'

'Not yet. He was shot once in the head, just like the Gerdners, so we have to consider the possibility that it's connected, although he wasn't on the list.' Gerry let out a long sigh. 'On the other hand, there could be a drugs connection — drug crime is flourishing like Japanese knot-weed at the moment, and rival dealers see firearms as tools of the trade. Let's face it, they're

189

not hard to smuggle in on a small boat around these parts.'

Wesley nodded. It was a problem that had spread its unpleasant tentacles into all sorts of rural areas unaffected by that sort of thing until a few years ago.

'Geoff Weston called to say that Colin's doing the postmortem at Morbay Hospital later this morning. Hopefully by then we'll have an ID. Dead man's probably in his early twenties; shaved head with a distinctive tattoo, so it shouldn't be hard to find out who he was. Morbay are going through all their missing persons, so . . . '

'Nathan Hardy has a tattooed snake crawling over his head,' Wesley pointed out. 'And his car was seen near the hotel shortly before Teresa Nilsen went missing, so if it's him, there could be a connection.'

'You're jumping the gun a bit, Wes. Even if it is Hardy, he'll have made some dodgy contacts over the years — the sort of contacts who'd think nothing of shooting someone in an alley. And we don't know whether the sighting of his car near the Cliffpiper's Rest had anything to do with Teresa Nilsen. He could have been there for a spot of thieving. It has been known.'

Ten minutes later, Gerry was giving his morning briefing, emphasising the urgency of finding any connection, however tenuous, between the people whose names were on the Darkhole Grange list, something they'd so far failed to do. At least Susan Elwood was safe, with a patrol car checking her address at regular intervals. According to Trish, Susan was baffled by the whole thing and insisted that her name must have been chosen at random. Wesley wasn't convinced.

When his phone rang, he saw Neil's name on the

caller display and was tempted to ignore it. He'd only spoken to Neil the previous evening but his friend was in the habit of ringing him if he'd found anything archaeologically exciting. Although Wesley usually welcomed this sort of information, on this occasion he didn't have time for distractions. He stared at the ringing phone for a few moments before yielding to temptation.

'Hi, Neil. Is it important?'

'I don't know yet. You were looking for Nathan Hardy?'

'Yes.' Wesley was tempted to mention the new development, but decided against it until they had a firm ID and the next of kin had been informed. 'Has he turned up?'

'No. He hasn't shown his face for a few days.'

'Perhaps archaeology isn't his cup of tea.'

'It's probably nothing, but his mate, Tel, seems worried. I don't think they're bosom buddies, but he wants to know whether you've located him yet.'

Wesley decided an explanation couldn't be avoided any longer. 'A body's turned up in Morbay and it fits Nathan's description. If Tel can ID him . . . I'll send a car over to fetch him.'

'I'll let him know.'

'Thanks. It would be far better coming from you than a uniform turning up out of the blue and hauling him off to the mortuary.'

'Will do.'

Neil rang off, leaving Wesley staring at the phone.

33

Tel seemed nervous, which wasn't surprising. Being inside a mortuary had that effect on people. Wesley had become used to it over the years, but he couldn't forget how he'd felt on his first visit. He'd been sick after watching the procedure, something he'd never shared with his parents or his sister.

Tel's only role on this occasion was to conduct the identification from behind glass with the body respectfully covered until the sheet was folded back to reveal the face. Even so, when he saw the small, neat bullet hole in the dead man's forehead, he turned ash pale and looked as though he was on the point of fainting.

The post-mortem itself held few surprises. Nathan had been an occasional drug user and his diet had been atrocious. A sad life, Colin said matter-of-factly. The bullet wound he'd sustained was very similar to those of the Gerdners, and the body showed no signs of having been moved, so he'd probably died where he was found. He had been shot at fairly close range — again just like the Gerdners — and when Wesley pressed Colin about the likelihood of the same weapon having been used, all the pathologist would say was that he couldn't rule it out. The bullet had been found in the alley, so they'd have to wait for the ballistics report to see whether it was a match.

When Wesley and Gerry emerged from the hospital, they found Tel at the entrance, smoking a cigarette. He wasn't the only one indulging in this particular vice. Patients in hospital gowns and pyjamas, some hooked up to drips, were also puffing away against medical advice, in spite of the chill in the air.

Tel stubbed his cigarette out on the ground when he saw them walking towards him.

'Thanks for waiting, Tel,' said Wesley.

'Saves us coming to look for you,' Gerry chipped in, giving the lad a threatening stare.

'You OK?' Wesley asked, wishing Gerry would abandon the role of nasty cop. They needed Tel's co-operation.

'Suppose so.' His manner told Wesley that his recent experience at the mortuary had left him shaken.

'Want a coffee? There's a café nearby. Or maybe you could do with something stronger.'

'Cup of tea'd be good,' said Tel, casting a cautious look in Gerry's direction.

'I expect you have to get back to the incident room, Chief Inspector,' said Wesley, hoping Gerry would take the hint. He knew he'd get more information out of Tel if they spoke alone, good cop to potential witness. And he couldn't trust Gerry not to ruin any atmosphere of trust with one of his sharp remarks.

To his relief, Gerry said he had to update Noreen Fitton on the latest development so he'd get a patrol car to take him back to Tradmouth.

Wesley and Tel walked in silence to the café, which stood round the corner from the hospital. It was an unpretentious place, one up from a greasy spoon. The tea was strong and the tannin stung the roof of Wesley's mouth. But Tel was looking more relaxed and that had been his intention.

'You're enjoying the dig?'

Tel's eyes lit up with enthusiasm. 'Yeah. It's great.'

'My degree's in archaeology. I studied with Neil

Watson.'

'Then why did you . . . ?'

'They say that inside every archaeologist there's a detective waiting to get out. It's all about piecing together clues. Archaeology's got a lot in common with police work.'

Tel looked sceptical. 'Yeah. Suppose it has.'

'I need to ask you about Nathan. Who were his closest mates?'

'He talked about mates up in Manchester, but he didn't know many people round here. Said he came down 'cause he fancied living by the seaside.'

'Long way to come.'

'He lived here for a while when he was a kid. He was in care and he was put with a foster family he liked. He came down to find them, but they weren't around any more. Moved abroad somewhere.'

'But in spite of that, he decided to stay.'

'He used to talk about going back up north, but . . . '

Wesley suddenly felt sad for Nathan. Life had dealt him a rotten hand and he'd ended up dying in a back alley with only a killer and a loaded gun for company.

'We got offered that place on the dig, but Nathan was never keen. Saw it as a skive.' Tel looked up from the mug of tea he was nursing. 'He had problems. Someone from the charity arranged for him to see someone — a therapist.'

Wesley remembered Neil mentioning the charity a while ago, but he hadn't been taking much notice at the time.

But he did recall the name of Neil's contact.

'Does someone called Pixie work there? Purple hair?'

Tel sniffed. 'Yeah. She comes round to the hostel

sometimes.' He gave a bitter little laugh. 'One of the blokes there says you could swear you'd been framed by your pet unicorn and she'd swallow every word.'

Wesley had to smile at the mental picture. 'Might she be able to tell us more about Nathan?'

Tel shrugged. 'Doubt it.'

'Was it her who arranged for him to see the therapist?'

'Dunno. But I told him to do it if it kept them happy.'

'What's the name of the charity?'

He hesitated, as though the question needed some thought. 'It's something like Starting Again . . . or Making a Fresh Start. Dunno where their office is, but I guess they must have one.'

'Did Nathan tell you anything about the therapist?'

'He never said much, but he was like that. Kept himself to himself.'

'We'll have to speak to the other residents of the hostel. Were any of them particularly close to Nathan?'

Tel shook his head. 'Doubt it. They'll only tell you what I've said. He was good at keeping shtum, was Nathan, so nobody knew him that well.' He leaned forward and lowered his voice. 'I heard he was the same inside — never said much, not even to his cellmate.'

Something about the way he said the words convinced Wesley he was telling the truth. Nathan had been an enigma to his fellow residents, but there was always a chance he'd opened up to the therapist the charity had arranged for him to see.

'You don't know if he'd got on the wrong side of someone? A dealer, maybe?'

The answer was a shrug of the shoulders.

'Did he have any enemies? Anyone he'd double-crossed?'

Tel shook his head and drained his mug. Wesley's was still half full and getting cold. There was a pause before Tel spoke again. 'I'll tell you one thing — Nath was never short of dosh. Must have got it from somewhere, but I don't know where. Look, I'd better be off. Ta for the tea.'

'I'll get someone to give you a lift back to the dig if you like.'

Tel considered the offer for a few seconds. 'Ta.'

Wesley made the call and saw Tel into the patrol car when it arrived. If he hadn't wanted to seek out the woman called Pixie at the ex-offenders' charity, he would have been tempted to take Tel back to the dig himself and see how Neil's work was progressing.

It took a few phone calls to track down the charity's address. The Morbay Fresh Start Trust had an office in a back street half a mile from the hospital, not far from where Nathan's body had been found. It was a fine day, so the prospect of walking there appealed to him. Walking gave him time to think.

The charity's offices were in a converted shop, the interior concealed behind grubby vertical blinds. Wesley pushed the door open and saw a young man sitting at the desk nearest the door. He had a ponytail, and a welcoming expression on his chubby face as he looked up expectantly.

'How can I help you?' he said, oozing sympathy.

But as soon as Wesley showed his ID, the sympathy vanished.

'I'm looking for Pixie.'

'Why? What's she done?' The young man sounded nervous, as though he feared Pixie had slipped into wicked ways.

'I'm hoping she might be able to help me, that's all. I'm enquiring into the murder of Nathan Hardy.'

He let the words sink in, watching the man's face.

'Nathan? He's . . . ?'

'He was found in an alleyway behind some empty shops not far from here.'

'That's terrible. Although I didn't know Nathan. He was one of Pixie's clients, you see. She's in the back office. I'll fetch her for you.'

All hostility vanished, the young man hurried through to the back of the shop and returned with a young woman, tall and athletic, with a long face concealed behind a pair of large glasses with heavy black frames. But the most unique thing about her was her shock of curly purple hair.

'I'm DI Wesley Peterson from the major incident team in Tradmouth. Can we talk — Pixie, is it?'

'Yeah. Come through.'

He followed her into a back office. There was a framed photograph of a smiling blonde woman on her neat desk — in contrast to Pixie, the subject was conventionally dressed in a smart trouser suit.

She saw Wesley looking at it. 'My partner, Tasha. She's a solicitor.'

'Must come in useful in your line of work.'

Pixie gave him a disapproving look, as though she judged his comment to be inappropriate. 'Matt's just told me about Nathan. Are you sure it was murder? Nathan was a troubled soul. Drug user. Nightmare background like a lot of our clients. In care from an early age. Alcoholic mum. It's hardly surprising he ended up in prison.'

Wesley nodded sympathetically. He'd always

favoured dividing offenders into two categories — the weak and the wicked — even though the legal system often didn't acknowledge the difference.

'What else can you tell me about him? Did he have any enemies, for instance? Was he involved in anything untoward?'

'Some of our clients are open with us and we get to know all the ins and outs of their lives, but not Nathan. He mentioned once that he had a sister, but he never told me anything about her. Like I said before, he was a troubled soul.'

'Is that why you recommended a therapist?'

Wesley thought he saw a momentary look of unease pass across her face, but it vanished so quickly that it might have been his imagination.

'I've sent clients to Rosemary before. She's helped a lot of people.'

'Did she help Nathan?'

'All consultations are strictly confidential, so wouldn't know.'

'I'll need to speak to her. Can I have her contact details?'

'As I said, whatever Nathan shared with her was confidential.'

'Nathan's dead and I'm afraid the dead don't have any privacy. Not when they've been murdered.'

There was a moment of hesitation before she took a file from one of the cabinets that lined the far wall of the office. She consulted it before writing down an address and handing it to him with a heavily ringed hand.

As soon as Wesley left the offices of the Morbay Fresh Start Trust, he tried the number Pixie had given him, but it went to voicemail. He left a message. Could Rosemary call him back urgently?

On Wesley's return to the incident room, Gerry rushed out of his office to greet him.

'How did you get on with Tel?'

'He said Nathan was the secretive type but he was never short of money, which suggests he was up to something. I want to have a word with the therapist he was seeing. I've left a message.'

'Good. We've had news.'

Wesley should have known from the excited look on the DCI's face that there'd been a development. 'What is it?'

'You know the cops in the States have been trying to contact Teresa Nilsen's mum? Well, we've found her. She isn't in the States. She's here in Devon — been living in a retirement home here for the past six months. Her daughter was over here to visit her, and when she stopped turning up, she started to worry. But Teresa had told the matron that she wanted to do a bit of sightseeing while she was here, so she assumed that was where she'd gone; that maybe she'd told her mother but she'd forgotten. She said people often do when they reach her age. Then one of the staff at the home took some time off and saw a report about Teresa's disappearance and rang the matron, who contacted us. The old lady hasn't been informed yet in case it upsets her.'

Wesley sank into the seat by his desk, his face solemn. 'Then we'd better pay Teresa's mum a visit. Break the news.'

'How do you tell an elderly woman that her daughter's missing and possibly dead?' Gerry asked nobody in particular.

'I'll go with Rachel if you like.' Rachel had a lot of experience in family liaison, so she seemed the obvious choice.

'There's something else. According to the matron, the mother's a formidable lady. Doesn't suffer fools gladly. Just wanted you to be prepared.'

20 September 1956

They say I have to go away. They're sending me to a place on Dartmoor and they tell me it's for my own good. They don't want me here risking the family reputation. Not a girl who did what I did. I'm a disgrace, and disgrace is something that isn't tolerated in this family.

Mother says nothing on the subject. Since she found out, she won't even look me in the eye. Father makes me take my meals in my room and has told Mrs Potts to leave the tray outside my door. He must think my moral pollution can spread like an infection, even to our housekeeper, who must be fifty if she's a day.

Ursula caught me with Elena's letters. She burst into my room as though I'm no longer entitled to any privacy because of what they think I did. She snatched one of the precious parchments from my hand. I told her to be careful, but she was too excited to take any notice.

In the end, she agreed that I could keep them for the time being because she hadn't finished transcribing the others yet. But as I struggle with the unfamiliar writing, I realise how much I need her help. The work is slow and today I've only managed a few paragraphs.

My right trusty Sir Nicholas, *Elena writes,* I beseech you to intercede with my father for I have no wish to marry the man for whom I am intended. There is another who pleases me

201

greatly — one Denyes, a learned man from Oxford and tutor to my brothers. He is of good family and I have a great affection for him. You have ever been my friend and I beg you to plead for me in this matter.

I can only conclude that the letter was intercepted by her family and never delivered to the priest. Poor Elena.

34

Arthur Penhalligan dreamed about Elena de Judhael most nights. He dreamed he was locked in with her; confined in that small stone chamber. Both of them were naked and he could hear chanting in the background; life going on outside her prison. He woke up sweating, tangled in damp sheets. Trapped as though his nightmare had come true.

During their therapy sessions he'd asked Rosemary's advice and she'd listened patiently while he described his dreams, even though that wasn't the primary reason he was there. His aim had been to cure the claustrophobia that had restricted his life for years. It was growing worse, and now the very sight of a lift brought on a panic attack. Rosemary had claimed she could help him. And her gentle confidence had made him believe her.

Discovering Elena's story amongst the sheaf of manuscripts from the house clearance had only made things worse. Alone in the shop he had a lot of time to think about what had happened to her and he was beginning to wish he'd never come across her story. He'd shown it to Dr Watson, who'd suggested he should donate all the documents to the county archives. But Arthur couldn't resist the thrill of possessing one in particular, poring over it like a miser with his gold. To him, the ancient writings of a humble Devon priest were treasure. Not to be shared lightly.

He thought of Elena's story as his and his alone. In his imagination she was a damsel in distress he had to save from her tormentors. There had even been shameful dreams where he'd treated her as a lover. Elena the innocent. Elena the beautiful. Elena the wronged.

Arthur had never been at ease with women and his own marriage had been a disaster. But the Elena de Judhael of his imagination was the kind of woman he'd happily kill for.

* * *

Before Wesley and Rachel set off, he looked up Wood-tarn House on the internet but found nothing. It was unusual these days for an establishment not to have some sort of website, and it meant he had no idea what they'd find when they got there.

The address was on the other side of Chabliton, and as they were driving down a wide tree-lined lane, Wesley spotted a sign by the roadside, so discreet that he almost didn't see it. He told Rachel to stop, and she braked sharply.

'Go down here,' he said.

'Is this it?'

He didn't reply, and she turned into a well-kept drive. They didn't catch sight of the house itself until they turned a sharp bend and saw a low stone manor house.

'I think this is the wrong place,' said Rachel as she put the car into gear, preparing to turn round.

'This is Bartonford Manor. Teresa Nilsen was looking it up on her laptop.'

'So where's Woodtarn House?'

'I'll ask,' Wesley said, remembering what Neil had said about the Manor being owned by a rapper. 'You stay here if you like.'

He made for the great oak front door. In the past, policemen had been expected to use the tradesman's entrance, but those days were long gone.

The door opened to reveal a woman with poker-straight long blonde hair and lines on her face that belied her youthful looks. She wore skin-tight leather trousers and she was smoking something that smelled illegal. She looked Wesley up and down as though he was an under-footman who'd been caught stealing the family silver.

'The house is only open to the public at weekends.' She sounded bored, as though she was used to turning away unwanted visitors.

Wesley thought it best to show his ID to prevent misunderstandings. The woman blushed and made a feeble attempt to hide the joint behind her back.

'I'm looking for Woodtarn House.'

'You've come to the wrong place.' Wesley could sense her irritation. 'Back down the drive, turn right and it's the next turning on the right.'

'Thank you, Ms . . . er?'

'Lois,' she said evasively, as though she was unwilling to give her full name to the police.

'Have you lived here long?' Wesley couldn't resist prolonging the conversation.

'I don't live here.'

'Who does?'

'Paul Cummings — MC Button.' She said the words as though they explained everything.

Wesley feigned ignorance and looked at the woman enquiringly.

'The rap artist,' Lois said with exaggerated patience when she saw how out of touch he was with her world.

'I'm his PA. Is this about that shooting nearby? We've already spoken to the police.'

'It's not about that. Do you mind if I ask you a few questions?'

She suddenly looked anxious, as though she feared she was about to be arrested.

'I'm not interested in what you smoke in your spare time. I just want to know about the house.' He nodded towards the joint, now almost burned out. She sighed and threw it to the ground outside the front door, where Wesley stamped out the glowing stub.

'I don't know what I can tell you. Paul only moved in a couple of years ago. I'm usually based in London, so . . .'

'A medieval manor house in the middle of nowhere?' said Wesley. 'Doesn't seem very rock and roll.'

'Rock and roll?' She looked at him enquiringly. He knew he'd said the wrong thing. 'Paul has to spend a lot of time in London and this place suits him. He likes to get away from the hustle and bustle.' She didn't sound too enthusiastic about the idea.

'We're investigating the disappearance of a woman called Teresa Nilsen. You may have seen it on the news.' She shook her head. 'Ms Nilsen's American and she was taking a great interest in this place. Has she called here at all? Or visited when the house was open to the public?'

He took Teresa's photograph from his pocket and held it out for Lois to examine. She gave it a cursory glance and shook her head before rolling her eyes.

'Paul opens the place to visitors, but I think it's a big mistake. What if an obsessive fan finds out he lives here? Some people will always find a way of —'

'I don't think Ms Nilsen was a fan. She might have

been interested in the house and its history.'

For a second there was a look of disbelief on Lois's face, as though she found it hard to credit that someone would prefer an old house over her rap star employer. 'I don't know anything about that. You'll have to speak to Paul. He's into all that sort of thing for some reason. He's here if you want to ask him.'

To Wesley's surprise, she stood aside to let him in, then led him through an arched oak door into what had once been the great hall. Somehow he had expected an unsympathetic conversion into a modern nightmare of leopard skin and clashing modern artworks. Instead, the room was furnished with comfortable leather sofas and antique furniture. On one of the sofas sat a man reading a novel while classical music oozed into the room from hidden speakers. He was mixed race, with sharp features, and he wore a neat polo shirt and jeans. When Wesley entered, he looked annoyed at the interruption — and something else. Embarrassed, perhaps.

'Yo, bruv,' he said, raising a fist in greeting. Wesley had the impression of an actor slipping into a familiar role.

As soon as Wesley introduced himself, however, the cool rapper persona vanished and a look of relief appeared on the man's face. The Paul Cummings who now sat before him could have been a member of any of the more conventional professions, with his intelligent eyes and his neutral accent.

'Sorry about that,' he said. 'I was afraid you might be a journalist.' When he saw that Wesley looked confused, he explained, 'Respectability doesn't sell.'

'It's all an act?'

'I got into it as a joke when I was at uni. A friend

of mine knew a record producer and . . . the rest is history. But for God's sake don't tell anyone my dirty little secret. As far as the record company's concerned, I used to be a drug dealer in Brixton. If they found out that my dad's an architect and my mum's a teacher, the whiff of middle-class suburbia would be the kiss of death to my career.'

Wesley smiled. 'Don't worry. My lips are sealed.'

'How can I help you? Hope I'm not in trouble.'

'Not at all.'

'Is it about those terrible murders? A constable called last week to ask whether I'd seen anything suspicious — which I hadn't.'

'We're investigating the disappearance of an American lady from a hotel near here. The Cliffpiper's Rest.'

'I know the place. Was she a fan?'

'We don't think so.' Wesley went on to explain how the victim had been taking an interest in Bartonford Manor, and Paul listened carefully before speaking.

'The Manor was built in the fourteenth century by the de Judhael family. They chose the wrong side in the Civil War and lost the place to one of Cromwell's cronies, then a descendant of the Judhaels bought it back in the nineteenth century — regained the ancestral home. I like to open it to the public a couple of days a week, though I have to keep out of the way, of course, so some retired volunteers from the village take the actual tours. We try to keep it quiet that I own the place, but it's of great historical interest and it doesn't cause much disruption – we're hardly Longleat or Chatsworth.'

'That's very generous of you,' said Wesley, impressed. 'Does the name Teresa Nilsen mean anything to you?'

A look of recognition appeared on his face. 'I don't

think I've heard of a Teresa, but when I bought the house, I did some research into the former owners. I told you the de Judhaels bought it back in the nineteenth century, but they didn't hold onto it for very long. They ran out of money and sold it to an industrialist called Ebenezer Crane in 1899. Then in 1997 it was sold by an Ursula Nilsen to a hedge fund manager who bought it as a country retreat. Ursula had inherited it from her parents, but she was living in the States so I don't suppose it was much use to her. Could this Teresa Nilsen be a relative of hers? Could that be why she was taking an interest?'

'It's possible,' Wesley said, pleased that the picture was becoming clearer. If Teresa's family had owned the Manor at one time, it was hardly surprising that she'd want to visit if she was in the vicinity.

'Do you recognise her?' He produced the photograph again and Paul studied it for a few moments.

'I'm afraid not. But if she was on one of our guided tours, I wouldn't necessarily have seen her. Sorry.'

Wesley was struck once more by the contrast between his initial impression of the man and the reality. 'What did you study at university?' he asked.

'Law, at St Andrews. I might go back to it when all this is over. It's always wise to have something to fall back on.' Paul smiled, showing a set of unnaturally perfect teeth. 'In the meantime, MC Button puts a roof over my head — and not a bad roof either.'

'It's a lovely place,' Wesley agreed, before returning to the reason for his visit. 'We've been told that Teresa's mother now lives at Woodtarn House. Is it round here?'

'Their sign's very near our entrance, so people sometimes call here by mistake looking for it. That's why I get Lois to answer the door if she's here. She's better than any guard dog. Woodtarn House used to be the dower house, where the de Judhaels put their unwanted widows and maiden aunts, but now it's a private retirement home. Very exclusive. No connection with the Manor at all these days.'

'None?'

Paul laughed. 'I might be thinking about what I'll do when my rapping career comes to an end, but I can assure you running a retirement home isn't one of my options.'

Wesley stood up and handed Paul his card. 'If you think of anything else, give me a call. And by the way, a friend of mine is in charge of the dig near here.'

His eyes lit up. 'Dr Watson? I've met him. He told me about the connection between his dig and the de Judhael family. They were the lords of the manor, of course. Had the old church built.'

'I believe there's a legend that someone was walled up in this house in the Middle Ages.'

Paul shook his head. 'I've heard it. Some girl who got pregnant by her brother, wasn't it? But they've got it all wrong. The surveyors I employed before I moved in were very thorough, and I'm pleased to say they found no unexpected sitting tenants, alive or dead.'

'You were a long time,' said Rachel when Wesley returned to the car, where she'd been waiting patiently, scrolling through the messages on her phone.

'The owner was keen to help. Ever heard of MC Button?'

'My nephew likes him. Had the Brit Awards on when I was round there once. All gold chains, sparkly trousers and dark glasses — MC Button, not my nephew.'

'He's the owner.'

Rachel's eyebrows shot up in surprise. 'Really? What was he like?'

'Nice bloke. And as for the gold chains and sparkly trousers, appearances can deceive, but I suppose we should know that in our job.'

Rachel rolled her eyes. 'Did he tell you how to get to Woodtarn House?'

'It's the next entrance down the lane. I'm glad we took our little diversion, though, because I discovered that Teresa might have a family connection with Bartonford Manor.'

'What connection?'

'It's possible that her family owned it at one time, which explains why she was looking it up on her laptop. I think it might be important.'

Rachel nodded. 'And it gives you the perfect excuse to snoop around an old manor house.'

35

A few minutes later, Rachel parked in front of a fine Georgian house — the sort of place once referred to as a gentleman's residence. If this was where the unwanted females of Bartonford Manor had been banished to, they hadn't done too badly for themselves.

It didn't resemble any other retirement home Wesley had visited. There was no scuffed paintwork or smell of stale cooking; nothing to suggest it wasn't a fine Georgian house in wealthy private hands. There were no telltale institutional signs either; no staff in uniforms bustling around, and if it weren't for the unlocked front door, Wesley would have assumed they'd come to the wrong place and be thinking up his apologies for the intrusion.

The polished mahogany door to their left was standing ajar, and he knocked before pushing it open because it seemed like the right thing to do. The room was traditionally furnished with antique furniture and comfortable chairs. In the large bay window four elderly people were sitting around a polished table playing cards, two Zimmer frames placed to one side. They were deep in concentration, but every so often one of them would say something about trumps as another kept the score. Wesley didn't know much about bridge, but he guessed that was what they were playing.

He was reluctant to interrupt their game, but he had no choice. 'Excuse me, we're looking for the person in charge.'

One of the women looked up. She was a lot younger

212

than her companions, probably in her fifties, with severe permed hair that made her look older. 'I'm Mrs Wardle, the matron. What can I do for you?'

When they showed their ID, she rose to her feet wearing the co-operative smile of the honest citizen. But there was worry behind that smile, as though she was wondering how best to handle the situation.

'Thank you for coming. We only discovered this morning that the missing woman is the professor's daughter, and I called you as soon as I found out. We don't watch the news here because it tends to upset our guests, but my member of staff was taking a few days off, and when she caught the report at home she let me know right away.' Mrs Wardle looked genuinely upset. 'Poor Professor Nilsen. She's been doing so well, but this will set her back. I'll show you to her room.'

'Would you like us to break the news?' Rachel asked.

'No. It's probably better coming from me.'

'How often did Teresa visit her mother here?' said Wesley.

'She was staying at a hotel about a mile away and she visited regularly until a few days ago. She did mention that she intended to do some sightseeing in Cornwall while she was over here, and her mother assumed that was where she was, as did the rest of us, although the professor didn't remember her saying she was going. The poor lady has mobility problems, I'm afraid. She's eighty-three and mentally sharp, but even so, she forgets things from time to time. Happens to the best of us. The spirit is willing but the flesh is weak, as the good book says.'

'Must be frustrating for her,' said Wesley sympathetically.

'She was a scientist – worked for a big multinational

company at a time when it was rare for a woman to progress that far in her career. She taught at a top university in the States too. She was very highly regarded in her field, I believe.'

This explained how she was able to afford such a well-appointed and obviously exclusive retirement home.

'Her family once owned the manor house next door, you know,' Mrs Wardle added with a hint of pride that someone from such a background should have chosen to spend her twilight days in her care. 'She inherited it when her parents died but sold it shortly afterwards because she was living in the States at the time. A pop star lives there now, I believe, but he doesn't give us any trouble.' She thought for a moment. 'The professor said she wanted to come home to die. It's not unusual for people to feel like that in my experience.'

'She's dying?'

'We're all dying, Inspector. Only some of us will die sooner than others. Since the professor's mobility problems have worsened, I fear she's been losing the will to live. And now with her daughter missing . . . You've no idea what's happened to Ms Nilsen?'

'I'm afraid not.'

'You're quite sure she hasn't gone off sightseeing?' she asked hopefully.

'Quite sure, I'm sorry to say.'

Mrs Wardle shook her head. 'She seemed such a nice woman. Do you think she's met with an accident? Or . . . ?'

'That's what we're trying to establish,' said Wesley gently.

There was no point mentioning the state of the hotel room and the bloodstained ashtray.

They allowed Mrs Wardle to lead them up the graceful sweeping staircase to the first floor, where she gave a light tap on one of the doors on the landing before opening it with a cheerful greeting. 'Hello, Professor Nilsen, you have some visitors.'

'My daughter?' Wesley couldn't see inside the room yet, but he heard the hope in the woman's question.

'I'm afraid not.' There was a long pause, and Wesley and Rachel stood on the threshold, listening.

'I'm sorry, Professor, but the police would like a word with you.'

The matron went further into the room, and the rest of the conversation was muffled. Wesley looked at Rachel. 'You'd better do the talking.'

It was a full five minutes before Mrs Wardle came to fetch them, telling them in a whisper that she'd broken the news. When they crept into the room behind her, they saw the old woman lying in bed, propped up against the pillows with a tissue clutched in her right hand. Her rheumy blue eyes were bloodshot and glassy with tears, but when she saw Wesley and Rachel, she rearranged her features, putting on a mask of bravery.

'We're doing our best to find your daughter, Professor Nilsen.'

'I know people mean well, but I should have been kept informed. I'm not a child who needs to be shielded from unpleasantness.' She spoke with an American accent. Educated East Coast.

'We've only just found out that Teresa was over in this country to see you, or we would have been in contact earlier,' said Wesley apologetically.

She nodded in acknowledgement. 'Mrs Wardle's explained the situation, and anything I can do to help . . .'

'Thank you.' Wesley caught Rachel's eye and she cleared her throat, ready to ask the first question.

'Can you think of anyone who'd want to harm Teresa, Professor?' She guessed that Professor Nilsen would want to be addressed by her proper title, an acknowledgement of what she'd achieved during her long and successful life.

'Nobody. Teresa was divorced from her husband, but the split was amicable. He married again, but she didn't. She said she'd done with men.'

'While she's been over here, has she consulted a private investigator? A man called Gerdner?' From what the matron had said about the residents being cocooned from the news and the world's unpleasantness, Wesley didn't expect the professor to recognise the name unless Teresa had mentioned it.

'No. Why would she do that?'

'Have you any extended family?'

She hesitated. 'No,' she said rather too emphatically.

'Teresa had a family tree on her computer. According to that, you had a sister called Perdita.' 'She died when she was a child,' she said quickly. 'I never really knew her.' 'When she came to see you, was there any suggestion that she was afraid of anything?'

'No.'

It was Wesley who asked the next question. 'Did Teresa mention visiting a place called Darkhole Grange?' There was no mistaking the flicker of horror in the old woman's eyes, swiftly hidden. 'No.' 'You've heard of Darkhole Grange?'

'I don't think so. What is it?'

'A former asylum, on Dartmoor.'

'Why would I have anything to do with a place like

216

that?' She turned her head away.

'Does the name Charles Maddox mean anything to you?'

She shook her head. She looked beyond the two police officers to Mrs Wardle, who was hovering by the door as though she feared the questioning might be too much for the vulnerable old lady. Although Wesley had the impression that, mentally at least, Ursula Nilsen was stronger than most.

'I'm sorry, I don't feel up to answering any more questions,' she said, sinking back into her pillows. 'Could you leave me now, please.'

'Of course. I promise we're doing our best to find Teresa,' said Rachel gently. 'Thank you for your time.'

'Time is the one thing I have a lot of,' Ursula said before closing her eyes, a sign that the interview was over.

'What did you make of that?' Wesley asked as they left the building.

'I think she recognised Charlie Maddox's name. And I didn't believe her when she said she hadn't heard of the Gerdners either. Did you see her face when you mentioned Darkhole Grange?'

'If she was lying to us,' Wesley said, 'we need to know why.'

36

On the journey back to Tradmouth, Wesley felt puzzled. If Ursula Nilsen had been lying to them, it would be the first time in his police career that the mother of a missing child, however old that child might be, didn't try to help the police in every way possible. He said as much to Rachel, and she agreed. Neither of them wanted to leave themselves open to accusations of bullying a frail elderly woman, but Wesley needed to have another word with Professor Nilsen.

Gerry greeted them as soon as they walked into the incident room.

'We've heard from that therapist Nathan Hardy was visiting — the one the Pixie woman put us onto. She said she'll be home around five o'clock if we want to go round for a word. She lives in Neston.'

Wesley had been nursing hopes of catching up with his paperwork, but it seemed another trip out was unavoidable. He followed Gerry into his office. The boss needed to be brought up to date with what they'd learned from Professor Nilsen.

'So you thought she recognised the Gerdners' and Maddox's names but wasn't letting on?'

'That's the impression I had, although I could be wrong. And she said she wasn't aware that Teresa had consulted Robert Gerdner in a professional capacity.'

'We don't know whether she did, but she had his business card and they were both on that list, so there must be a connection.'

'Darkhole Grange definitely meant something to

the professor,' Wesley continued. 'Could she be J. Jones, the anonymous provider of the free tickets? Did she want those people to go there for some reason?'

'We can check whether one of the staff at Woodtarn House obtained the cash and posted it to Darkhole Grange for her — presumably she couldn't do it herself.'

Wesley shook his head. 'According to the matron, she has mobility problems.'

'Darkhole Grange used to be an asylum. Could a member of her family have been a patient there? What about her sister — the one on Teresa's family tree? Penelope, is it?'

'Perdita. The professor said she died in childhood.'

'Believe her?'

'You mean she might have been lying?' All sorts of half-formed possibilities had been swirling around Wesley's brain, and this had been one of them.

'Trish has been to see Susan Elwood again, and asked her whether she has any family connection to Darkhole Grange. Maybe she had a relative who was sent there. Susan said she wasn't aware of anything like that, but there was a time when families kept that sort of thing quiet.'

'What does Trish make of Susan?'

'She's a retired teacher who's set herself up as an artist, and she's convinced that nobody could be remotely interested in murdering her. She's mystified by the whole thing.'

Gerry looked at his watch. 'I think it's time we spoke to this therapist. Rosemary Harris, her name is. Ever visited a therapist, Wes?'

'No.'

'Me neither.'

'Although Della has. Many times.' The words conjured a mental picture of his mother-in-law, who'd stayed with them while convalescing from a car accident, an unforeseen result of one of his previous cases. She hadn't been the easiest of house guests, so it had come as a great relief when she'd moved out.

'Has all this therapy done her any good?'

'Not that I've noticed,' Wesley replied, thinking that no amount was likely to cure Della's self-absorption and impulsive behaviour. His mind strayed to his own little problem. He'd heard that therapists could cure phobias, and Neil had mentioned that someone he knew, a bookshop owner called Arthur Penhalligan, who shared his fear of confined spaces, had consulted this Rosemary woman. But it was something he'd learned to live with over the years. Besides, he was embarrassed to raise the subject in front of Gerry.

As Wesley drove to Neston, the traffic was becoming heavy; it was home time for most, although he knew his own working day wouldn't come to an end for a few hours yet.

Rosemary Harris lived in a cottage on the fringe of town, across the bridge that spanned the river and down a small lane adjacent to open countryside. It was a small whitewashed building with the date 1789 picked out in black paint above the front door. The year of the French Revolution, Wesley thought, allowing himself to be distracted. A silver Toyota was parked outside the cottage, and he pulled up carefully alongside it.

'Let's hope she'll give us chapter and verse on Nathan, because at the moment, he's a bit of a mystery.'

'You're right,' Wesley agreed, thinking of Tel's verdict on his fellow ex-offender. He watched Gerry lift the wrought-iron knocker and let it fall.

After a few moments, the door opened to reveal a thin woman whose bone structure suggested that she had once been stunningly beautiful. Her grey hair was tied back into a ponytail, and she wore a brightly coloured floor-length skirt with a long-sleeved black T-shirt and chunky silver jewellery adorning her neck and wrists.

She invited them in with a professional smile and led them through to a small back room brightly decorated with an array of Indian throws and wall hangings. They sat on the low sofa while she opted for a beanbag, which looked distinctly unstable. The place smelled faintly of patchouli — one of Della's favourite scents.

'We'd like to ask you about Nathan Hardy,' Wesley began as he adjusted the garish cushions on the sofa in an attempt to get comfortable.

'Let me make it clear, Inspector, that I'm only willing to discuss him because he's passed away. Confidentiality is vital in my work, as is trust.'

'Of course,' said Wesley, catching Gerry's eye. 'We understand.'

'He was murdered and we're trying to find out who did it,' said Gerry with the hint of a growl.

'I did wonder why the police were so interested,' she said calmly. 'I assumed at first that it was an overdose. Sadly, such things happen to the likes of Nathan.'

'He was shot.'

'I see,' she said, sitting with her hands resting on her lap, the picture of calm.

'He was seen at a hotel on the coast not far from Bereton, and a woman called Teresa Nilsen went missing from there soon after. Does that name mean

221

anything to you?'

'I'm afraid not. Who is she?'

'An American lady; the daughter of a professor who was born here but moved to the States. The professor returned to Devon recently to live in a retirement home and Teresa was over here to visit her. There's evidence that she was abducted from her hotel room.'

'Perhaps she invited someone into her room and that's how her trust was repaid. People in a strange country are often less cautious than they would be at home. Psychologically they let their guard down, get into holiday mode. The threats don't seem as real in unfamiliar surroundings.'

'You could be right,' said Wesley.

'I know I'm right. It's my job — the workings of the human mind.' She gave him a dazzling smile. 'I expect you want me to tell you everything I know about Nathan.'

'That'd be helpful,' said Gerry. He too appeared to have fallen under the woman's spell.

'It's the usual sorry tale, I'm afraid. Single mother with an alcohol problem. In and out of care. Fell in with a bad crowd and got into drugs. Started stealing to fund his habit. Became bolder and used violence. Ended up in a young offender institution, followed by prison. For the likes of poor Nathan, that was like progressing from sixth form to university would be to those from a more stable background. He originally came here from up north to find a foster family he'd been happy with for a few years when he was younger, only to discover they'd moved away. The poor boy had a rotten start in life, but I did my best to provide strategies for him to cope with life outside prison. I was hoping that therapy would encourage him to think 'more carefully about the consequences of his actions.'

'He was taking part in the excavation at Long Bartonford, near the village of Chabliton. My friend Dr Neil Watson is in charge of the site.'

'I thought the dig would be good for him. Give him a purpose and let him experience a life away from crime and the people he used to hang around with. Once they start seeking refuge with their old friends, there's not much anyone can do to shake off their influence. Breaking the cycle is the key, Inspector, as I'm sure you know.'

'Who were his mates?' Gerry asked.

'He had friends up north where he used to live, but I don't think he knew many people down here. Only his fellow residents at the hostel in Morbay, I imagine.'

She stood up, a sign that the interview was over. But Wesley had more questions. 'Does the name Darkhole Grange mean anything to you?'

Wesley was sure he saw a flicker of recognition in her eyes, there for a split second then gone.

'I've heard the name. It used to be an asylum; a private institution, I believe.'

'Have you ever come across any former patients in the course of your work?'

'It closed many years ago — before I came to the area.' There was something evasive about her reply, and that aroused Wesley's curiosity.

'Have you heard of Robert and Greta Gerdner?'

'Aren't they those poor people who were murdered? I heard the names on the news.'

'Or Charles Maddox?'

She shook her head.

'I think that's all,' said Gerry, heaving himself out

223

of his seat. 'Thanks for your time.'

She saw them to the front door, but as Gerry was making for the car, Wesley hung back. 'Can I have a word?'

'Of course,' she said with an efficient smile.

'My friend at the Long Bartonford dig told me you'd treated somebody he knows for claustrophobia.'

The look in her eyes told him she'd understood what he wanted before he'd had a chance to put it into words. 'You suffer yourself?' She continued before he had a chance to reply. 'The treatment's simple and effective,' she said. 'Usually desensitisation or sometimes hypnotherapy. I'll give you my card.' She took a business card from her pocket and handed it to him.

'And I'd better give you mine,' he said with a smile, passing over one of his own cards. 'If you remember anything about Nathan, please give me a call.'

'Will do, Inspector,' she said with a charming smile. 'And I look forward to hearing from you.'

Gerry was waiting by the car tapping his foot. Patience had never been his strong point.

37

Rachel had been waiting for Wesley's return, twisting her head every so often to look at the office door in the hope of seeing him. This was something he needed to know about.

She felt her baby kick inside her and instinctively placed her hand on her swelling stomach. At that moment the door opened and Gerry marched in with Wesley following in his wake.

'Right, troops. Anything new to report?' the DCI boomed, scanning the room for anyone who didn't appear to be paying attention.

Rachel rose to her feet, a sheet of paper in her hand. 'I've been looking into Charles Maddox's background.' She paused. 'There isn't much on Charlie himself that we don't already know about. But his father, Rupert Maddox, the one he inherited all that money from, was a colourful character by all accounts.'

'Charlie's widow told us that he was a bit of a lad,' said Gerry, earning himself a disapproving look from Rachel.

'He had a couple of paternity claims against him that went to court.'

'So that confirms Angie's claim that her father-in-law couldn't keep his trousers on. Is it relevant?'

'There's worse. A nanny employed by the family made an allegation of rape against him in the 1980s, but it never came to court. The Maddox family were very wealthy; made their fortune in biscuits, apparently. Rupert's father — Charlie's grandad — was

225

a Member of Parliament. One of the great and the good.'

'So Rupert was the wayward son.'

'He was a rapist,' Rachel snapped. 'He ruined the life of at least one woman we know of. Probably more.'

Wesley saw Gerry bow his head in penitence.

'Sorry. Of course he was a bad 'un. And I expect his money helped him to get away with it. But what's it got to do with his son's murder?'

'Revenge?' Rachel's suggestion was tentative.

'The sins of the fathers being visited upon the children?' said Wesley. 'As far as we know, Charlie wasn't in the least bit like his father, so is it likely?'

'I suppose we've got to consider every possibility,' said Gerry. 'Any chance of tracing this nanny or her family?'

'I've already put someone onto it,' said Rachel with a hint of pride. 'Her name, according to our records, was Charity Benson, and if she's still alive, she'll be in her sixties. She was a local girl who went to work for the Maddox family at their big house near Bereton. I've had a look at the house online. It's an outdoor pursuits centre now, which gives you an idea of the size of the place. The family had a house in London too. Mayfair.'

'Not short of a bob or two then. Have you found out how much Charlie inherited?'

'A tidy sum, but nothing like the fortune you'd expect. Seems money slipped through Rupert's fingers.'

'I presume the nanny was looking after Charlie?' said Wesley.

'Probably. Angie told us that his mother's no longer with us so it looks like Charlie was the last of the Maddox line. Apart from his daughter, Ophelia.'

'And whatever other children Rupert Maddox fathered on the wrong side of the blanket,' said Gerry.

'That's a very old-fashioned phrase,' said Rachel with a frown.

'Contrary to rumour, Rach, we dinosaurs aren't extinct. Anything else?'

'Not yet. But I've been looking at the benefactors who funded Darkhole Grange when it was an asylum. Turns out the Maddox family had a big interest in the place, because one of those benefactors was Abel Maddox, Rupert's father.'

24 September 1956

Mother came to my room this morning, knocking so quietly that I hardly heard it. I presume she didn't want Father to know she was speaking to me, because he'd told her not to. I was to stew in my own juice, he said.

My sister's going back to Oxford next week. I hate the way everyone thinks she can do no wrong. There are times when I'd like to kill her. She's translated more of the papers, though, and reluctantly I let her take Elena's unsent letters too, because my head was aching from the effort of making sense of them. I know they were private to Elena, but after five hundred years, I don't suppose it matters. Ursula says they're important historical documents — like the Paston Letters, whatever they are — and that Father should show them to a museum. But I said that Father's got more important things to worry about — like me. I hope she forgets about the museum idea. Now that I'm locked away, Elena has become my special thing. A story that's mine and mine alone.

According to my sister, Elena must have been well educated to write letters. In those days, even rich women were often illiterate, unless they were nuns, which makes my discovery even more surprising. But what do I know about how things were back then?

Mother's allowed me to have the notebook and pen I asked for — that's why I'm able to write this. I think she'd like to be kinder to me but she's afraid of Father. We're all afraid of Father.

She hasn't mentioned Rupert for some time. I sometimes wonder whether she knows the truth about what happened.

38

The atmosphere at the Long Bartonford dig had been subdued since the news of Nathan's death had filtered through the grapevine. Although Neil noticed that Tel didn't seem much affected by the loss.

Once the excavation of the graveyard was under way, Neil walked to the anker cell, the trench he was keeping to himself in the hope that it would contain a major discovery. Everyone else was hard at work, and the only sounds he could hear were birdsong and the industrious scraping of trowels against earth as he shifted the tarpaulin away from the trench he'd abandoned before the weekend because he'd been occupied with other things.

The small rectangle in the centre where the stone flags were missing still looked to him like a grave, but the remainder of the floor had to be exposed before he investigated further. Or perhaps he was putting it off because he had a bad feeling about what he'd find.

★ ★ ★

'There's someone asking for you at the front desk, sir,' said the female voice on the other end of the line. 'Says it's about Nathan Hardy. Wants to see the person in charge, but DCI Heffernan's phone's engaged.'

'Did this person give a name?' Wesley asked.

The woman lowered her voice. 'She says she's his sister, sir. Will you come and have a word?'

Wesley said he'd be down right away. He was glad

of the distraction from trawling through paperwork: overtime budgets and statements from contacts of all the victims. As far as he could see, there was nothing amongst them that had moved the case forward, and even tracing the relatives of the women Charlie Maddox's father had wronged seemed to be clutching desperately at unlikely possibilities. They'd discovered that Charity Benson, the nanny, had died ten years ago leaving no relatives. It seemed that this particular line of enquiry had hit a dead end.

In his despair, he'd even taken Rosemary's business card from his pocket and stared at it for a few moments. Banishing his irrational fear of confined spaces might be a good idea, if he ever had time to follow it up.

As he was leaving the incident room, he glanced into Gerry's glass-fronted office and saw the DCI was still on the phone. The expression on his face told him that it was an unwelcome routine matter rather than a new development in the case. He guessed the call was from the chief superintendent — or even someone higher up the food chain. He raised a hand in greeting, and Gerry pointed to the receiver and rolled his eyes.

Down in the reception area, Wesley saw several people waiting for attention, perched nervously on the blue plastic benches provided for visitors. There were two young women, either of whom might be Nathan Hardy's sister, so Wesley sidled up to the civilian officer behind the reception desk and asked which one it was. The last thing he wanted was to make an embarrassing mistake.

Once he'd been pointed in the right direction, he approached the woman sitting nearest the door. She had scraped-back dark hair and an anxious pasty face, and she rose to her feet when she saw him walking towards her, her eyes, pale as Nathan's, wide with fear.

'You wanted to speak to me about Nathan Hardy,' Wesley said after he'd introduced himself.

She gave a nervous nod.

'Let's go somewhere more private,' he said, trying to sound reassuring. He punched out the code that admitted him to the part of the station the public didn't usually see, and led her through to the comfortable interview room reserved for victims and innocent witnesses. There were tea-making facilities, but the girl declined his offer of refreshment. Tea was clearly the last thing on her mind.

'I'm sorry, I didn't catch your name,' Wesley said once they were seated comfortably.

'Michelle Dooley, but I'm usually called Shell.'

'Not Hardy?'

'Nath and me had different dads. But we were close once upon a time — when we were little. We got split up when we were put in care, but I got back in touch with him last year. He was my brother after all, and blood's thicker than water. Isn't that what they say?'

'It is,' said Wesley quietly. 'Tell me about him.'

'I live in Bristol, but we kept in touch. Nath had his problems. Drugs and all that. But he was trying to get back on track. He was seeing some sort of therapist and he'd started this archaeology; digging for old things. It was something to do with a charity. But then . . .'

Wesley shuffled to the edge of his seat. She had been speaking so quietly that he could hardly make out what she was saying. But those last two intriguing words made him listen intently.

'But then?' he prompted.

'A few months ago, he met this guy. Started doing odd jobs for him. I came down to see Nath last week — met him at a café in Morbay near his hostel. I wanted to tell him that my boyfriend had moved out 'cause we'd had a row, so if he wanted, he could sleep on my settee now Lee wasn't there to moan. I didn't like Nath being in that hostel. There are some bad sorts in there and I didn't want to think of him getting back into . . . you know.'

'You cared for your brother. You wanted to help him.'

She looked embarrassed. 'Yeah . . . I suppose. But some people can't be helped, can they.'

'This guy he did odd jobs for . . . ?'

'Nath never said much about him. Only that he runs a shop and he needed odd jobs doing.'

'Drugs-related jobs?'

She shrugged her shoulders. 'He said he delivered things. Handed them over. So it could have been drugs.' She thought for a moment. 'Must have been, when you think about it. He said it was easy money.'

'Can you tell me anything about this man?' Wesley held his breath, waiting for the answer and hoping it would be the lead they'd been waiting for.

'He asked Nath to keep an eye on someone for him.'

'Who?'

'Don't know. All he said was that it was like being a private eye.'

'I don't suppose he told you the man's name? Or what kind of shop he ran?'

'No. But he said the boss in charge of the archaeology thing came into the shop once while he was in

233

the back.'

'The dig near Chabliton? Was the boss Neil Watson?'

Shell frowned in an effort to remember. 'The name rings a bell.'

'Where was the shop?'

'I think it was Neston. But that's all I know. Sorry.'

'Thanks, Shell. You've been very helpful.' He smiled, anxious to get in touch with Neil. Neil had probably visited a lot of shops recently, but Wesley needed a list as soon as possible.

As he escorted Shell out, he saw tears welling in her eyes. 'Will you be all right?' he asked, suddenly concerned for her.

'I'll be fine,' she said bravely. 'Nath wasn't much of a brother, but I'll miss him.'

'Take care,' Wesley said as she walked away.

Once she was out of sight, he called Neil's number, but there was no reply.

* * *

As DC Trish Walton flicked through the files on her desk in search of inspiration, the notes she'd made of her last call to Susan Elwood caught her eye. Over the past few days Susan had become increasingly chatty and open, intrigued by the mystery of her free ghost tour ticket. During the course of their most recent conversation, she'd mentioned that before her retirement she'd worked with a woman called Della whose son-in-law was a policeman in the Tradmouth area — an inspector, she thought. Trish hadn't taken much notice at the time, but now she remembered that Susan was a retired teacher — further education.

And as the realisation dawned, a smile spread across her face.

She knew Wesley's mother-in-law was called Della and that she'd once taught in a further education college, and there weren't that many in the area. Coincidences were more common than people assumed, and this could possibly be one of them.

As soon as Wesley returned to the incident room, she hurried over to greet him. This was something he'd want to know.

39

Neil arrived at the dig early on Tuesday morning, thinking of the call he'd had from Wesley the evening before. Had he visited any shops in Neston? The answer was simple. The only shops he'd been to were the big supermarket to buy some essential groceries to take back to his Exeter flat, and Arthur Penhalligan's bookshop. When he'd asked Wesley why he wanted to know, his friend said it was something to do with the case he was working on.

As soon as he'd checked the site hut, Neil uncovered the anker cell trench and adjusted his kneeling mat before starting to scrape away the soil, wondering if he could be wrong. He'd cleared the floor the previous day and found all the other flags in place, which convinced him more than ever that it was a grave cut — a rectangular gap in the floor of the strange little chamber, as though someone had lifted the stones in that particular place in order to dig a grave. But he knew he could be wrong, that those few stones might have been removed to be reused when the church was abandoned.

He'd only dug down eighteen inches when he saw a cream-coloured dome that looked very like a skull. He'd concentrated on the west end of the rectangle, the end where the head would lie in any medieval Christian burial — unless it was a priest, who would have been buried the other way around so he'd be facing his congregation when the dead rose on the Day of Judgement — and it seemed his hunch had paid off. The grave seemed unusually shal.low, far nearer the surface than the ones being excavated outside in the disused churchyard. He ran through the possibilities in his mind as he called Dave over. He wanted a second opinion on this particular burial.

* * *

It was a long time since Susan Elwood had seen her old colleague Della Stannard, but she'd been reminded of her when the police made contact. Della's daughter, Pam, she remembered, was married to a police inspector — much to Della's disappointment, as she'd hoped her only child would have chosen someone with fewer links to the Establishment she'd always claimed to despise. Della had told her that Wesley — that was the son-in-law's name — also had a sister who was a vicar's wife, so enough said, she'd added meaningfully. When Della said she feared Pamela was becoming middle-aged before her time, Susan had nodded gravely in agreement, knowing that Della hated to be contradicted.

It wasn't Della's son-in-law who'd asked her about the free ticket for the ghost tour at Darkhole Grange. It was a female officer called DC Trish Walton, who'd been in constant contact ever since, checking she was safe. She liked Trish, as she now called her, but was getting tired of being warned to be careful and to call 999 if anything suspicious occurred. She wasn't quite sure what she needed to be careful of. Going out after dark? Strangers lurking in gloomy alleyways? Walking too near unguarded cliff edges when she exercised the dog? The possibilities for danger were endless, but Susan had no idea which one she should fear. Neither, she suspected, did Trish.

Now that Susan's contact with the police had brought Della to the forefront of her mind, she decided to call her to suggest they get together; two retired teachers at a loose end. She'd expected Della to offer to meet for lunch at some convenient café, but instead she surprised her by saying she fancied a session in the flotation tank at the new healing centre in Neston, a New Age town with an impressive reputation for the innovative. It was something she'd been wanting to try for ages, she said. Was Susan up for it?

Susan hadn't liked to say no, not after Della had accused her own daughter of unspeakable dullness. Swept along by Della's enthusiasm, she'd agreed to meet her in Neston, hiding her misgivings. Perhaps she shouldn't be driving. Perhaps someone would follow her on a lonely lane and force her off the road like they did in films.

Trish Walton had asked her whether she knew of any family connection to Darkhole Grange and she'd said she didn't. But now that she'd had more time to think about it, the question had triggered a long-buried memory. Susan's father was a retired doctor, in his nineties now and housebound, and she was sure she remembered her late mother mentioning that he'd worked in some kind of mental hospital many years ago, though the name Darkhole Grange had never been mentioned. Susan had never showed any curiosity about her father's job — as far as she was concerned, he was an ordinary GP — but she knew he still had some papers from his working days. She'd wondered if she should tell Trish, but had decided against it because she could be wrong and she didn't want to make a fool of herself. Besides, she didn't want her father bothered — not at his age.

Susan's journey to Neston was uneventful, even though a nondescript grey car had slipped in and out of view behind her, as though it might be following her. But once she reached Neston, she relaxed a little, and after she'd found a parking space, she managed to locate the healing centre easily enough. The sign outside depicting a calm pool dotted with water lilies encased in a pair of caring cupped hands told her she was at the right place.

Della was waiting for her at the entrance and greeted her with a hug, enveloping her in the huge woollen scarf she was wearing, a garment that could have doubled as a blanket.

'I had a call from the fuzz last night — well, the fuzz in the shape of my son-in-law. He said your name had come up in his investigation. He asked if I knew you.'

Susan sighed. She'd hoped the outing would be an opportunity to forget all about DC Walton's warnings, but now it looked as though she couldn't escape them.

'He wanted to know all about you,' Della continued, 'but I told him to bugger off and mind his own business. We don't live in a police state yet.'

Della looked pleased with herself, but her words had only made Susan more nervous. If the inspector was asking questions about her, then perhaps she was more deeply involved in whatever was going on than she'd first imagined.

Susan didn't like the flotation tank. Being shut in a tank of water, floating aimlessly to the accompaniment of whale song, made the time drag slowly, and she was relieved when her session was over. Della, in contrast, seemed elated by the experience and was keen to book another appointment. Susan stayed quiet, suddenly longing for the comforts of home.

After lunch in one of Neston's many vegan cafés, Susan drove back to Plympton, having told Della that she wasn't free to repeat their appointment the following week because she had to visit the hairdresser. A little white lie.

When she arrived back at the bungalow she shared with her husband, John, he greeted her at the door, his face ashen. Something was wrong and she cursed herself for yielding to the force of Della's stronger personality and allowing herself to be dragged off to pursue an expensive activity that she hadn't particularly enjoyed.

'Your phone was off,' John said accusingly.

'I put it on silent — forgot to turn the sound back up. What's the matter?'

'I've had a call from your father's cleaner.' He paused. 'Your dad's dead.'

Susan's hand went to her mouth. Death wasn't necessarily unexpected for someone of her father's advanced years, but the news still came as a shock.

John hesitated before speaking again. 'There were signs of a break-in, and she called the police.'

Susan's head began to swim. The last thing she remembered was hitting the hard wooden floor.

40

Andy Fulford hadn't seen anything of the police for a couple of days. They'd finished whatever they were doing at Hawthorn Barn, and when he'd passed the place in his tractor, it was still festooned with blue-and-white crime scene tape but otherwise deserted — which had come as a relief. The police made him uncomfortable.

Claire had told him that Rachel Tracey — now married to Nigel Haynes of Garfleet Farm — had interviewed her in the wake of the Gerdners' murders. The Traceys knew everyone in the farming community, and he'd heard that Rachel was sharp, which made her dangerous.

He stopped the tractor outside the dilapidated building that had been a cowshed until the new one had been built nearer to the house. He recalled the time he'd caught Robert Gerdner snooping round there, trying the padlock. But the sight of the shotgun over Andy's arm had sent Gerdner scurrying off like a frightened rat.

Then a few days later, the problem went away. Andy approached the door, key at the ready. This was his secret. His and Claire's.

★ ★ ★

Wesley wanted to follow up Shell's statement. Her brother had been working for a man who owned a shop in Neston, and according to Neil, it was highly likely that that shopkeeper was Arthur Penhalligan. Nathan and the antiquarian bookseller seemed an unlikely combination, but Wesley was eager to pursue it.

Before the morning's team briefing, he had spent half an hour in Gerry's office going through everything they had. He was sure that Darkhole Grange would provide the key to the puzzle, and Gerry had requested the patient files. However, he was told they'd been either hidden away somewhere inaccessible or destroyed, leaving both men frustrated. How could the management of the place have been so cavalier about their records? Unless it was deliberate.

Gerry volunteered to go with Wesley to see Penhalligan. He said he was desperate to get out of the office, and pointed out that Rachel was quite capable of dealing with anything that arose in their absence.

When they arrived at the shop, Penhalligan hurried out to greet them, assuming that anyone who set the bell on the door ringing was a potential customer.

'How can I help you gentlemen?' he said, trying to hide his disappointment, without much success.

'We'd like to ask you about Nathan Hardy. You knew him?' said Wesley, hoping he'd got this right.

There was a long silence, as though the man was trying to decide how to answer. In the end, he nodded slowly.

'I knew Nathan. My therapist introduced us, if you must know.'

'I know about Rosemary,' said Wesley.

'How? All her consultations are strictly confidential.'

'I'm a friend of Neil Watson's. He told me about her.'

242

'I see.' Penhalligan took a deep breath. 'Well, Rosemary thought a bit of honest work would help keep Nathan on the straight and narrow — not that I had much work for him to do. Just bits and pieces.'

'What sort of bits and pieces?' asked Gerry.

There was another silence before Penhalligan replied. 'He made some deliveries for me. I wouldn't have trusted him with cash, you understand, but there's not much temptation with a bank transfer — or even a cheque, though they're getting rarer these days.'

'We've spoken to Nathan's sister.'

'I didn't know he had one.'

'She said you were paying him to keep an eye on someone for you. Is that right?'

Penhalligan bowed his head, like a naughty schoolboy who'd been caught doing something unspeakable behind the bike sheds. 'I asked him to keep an eye on my old house,' he said after a lengthy silence. 'My ex-wife still lives there, you see. She got everything when we divorced. All I was left with was this shop, and she would have taken that too if she could. To tell you the truth, I wanted to know if she had another man.'

'And has she?'

'Not according to Nathan,' he said, as though the young man had let him down. 'He said he never saw anyone going into the house apart from workmen. She's having a new conservatory built,' he added.

'You paid Nathan to watch her?'

'He wanted money for his trouble. It was a simple transaction. But it couldn't have had anything to do with his death, could it?' He looked from Wesley to Gerry, anxious to be believed. 'Look, I feel guilty that I gave him money that he probably spent on drugs,

243

but I can't be held responsible for his choices, can I?'

'Why didn't you come forward with this information before?' Gerry asked.

'Because I didn't know anything else about his life. Nathan probably mixed with some unsavoury people, so I expect his murder was drugs-related. It has to be.'

'Have we your permission to search these premises?' said Wesley reasonably, noting the look of shock on the man's face.

'Certainly not.' Penhalligan sounded alarmed at the suggestion. 'There are valuable manuscripts in my stockroom and I don't want them pawed by people who don't know what they're doing.'

'We'll make sure nothing gets pawed,' said Gerry, glancing down at his large hands before thrusting them into his pockets.

'Did you send Nathan to the Cliffpiper's Rest Hotel?' Wesley asked, watching Penhalligan's face carefully. 'Did you ask him to keep an eye on a woman called Teresa Nilsen?'

'Absolutely not,' was the swift reply.

Wesley wasn't sure whether to believe him.

Gerry's phone rang and he left the shop to answer the call, leaving Wesley alone with Penhalligan.

'Did you find Rosemary helpful? Professionally, I mean?' said Wesley after an awkward silence.

Penhalligan was still agitated, but Wesley's question was so reasonable that it would have been churlish to do anything else but give a civil answer.

'Yes,' he said. 'All my life I've suffered from terrible claustrophobia, fear of enclosed spaces, but a couple of consultations with Rosemary did wonders.'

Before Wesley could ask any further questions,

Gerry barged back into the shop. 'We've got to go.' He looked at Penhalligan. 'Don't leave town, will you, Mr Penhalligan.'

41

'Do you think Penhalligan has something hidden on the premises? Drugs?' Wesley asked as he broke into a trot to catch up with Gerry. It wasn't like the DCI to move so fast; the call he'd taken must have been urgent.

'I'm willing to bet we'll find more than a load of old books in that shop, but it'll have to wait. That call I've just had was from Dukesbridge. There's been another shooting. Retired doctor in his nineties. Name of Peregrine Birtwhistle. He lived alone, but a cleaner came in every day. She arrived at lunchtime, saw signs of a break-in and called

999. When the patrol went in, they found him dead in bed and sealed off the scene. He'd been shot in the head and they want us over there asap.'

Wesley stopped walking. 'The name Birtwhistle hasn't cropped up before.'

'True, but we don't get many shootings around these parts, Wes. This isn't Chicago. And if it turns out to be the same gun . . . ' Gerry didn't finish the sentence.

Neither man said much during the journey, and when they arrived at the modern detached house on the outskirts of Dukesbridge, they saw that it hadn't taken long for it to become a fully fledged crime scene.

The house was of 1960s vintage and seemed too large for one elderly man on his own. Wesley, however, knew that family homes where people had raised their children held a host of memories and couldn't easily be abandoned.

He and Gerry reported to the crime-scene manager and donned their protective suits. The process was becoming far too familiar, he thought, and one glance at Gerry told him he was of the same opinion. They spotted DC Trish Walton, who was already in her white scene suit, holding a clipboard and organising a group of uniformed officers who were about to embark on house-to-house enquiries at the nearby properties. She nodded to Wesley without smiling.

They were directed up the stairs, where a stair lift sat waiting at the top. When they reached the front bedroom, they found Colin already at work while a police photographer recorded every detail. The pathologist was bending over the figure in the bed, but as soon as Gerry greeted him, he turned.

'Bad one this, Gerry,' he said. His face was solemn. 'Single shot to the head. Execution style. Reminds me of the Gerdners. And the lad in that alleyway. But we won't know if it's the same weapon until ballistics have done their bit.'

'They're taking their time,' said Wesley. 'I understand the victim's a retired doctor.'

'So I believe, although I've never come across him professionally. He was in bed when he was shot, but it looks as though he was awake and possibly trying to get up — maybe to challenge the intruder.'

Wesley studied the body. Peregrine Birtwhistle's startled grey eyes were wide open in surprise, and when Colin saw Wesley looking, he closed the eyes gently. For a man of his age, he looked as though he'd been vigorous in life. Slim rather than skinny, with a shock of white hair. However, the stair lift and the Zimmer frame by the bed indicated mobility problems, and Wesley felt angry that someone had ended the life of such a defenceless victim.

'It looks as though he was shot before he could get out of bed. The bedside light was on when he was found by his cleaner.'

'So he might have heard an intruder, put the light on and started to get up before the killer burst into the room and shot him,' said Gerry, getting the likely scenario straight in his head.

'There are signs of a break-in downstairs,' said Colin helpfully. 'Back door.'

'Anything missing?'

He gave a sad smile. 'Not my department, Gerry. You'll have to ask the CSIs.'

Gerry didn't move, so Wesley left him and made his way down the staircase. He found a CSI examining the kitchen. The window in the back door had been broken, and there were shards of glass scattered over the linoleum floor. He'd seen the CSI before, at the Cliffpiper's Rest Hotel, and the young woman gave him a small smile of recognition.

'Hi,' said Wesley. 'Do we know if anything's missing? Is there any indication that the place has been searched for valuables?'

The CSI stopped what she was doing. 'No. That was the first question the patrol asked the cleaner who found him. And look.' She pointed towards the kitchen table with a gloved hand. 'There's a wallet over there with forty quid still in it. If robbery was the motive, surely the killer would have nicked it. It looks like an assassination, but someone said the victim was a retired local GP – hardly a Mafia don.' She tilted her head to one side. 'Unless he still had connec.tions in the pharmaceutical industry and was supplying drugs or . . . ' She let the suggestion trail off, as though she realised she was letting her imagination run away with her.

'Where's the cleaner who called it in?'

'With one of the neighbours. Someone said she'd called the victim's daughter.'

He wandered across the hall into the living room. It was gloomy in there because the curtains were still drawn, but as Wesley's eyes adjusted, he could make out three CSIs in their white scene suits going about their work.

'Anything interesting?' he asked as he crossed the threshold.

'Nothing yet,' was the reply.

'Is it OK if I draw the curtains?' Wesley asked, reluctant to disturb the scene without permission.

'Don't see why not.'

He picked his way over the carpet. The room was neat and there was absolutely no sign of disturbance. Which seemed to confirm once and for all that the intruder had been more interested in the house's sole resident than in theft. The doctor had been the target, and the word 'assassination' kept echoing through Wesley mind. The MO was so like the murders of the Gerdners and Nathan Hardy that as he stood looking round the long room with its comfortable, old-fashioned furniture, he was more convinced than ever that the same killer was responsible. And they needed to find him before he killed again.

He heard a familiar voice behind him. Trish Walton had entered the room.

'I've got a team out visiting the neighbouring houses. Hopefully someone will have noticed a strange car or . . . Hang on . . . ' Trish came further into the room and walked slowly over to the sideboard, her eyes focused on a group of framed photographs arranged neatly on the top. She stopped and pointed at one of them.

'I know her. That's Susan Elwood.'

Wesley hurried over to take a look. The woman smiled out at him from several of the pictures, some taken with the dead man upstairs and others alone. There were a few of a younger Susan too, with a couple he presumed were her parents, a youthful Dr Birtwhistle standing beside a handsome dark-haired woman. There was also a wedding photograph with Susan as the bride, arm in arm with Dr Birtwhistle.

If Susan Elwood was the victim's daughter, they had their connection to the Darkhole Grange list.

42

Neil had been too preoccupied to contact Wesley. But that didn't mean he wasn't curious about the fate of Nathan Hardy. He'd known Nathan, and now he was dead. Neil wouldn't have been human if he hadn't wanted to know why.

The excavation of the skeleton in the anker cell was going well, and the others were busy with the burials in the old churchyard, lifting each with great care and packing the remains away respectfully until they could be examined back in the lab in Exeter before being reinterred in consecrated ground at a later date. The skeleton he'd just uncovered was definitely female and she would ultimately be treated in the same way, but in the meantime, he wanted to solve the mystery of why she'd been buried in such a shallow grave in what appeared to be a sealed room.

He'd almost finished separating the woman's skeleton from the clinging earth, noting that her exposed pelvis bore none of the signs that she'd ever given birth to a child. He stared at her skull, willing her to give up her secrets, before photographing the bones *in situ*.

'How are you getting on with yours?' The sound of Dave's voice made Neil jump.

'Nearly ready to lift,' Neil said calmly. 'Strange grave. Shallow doesn't begin to describe it.'

'Medieval graves weren't as deep as burials these days, but that one looks like a health hazard,' Dave said as he stared down at the bones. 'Shallow grave. Murder victim?'

'If I was trying to get rid of a body, I wouldn't do it in a building where the entire village met on a regular basis.'

'Is there bedrock under it? Perhaps they couldn't dig any deeper?'

'Far from it. It's good soil under the stone flags.' Neil couldn't take his eyes off the bones. They looked so small, vulnerable. 'I can't see an obvious cause of death. No head injury. No rib nicked by a bladed weapon. Hyoid bone intact. But not every murder leaves a trace on the skeleton.'

'Looks as though she just lay down to die and nature covered her body over the centuries,' Dave said. 'Not much chance of solving the mystery after all this time, is there?'

Neil sighed. 'Once I've dealt with these bones, we'll need some help out there to clear the interior of the main church.'

'We're bound to find some more burials in there — the posh buggers who could afford an inside tomb.'

Dave walked away, and Neil squatted down again. He felt suddenly reluctant to disturb the mystery woman's bones. For a split second it was almost as if he could feel her anguish. And the emotion surprised him.

Then he spotted something gleaming in the soil. The telltale glint of gold.

★ ★ ★

Susan Elwood steered the car automatically towards her father's house, hoping her stunned state wouldn't make her a danger to other road users.

She'd been told there'd been a break-in and that her father was dead, and all sorts of possibilities flashed through her mind during the journey. If they'd hurt him, if they'd made his last moments on earth full of pain and fear, she didn't think she could ever forgive whoever had done this dreadful thing. She could barely think of the perpetrator as human. It was a creature, a monster.

As she brought the car to a halt, the sight of the police vehicles and the van with the words *Crime Scene Investigation* emblazoned on the side brought a wave of nausea. This couldn't be happening. Not to her gentle father who hadn't an enemy in the world. He was elderly and harmless. The last person anybody would want to kill — unless they were totally evil or so high on drugs that they were no longer responsible for their actions.

When she emerged from the driver's seat, she was relieved to see Trish Walton walking towards her accompanied by a good-looking black man with a kind, intelligent face. This must be Della Stannard's son-in-law, Wesley; the man Della had been so scathing about.

Most of the people milling around were wearing white crime-scene suits, but Trish Walton and her companion had discarded theirs. Susan knew this would just be another job to them, but she was still glad of the gentle and solemn expressions on their faces. Trish introduced DI Wesley Peterson before they led Susan to the house next door, where her father's neighbour was waiting to provide tea and sympathy.

'I know your mother-in-law, Della,' was the first thing she said to Wesley once the neighbour had left them alone. She suspected she was trying to delay the dreadful moment when she'd have to face the reality of her father's death.

'So I understand,' Wesley said, glancing at Trish.

There was a short silence before she spoke again. 'How did my dad die? What did they do to him?'

Wesley decided on complete honesty. 'He was shot. His death would have been instantaneous. He wouldn't have suffered.'

Susan had been sitting bolt upright, but now she seemed to relax. 'Thank God for that. I thought they might have . . . You hear of all sorts of things happening — people being . . . mistreated so they'll reveal the whereabouts of their valuables.'

'Nothing like that happened to your father, I promise,' said Wesley, swift to reassure her. 'He suffered a single shot to the head. He was in bed. He might even have been asleep, so he wouldn't have been aware of what was happening.' He felt it was worth bending the truth a little to avoid more distress. Besides, it made no difference.

Susan looked at Trish. 'Do you think this has anything to do with that list? Were they after me and got Dad instead?'

'We don't know yet,' said Trish, putting a comforting hand on her arm.

Wesley waited a few moments before asking his next question. 'Your father was a doctor. Do you know if he ever had any dealings with Darkhole Grange?' He'd been going through all the possibilities in his mind, and this was the one that kept popping up.

'I've already told Trish that he never mentioned that place to me.' Susan hesitated. 'But there are some of his old records in the loft. When she was alive, my mother was always nagging him to get rid of them,

254

but he said he might get round to writing his memoirs one day.' She gave a sad smile.

'In the loft, you say?' Wesley caught Trish's eye and stood up. 'Is it all right if I leave you with Trish? There's something I need to do.'

★ ★ ★

Wesley hurried back to Dr Birtwhistle's house, where he found Gerry saying goodbye to Colin Bowman. Colin raised a hand in farewell as he climbed into his car, and Wesley stood beside Gerry watching the pathologist drive away.

'What's new, Wes? Has the daughter told you anything?'

'It seems the good doctor kept records from his working life in his loft.'

Gerry raised his eyebrows. 'And you think they might contain something that led to someone killing him. If that's what the murderer was after, he didn't find it. There's no sign that the loft was accessed, but then we haven't had the hatch off to look in there yet. It hasn't been a priority.'

'I think it should be now,' said Wesley. 'His daughter was sent a ticket to Darkhole Grange. If we find he once worked there . . .'

'If that's the case, why not send the doctor himself a ticket? Why his daughter?'

'Perhaps they knew he'd be too frail to go and they wanted to get to him via Susan. Teresa Nilsen was sent one and her mother wasn't. In which case Susan Elwood might still be in danger.'

'There's no might about it, Wesley. She should be given protection.'

255

'But we haven't the faintest idea what we'd be protecting her against. Even though we're still awaiting confirmation from ballistics that the same gun was used, we can be pretty sure Birtwhistle's death is linked to the others.' Wesley sighed. 'All the licensed guns round these parts have been checked and none of them fit the bill. Didn't ballistics say it was a revolver? Possibly an old one from World War Two.'

'So it might have been in someone's attic for decades and nobody's ever bothered to register it. There must still be a few wartime souvenirs floating about, either forgotten about or deliberately hidden.'

'Talking of attics, I'll have a word with the search team — ask them to open the loft. We need to find those records . . . if they exist.'

Wesley went off to give the order, and while he was on his way back to join Gerry, his phone rang. It was Rachel.

'Penhalligan relented and gave us permission to search that bookshop, although he wasn't pleased about it. We didn't find anything related to Nathan Hardy and there was nothing to suggest any drugs connection. Penhalligan's not a dealer. We searched his home address as well. Nothing there either.'

'I didn't expect there would be,' said Wesley.

Before he could say any more, a constable in a white crime-scene suit interrupted him. From the look on his face, Wesley knew he had news.

'We opened up the loft like you said, sir. There are boxes full of papers up there.'

'Have them taken to Tradmouth, will you.'

'What's going on?' said Rachel on the other end of the line.

'We'll need somebody to go through the latest victim's papers.'

'As long as it's not me,' Rachel said quickly.

As Wesley ended the call, he suddenly felt more optimistic than he had done for days.

2 October 1956

I've been reading Ursula's translation of Elena's letters, and to my surprise, some of them weren't written to Sir Nicholas, the priest, but to Denyes himself, the man she loved. She was definitely a victim of her passions. That's a good line, isn't it? Maybe I should write a book.

Here's what Elena wrote to him, pouring out her heart, willing him to understand. My sister translated it for me into the sort of words we use today, so perhaps she really is as clever as everyone says.

When you came to me in the garden and asked if I would walk with you a while, I said I would even though my father would have been displeased if we were discovered. I thought your countenance pleasing and I welcomed your company. My mother had spoken well of you so I thought no harm would come of my boldness.

Now I think of you all my waking hours. I long ever to be in your company and yearn to see your dear face. I loiter near the schoolroom to catch a brief glimpse of you, my dearest love. I desire our next meeting more than life itself.

How like me Elena was. I thought no harm would come of my actions either. Although Father says different. He says I am a cheap little whore whose existence must be wiped from the family memory.

43

Wesley tried to ignore the horrified looks on the faces of Rob Carter and his fellow DC who'd been given the task of searching through Dr Birtwhistle's files. He left them to it. The last thing they needed was somebody standing over them while they worked.

It was coming up to six o'clock, and Rachel was still sifting through paperwork. Wesley walked over and perched on the edge of her desk.

'What did you make of Arthur Penhalligan?'

'He didn't like us searching his place — not that anyone does, but he was particularly jumpy. He's protective of all those old books. I suppose they're valuable.'

'Has anyone spoken to his ex-wife?'

Rachel searched through the papers on her desk and pulled one out. 'Yes. Someone checked out his story about Nathan and it turns out he was telling the truth about her having a conservatory built. And what's more, she noticed Nathan hanging about on the other side of the street, so covert surveillance wasn't his strong point. At least that confirms Penhalligan wasn't lying to us — not about that, anyway.'

Wesley thought she looked tired. The colour had drained from her face and there were dark circles beneath her eyes. 'Why don't you go home? Put your feet up. Gerry won't mind.'

Their eyes met and she smiled. 'I think I will. To tell the truth, I'm shattered.'

Wesley wandered over to Gerry's office. When he

announced that he'd sent Rachel home, the DCI nodded slowly. 'Quite right. I've been a bit worried about her. Not that I'd ever dare tell her that,' he said with a meaningful look. 'Why don't you get off home and all?'

Wesley took him up on his offer, and when he arrived home just after six thirty, Pam greeted him with surprise. 'You're back early.'

'Don't sound so disappointed,' he said as he kissed her on the cheek. 'How are things? How's Michael?'

Before she could reply, Amelia came bounding downstairs to greet her father. It wouldn't be long before she reached the teenage years, but she hadn't quite got there yet, which meant she was still pleased to see him, throwing her arms around him and chattering about what she'd been doing that day. Wesley hated the thought of her losing her childish enthusiasm. It was precious, and work had caused him to miss far too much of it over the years.

Once Amelia had skipped off to the kitchen in search of a biscuit, Pam answered his question.

'No change. Although he did eat a bit of dinner earlier. I rang the surgery to see whether the blood test results have come back, but no luck.' She paused. 'I don't like to keep calling Maritia. She's got enough on her plate, what with her work and Mark's parish, not to mention a toddler.'

'She won't mind if you're worried,' said Wesley, sounding more confident than he felt. His sister sometimes reminded him of a swan, serene on the surface but paddling frantically beneath the water.

He squeezed Pam's hand before climbing the stairs to Michael's room, where he found his son lying on his bed with his eyes shut. He was fast asleep, so

Wesley didn't disturb him. He shut the door quietly and crept downstairs, suddenly realising he was hungry. He hadn't eaten since he'd gobbled down a quick tuna sandwich at lunchtime.

Still worried about Michael, he called his sister from the kitchen. She sounded harassed, and he could hear little Dominic crying in the background, but she promised to make some enquiries and told Wesley not to worry, adding that some viruses could be debilitating. Best to wait until the blood test results were back. He didn't feel like thanking her, but the manners their parents had taught them in childhood meant he said the words anyway.

Pam had made chilli con carne, and he carried his plate over to the kitchen table. She'd eaten with the children, not expecting him home so early, and she leaned against the fridge and watched him, arms folded, enjoying a few moments of peace.

'I saw my mother today,' she said.

'How is she?' said Wesley before shovelling the first forkful into his mouth.

'Same as ever. She'd been to some healing centre with a friend. Flotation tank. Made me think of you and your little problem.'

'I haven't got a problem.'

'You don't like going in lifts, Wesley. That's a problem if you find yourself in a high-rise building.'

'I use lifts,' he said defensively.

'But you're not comfortable with it.'

'Who is?'

'My mum recommended someone from Neston who cures people with crystals.'

'Using the stairs is good exercise. Besides, someone's already been recommended to me.'

'But will you do anything about it?'

'Possibly,' he said, thinking that making an appointment with Rosemary might enable him to raise the subject of Nathan Hardy. If anybody knew the inner workings of his life, it would be her. Who knew what he'd revealed during their therapy sessions?

Once he'd finished eating, he found Rosemary's card and rang her number. She had a space in her diary for the following evening. She'd be expecting him.

44

Wesley didn't intend to tell Gerry about his appointment with Rosemary. It was something he wanted to keep quiet if possible. After Gerry's morning briefing at seven thirty, he sat down at his desk and sorted through the paperwork that had come in overnight.

The two unfortunate Detective Constables were already back at work ploughing through Dr Birtwhistle's files. They'd put some of them to one side and Wesley wondered whether this meant they'd found something relevant. He was tempted to go over and ask, but before he could stand up, the phone on his desk began to ring.

'Hello,' said a woman's voice on the other end of the line. 'Can I speak to someone about the murder cases? I had a visit from the police yesterday and the officer asked a lot of questions.'

'What's your name, please,' said Wesley trying to sound encouraging. He had a feeling this woman, whoever she was, might be about to tell him something important.

'Shona Penhalligan. I know it's early, but the officer asked me about the boy my ex-husband paid to watch me.' There was a bitterness behind the blunt words and Wesley could understand why. Being stalked by your ex — even by proxy — would be a disturbing experience at best. At worst, he knew from past investigations that it could be downright dangerous.

'Your ex-husband is Arthur Penhalligan? He owns a bookshop in Neston?'

'That's right. I told the officer I saw the boy with the snake tattoo on his head watching the house, but I had no idea it was Arthur who'd put him up to it. I was afraid he might be planning to break in. I'm having building work done, you see, and if I'm out when the builders leave, they sometimes forget to set the alarm. I wondered whether to report it to the police, but . . . '

'Why didn't you?'

'My neighbour said it would be a waste of time.' There was an embarrassed silence before she carried on. 'Your lot don't bother coming out to burglaries these days. Just give the victims a crime number for the insurance and blame government cuts. You'd hardly rush to arrest a lad who's done nothing more than hang around looking suspicious, would you?'

'Probably not,' said Wesley. There was some truth in her words and he couldn't help feeling a little awkward about the force's shortcomings, even though they weren't his fault.

'There's something you should know,' she said. 'These people who've been murdered — they were shot, is that right?'

He straightened his back, all attention. 'Yes.'

'In that case I should tell you that Arthur was a member of a shooting club. His first love was musty old books, then guns. I came a poor third,' she added resentfully.

'We've checked all the licensed gun owners in the area and his name didn't come up.'

'Not everyone bothers getting a licence.'

'If he was a member of a shooting club . . . '

She hesitated. 'That was a few years ago, so he might have let his licence lapse since we split up. But that doesn't mean he couldn't have got hold of a gun somehow.'

'His shop and flat have been searched, but nothing was found.'

'Have you searched his lock-up?'

'He has a lock-up?' He glanced at Gerry's office. This was news he'd want to know as soon as possible — before Penhalligan had a chance to get rid of any evidence he might be hiding in there. 'Where is it?'

'Industrial estate on the edge of Morbay. Storage pods, they call them. He keeps stock there — including the most valuable items. I only found out about it by accident when we split up. I knew he wasn't declaring all his assets, so I put a private detective on to him,' she said smugly, obviously pleased with her own cleverness.

'What was the detective's name?' He held his breath, waiting for the answer.

'It was a man in Morbay. I heard on the news that he'd been shot.'

'Robert Gerdner?'

'That's it. He used to be a detective at Scotland Yard.'

Gerdner had been elastic with the truth about his police career, but Wesley didn't feel inclined to disillusion her. 'When did you last see Mr Gerdner?'

'Must have been about three months ago.' She paused. 'When I heard he'd been shot, I thought it must have been to do with his time at Scotland Yard. A gangland revenge killing.'

Wesley imagined her giving a little nod, pleased with herself for solving their case.

'Did your husband know you'd put someone on to him?'

Shona Penhalligan caught on quickly. 'You don't think — '

Wesley interrupted her. 'We'll get a warrant to search the lock-up. And thanks for calling. You've been a great help.'

'Don't fall for that flaky antiquarian bookseller act. Arthur's got a nasty streak. I was married to him, so I know.'

As soon as the call ended, Wesley hurried to Gerry's office to tell him about the conversation. Shona Penhalligan was a bitter ex-wife and normally this would have made him sceptical. But her story sounded convincing and needed to be checked out. And the news that Robert Gerdner had been involved opened up new possibilities.

Gerry listened carefully, then began to rifle through the papers on his desk: reports, budget forms, all in no particular order. There had been many times when Wesley had despaired of the DCI's disorganisation, but he'd learned from experience that there was some kind of method to the apparent chaos. After a few moments, Gerry pulled out a statement form and brandished it triumphantly.

'Thought I'd seen it somewhere. As a matter of routine, Penhalligan was asked where he was on the dates of all the murders, and he either said he couldn't remember or that he was at home watching TV. Looks like he hasn't got alibis for any of them. Once we get that lock-up searched, we'll bring him in.'

'And his motive?'

Gerry shrugged. 'No doubt he'll have one.' He thought for a couple of seconds. 'Or maybe not. Some people just enjoy killing for the sake of it.'

45

Wesley arranged for a team to search Arthur Penhalligan's lock-up, on the lookout for anything that might link him to the recent victims. Penhalligan's wife had hired Robert Gerdner to investigate his assets, which gave him a motive, of sorts, for Gerdner's murder. Greta had been collateral damage. If they found anything, they'd bring Penhalligan in for questioning. In the meantime, they had Peregrine Birtwhistle's post-mortem to attend.

He was glad to see that Rachel looked considerably better this morning. Perhaps her husband had urged her to have a lie-in instead of getting up at four in the morning to help with the milking. Wesley was sure her insistence that she was used to rising at such an antisocial hour was born of her natural stubbornness. Rachel had never been one to give in, which had proved beneficial in many past investigations.

'Colin's expecting us at the mortuary in twenty minutes.' The DCI interrupted his thoughts with inappropriate cheerfulness.

Wesley picked up his coat and followed Gerry out of the station. From the incident room window he'd seen that the weather had turned dull and drizzly. And once they were outside, the wind picked up, setting the bunting draped between the lamp posts on the waterfront fluttering like butterflies. He zipped his coat up to the chin, but as they walked beside the choppy grey river, the chill wind bit through his clothes so he was glad when they reached the shelter of the hospital.

It wasn't long before Colin was able to confirm what they'd already assumed. Dr Peregrine Birtwhistle had died from a single shot to the forehead, fired at close range. The killer must have stood there with the gun pointing at the old man's head before pulling the trigger, and Wesley was horrified by the cold-blooded nature of the act.

The bullet found at the scene, embedded in the bloodstained mattress, appeared to be a .38, the same as the others. However, they'd have to await the definitive verdict from ballistics to be sure that it had been fired from the same gun.

A retired civil servant and her former traffic policeman husband who'd set himself up as a private eye, the popular owner of an escape room, a young ex-offender, and now Dr Birtwhistle — not to mention Teresa Nilsen, who still hadn't been found. They appeared to have nothing in common, but Wesley knew the police must be missing something.

Once the post-mortem was over, Gerry stayed at the mortuary to enjoy a cup of tea with Colin – and to avoid the chief super, who was starting to ask awkward questions about the investigation budget. Wesley, however, put duty above pleasure and hurried back to the station, pausing for a while to watch the boats on the river. The ferries glided to and fro oblivious to the conditions, but the smaller yachts and cabin cruisers moored up at the pontoons danced up and down as they were tossed about on the rough surface of the water.

As soon as he reached the incident room, DC Rob Carter rushed up to him. He had news.

'We've been through all those files from the doctor's loft.' The words came out in a rush. 'Most of

them are about routine family and work stuff, but . . . '
he paused, 'one box contains records from Darkhole
Grange dating back to the 1950s, when it was a private asylum. His name's on the forms, so it looks like
he worked there. You said you wanted to find a connection.' He looked at Wesley hopefully.

'He must have been very young at the time. Newly
qualified?'

'Probably,' said Rob, who clearly hadn't bothered
doing the sums in his head. 'There were files on seven
different people — notes about treatments.'

'Any familiar names?' 'Yes. There's one name
from that family tree on Teresa Nilsen's computer.
Crane — Perdita Crane.'

Professor Ursula Nilsen had told them her sister had
died in childhood; that she'd barely known her. But
she must have lied. And it seemed they'd now found a
link between Teresa Nilsen and Dr Birtwhistle.

Normally they'd think very carefully before barging
in and interrogating an elderly lady in a care home,
especially someone who was bound to be frantic with
worry about her missing daughter. But it couldn't be
avoided.

As soon as Gerry returned from the mortuary, Wesley broke the news.

'Perdita's an unusual name,' Gerry said, sitting
down heavily in his executive leather swivel chair,
which lurched under his weight.

'It's from Shakespeare,' said Wesley. *The Winter's
Tale*. It means 'lost'.'

'Very appropriate in the circumstances.'

'Want to come with me to Woodtarn House?'

'No, Wes. You've got a better bedside manner than
me.'

'In that case, I'll take Rachel. She spoke to Professor Nilsen last time, so a familiar face . . . '

Gerry nodded. 'Good luck. And by the way, I've just had a message to say they've dropped all charges against Steve Masters.'

'That'll be a weight off his mind.' Wesley had felt some sympathy towards the young plumber.

Rachel was eager to abandon her paperwork, and as soon as they arrived at Woodtarn House, the matron, Mrs Wardle, emerged from her office to greet them.

'What's it about? The professor was rather upset after your last visit,' the woman said, looking from one to the other like a lioness protecting her cubs.

'Her daughter's missing, so that's understandable,' said Wesley, trying to smooth the waters. 'I'm afraid we do need to have another word with her.'

Mrs Wardle hesitated for a moment before instructing them to remain in the hall. She'd tell the professor they wanted to speak to her. Her tone implied that if Professor Nilsen wasn't feeling up to an interview, they'd have to come back another time.

The wait seemed long and Rachel took a seat on an uncomfortable wooden hall chair, possibly a relic of the days when Woodtarn House had been the dower house for the Manor. Neither of them spoke for a while. Wesley knew that Rachel wouldn't welcome any enquiry about her health. But when the silence grew too much, he broke it with a question about the case.

'Have you heard anything about the Fulfords on the farming grapevine?' Rachel looked up. 'Funny you should say that, Nigel mentioned Andy Fulford only last night. Said he'd heard he'd just bought some flashy new equipment for his milking parlour — and a new Range Rover. Looks like the farm's been doing well since he took over from his parents. Better than it ever did in their day. My mum said she doesn't know where the money's coming from.'

Wesley raised his eyebrows. 'Suspicious?'

She shrugged her shoulders. 'They might have made a pile from selling that barn to the Gerdners.'

Before Wesley could say anything else, the matron returned.

'You're to go up, but don't be long. She tires easily, and she's anxious about her daughter. I hope you have news,' she added as they were about to climb the stairs.

Rachel and Wesley glanced at each other but said nothing.

When they reached Professor Nilsen's room, they gave a token knock before letting themselves in. The professor was fully dressed, sitting in a high-backed chair next to a round side table by the tall window. In the weak sunlight trickling through the glass, they could see the lines deeply etched on her pale face. Only the eyes were bright and sharp. Wesley started by apologising for disturbing her again.

'You have news of Teresa? You've found her?'

'I'm afraid not. But we're following a number of leads,' said Wesley, feeling helpless. There were still no clues to Teresa Nilsen's whereabouts. He'd had hopes that the search of the neighbouring caravan park would turn up something, but the place had been clean. There was nothing he could do but evade the subject and come straight to the reason for their visit.

'Have you ever heard of a Dr Birtwhistle? Dr Peregrine Birtwhistle?'

'I don't think so,' Ursula said, turning her head away.

'He was murdered yesterday. Shot.'

She turned back to look at them, but there was no shock on her face and certainly no grief, merely an expression of mild interest. 'It's a very wicked world, but I don't see what it has to do with me.'

'I think you did know Dr Birtwhistle, because you had a relative in Darkhole Grange.'

He watched her carefully as she gave a reluctant nod.

'I think the relative was your sister, Perdita. She didn't die when she was a child, did she? She became a patient at Darkhole Grange.'

The woman's eyes widened for a second before she resumed her calm expression.

'What can you tell us about Perdita?' said Rachel, glancing at Wesley, who was sitting forward listening carefully, breath held.

'She was my sister. A couple of years younger than me but . . . very different.' She bowed her head. 'She was ill. That's why she was put in that place.'

'What was the matter with her?'

'I'd rather not talk about it.'

Rachel walked over to the woman and squatted down beside her chair. Her growing abdomen made the action look awkward, and Wesley watched with concern as she placed her hand on top of the professor's gnarled fingers.

'Please,' she whispered. 'We're pretty sure that whoever killed the doctor also abducted your daughter. Please,' she repeated.

The professor seemed to soften as she studied Rachel's smooth hand. 'Poor Perdita — or Perdy, as she liked to be known. My parents despaired of her. If there was trouble, Perdy would find it. She was

272

wild, promiscuous, and she hung around with all the undesirables in the area. She didn't care what people thought about her.'

'Most wild teenagers go on to live perfectly normal lives when their hormones settle down,' said Rachel with a smile. 'Tell us about Perdy.'

'She was in an unsuitable relationship with a married older man. She was out of control.'

'What was the man's name?'

The professor hesitated. 'That doesn't matter. Not now. He turned her head.'

'So she had mental health problems and needed help,' said Rachel, filling in the blanks. 'What happened to Perdita, Professor Nilsen?'

'She died in Darkhole Grange,' was the whispered answer. 'She went in there and never came out.'

46

The journey back to Tradmouth allowed Wesley and Rachel the opportunity to discuss what they'd learned.

'I can't believe Perdita's family put her away in an institution just for getting involved with a married man,' said Rachel.

'Morality could be cruel back then,' said Wesley. 'If you made a mistake, you paid for it.'

'It sounds like Perdy Crane made more mistakes than most. The poor girl died in Darkhole Grange. Do you think that could have anything to do with what's going on now?'

Wesley confessed that he had no idea.

Rachel's phone rang and she pulled the car into a passing place to answer the call. After a short conversation, she turned to Wesley. 'That was one of the team I sent to search Arthur Penhalligan's lock-up. He says it's like Aladdin's cave in there and he suggests you go over and take a look, seeing as you used to work in the Art and Antiques Unit at the Met.'

'OK. Let's get over there now.'

'Do you think we're barking up the wrong tree with Ursula Nilsen?' Rachel asked. 'Is Penhalligan our man? His wife got Gerdner to spy on him. That would be motive enough for some people.'

Wesley didn't answer. Ursula was connected with the Gerdners through her daughter's name being on the list sent to Darkhole Grange, and she was also linked to Dr Birtwhistle through her sister. Although all this didn't mean Arthur Penhalligan was beyond suspicion.

As they neared Morbay, they came to what the high-ups in the town hall liked to call the business park. It was identical to the industrial estates found on the outer fringes of most towns, gnawing away at the surrounding countryside. Somewhere in these streets of barn-like windowless units stood the storage facility containing Penhalligan's rented lock-up. Wesley couldn't help wondering what he'd find there; more than old books if the search team were to be believed.

The sign outside a big blue warehouse to their right told them they'd reached their destination; as did the pair of police cars parked in front of the building. Lock-Ups 4 U had a glass-fronted entrance where a couple of uniforms appeared to be lurking aimlessly while the spotty lad on the reception desk looked decidedly nervous.

Wesley and Rachel were directed to one of the nearby units. The previously padlocked door was standing ajar, and they donned crime-scene gloves before venturing inside the small room lit by a buzzing fluorescent tube.

One wall of the room was lined with steel shelves, and as Wesley's eyes travelled over them, he saw wonderful things. A triptych, probably fifteenth-century Flemish, depicting a serene Madonna graciously receiving gifts from exotic-looking Magi. Two wooden saints painted with faded medieval pigments. A silver box engraved with hunting scenes. An ivory goblet decorated with carved cherubs. A gold crucifix with a delicate ivory figure of Christ. There were books too. Ancient precious volumes illuminated in monasteries before their brutal destruction by Henry VIII.

He could see Rachel looking round, eyes wide and

mouth agape. Eventually she broke the heavy silence. 'What the hell's Penhalligan been up to?'

'My guess is that we'll find this lot on the Art Loss Register. I suspect Penhalligan was acting as a middle man. A fence, if you like.'

'He hasn't got a criminal record.'

'Then he'd be the ideal choice. His little shop's been a front for his activities.'

'I presume his ex-wife wasn't aware of all this?'

'There's no love lost between those two, so he wouldn't want her to benefit, would he.' He paused, unable to take his eyes off the treasures lined up before him. 'But if Gerdner found out and threatened to tell the wife or the authorities, it gives Penhalligan a whacking great motive for silencing him, and it gives us a whole new angle to the murder of Nathan Hardy. If he was working for Penhalligan . . .'

'He came to know too much. Which puts Arthur Penhalligan in the frame again.'

Wesley said nothing. Rachel was right, but it still didn't explain how Penhalligan was linked with the murders of Dr Birtwhistle and Charlie Maddox — or the disappearance of Teresa Nilsen — unless he too had some connection with Darkhole Grange that was yet to be discovered.

'Where on earth did he get all these things?' Rachel asked, walking slowly round the confined space.

'I'd guess they've all been stolen from places around Europe — museums and churches. It shouldn't be difficult to reunite the items with the legal owners. Unless they were owned by collectors who'd rather the authorities weren't aware of what they were hiding away. I think it's time we had a word with Arthur Penhalligan,' he added, looking at his watch. 'This lot needs careful handling, so it might be best to get in touch with the local museum. We don't want anything damaged.'

They secured the padlock as they left. If Wesley was right about the value of the treasures inside, there would be people who'd be anxious not to see their investment fall into the hands of the police.

★ ★ ★

Arthur Penhalligan had been brought in by a patrol car and he was saying nothing. Once Wesley's old colleagues at the Met confirmed that the goods in the lock-up had been stolen, they'd have enough to charge him. He was waiting for them to call back when Rachel hurried up to his desk.

'I've just been speaking to Nigel. He's been hearing rumours about the Fulfords.'

'You said you thought they'd come into money.'

'Apparently Andy Fulford's been diversifying, but it's all very mysterious. I think we should take a look at what he's up to.'

Wesley had almost forgotten about the Fulfords, but he reminded himself that the Gerdners had made Andy Fulford's life a misery with their carping complaints. It gave him a motive of sorts for wanting to see them out of the way, and even Rachel's husband suspected that there was something odd going on. He'd met Nigel many times, and he'd never thought he was a man who'd be inclined to let his imagination run away with him.

'I'm happy to visit the Fulfords. I can make the excuse that I want to see how Claire's getting on.' Rachel gave Wesley an uncharacteristic wink. 'After all, it must have been a terrible shock having a murder on her doorstep like that.'

Wesley looked first at his phone and then at Rachel. 'I don't think you should go alone. I'm expecting a call from the Met. As soon as it comes through, I'll come with you.'

'That would make it look official. Leave it to me.'

Wesley's phone rang and he picked up the receiver. It was the call he was waiting for. But when he'd finished talking, he looked round and saw that Rachel had gone.

4 October 1956

My sister warned me that some of Elena's letters were 'passionate in nature'. Ursula has always been a prig. At one time I was glad I wasn't like her, but she is studying at Oxford and bound for a brilliant future, while I am bound for . . . God knows where.

When she delivered the next transcriptions to my room, I fell on them like a hungry beast. What did Elena do next?

Remembering my time with Rupert, the new letters held few surprises.

My most cherished Denyes, your very name is so dear to me. I think often of when we met at our private place in the wood near our garden and you swore to make me your wife. There I yielded my body to you and the memory of your flesh upon mine excites me in my solitude. My love, when will we meet again? How I long for each new tryst, for we are lovers for eternity. Man and wife. I am yours and you are mine.

I smile at her words, because that was exactly how I felt when Rupert and I first made love. I think now that love is like a ripe fruit — beautiful when new but rank and stinking when it rots.

Ursula goes back to Oxford today and she's taken the rest of the letters with her. I feel as though she's stolen a piece of my soul.

47

The ring they'd found the previous day was the most exciting thing that had turned up at the dig so far. The small circle of gold Neil had removed with great care from the bony finger of the woman's skeleton was plain and dulled from years of burial in the Devon soil. But nothing could rob gold of its characteristic glow.

Even better, there was an inscription inside the golden circle. The old magnifying glass he kept in the site hut had been pressed into service to decipher the tiny words, and he'd translated them from the Latin. *Lord have mercy on a sinner.* The pious sentiment fitted with the document Arthur Penhalligan had showed him. Elena de Judhael had undergone the ritual that took her from the land of the living to the land of the dead. They'd recited her requiem mass in the church of St Leonard, the patron saint of prisoners, and the archaeological evidence suggested that she'd been sealed into the small stone chamber at the side of the church to serve as an anchoress.

There would have been a gap in the wall so that someone could provide food and see to her personal needs. She would also have had a squint window giving a view of the church altar so she could hear mass, but that would have been the tiny world where she was confined for life. However, those words carved on the wall suggested that she hadn't dealt well with her voluntary isolation — if indeed it was voluntary.

It was time to see what Arthur Penhalligan had to say for himself. He'd been taken down to the interview room, and Wesley and Gerry found him sitting beside the duty solicitor sipping beige tea nervously from a plastic cup.

'I'll come clean,' he said before they'd even had a chance to sit down and introduce themselves for the benefit of the tape machine at the end of the table.

'You want to make a statement?' said Gerry.

'Yes. Some men came into the shop a couple of years ago saying they had a proposition for me.' The words came out in a rush and Wesley noticed that the solicitor was glaring at his client in despair.

'What was this proposition?' Gerry asked.

'They had things they wanted me to look after. I just had to store them in the lock-up and they'd pay me more than the shop could make in a whole year. The divorce wiped me out financially and the shop only just keeps afloat.' He looked from one detective to the other, desperate for them to understand.

'Who were these men?' Wesley asked.

'Don't know their names. They never said. All I know is that the stuff was brought into Tradmouth on a private yacht and I had to keep it until someone came in a van to collect it and pay me. That's all I know. Honestly.'

'Can you tell us anything about the death of Nathan Hardy?'

Penhalligan looked shocked. 'Absolutely not.'

'Have you ever heard of Darkhole Grange?'

He frowned. 'Isn't that the ghost place? I've seen adverts for it.'

Wesley caught Gerry's eye. Penhalligan sounded as though he was telling the truth, but Wesley intended to keep an open mind.

His former department at the Met had confirmed that the items from Arthur Penhalligan's lock-up did indeed feature in the Art Loss Register. Some had been stolen from churches in Europe and some from private collections. All would be reunited with their owners once the case had been cleared up. But there'd been no sign of a gun.

The duty solicitor said nothing when Gerry charged Penhalligan with handling stolen goods. Wesley wondered whether there would turn out to be more serious matters to add to the charge sheet. Arthur Penhalligan had been in possession of a secret. But had he killed in order to keep it?

While Wesley was dealing with this, he kept thinking of Rachel. She'd left for the Fulfords' farm before he'd had a chance to stop her, and he was starting to feel anxious. He wanted to check she was safe, even though he knew he'd be risking her wrath. He went to Gerry's office to tell him where he was going, but Gerry was deep in conversation on his phone and Wesley hadn't time to waste, so he plucked his coat off the stand by the door and hurried downstairs to the car park.

The journey to Chabliton seemed to take an age, although he knew it would have been a lot worse in the middle of the tourist season. He gripped the wheel as he steered as fast as he dared down the winding Devon lanes. When he reached the Fulfords' farm, he saw Rachel's car parked in the farmyard, but when he knocked on the front door, there was no answer, only the distant barking of dogs inside the house. He tried the converted stable block that was home to Andy's parents, but again there was no reply.

He looked around for signs of life, cursing himself for allowing Rachel to wander alone into possible danger. Farms were hazardous places, and anything could have happened to her. And Andy Fulford, in common with most farmers, had guns.

He stood still and listened to the sound of birdsong and the distant lowing of cattle. No screams, no shouts for help. Summoning his courage, he walked towards the group of outbuildings behind the house, keeping to the side wall of the farmhouse in the hope that he wouldn't be spotted. There was a large barn full of farm machinery and various smaller brick buildings that must once have served a useful purpose, but their windows were now opaque with dust. When he stopped and listened again, he could hear the hum of something electric — a freezer, perhaps, or a ventilation system. He headed for the source of the sound, a large brick outhouse standing apart from the other farm buildings.

As he approached, he heard voices, although he couldn't make out what they were saying. He put his hand on the door and pushed gently. It creaked open and the voices fell silent.

He'd expected to step into gloom, but instead the space was filled with bright fluorescent light. He could see Rachel standing facing Andy Fulford, who was pointing a shotgun straight at her.

'Don't be an idiot, Andy,' she said. 'I know you don't want to hurt anyone.'

It had taken Fulford a few moments to realise that Wesley had come in, but as soon as he did, he swung the gun in his direction. Wesley took a deep breath and took in his surroundings. The building was full of healthy-looking plants, but they weren't the farmer's usual crop. Machinery hummed around him, technology to keep the plants flourishing.

'A cannabis farm,' he said calmly. 'Must be lucrative.'

The shotgun shook in Fulford's hands. He wasn't used to this sort of situation, and Wesley knew he wasn't sure how to get out of it.

'Come on, Andy, this isn't doing any good,' said Rachel quietly. 'Pointing a gun at a couple of police officers will only make things worse.'

'Rachel's right, Andy,' said Wesley.

Slowly Andy Fulford lowered the gun and placed it on the ground. Rachel bent down to pick it up, breaking it expertly and taking out the cartridges to make it safe. The man stood, bowed and defeated. Wesley suspected that if he raised his head, he would see tears forming in his eyes.

Rachel handed Wesley the gun before stepping forward to take Fulford's elbow. Wesley saw sympathy in her eyes as she led him outside. Andy Fulford, he felt, would fall under his category of weak criminals rather than wicked. Unless he'd been hiding more than a sideline in drug production. He called for a patrol car to pick up their prisoner, and at the same time he requested a search team to go over the house. If they found a revolver on the premises, the situation would change. After all, there'd been no love lost between Andy Fulford and the Gerdners.

Once Andy had been taken off to the police station to be questioned, Rachel announced that she was going to stay and wait for the search team, but he knew she wanted to talk to Claire, farmer's wife to farmer's wife. Claire would open up to her, she said, and Wesley knew she was right. He was an outsider, so his presence was bound to make things awkward.

Forty-five minutes later, he was back in Tradmouth, sitting in Gerry's office.

'That's a turn-up,' Gerry said. 'Rachel seemed sure the Fulfords had nothing to do with the Gerdner shooting.'

Wesley sighed. 'I hate to say it, but I think she's biased. She's known the family for years.'

'Maybe you shouldn't have left her there.'

Wesley stayed silent for a few seconds, beginning to doubt his own judgement. Then he spoke. 'Rachel's a professional. She's sympathetic to the Fulfords' problems, yes, but that means they're more likely to confide in her. The farmhouse is being searched, along with the parents' place — the converted stables. What parent wouldn't cover for their child?'

'You think they were all in on this new example of farming diversification?'

'Who knows? But it would be a hard thing to keep quiet from the other people who lived on the premises.'

Wesley's phone rang. It was a number he didn't recognise, and he hesitated before answering the call. The unfamiliar male voice on the other end of the line asked if he was through to DI Peterson, and when the caller said his name was Paul Cummings, it took Wesley a few moments to place him. MC Button was calling, which meant he must have information.

'I've been speaking to one of our guides,' he began. 'Her name's Letty Jerome, and she takes visitors round when we're open to the public. She's in her nineties but still remarkably sprightly, and I'd never dare tell her she's past it, if you know what I mean. Anyway, she remembers the Crane family who used to live here, so if you want to speak to her, she'd be more than happy to have a chat.'

'Can you give me her number?'

Paul Cummings, aka MC Button, obviously had Letty's number to hand, and Wesley wrote it in his notebook. As soon as the call was ended, his phone rang again. Andy Fulford had been taken down to the cells prior to being interviewed. Wesley immediately broke the news to Gerry, who reckoned it was best to let him stew while they worked out a strategy for the interview. Arthur Penhalligan was in the cells too while further enquiries were made into the treasures in his lock-up. Two suspects for the price of one, Gerry said cheerfully.

Wesley said nothing. Both Fulford and Penhalligan had things to hide, things many would kill to conceal, but his gut feeling told him the answer to the recent murders lay with Ursula Nilsen's family history. And he'd have a good chance of finding out what that answer was from the elderly tour guide, Letty Jerome, who according to Paul Cummings would be looking forward to his visit.

Gerry told him he had a lot to sort out before Andy Fulford was interviewed, so it would be best if Wesley went on his own. One elderly lady, after all, hardly posed such a threat that two officers were needed.

'You never know,' Wesley said with a grin as he left the DCI to his paperwork.

48

When Wesley reached Letty Jerome's address, it turned out to be everyone's idea of the perfect English cottage: thatched, with small latticed windows, the front garden crammed with colourful spring flowers. To Wesley it looked slightly unreal, like a house from a film set. As he opened the gate and walked up the crazy-paved path, he felt clumsy and oversized, like a child in a model village.

The tiny woman who answered the door had youthful eyes set in a wizened face. She looked him up and down with wary curiosity and spoke before he had a chance to introduce himself.

'You must be the policeman Mr Cummings told me about.' A smile spread across her face. 'Well don't stand there on the doorstep or the neighbours will think you're one of those con men who go around preying on the elderly. Come in, come in.'

As she grabbed his sleeve and pulled him inside, Wesley wasn't sure whether to feel insulted by her suggestion that he looked like a criminal or glad that she was exercising caution. Once he was in the sitting room with beams so low that he had to bow his head, even though he wasn't unusually tall, she invited him to sit and offered tea.

Although Wesley was impatient to find out what she knew about the Cranes, he accepted her offer. Once his tea was in front of him, he came straight to the point. 'You told Mr Cummings you knew the Crane family.'

287

'Oh dear, yes. I was a very young teacher at the village school when they lived at the Manor. Mr and Mrs Crane were a cold pair. I never liked them much — or their attitude to their daughters. The girls attended the village school until they were eleven, and then they were sent off to a boarding school. That was what happened in those days for those who could afford it. It meant I came to know the family quite well, of course.' She paused. 'Ursula, the elder girl, was very clever. A joy to teach and way ahead of her classmates.'

'And the younger girl, Perdita?'

Miss Jerome smiled. 'Little Perdy was the opposite of her sister. Nowadays I'm sure she'd be diagnosed with something like attention deficit disorder, but back then . . .'

'Tell me about her. What kind of things did she do?'

'She was impulsive. She found it hard to concentrate on her school work. Always getting into scrapes. She climbed up on the school roof once and the caretaker had to carry her down. She thought it was hilarious and so did the sillier boys in the class. Her parents didn't, of course. She was frequently in trouble, and when she was sent away to school, she managed to get herself expelled from several establishments. In the end, her parents sent her to the local high school because nowhere else would have her. She attracted the wrong kind of friends like a magnet. Undesirable boys with motorbikes. Lads who got in trouble with the police. It was a shame, because she was such a pretty girl. Beautiful. Far more attractive than her sister.' She took a deep breath.

'Eventually Ursula went off to Oxford, while Perdy was sent away to an aunt in another part of the country. I don't think it's hard to guess why,' she said meaningfully. 'Anyway, Ursula enjoyed a flourishing career, got married and moved to America, while Perdy was never heard of again. When the parents died, Ursula sold the Manor and that's the end of the story, Inspector.'

Wesley knew there was something she was holding back. He said nothing for a few moments, hoping she wouldn't be able to resist the urge to fill the silence. His patience was rewarded.

'I said it was the end, but...Well, I heard things — rumours.'

'What kind of rumours?'

'I heard that Perdy had been conducting an affair with a much older man. And I heard — although I don't know if this is true — that the story about the aunt was false and that she'd got herself into trouble and ended up in an institution. There was even talk that the man she was involved with had arranged it all. I had the impression her parents were only too pleased to be rid of her. Some children are born troubled, Inspector.'

'It's a sad thing to say.'

'But I'm afraid it's true. And Perdita Crane was one of those children. Do you know whether she's still alive?'

'According to her sister, she's dead. Ursula has come back from the States. She's living in Woodtarn House.'

Letty raised her thin grey eyebrows. 'I had no idea. I presumed she was still in America.' A wistful look appeared in her eyes. 'As she's so local, I might pay her a visit. I'd like to see her again. It's good to speak to the people who remember. You'll find that out if you reach my age.' She sighed. 'That's it, Inspector. I've told you everything I know.'

Wesley recognised a dismissal when he heard one. But he had another question. 'Who was the father of Perdita's child?'

She hesitated before replying. 'It was a man called Rupert,' she said quietly.

'Rupert Maddox?'

'That's right.'

He recalled what they'd discovered about Charlie Maddox's father, the alleged rapist, and suddenly he felt as though another piece of the puzzle had fallen into place.

'I didn't know him, of course,' Letty continued. 'But I knew of his reputation. I heard that his wife died shortly before Perdita went away. It was a terrible tragedy.' She leaned forward as though she was about to share a confidence. 'I'm surprised Perdita's family didn't put pressure on him to marry her once he was free — if he was indeed responsible for her predicament. Or perhaps they did and he refused. I heard Rupert Maddox wasn't bound by conventions where women were concerned. There were some terrible rumours about him. They say he married again some years later and that he . . . assaulted his child's nanny, although I don't know how true that is.' She shook her head in disapproval. 'So you see, Inspector, Rupert Maddox was a bad man — the worst type poor Perdita could have got involved with.'

'Could the institution Perdita was put in have been Darkhole Grange?'

Letty gave a little shudder. 'I don't know, but if that's where the poor girl was forced to have her baby, no wonder she died.'

Wesley could see tears forming in her eyes, the first hint of emotion she'd shown during their interview. He thanked her and prepared to leave her to her thoughts of her wayward former pupil. The wild girl who hadn't played by the rules.

When he reached the front door, though, he paused, stooping a little to avoid banging his head. 'If Perdita *was* pregnant, you don't happen to know what might have become of her baby?'

'The Crane family were hardly likely to confide in me, were they?'

He was about to step outside when, unexpectedly, she called him back, her voice wavering a little.

'I have a confession to make, Inspector.'

He turned, wondering what she was about to tell him.

'I took something from the Manor. It was with Mr Cummings' permission, so it wasn't stealing, but . . .'

'What did you take?'

'When Mr Cummings moved in, he was a little overwhelmed by the contents of the muniment room, where all the old estate documents were stored. It's out of the way, near the old servants' quarters, and it had become a bit of a dumping ground over the years. Ursula never bothered with it when the house came to her, and the next owner used the Manor as a second home and took little interest in the place, other than somewhere to bring his friends at weekends, so the room was left untouched. He probably didn't even know it existed.

'Mr Cummings decided to open the house to visitors and he asked me and a couple of the other guides to sort things out. I came across an exercise book in there and I recognised Perdita's handwriting. It's a diary of sorts, and when I told Mr Cummings about it, he suggested I keep it as I'd known her and he had no use for it. He's a very nice young man in spite of . . . how he makes his living.'

Wesley's heart began to beat faster. 'Do you still have it?'

She sniffed. 'In spite of everything, I was very fond of Perdita. I wouldn't have dreamed of destroying it.'

'May I borrow it?'

She considered his request for a few moments. 'As long as you agree to return it.'

'I will. As soon as I can.'

She fetched a little soft-backed exercise book from a drawer, the type of book commonly used in schools in days gone by, and handed it to Wesley.

'Must you rush off? Won't you stay for another cup of tea?'

'Thank you, Miss Jerome. I'd love to, but I really must get back to the station.'

He tried to ignore the look of disappointment on her face and gave her a reassuring smile before hurrying down the garden path, making for the car.

49

Instead of heading straight back to Tradmouth, Wesley found a grass verge at the side of a quiet lane, a good place to stop the car. He switched off the engine and began to read Perdita's diary. He wasn't sure whether he'd find anything that would help him with the case, but he needed to make sure.

To his delight, the book contained not only details of her affair with Rupert Maddox, but comments about some of the residents of the village. Miss Jerome, the schoolteacher, was treated kindly although other observations were harsh and sometimes downright bitchy. The wife of the village policeman, for instance, had reminded Perdita of one of the hags who knitted by the guillotine during the French Revolution — judgemental and revelling in the misfortunes of others. This woman, Mrs Maltrit, didn't have children, and Perdita would have pitied any child unlucky enough to have her as a mother.

Perdita's prose style was sharp and entertaining, and hinted at a keen intelligence. Perhaps once she'd outgrown her troubled adolescence she would have proved as successful as her brilliant sister. But fate had decreed that this hadn't happened, and as he read on, one question kept nagging at the back of his mind. If Perdita had been pregnant, what had become of her child?

He found that the diary didn't contain only Perdita's story. Several of the entries concerned someone who'd lived at the Manor many centuries ago. When, in an effort to curb her undesirable behaviour, Perdita's parents had confined her to the house, she'd become bored and, to fill her time, had trawled through the old documents stored in the neglected muniment room, finding some that dated back to the time the house was built. It seemed an unlikely pastime for a girl like Perdita Crane, but in those days, of course, there was no internet to occupy a teenager, so any form of entertainment was better than none.

Perdita had discovered the story of Elena de Judhael, who'd lived at the Manor in the fifteenth century; the girl who according to legend had been walled up somewhere in the house. As Wesley read on, he formed the impression that Perdita had become a little obsessed with her. According to Neil, rather than being imprisoned in her own home, Elena had apparently become the anchoress of St Leonard's Church in Long Bartonford, and had lived and died in what amounted to solitary confinement. Wesley had seen the words she must have carved on the wall — her statement of despair — and suspected that if this was indeed Elena's work, hers was no religious vocation. Somebody had placed her in that situation against her will.

In Perdita's own account, Wesley reached the point where she'd discovered she was pregnant. The entry was intriguing.

They're going to send me away. I asked where I was going and they told me I was going to stay with my father's cousin in Wales. They said this cousin lives at the seaside, only I've never heard of her so I don't think she exists. I am going to sneak out of the house to see Rupert. It's his child and I have to make sure the three of us can be together for always. It won't be easy, but I must be brave. There is only one way to secure my happiness. I won't lose him. We will have a future.

He skipped to the final page.

My parents told me I was going to be taken somewhere safe, somewhere out of the way where nobody will ever find me. It's a private hospital in the countryside and they say it's for the best. Rupert has made the arrangements because his family have influence there. It shows he cares for me very much and wants to protect me. It won't be for very long, and once the fuss dies down we'll be together again. I know we will be happy one day — us and our child.

As he stared at the determined words, it was hard to believe that shortly after she'd written them in her distinctive sloping handwriting, she'd been confined in the institution where, according to Ursula Nilsen, she'd died. The hospital she referred to had to be Darkhole Grange, the asylum that had boasted Rupert's father as its benefactor.

It was getting late, but he wanted to speak to Professor Nilsen again. She was Perdita's sister and he needed to hear the whole story, not the edited version he'd been given. He took his phone and rang Rachel's number. If there was anybody who could get the truth out of Ursula, it was her.

50

When Rachel answered, she sounded tired.

'Any word on the search for Teresa Nilsen?' she asked.

'Not yet. None of the appeals have turned up anything useful, and they've been out with tracker dogs again, but no luck.'

'Think she's dead?' she said quietly.

'Let's hope not.' Wesley was reluctant to give up hope just yet. 'How's it going?' he asked.

'Claire Fulford denies knowing anything about the cannabis farm. Andy told her he was experimenting with hydroponics — growing plants without soil under artificial light. He said if he could develop new techniques there might be money in it. I believe her, Wes. Her in-laws don't know anything either, I'm sure of it.'

Wesley knew the situation was awkward for her, but he hoped she wasn't accepting Claire's word just because it was what she wanted to believe. Perhaps somebody else should have conducted the interview, but he was reluctant to press the matter for the moment. He gave her a quick account of his meeting with Letty Jerome and asked her to join him at Woodtarn House. They needed to speak to Ursula again.

'She looked quite frail when we last saw her. Are you quite sure about this, Wes?' she asked.

Her question made Wesley hesitate. Then he answered with a confidence he didn't feel. 'She must know more than she's told us, and whatever she's holding back might lead us to Teresa. And now I've found Perdita's diary . . . '

He heard Rachel give a weary sigh and he suddenly wondered whether he should be dragging her away from her desk on what amounted to a whim. But she said she'd meet him at Woodtarn House in half an hour.

He waited on the verge for a while, filling the time by rereading Perdita's diary, looking for some clue to what had happened to her. But after that poignant last entry, there was nothing.

When he arrived at Woodtarn House, Rachel's car was already there in the small car park. She was sitting in the driver's seat, casually tapping her phone. Wesley suspected that she was enjoying the rare moment of peace and enforced idleness. He knocked on the car window and she looked up and smiled before opening the door.

'I'll let you do the talking,' she said. 'I think that matron fancies you.' The playfulness in her words surprised him.

'I doubt it,' he said dismissively.

She laughed. 'You don't know the effect you have on people, Wesley Peterson.'

Wesley couldn't think of an answer, and he was a little relieved when they were waylaid at the door by Mrs Wardle, whose tightly permed hair seemed to have stiffened since their last meeting. She looked at her watch. 'It's getting late. The residents have just had their evening meal.'

'I'm afraid we do need to speak to her. I know she'll want to help us find her daughter.'

Mrs Wardle gave in and led them upstairs to the professor's room. As they entered, muttering

297

apologies for disturbing her again, the old lady looked up hopefully.

'Have you found her? Is she safe?'

'I'm sorry,' Wesley said, bowing his head. 'There's no news yet. But we're doing our best.' He was reluctant to admit that all their efforts had so far come to nothing; that Teresa Nilsen appeared to have vanished off the face of the earth.

'If you haven't come with news about my daughter, what do you want?' Ursula said. 'I've already told you everything I know.'

'I've read Perdy's diary,' Wesley began quietly.

The professor's expression gave little away. 'How on earth did you get hold of that?' she asked, as though she thought he might be lying.

'It was found in the muniment room of Bartonford Manor when one of the house guides was tidying up in there.' He decided not to mention Miss Jerome's name for the time being. 'Perdita must have left it there, thinking she'd come back. But instead she died in Darkhole Grange.'

The professor stared out of the window again, as though the view of the twilit garden outside held a deep fascination.

'Perdita was pregnant, wasn't she?' Rachel said.

'Times were different then, Detective Sergeant.' Ursula gave her a sad smile. 'You're wearing a wedding ring, I see, so if you were expecting a child back in the 1950s you'd be fine. But if there was no ring on your finger, and no husband . . .'

Rachel caught Wesley's eye. The world had changed so much in the sixty or so years that had passed since the time the professor was talking about, and attitudes common then were barely credible now.

'You probably can't see what the fuss was about, but in a family like ours, with a girl like Perdy . . . '

'Your parents were strict?' Wesley asked.

'My parents' attitude wasn't out of the ordinary in those days, and they had a position to maintain in society. We lived in the manor house. And the circumstances surrounding Perdita's . . . ' she searched for the right word, 'lapse of judgement were scandalous to say the least.'

'Can you tell us what happened?' Rachel asked gently.

'I'm going to use a word you probably think went out with Jane Austen. She was *seduced*. Although I don't imagine she put up much resistance. He was a very persuasive man.'

'You're talking about Rupert Maddox.'

Ursula caught her breath as Wesley said the name. 'Tell me about him.'

'He was fifteen years older than Perdy — sophisticated, worldly, and married to a very rich wife who didn't give a damn what he got up to as long as she could lead her own life. I must admit he possessed a certain glamour. He was charming. I even felt the heat of his charm myself, but I was a plain, bookish teenager and therefore of no interest to him, I'm relieved to say. He was handsome, with a flashy sports car. Just the sort to turn an impressionable girl's head. Perdy lied and said she was going away for a few days to stay with a respectable friend. But it turned out Rupert had taken her off to London, where they stayed in an expensive hotel and he wined and dined her. In different ways it was a game to both of them. Only Perdy was the loser.' She shook her head. 'This is private family business. I really shouldn't be talking about it.'

'It might not seem relevant, but it could help us find Teresa,' said Wesley, wondering if he was speaking the truth. 'Anything you tell us will be treated in the strictest confidence.'

'I was raised not to wash my dirty linen in public, Inspector. My parents were very particular about keeping up appearances. That's why Perdy was such a disappointment to them. She didn't care, you see — just did what she wanted. My parents reckoned there was something . . . lacking in her; that she possessed no self-control. My father had words with Rupert, of course, but he laughed in his face. He actually punched my father. I remember coming down the stairs and seeing Father with blood all over his face while that horrible man stood there laughing. My mother was screaming at him to get out. It was terrible.'

It sounded to Wesley like a scene from a Victorian novel: the dastardly seducer confronted by his victim's unhappy parents. But this story had happened within living memory. Had the world really changed so much since then? He wasn't old enough to remember the 1950s, but he guessed it probably had, although Rachel was looking sceptical.

'What happened next?' she asked, as though she was keen to hear the rest of the story. 'Perdy was pregnant. Presumably Rupert was the father, because he said he'd make arrangements.'

'A termination?' Wesley asked tentatively.

'That sort of thing was illegal and highly dangerous in those days. My parents would never have agreed to it. They thought it best if Perdy went away to have the baby and then it would be adopted. That was how things were done back then. Discretion. A girl would

300

vanish mysteriously for a few months to a relative's at the other end of the country and return as though nothing had happened.'

'But that didn't happen in this case. She was admitted to Darkhole Grange as a patient.'

'Yes.'

'Do you remember Dr Birtwhistle?'

Ursula's expression gave nothing away, and it was a full thirty seconds before she answered. 'He was young, but . . .'

'But?' Wesley glanced at Rachel. He had the feeling he was about to learn something important.

'Birtwhistle was keen to try new treatments. Experimental treatments. He was full of ideas and eager to put them into practice.' A grim smile played on Ursula's lips. 'He was rather handsome, as I recall. But appearances can deceive.'

'Did Rupert Maddox have anything to do with Perdita once she was in Darkhole Grange?'

'Not that I know of. He merely arranged her stay, with the connivance of my parents. I found out later that his family had a connection with the place. His father was a benefactor, so he had no difficulty getting her admitted. They said she was suffering from moral degeneracy — you could be confined in a mental institution for that in those dark days. But the truth is she was an inconvenience to him. She'd threatened to make their affair public, you see. Shout it from the rooftops. His wife controlled the purse strings, so that wouldn't have suited him at all.'

'But your parents went along with it?' Rachel said, as though she found it hard to believe.

'Perdy had long been an embarrassment to them, so they told themselves it was for the best and her name was never mentioned in the house again. Rupert was a ruthless manipulator and people tend to believe what they want to believe, don't you find? Perdy assumed that once his wife was dead he'd marry her right away because of the baby. But that wasn't part of his plan. He'd always told Perdy that his wife was Roman Catholic and refused to divorce him, but in my opinion, that was just an excuse. The truth was that he didn't want to forfeit her money. He married another woman soon after he was widowed — once Perdy was safely out of the way. I heard the new wife had money of her own too. Unlike Perdy.'

'How did his wife die?'

'She had an accident. Fell off the cliff onto the rocks below. It had been raining heavily earlier that day and the path was treacherous.'

'When did it happen?' The mention of another death had aroused Wesley's interest.

'About three weeks before they sent Perdy away.'

'What happened to Perdita's baby?'

'I presume it was adopted. I heard it was a girl but my parents never spoke of it and I was never allowed to see Perdy after the birth because I was told she was too ill.'

'But you tried to visit her?' said Wesley. If it had been his own sister, he would have moved heaven and earth to see her, but this was a different family — and different times.

He saw a shadow pass across the professor's features, a momentary look of deep sadness that suggested she'd felt more for her sister than she'd so far admitted.

'I went to the hospital several times and spoke to the nurse in charge of Perdy's ward. But every time

I called, I was told that Perdy wasn't well enough to receive visitors. I can be quite forceful, so I did manage to see her on a couple of occasions when her pregnancy was well advanced. After that, though, there was always some excuse, then my parents told me she'd developed an infection and died after the baby was born. They kept the details vague to stop any awkward questions. I suspected it was a lie, but all my questions were met with obstruction and my parents were furious when they found out I was trying to discover the truth, so, to my shame, I eventually gave up. I moved to London, and my studies occupied all my available time. When I was in my thirties, I met Dwight Nilsen at a symposium in the States and we married. A year later I had Teresa. Then I started applying for academic posts in the States. As soon as I was appointed, we moved over there.'

'So you never discovered what really happened to Perdita?'

She paused. 'Eventually I found out that my suspicions were correct and she hadn't died after the birth as I'd been told. But her time in that terrible place took its toll. They experimented on her with different treatments: brain surgery — a lobotomy that reduced her to a shell of a human being; electric shocks; plunging her in cold water. That doctor you mentioned — Birtwhistle — was very keen on new medical developments, and he performed the operation himself. He was full of bright ideas,' she added bitterly. 'Poor Perdita . . . ' She bowed her head.

'She died?'

'Who would survive something like that?'

'How did you find out about this?'

'I was over here for a conference and I met a doctor

who'd worked there for a short time until he became disillusioned. He told me what really happened.'

'Dr Birtwhistle's dead.'

'Good. My sister suffered terribly because of his scientific curiosity.'

'Why did you decide to return to Devon?'

'I wanted to die here,' she said simply. 'At my age, you realise what's important. Your roots.'

Wesley could see tears forming in her eyes, her tough carapace finally melting as she acknowledged the enormity of what had happened to her sister.

She flapped her hand as though Wesley was an annoying insect. 'I've had enough now. I want to be left in peace.'

'We understand,' he said, trying his best to sound sympathetic. 'You're sure you don't know what became of your sister's child?'

'No.' She stared out of the window, a signal that the interview was at an end. 'I've no idea what became of her. I only wish I had.'

'So the child was a girl,' said Rachel sharply.

Ursula looked up. 'That's what I heard. All I know for sure is that the baby was adopted.'

'Was the adoption arranged through an agency?'

'I don't know.'

'Have you tried to trace her?'

She shook her head, then opened her mouth as though she was about to say something before looking away. Wesley could tell the question had disturbed her.

'You have tried to trace her, haven't you?' He felt he had no choice but to press the matter.

'No,' she said after a while. 'I haven't. I've been in the States and it's sometimes best not to rake up the past.'

'Has Teresa tried to find her?'

She shook her head.

'Has Perdita's child tried to find you?'

She didn't answer the question. Instead she closed her eyes. 'I'm tired. You'll have to go.'

They left her alone and went in search of the matron. There was something Wesley needed to know.

'I hope you haven't been tiring the professor,' said Mrs Wardle. 'She isn't well, you know.'

'Has she had any other visitors?' Wesley asked before she could chide them further.

'There was her daughter, of course, the one who's missing.'

'Anybody else?'

She thought for a moment. 'Now that you come to mention it, there was someone. A woman. She said it was a private matter.'

'Did she give a name?'

'She said she was a Ms Crane. The professor wasn't well that day, so I didn't want to disturb her. The woman said she'd call again, but she never did.'

'When was this?'

'A couple of weeks ago.'

'Can you describe her?' Rachel chipped in, infected by Wesley's excitement.

'Middle-aged. Greying hair. Quietly spoken, with a slight local accent. Tall, slim. Long black skirt. Unremarkable.'

The description could have fitted a great many people in the area. But the name, Ms Crane, told Wesley he was on the right track. The fact that this mystery woman shared a surname with the professor was unlikely to be a coincidence. All his instincts cried out that this might be Ursula's long-lost niece.

Perdita Crane's daughter.

Mrs Wardle put her hand to her mouth. 'Oh, I almost forgot, one of my staff has just told me that a man was asking about the professor about three weeks ago. I told her she should have mentioned it before, but she's been off work until today and she says she's only just remembered.'

'What did she say?'

'Only that he spoke to her outside when she was putting rubbish in the bins and she told him that the professor hadn't been receiving visitors apart from her daughter and he'd have to see me. Then he said he'd speak to the daughter and asked where he could find her.'

'She told him about the hotel?'

'Yes. He told her he was a former policeman and he was working for a company that traced people's relatives.'

'And she believed him?'

'She said he seemed very businesslike. He told her he'd been trying to trace the professor to tell her something to her advantage, so she thought it'd do no harm. She's rather naïve, I'm afraid. He gave her his card; I have it in my office. Wait there.'

She hurried away and returned a few minutes later with a business card. When she handed it to Wesley, he saw the words *RG Investigations*. This was how Robert Gerdner had found Teresa Nilsen. But who had paid him to do it?

As they left, Wesley put in a call to the incident room. Could someone get hold of Perdita Crane's death certificate, and contact all the relevant agencies to try to trace who had adopted a baby girl born to Perdita at Darkhole Grange in early 1957.

16 October 1956

I was surprised when I received a fat envelope with an Oxford postmark this morning. My sister had translated more of Elena's letters — the ones that were never sent. These particular ones, though, weren't addressed to her lover, Denyes, but to her father, and were dated two months later.

Most honoured and best beloved father, *she began.* I know I have sinned gravely, but the choice you give me saddens my heart, for I am no holy sister who yearns for such a life. I am but a poor sinner who would keep her liberty. Yet I know I must bow to your will, although I pray you not to be hasty, for the cell is a prison like any castle dungeon.

I didn't understand what she meant. Did she go to prison for loving her brother's tutor?

Is what lies ahead for me any better than a prison? I thought it would be some discreet nursing home where I could have my baby before returning to my life here — or even a different part of the country where nobody knows me. But instead they plan to send me to an asylum and they say it's for my own good.

The place is called Darkhole Grange, and I found out from Mother that Rupert's father is one of the chief benefactors. She says Rupert himself has made the arrangements, but I cannot believe he'd betray me like that. He loves me. He told me so.

51

Neil received the call from Annabel while the bones he assumed belonged to Elena de Judhael were being photographed *in situ* before being placed reverently into a box. This had been a living woman, after all; an anchoress who must have been respected by the village community, however she might have felt about her situation in life.

'Neil, I've got news.' Annabel sounded excited, not her usual cool self. 'I've found your Elena in the ecclesiastical court records. Seems she was a very naughty girl.'

He pressed the phone closer to his ear, trying to drown out the sound of the small digger that was opening up a new trench on the far side of the site. 'Go on.'

'Elena de Judhael was appointed as anchoress at St Leonard's Church, Long Bartonford, in 1459 at the request of her parents. She went through a ceremony, a requiem mass, as though she'd died, and then she was incarcerated in a cell.'

'I know that already.'

He'd expected Annabel to be disappointed, but instead she sounded a little smug. 'But you don't know why she became an anchoress, do you?'

'I'm sure you're going to enlighten me.'

'She was the daughter of the lord of the manor but she fell in love with her brother's tutor and planned to run away with him. His name was Denyes.'

'Reminds me of the story of Abelard and Héloïse.

What happened?'

'Elena's father had already arranged an advantageous marriage for her, so he was furious when he found out. There's no more mention of Denyes, and I wonder if he was paid to go away — or if Elena's father and brothers dealt with him.'

'Murder?'

'It's possible. Anyway, Elena found she was pregnant by Denyes, and the man her parents had arranged for her to marry refused to go ahead with the wedding. There's no record of the child, so either it was born dead or . . . '

'Perhaps she was lying about being pregnant to get out of the arranged marriage,' said Neil, recalling how the skeleton in the shallow grave showed none of the signs of having borne a child.

'Possibly. Anyway, Elena became an anchoress, but she didn't take her fate lying down. According to correspondence from the parish priest of St Leonard's, she made two bids for freedom and had to be brought back to her cell. The second time they actually sealed up the small door into the church so she couldn't escape again.'

Neil stood there, lost for words. The archaeological evidence backed up Annabel's findings, but he could barely believe that a woman whose worst sin was to fall in love with the wrong person would be subjected to such brutal treatment.

'So she died in there,' he said sadly.

'Looks like it. You're right, it is a bit like Abelard and Héloïse. Only in that case, Héloïse fell in love with her tutor, and when her family's thugs castrated him, she ended her days as an abbess, which seems considerably better than being locked away in solitary confinement.'

'If there's no further record of Denyes, maybe the de Judhaels had him murdered. Can you keep looking?'

'You don't have to ask. If I find anything else, I'll be in touch.'

As Neil ended the call, the skull of Elena de Judhael was being lovingly placed in the box with the rest of her bones. He looked up to see Tel standing near the edge of the trench, watching with morbid fascination.

★　★　★

When Wesley and Rachel arrived back in the incident room, Gerry waved them into his office, hungry for news.

'I could be wrong,' said Wesley once he'd closed the door, 'but I think Professor Nilsen knows more than she's admitting. I think the daughter of her dead sister, Perdita, went to Woodtarn House to visit her. Adopted children are allowed to trace their birth family, and I think Perdita's daughter has done just that.'

'Then why didn't the professor mention it?' said Gerry with disbelief. 'What's the big secret in this day and age? She's her niece, for heaven's sake. Most of her family are dead and her daughter's missing. You'd think she'd be glad to find another relative. You'd think she'd be shouting it from the rooftops.'

'She didn't mention it because the niece never got to see her,' Rachel said. 'The matron told her that Ursula wasn't receiving visitors. She said her name was Crane — that's Ursula's maiden name — and that she wanted to see her on a personal matter. She told the matron she'd call back, but she never did.'

310

'I wonder why,' said Wesley, staring at Gerry's desk as though seeking inspiration. 'Unless she just wanted to establish that the professor was actually there.'

'I'll ask one of the DCs to trace everyone in the area called Crane. And I've asked someone to contact all the adoption agencies to see if they can help us find out more about Perdita's daughter.'

'You'll be lucky. They're big on confidentiality,' grumbled Gerry.

'There might be official documents, so I'm not giving up hope,' Wesley said. An idea suddenly struck him. 'Unless the adoption was a private arrangement. Something Perdita's family organised and hushed up. Things weren't as regulated back then.'

He needed to think. He returned to his desk and took Perdita's diary from his pocket. Then he made a call. There was someone else he needed to trace, and given that this person was a retired policeman, he knew it shouldn't be difficult. The man in question might well be dead, but there would still be records somewhere. Once he'd made his calls, it was just a question of waiting patiently.

But if he wanted to find Teresa Nilsen alive, perhaps patience was one thing he didn't have time for.

★ ★ ★

Sadly for DC Rob Carter, most police enquiries succeeded through solid grunt work: details followed up, statements trawled through for discrepancies. Gerry thought Rob needed to learn this valuable lesson, so after the detective constable had established that there were no Cranes in the area who answered the description given by Mrs Wardle, Gerry had another

311

job for him. He asked him to make a start tracing various births, marriages, deaths and adoptions. Dull stuff, but without it they'd get nowhere.

Wesley, in the meantime, sat at his desk trying to concentrate. He'd established that PC Walter Maltrit, Chabliton's village policeman back in the 1950s, had moved away to Cornwall around the time Perdita's child must have been born. He'd passed away a few years later, leaving his widow and a child — a daughter called Mary. Either the childless and bitter Mrs Maltrit, mentioned in Perdita's notebook, had been blessed with a late pregnancy, or the couple had adopted a child who would have proved an embarrassment to the family in the manor house if she'd stayed in the village. Wesley suspected the latter.

Mrs Maud Maltrit had continued to receive her widow's pension until five years ago, when she too had died. Of Mary there was no further record. He looked at the clock on the wall. Another late night for everyone. He stole a glance at Rachel, who was tapping the computer keys at her desk. She looked weary and he wished he could tell her to go home and get some rest. But he had a feeling that their visit to Professor Nilsen had opened a new line of enquiry for them. He put his head in his hands and closed his eyes, trying to tie everything together.

The first death had been that of Charlie Maddox, son and sole heir of Rupert Maddox, the father of Perdita's child. Charlie hadn't been shot, which must be significant. The killer must have been familiar with the escape room and the whereabouts of the boiler and its flue, which should have narrowed the field a little. But the employees there had been interviewed and eliminated. All of them had spoken well of Charlie and none appeared to have the remotest connection with Perdita Crane or any of the other victims. There must be something he'd missed; something obvious. But he couldn't for the life of him think what it was.

He made a call to Morbay. He wanted someone to go round to the escape room to check the names of every visitor. All the ones on record had already been spoken to, but there was a chance there'd been others who hadn't bothered to sign in. He remembered the girl on reception, Grace the goth. If he was right about her powers of observation, she might be the key to this, and when he told Inspector Weston what he wanted, his counterpart in Morbay happily agreed. He'd let Wesley know as soon as he had any relevant information, but it would probably be the following day.

It was eight thirty now, and there was little more they could do that day, so Gerry ordered everyone to go home and get some rest. Rachel was the first out of the door, rushing out as though she was desperate to get away.

Before he could follow her example, Wesley's phone made a pinging sound that reminded him of the bell fixed to the door of Arthur Penhalligan's bookshop, put there to announce the arrival of a customer. He fished his phone from his jacket pocket and saw that it was a reminder. He had an appointment with the therapist, Rosemary, that he'd miss if he didn't hurry. He'd been brought up to be conscientious about keeping appointments, something instilled into him by his GP mother, who'd often been annoyed by thoughtless patients who failed to turn up at her surgery as arranged.

He borrowed a pool car and drove to Neston. He

parked outside Rosemary's cottage, then sat for a while, gathering his thoughts. There was something he needed to do while he was there. And he had to figure out the best way of going about it.

Ten minutes later, he was sitting in an armchair in Rosemary's consultation room, which was arranged so that he and the therapist were facing each other, creating an atmosphere of intimacy. Her voice was soft and hypnotic, and in spite of himself, he found it hard not to relax and confide his innermost thoughts.

'Do you remember the first time you felt like that?' she asked.

He closed his eyes as instructed, and soon in his mind he was eight years old again, playing hide-and-seek with his sister, determined to win the game. There was an empty cedarwood chest in the spare bedroom, one his mother had recently bought from an antique shop to store bedding. He climbed into it and closed the lid. He could hear Maritia calling his name, then she was in the room and he opened the lid half an inch to peep out, but it closed with a crash and he heard his sister's laughter receding as she shut the door behind her. He tried the lid again, but it wouldn't open. It was pitch dark, and he felt hot as he struggled for breath, terrified that the air was running out. His frantic limbs flailed against the sides of the box like a bird in a solid cage, until his mother found him and pulled him out, hugging him against her breast as he sobbed helplessly. From that day on, the very smell of cedarwood brought on a sense of panic.

'Your sister knew you were there?' Rosemary asked quietly.

'I suppose she must have done.'

'How do you feel about her now?'

'Fine,' Wesley said quickly. 'We're very close.'

Rosemary nodded sagely, but Wesley could sense her scepticism.

He glanced up and noticed a framed photograph on the mantelpiece: Rosemary with a younger woman whose mousy hair was tied back in a ponytail, both of them smiling but looking slightly awkward.

He was struck by a resemblance he hadn't noticed before. Rosemary certainly fitted the description he'd been given of Ms Crane, the woman who'd tried to visit Professor Nilsen. Although he might have got it completely wrong.

'Would you like to make another appointment for when you have more time?' she asked with a professional smile.

It was time to act. He said he'd consult his diary but first he had to call his wife. He took his phone from his pocket, but instead of selecting Pam's number, he pressed Rosemary's. To his relief, her landline in the hall began to ring and she left the room to take the call. Surreptitiously he crept over to the mantelpiece and captured the image on his phone, hoping she wouldn't return and catch him in the act.

He was lucky. She returned after a few moments, looking puzzled.

'I'm so sorry.' Wesley tried his best to sound apologetic. 'That was me. I called your number by mistake. My fault. I intended to call my wife to ask her to check our calendar in the kitchen and tell her I'm on my way home, but I pressed the wrong number. I'm so sorry.'

This meant he had to call Pam as Rosemary looked on. It was a brief conversation and Pam sounded a little puzzled at his request, but he had what he wanted and he could make his explanations as soon as he arrived home. Before he rang off, she spoke again. 'I've got news. Tell you when you get home.'

52

When he arrived home, Pam came out to greet him, a glass of wine in her hand. For the first time in a couple of weeks, the strained look on her face had gone. She was smiling.

'You said you had news.'

'Yes. Michael's test results have come back.'

'And . . . ?'

'It's glandular fever. Maritia says it's nothing to worry about. I think she feared it might be something much worse. A lot of adolescents get it apparently. It's caused by the Epstein–Barr virus and it's debilitating while it lasts, but at least we know what we're dealing with. When I let his school know, they said a couple of other kids in his year have come down with it. They're going to send him work so he doesn't fall too far behind. Maritia says it's just a matter of being patient and letting him take things at his own pace.'

'That's great,' Wesley said. 'Did Maritia say when he's likely to improve?'

'It could last weeks and he might be tired for a while after that, but she says he'll be fine, Wes.'

They came towards each other, reaching out then embracing in a comforting hug of sheer relief. Wesley could tell that all sorts of dreadful possibilities had been preying on Pam's mind, possibilities he'd tried his best not to consider.

'I'll go up and see him,' he said once they'd shared a brief kiss. 'Amelia asleep?'

'Yes. She said she'd had a hard day at school. Double

317

PE.' She looked him in the eye. 'How did the appointment with the therapist go?'

'Well . . . I think,' he said, his mind on his suspicions rather than the actual session with Rosemary.

'Good. It's time your little problem was sorted out,' she said with a sigh.

He gave her hand a squeeze and went upstairs to Michael's room, where he found his son scrolling through phone messages, his face occasionally breaking into a smile. The atmosphere in the room seemed lighter.

'Mum's told me the diagnosis. My mate Kieron's got it too.' There was a long pause as Michael checked his phone again. Then he looked up at his father.

'Never thought I'd get sick of being stuck in my room,' he said with a twinkle Wesley hadn't seen for days.

Wesley grinned. 'Solitary confinement isn't all it's cracked up to be — even with a smartphone for company.'

* * *

Neil Watson returned to his Exeter flat later than he'd expected. He'd gone out for a post-dig drink with Chris and Dave in the city centre and lost track of time. Now, after four and a half pints of what he'd convinced himself was well-earned best bitter, he felt a little drunk. Tipsy was the word his grandmother would have used.

He let himself into the flat and searched the fridge for something to eat, finding only a lonely carrot and a pack of cheese slices a day past their sell-by date. However, there was bread and half a tub of low-fat spread, so at least he could make a sandwich. Once he'd devoured it, he scrolled through the messages on his phone, hoping to see one from Wesley. But there was nothing.

He picked up the TV remote and flicked through the channels on the small portable in the corner, settling on an archaeology programme fronted by an unfeasibly glamorous presenter wearing full make-up and a skin-tight vest top. But before he could find out what sort of site she was talking about, the doorbell rang, and when he answered it, he was surprised to see Annabel standing there with an excited look on her face.

'I found it in the cathedral archives,' she said, stepping into the hall. 'I've made a copy for you.' She held out a plastic file with both hands, like an offering.

'I've been having a drink with friends and I thought you'd like to see it sooner rather than later, so I decided to call in on my way home. It explains why your friend Elena ended up as an anchoress. Lucky she came from a wealthy family who used their influence with the authorities, or it could have been a lot worse for her.'

'What could be worse than being walled up in a cell?'

Annabel gave him a meaningful look. 'I'll leave you to it.'

'Sure you won't stay for a drink?' Suddenly he didn't want to be alone.

'Thanks, but I'd better get back.' To his surprise, Annabel leaned forward and her lips brushed his cheek. 'Take care,' she said before leaving him.

Confused, he looked down at the file he was holding. At least he had something to read in bed.

The document Annabel had given him was a letter written by Sir Nicholas, the priest at St Leonard's, seek.ing his superiors' advice. A young woman of noble birth had sinned grievously, a crime so dark that she should have paid with her life, and she had the choice of facing death or showing true repentance by withdrawing from the world. The reply was that it was up to Sir Nicholas to decide whether to accept her as an anchoress. And that was what he did.

Their assumption that Elena had been punished for flouting the moral code of the day was probably wrong. Elena's sin might have been much worse than he and Annabel imagined.

★ ★ ★

Wesley slept well that night. He wondered whether it was because the dark shadow of worry about Michael's health had been lifted. Or because he felt he was about to make some progress in the investigation. He told himself it was probably a mixture of both.

As soon as he reached the incident room, he called Mrs Wardle at Woodtarn Hall.

'I'm calling about that woman who visited the professor a couple of weeks ago — Ms Crane. If I send you a photograph by email, can you tell me whether it's her?'

There was a pause. Then, 'Very well.'

After she'd recited her email address, Wesley thanked her and set to work. Five minutes later, he had his answer. The mystery woman who'd asked to see Professor Nilsen had been Rosemary Harris. No doubt about it.

53

Wesley felt quietly pleased with himself that his subterfuge the previous evening had paid off. The fact that Rosemary had used the name Crane when she'd tried to see the professor and that she was around the age Perdita's daughter would have been convinced him he was on the right track. When he broke the news, Gerry seemed positively excited and was eager to bring Rosemary in for questioning. And as she'd also been Nathan Hardy's therapist, the DCI suggested it might be wise to conjure up a search warrant for her premises.

Gerry reminded Wesley of a child on Christmas Eve, waking every hour to check whether Santa had been. Wesley felt impatient too, but he was more skilful at hiding it.

He'd already confided in Rachel but he'd asked Gerry not to say anything to the wider team about his visit to Rosemary the previous evening. He didn't want it getting round the station that he'd consulted a suspect on a personal matter; a weakness he'd always done his best to hide. And he certainly didn't want it known that he'd fallen under the woman's persuasive spell and opened up to her. Now, in the mundane atmosphere of the incident room, the memory of the confidences he'd shared made him feel embarrassed — and a little disloyal to his sister. Maritia had only been seven years old at the time, but he'd had the impression that Rosemary thought she was to blame for his problem.

He sat at his desk and stared at the picture again. In it, a smiling Rosemary had a protective arm around the younger woman. There was a definite family resemblance between the pair, and it struck him that he knew nothing about Rosemary's domestic situation. He'd made the assumption that she lived alone, and there'd been no mention of a partner or other family. But these days the authorities kept records of who lived where, so he asked Paul Johnson to find out what he could.

Rachel had barely said a word since she arrived at work, and Wesley saw that she was frowning in concentration. After a while, she stood up slowly, her hand to the small of her back, and walked over to his desk. He stood to greet her and fetched a chair from the side of the room, placing it down for her. He saw her frown, as though she was interpreting his thoughtful action as sexist gallantry. But she sank into the seat with a muttered 'I'm not an invalid, you know.'

'I've been going through old records,' she began. 'Some kind person has digitised a lot of stuff dating back to the 1950s. Too much time on their hands, obviously,' she added with a sniff. 'Anyway, I typed in Rupert Maddox's name and found the inquest into his wife's death. Rupert was out, and his wife, Heather, took the dog for a walk. The housekeeper told the inquest that Heather received a phone call shortly before she left. A few hours later, the dog was found barking on the clifftop near Chabliton and her body was discovered on the beach below. It was thought she'd slipped and fallen because it had been raining earlier that day and the path was treacherous. Rupert had an alibi for the time of her death. He said he was in Exeter.'

'And was he?'

'No witnesses, so he could have been lying.'

'So Heather Maddox might have been lured out by the phone call and it might have been Rupert?'

'The housekeeper answered the phone and said it was a woman, but this wasn't followed up.'

'You're saying the police suppressed it?'

'Ignored it, more like. They went for the easy option. Accidental death.'

'Which suggests that if it was murder, the perpetrator was someone with influence . . .'

'Like Rupert Maddox, the husband.' She paused. 'Perdita Crane was pregnant by him — what if he got her to make the phone call?'

'It's impossible to prove it after all this time.'

'It's Perdita I feel sorry for. She probably imagined Rupert wanted to marry her, but he clearly had other ideas.'

'She was the wild child of the Crane family. Unstable. Possessive. She'd probably become an embarrassment to Rupert as well as to her family. Rupert would have had a lot of influence with the management of Dark-hole Grange, so it wouldn't have been hard for him to have Perdita admitted there for her own good, with the connivance of the Cranes.'

'No doubt they all thought it was the perfect solution to their dilemma,' Rachel agreed. 'The Cranes didn't want the wayward daughter flaunting her condition when they had a position to maintain in the community, and Rupert was free of a woman he'd tired of.'

'You think it was a conspiracy?'

'Appearances were everything back then.' Rachel looked round as though she was about to share a secret. She lowered her voice. 'I haven't told anyone this before, but my mum found out recently that the woman she'd always thought of as her aunt was really her half-sister. Her mother, my grandmother, had a child a few years before she met her husband, and her mother brought the child up as her own. My great-aunt was really my aunt. According to my mother, it happened in a lot of families. Shame was a big thing in those days.'

Wesley raised his eyebrows, surprised that she had shared this unconventional piece of family history so readily. 'And you think that's why the Cranes abandoned their daughter in an asylum? Shame?'

'We need to know what became of the child. If she was born in 1957, she'll be around sixty-five now, with a lot of reason to exact revenge on the people responsible for the incarceration and the death of her birth mother.' She shifted in her seat, trying to get comfortable.

'I suspect the adoption, if there was one, was a private arrangement. Chabliton's village policeman, PC Maltrit, and his wife were childless, and they left the village to live in Cornwall around the time Perdita's child must have been born. The pension records mention that Maltrit died leaving a widow and a daughter called Mary.'

'And you think Mary is Perdita's child. Bit of a leap, Wes.'

'Rosemary's surname is Harris, but the matron of Woodtarn House says she gave her name as Ms Crane. I think she's Perdita's daughter.'

'Or another relative we don't know about. A cousin, perhaps; one Teresa hadn't got around to putting on the family tree?'

He'd expected Rachel to be more excited by the possibility and he felt a little let down by her scepticism. 'Nevertheless, we need to speak to her, if only to eliminate her from the inquiry.'

'You're convinced Perdita is behind all this?'

'Yes. But she's dead.'

'How do we know?'

Wesley hesitated. 'Her sister, the professor, told us, and I have no reason to disbelieve her. Has anyone found the death certificate yet?'

Rachel said she'd given the job to one of the detective constables. 'I've a feeling it might not be that straightforward, if Darkhole Grange took steps to hush it up,' she added.

Wesley nodded. No records from Darkhole Grange had yet been found, so she could well be right. 'Well, we'd better keep looking,' he said hopefully.

As Rachel hurried away, Wesley saw Rob Carter rise to his feet. His desk was by the window, overlooking the Memorial Gardens and the river. He'd bagged the best seat in the office when he first started in Tradmouth CID and was very protective of his territory. Gerry was relaxed about it, saying that if it kept him happy, he was OK with it. Others, however, were more resentful.

'I've found out more about Mrs Maltrit,' he told Wesley. 'In 1968, she was living in Redruth, in Cornwall, describing herself as widowed. Her husband was a serving police officer who'd died in 1964 of a heart attack. She had an eleven-year-old daughter called Mary Rose, who was taken into care. Maud Maltrit had been known to social services for a couple of years after first being reported by neighbours in 1966. Suspicions of child cruelty. Physical and mental. They'd heard the child screaming and found her wandering about filthy and in rags. One social worker's report says the mother had mental health issues, but another says she was just a nasty piece of work. I've been looking for a record of Mary Rose's birth or adoption, but I can't find anything.'

There was silence in the office as everyone took the information in. Then Wesley spoke. 'Well done, Rob.'

'Think it's relevant, sir?'

'It might be.' Wesley couldn't stop thinking of Rosemary and the fact that her name was Mary Rose reversed, which seemed like further proof that his theory was correct.

He took his phone out to study the photograph again, more convinced than ever that he could detect a resemblance between Rosemary and Professor Nilsen. And he was certain that he'd seen the young woman with Rosemary somewhere before, but he couldn't think where. His eyes travelled to Gerry's office. He was on the phone, holding an animated conversation. As soon as he put the receiver down, he loomed at his office door.

'Right. We've got the search warrant for Rosemary Harris's premises. Wes, coming with me? We need to ask the lady some questions.'

54

Gerry had assumed Wesley would want to go to Neston with him to interview Rosemary, but Wesley shook his head. 'It's best if Rosemary doesn't realise I'm responsible for all this. I want to keep her trust,' he said. 'If she thinks I'm on her side, she might be more open with me.'

A look of disappointment passed across Gerry's face before he acknowledged that Wesley had a point. Besides, he said, Rachel looked as though she could do with some fresh air.

The traffic was light as Rachel drove Gerry to Neston. Once the castle that dominated the town came into view, he broke the amicable silence.

'If we get there first, we'll wait round the corner for the search team to arrive,' he said, stretching out his legs as though he was preparing for a long evening in front of the TV.

'According to records, nobody else lives at her address, so hopefully we'll find her on her own,' said Rachel.

'Good. As far as she's concerned, the only contact she's had with the police was when she was interviewed regarding Nathan Hardy's drugs-related murder. Hopefully our visit will come as a surprise.'

As soon as the words had left his lips, a patrol car swept past with sirens and lights blazing.

'Bloody idiots,' Rachel muttered as the vehicle screeched to a halt in front of them.

Gerry emerged from his own unmarked car,

slamming the door behind him. 'I said discreet,' he bawled over the noise. 'You're about as discreet as a travelling circus.'

A pair of red-faced constables emerged from the patrol car, which was soon joined by more police vehicles, quieter ones this time. Rachel sent one of the officers round to the back while Gerry rapped on the front door.

Rosemary answered looking puzzled. 'Can I help you?' she said, every inch the law-abiding citizen anxious to aid the police. When Gerry produced the search warrant from his pocket, a look of fear flashed across her face.

'I don't understand. I've told you everything I know about Nathan.'

She stood aside to let them into the hall, and Gerry signalled for the search team to follow.

'Sorry about this, love,' he said as the officers crowded into the small cottage like an invading army. 'But this is a murder investigation.'

Some of the team went upstairs while others began their search downstairs. Rosemary looked alarmed. 'They won't make a mess?'

'They'll try and cause as little disruption as possible,' said Rachel reassuringly, knowing she'd just told a lie. She'd seen the mess even the most careful search teams could make.

When Gerry told Rosemary they were taking her down to the police station for questioning, she looked as though she was about to object, but instead she bowed to the inevitable. Half an hour later, the three of them were sitting in Interview Room 2 at Tradmouth police station. As previously arranged, Wesley was waiting behind the two-way mirror to observe the interview unseen.

It was Rachel who asked the first question. 'Why did you go to see Professor Nilsen at Woodtarn House?'

The woman didn't answer for a while, as though she was searching for the most suitable answer. 'Her daughter, Teresa Nilsen, saw my website and asked me to visit her,' she said at last. 'She wanted to know about therapies for anxiety. Strategies to deal with her mother's situation. Immobility can lead to depression.'

'The professor didn't mention this to the matron in charge.'

'According to her daughter, she's an independent woman. Not the type who appreciates everyone knowing her business.'

'How did the daughter contact you?'

'By phone.'

'You gave your name as Crane.'

'It's my maiden name. I still use it professionally sometimes.'

Rachel and Gerry exchanged glances. The explanation sounded plausible. But there was a caution about Rosemary's answer that suggested she wasn't telling the entire truth.

Before they could proceed any further, Trish Walton entered the room, Gerry announcing her arrival to the tape machine running at the end of the table. She bent down to whisper into his ear, and he paused the tape before following her out into the corridor.

There they met Wesley, who'd just emerged from the room next door. Trish had news from the search team and they both needed to hear it.

'They didn't find a firearm, but they did find an empty ammunition box hidden at the back of one of the dressing table drawers in her bedroom. According to ballistics, it dates from World War Two and the .38 bullets it contained are the kind that killed the four victims. They've also just confirmed that all the victims were shot with the same firearm.'

Gerry let out a low whistle. 'But where's the gun now? She hasn't got it on her, that's for sure.'

'I asked the search team to pick up that photograph I told you about,' said Wesley. 'The one of Rosemary with a younger woman.'

Trish shook her head. 'They couldn't find it. It wasn't there.'

'Never mind, I've got a shot of it on my phone.' He thought for a moment. 'If she went to the trouble of getting rid of it after my visit, it must be significant, don't you think?'

Before Gerry could reply, the door to the interview room opened and the officer who'd been standing there guarding the suspect poked his head out. 'Sir, you're needed. The suspect's told DS Tracey she wishes to make a full statement.'

Gerry signalled Wesley to join him and Rachel, and when he walked in, Rosemary looked up, surprised. 'Wesley. I didn't know you were involved in all this.'

Wesley said nothing. Rachel rose from her seat, looking relieved that he had arrived to take over while she took his place behind the mirror.

'The team searching your house found something in your dressing table drawer,' Wesley began, trying his best to give no hint of their previous acquaintance. It was difficult. The previous evening the woman in front of him had begun to delve into his psyche, which inevitably had created a kind of intimacy between them. But he tried hard to put this out of his mind.

Even though she looked like a harmless and sympathetic middle-aged woman, he had to remind himself that she was suspected of involvement in at least four brutal and calculated murders. And that one potential victim, Teresa Nilsen, was still missing.

'I realise that,' she said. 'That's why I want to confess to the murders.'

'Where's the gun?' Gerry asked.

'I threw it into the river. I wanted to get rid of it. It was my father's. He brought it back from the war as a souvenir and taught me how to fire it. I did target practice with it when I was young.'

Wesley and Gerry looked at each other. There was something about her story that didn't feel right.

'What was your father's name?'

She didn't answer.

'What about your mother?'

'She died when I was young.'

'Do the names Walter and Maud Maltrit mean anything to you?'

Wesley saw her flinch before rearranging her features into a neutral mask.

'I think they adopted you as a baby. There'll be records, so we can easily find out,' he said.

'This is irrelevant. Just charge me and get it over with.'

'Why did you kill those people?'

She opened her mouth to speak, but no words came out. Wesley suspected she hadn't thought this through.

'Very well, I'll ask another question.' He brought up the picture on his phone and placed it on the table in front of the suspect. 'Who is the woman you're with in this photograph?'

'It's just someone I met on holiday,' she said quietly. 'At a yoga retreat in Portugal. Her name's Jane. We lost touch.'

'But you went to the trouble of framing a picture of you together.'

'It was a happy time,' she said, her confidence returning. 'I wanted a souvenir. Is there anything wrong with that?'

'I saw it when I came to see you last night, but it wasn't there when our search team went over your property just now.'

'I broke the glass. I had to throw it out. The photo's still there somewhere amongst my papers.'

Again her explanation sounded plausible. But Wesley knew it was a lie. 'Where's Teresa Nilsen?'

She sat up straight and raised her chin like a martyr about to go to her death. 'How should I know?'

'Did you kill her too?'

'Just charge me. I want to get this over with.'

An idea had started to form in Wesley's mind. And if he was right, there was a good chance they'd find Teresa Nilsen. If she was still alive.

3 November 1956

They are taking me there today.

Ursula is back from Oxford, and she came to my room this morning and put the last translation into my hands. She said she was sorry, and I could see she was about to cry. When I asked her what would happen to my baby, she wouldn't answer. I think I know what will happen. I think I will go through the pains of giving birth, then my child will be torn from me and I'll never see it again. My sister says that such babies are always adopted by kind couples who can't have children of their own, but I remember overhearing Mother telling Father that Constable Maltrit and his wife are childless. The constable is a quiet man and respected in the village, but I do not like his wife. I heard she drowned a litter of kittens once, and I would not like to think of her having my baby. I pray she won't, for I would fear for the poor mite.

I have been told to pack my bags but I cannot bring myself to do it. Instead, I sit on my bed reading Elena's last letter.

I pray you, gentle Father, to have mercy, for I know I will hear my own requiem mass before entering the chamber built there for me. I will be dead to all and cut off from the world of men. You say I deserve my fate, but my heart rebels against it. My passions overcame me and I can do nothing but weep hot tears. For I must endure a terrible punishment.

55

When Gerry had first started in the force, in what he always referred to as 'the olden days', a suspect would have his or her fingerprints taken when they were arrested on suspicion of murder. Things had progressed since then, and nowadays samples of DNA were taken too.

As soon as this was done, Trish Walton went over to Woodtarn House to ask Professor Nilsen whether she was willing to provide a sample of her own DNA for comparison, just a simple mouth swab. Trish reported that the professor had agreed, her initial reluctance overcome when Trish convinced her that it might help them to find Teresa. It was an option no mother could refuse.

Rosemary was being held in a cell in the bowels of the station while the search for more evidence continued. All they had was her confession and the empty box that had once contained the same kind of bullets that had killed the victims. Although Wesley pointed out that they'd only have solid proof if they could produce the gun that had fired them. Rosemary had provided no plausible motive for the killings that would stand up if the case came to court, and any barrister worth his fee would be able to convince a jury that Wesley's suspicions added up to little more than a fairy tale.

Once both DNA samples had been obtained, they'd been sent to the lab with a special request for speed. Wesley hoped he'd conveyed the urgency of the matter. He always felt powerless when things were taken out of his hands. According to Pam, he was a control freak, unable to trust anyone else to do a job to his own exacting standards. Although she'd laughed at the time, he suspected she'd meant it.

In the meantime, he'd had the photograph on his phone enlarged and printed out by the tech people so at least he could fill his time by asking some questions.

He could tell from the exasperated expression on Gerry's chubby face that he didn't think they yet had enough evidence to present to the CPS. And when Wesley told him he was going out because there was something he needed to check, Gerry was too preoccupied to ask what it was. Wesley shared his frustration. If they didn't get something else soon, they'd have to let Rosemary go.

He drove to Morbay alone, taking the car ferry. It was a lovely late spring day, and sunlight dappled the rippling water as the vessel chugged its way over to the far bank. The good weather had brought out the yachts, skimming over the river silently like insects on a pond. It was a peaceful scene, far removed from the death and violence of the past weeks. He had a sudden mental picture of Dr Birtwhistle lying there with the bullet hole in his head, staring in surprise at his killer.

With fresh determination, he negotiated his way through the Morbay traffic and arrived at the escape room, relieved to find a parking space a short distance down the road. Once he was inside the building, he pushed open the door to the reception area and saw Grace the goth sitting behind the desk tapping on the keyboard of the laptop in front of her.

She looked up and gave him a wary smile. 'You're back.'

Before Wesley could reply, a group of five young people emerged laughing from the Dungeon. Grace asked them how they'd enjoyed themselves, and after a brief conversation and a request for them to tell their friends, the customers went away satisfied and Wesley had her undivided attention.

'How are things going?' he asked.

She looked at him suspiciously, as though she expected to be arrested at any moment. 'Not bad.'

'The place is doing all right — in spite of what happened to Charlie?'

'Bookings are up — almost doubled. I reckon some people just come out of curiosity. Bloody ghouls,' she muttered in disgust.

'Proves that no publicity is bad publicity,' said Wesley. 'I've got a photo here. Can you tell me if you recognise either of these women?'

He produced the photograph and she looked at it as though she suspected it was booby-trapped. She took it gingerly by the corner and studied it with a frown.

'I know her,' she said, pointing at the younger woman. 'She worked here as a temp for a couple of weeks. Showed me the ropes when I started.'

'Would she know about the boiler?'

'Everyone knows about that old thing. Angie says we'll have to get a new one now. About bloody time.'

'An officer came round to interview you about former staff. Why didn't you mention this woman then?'

'Because I wasn't here. It was my day off, so the policeman only spoke to Stanislaus, and it was before his time. Besides, she was a temp. Not on the books.'

'Cash in hand?'

Grace nodded as though she feared she'd said too much. But Wesley wasn't worried about minor tax fiddles.

'You wouldn't know where I can find her now?' he said, jabbing the picture with his finger to emphasise the urgency.

'No. But I did see her a few months ago. Her hair was completely different, but I never forget a face.'

Wesley had known the yoga retreat in Portugal was a lie. 'Do you know her name?'

'Can't remember. I only met her the once.' She thought for a few moments. 'I don't know where she works now, but when I saw her, she was with the solicitor who did the conveyancing when I bought my flat.'

Grace said the solicitor's name, and as Wesley studied the picture again, he wondered why he hadn't seen it right away. Now he knew the mystery woman's identity, he was annoyed with himself for not realising it earlier. But when there was something startling or unusual about someone's appearance, it was often the only thing you remembered about them.

'You've been a great help.'

'I don't like the police,' was Grace's comment as he turned to go.

Wesley swung round to face her. 'Well, at the moment the police like you. Thanks,' he said, feeling he'd just discovered the last piece of a particularly fiendish jigsaw.

★ ★ ★

337

Wesley's discovery wasn't proof, and his next move needed some thought, especially if the killer was armed.

He drove back to the station via Neston, because it was coming up to rush hour and he wanted to avoid the queue for the car ferry. It was too early for the DNA results to have come back, but he was impatient to get back. In an ideal world, Rosemary would have revealed Teresa's whereabouts — or at least the whereabouts of her body — and told the truth about the gun. But it wasn't an ideal world, and he knew that her confession had been a work of fiction, dreamed up to protect someone else.

'I told the lab I want those DNA results yesterday if not sooner,' said Gerry as soon as Wesley walked into his office. 'But they said it would be twenty-four hours. And that was doing me a favour.'

Wesley sat down heavily in the chair beside the boss's desk, preparing to break the news of what he'd discovered at the escape room. 'I know who the woman in Rosemary's picture is,' he began.

When Gerry heard the name, his eyebrows shot up. 'In that case, we've got a connection with one of the victims — two if you count Charlie Maddox. And judging by that picture, she and Rosemary are close. But how close?' He paused, his gaze straying to the crime-scene photographs on display in the outer office.

If they were to have a chance of finding Teresa Nilsen alive, their new suspect needed to be brought in as soon as possible. And although they'd take backup, Wesley insisted that there'd be no lights or sirens. This time it was vital that their visit came as a surprise.

* * *

With the holiday season about to commence, the streets of Morbay were busier than normal and the journey was frustratingly slow. When Wesley brought the car to a halt outside the building, he could see the patrol cars behind him in his rear-view mirror and felt reassured.

'Think we should have brought the armed response unit?' he asked, suddenly realising how potentially vulnerable they were if their target turned out to be armed.

'She's hardly likely to bring a gun to work,' Gerry said with a confidence Wesley didn't feel.

When they pushed open the door of the Morbay Fresh Start Trust, the three young people sitting at the desks raised their heads as one to look at the new-comers. But the person they were after wasn't amongst them.

'Where's Pixie?' Wesley asked after introducing himself.

'On leave,' said a young man with deathly pale skin and a shaved head. 'If it's about one of our clients, maybe one of us can help you.'

There was nodding all round. But when Wesley asked for Pixie's home address, the atmosphere changed.

'We can't give that out. Confidentiality.'

Gerry walked slowly towards the pale man's desk and loomed over him before explaining in simple terms that he was obstructing a murder inquiry. The man's manner changed at once from defiant to nervous, and he meekly looked up the address.

Wesley didn't trust Pixie's colleagues not to tip her

off that they were on their way, so he left a uniformed constable there to make sure nobody called her.

Ten minutes later, they arrived at her address a few streets from the sea, a flat in a Victorian stucco terrace that had seen better days. There was no answer. But Wesley had an idea.

It wasn't hard to find the solicitor's office, and he was soon face to face with Pixie's partner Tasha, the woman he recognised from the photograph Pixie kept in pride of place on her desk at work.

At first Tasha seemed cautious, although in Wesley's experience lawyers usually were. Then, after a long silence she began to speak, the words tumbling out in a rush, as though the chance to unburden herself came as a relief.

'Pixie hasn't been the same since she found out her grandmother was locked away in an asylum and had her baby snatched from her,' she began. 'It became an obsession, and recently she's talked about nothing else. Her mum was adopted by a woman who abused her and sneered at her, saying she'd been born in an asylum.'

'Is Pixie's mother Rosemary Harris, the therapist from Neston?'

'I'm sorry, I don't know. She never allowed me to meet her. All I know is that her mum met someone who used to work at the asylum, and this person told her exactly what had happened to Pixie's grandmother.'

'What was that?' Wesley asked gently.

'It was horrible. She was operated on — experimental brain surgery — and had to endure all sorts of terrible treatments that would never be allowed today. I'd say there were grounds for a public inquiry if it's all true. And to add insult to injury, the man who got her pregnant — that would be Pixie's biological grandfather — used to visit from time to time to make sure she was still locked up.'

'Pixie's mother told her all this?' Wesley said gently.

'She didn't hold back, and in the end Pixie became more and more fixated with what had happened and started talking about retribution. I told her there were legal avenues that would enable her and her mother to publicise what had gone on there and maybe get compensation for the victims, but she wouldn't listen.' Tasha took a deep breath. 'A few weeks ago, I walked out on her. She'd become a different person. Bitter, obsessive and bent on revenge.' She looked Wesley in the eye. 'Is she all right?'

He didn't answer. He didn't want to lie. 'Do you know where Pixie is? She isn't at work or at home.'

Tasha thought for a while. 'The only place I can think of is the hut. She bought it on a whim a couple of years ago. It's a bit run-down and quite isolated, but we used to go there on a nice day.'

'Where is it?'

'On the coast between Bereton and Dukesbridge. There's a caravan park not far away, but that section of the beach is very private.'

Wesley had a sudden flash of inspiration. 'Is the caravan park called the Chabliton View? There's a hotel nearby.'

She looked at him as though he'd pulled off an impressive conjuring trick. 'That's right. How did you . . . ?'

Wesley thanked her and returned to the car, where Gerry was waiting for him.

56

Wesley and Gerry arrived at the caravan park just as it was starting to rain. The place looked even more miserable and tawdry under the steel-grey sky. Wesley drove straight to reception. They needed to know where Pixie's beach hut was. During the journey, Gerry had discovered her car's registration number and found out that it had been picked up on traffic cameras on the main road heading that way an hour ago.

Paddy Smith greeted them with a snarl. Wesley hoped he was more welcoming to the people who were unwise enough to choose the Chabliton View as their holiday location from the touched-up and cleverly angled photographs in the brochure.

They didn't bother with pleasantries before beginning their questions. At first Smith pressed his lips firmly together and refused to answer. It wasn't until Gerry threatened him with arrest that he finally spoke. 'There's a track a few hundred yards beyond the statics, near the cliff. It's the only access to the beach by car and I saw one driving in earlier. Girl with purple hair it was; never even waved, snotty cow.' He sniffed and turned away.

'Have you seen her here much lately?'

'Funny you should ask that. I've seen the car passing most days. I was going to go and have a word, 'cause she drives too bloody fast. It'll soon be holiday season and we'll have lots of kiddies wandering all over the place. Stupid bitch.' The words were defiant, cocky.

'You're certain she's there now?'

Smith didn't look quite so sure of himself, but he nodded. 'Not seen her leave this way, so she must be.'

'Stay in here,' Gerry barked before they both went outside. To their relief, the man didn't argue.

Gerry told Wesley to call the armed response unit. If Pixie had a gun with her as they feared, it would be foolish to go in without backup. But that needn't stop them locating the track down to the seashore and keeping an eye on the beach hut until help arrived.

They followed the directions they'd been given. Once they arrived on the pebble beach, they had to walk some distance before they saw a battered Renault with the right registration tucked in next to an old wooden beach hut with a rotting veranda, some way from the main beach where holidaymakers would gather. As they drew nearer, they saw thin curtains drawn across the two dusty windows and no sign of life. They assumed Pixie was inside, but whether Teresa Nilsen was with her was another matter. The other possibility was that she was elsewhere — or she was dead. But Paddy Smith's statement that Pixie had been up there most days filled Wesley with hope. If Teresa was still alive she needed to be fed.

He left Gerry waiting in the shelter of the nearby cliff face and crept to the back of the hut, pressing his ear to the splintery wood with its flaking blue paint, hoping to hear voices or any other sound that would tell him what was happening in there. He stood quite still, the thin rain dampening his face, and after a few moments, his patience was rewarded.

'Get back in.' The words were a cold order barked to a prisoner.

Wesley tiptoed round to the other side, where he

could see Gerry whispering into his phone. He signalled to him. A thumbs-up. The gesture seemed inappropriate, but it was the only way he could think of to convey the message that their suspicions had proved correct.

Suddenly the hut door burst open with a crash that startled him. As Pixie appeared on the veranda, he concealed himself against the splintery wall while Gerry shot back into his hiding place.

Wesley heard the rattle of a key turning in a padlock and watched Pixie approach her car. She didn't appear to be armed, unless the gun was concealed in her jacket pocket, but he knew it would be wise to wait until the ARU arrived. However, there was a chance that a woman's life was at stake, and besides, they had the advantage of surprise.

Unaware of their presence, she bent to unlock the car. Wesley slowly took out his handcuffs, ignoring Gerry, who was signalling frantically from the other side of the path. He crept up behind her as the car door opened, and pushed her against the vehicle. Her reaction was to freeze for a second, then try to wriggle free, frantic as a trapped cat. She swore loudly as she kicked at his shins, and he winced each time her shoe came into contact with his leg.

'Police,' he said as he struggled to secure the handcuffs around her skinny wrists. As soon as the cuffs snapped shut, he managed to pin her against the car, and he was reciting the words of the caution as Gerry broke cover and jogged over to come to his aid.

'This is police harassment,' Pixie hissed.

'We need to see inside the hut.'

'You'll need a search warrant.' She was still struggling, her face red with fury.

'Not if someone's life's in danger,' said Wesley. He could hear the ARU sirens approaching, like the cavalry over the hill. 'Keys,' he said, before noticing that they were dangling in the car door.

He snatched them and tossed them to Gerry, who ran to the hut door while Wesley checked Pixie's pockets. She started to kick his shins again, but to his relief, he found she wasn't armed.

'Where's the gun?' he demanded as he tried to hold onto her. She was still wriggling like an eel, determined to slip from his grasp.

'What gun?' she said in a breathless hiss.

It seemed an age before the ARU cars appeared and their occupants leapt out, pointing their firearms and yelling orders. Wesley hit the ground and pulled Pixie down with him before placing his hands behind his head as instructed. The time for explanations would come later.

He stared up at the officer pointing a gun at his head. 'DI Wesley Peterson, Tradmouth CID. It was me who called you,' he said, trying to sound calm. 'This is the suspect. I don't think she's armed.' Even though he was an experienced police officer who knew he was on the right side of the law, he found the situation frightening.

He was frisked and instructed to produce his ID, and he obeyed the terse orders without question. Eventually the armed cop was satisfied and helped him to his feet, just as a patrol car screeched up to take Pixie away for questioning. As she was led to the car, the fight seemed to leave her. But Wesley's shins would bear the marks for some time to come.

Wondering why Gerry hadn't yet reappeared, he limped towards the hut and stepped into the gloomy interior. By the light trickling in through the closed curtains, he could make out two figures sitting on the bench seat at the far end. One was Gerry. The other was small and hunched and wrapped in a blanket.

'This is DI Peterson, love,' said Gerry gently. 'Don't worry. He's with me.'

Wesley's eyes were adjusting to the light, and now he could see that the woman was shaking, her eyes wide and desperate, as though they had witnessed unimaginable horrors. He recognised her from her photograph as Teresa Nilsen, though the glossy hair and make-up was gone and now she resembled a waif or the victim of some natural disaster. Only what had happened to her had been far from natural.

'I've called Rach and Trish. And an ambulance,' he told Gerry. He looked at Teresa. 'You'll be OK, love. You're safe now. It's all over.'

Rachel arrived at the same time as the ambulance and tried to help Teresa down the steps to the beach. But her legs were so weak that she collapsed to her knees and it fell to the ambulance crew to help her up with practised efficiency. Rachel went off with her to hospital, holding her hand, a comforting presence.

Once they'd gone, Gerry flung the curtains open and Wesley had a chance to take in his surroundings. Now he could see that the bench seat had a hinged lid that had been secured with a sturdy padlock.

'Good job she left the key on the side,' said Gerry as though he'd read Wesley's mind. 'I don't think Teresa could have survived for much longer in there.'

'You found her in the box?' A tingle of horror passed through Wesley's body. He'd thought the session with Rosemary had set him on the road to curing his fear of enclosed spaces, but the idea of being trapped inside that bench for days on end was a step too far. He turned away so he wouldn't have to see the thing. 'I thought this whole coastline had been searched.'

'It was. But if someone came and shone a torch through the windows of this hut, there'd be nothing to see. No sign that anyone was here. Pixie brought her food once a day and let her use the loo.' Gerry wrinkled his nose at the acrid smell of urine from the bucket in the corner. 'If you ask me, it'll take her a while to get over this. We should go to Woodtarn House to tell her mum she's safe. She probably thinks she's dead.'

'That was the whole point,' said Wesley. 'Pixie wanted to punish the people who hurt her grandmother, Perdita Crane. She didn't care how much Teresa suffered; she was paying the price for what Pixie thinks Ursula did to Perdita. She wanted retribution.'

As they left, Wesley glanced back and shuddered. Death was one thing, but a living death, in his opinion, was even worse.

57

The anchoress's cell, as Neil's team now called it, had been excavated, tidied up, recorded and photographed. Neil had sent the young woman's bones off to the lab, carefully packed. But as he looked into her shallow grave, he was surprised to realise that he was feeling bereft without her.

His next task was to open a trench in the interior of the church, where they were sure to find more burials; high-status ones with the promise of interesting artefacts befitting the deceased's station in life. Next season they'd tackle more of the churchyard and its burials, which would provide valuable information about the inhabitants of Long Bartonford: their diseases, their lifestyle and even the food they ate. Although all the lab tests in the world wouldn't tell them what had really gone on in their hearts and lives.

He was suddenly reluctant to leave Elena's grave — he was sure it was Elena — and he'd just squatted down to take another photograph of the graffiti when he caught sight of Annabel walking purposefully towards him.

'Hi,' she called. 'I've found more goodies in the cathedral archives that might interest you. The documents were all over the place, so they haven't been easy to find, but this one's a corker.'

The sight of one of Annabel's cardboard work files was always a welcome one, and he wondered what else there was to discover about Elena de Judhael. He took the file from her, and when he opened it, he saw another photocopy of an old document, the original no doubt a faded sheet of parchment.

'I'll give you the gist — save you spending hours trying to make out what it says. It's an account of a private hearing between the bishop's secretary and the father of Elena de Judhael. It turns out that Elena killed her lover, Denyes, her brother's tutor, when he revealed that he was already married. She was caught with a bloodstained dagger in her hand and she made no attempt to deny what she'd done.' She smiled. 'It wasn't Devon's answer to Abelard and Héloïse after all.'

'Elena was a murderer?'

'Denyes had been seen to quarrel with one of the lord's tenants, who was subsequently killed by a runaway horse. The lord of the manor, Elena's father, told the priest, Sir Nicholas, who must have owed his position to the de Judhael family, that it would be convenient for everyone if this dead tenant got the blame so that his daughter could go free. The reply to his request, however, was stern. If the young woman had committed the sin of murder, her life should be forfeit.'

Neil held his breath, waiting for the end of the story.

'They met with the bishop's secretary and reached a deal. Elena was to show her true repentance by 'dying' — leaving the world and becoming an anchoress. But as we already know, she couldn't hack it. She managed to escape twice, and each time she was brought back. Eventually she was walled in.'

'That's the one thing we do know from the archaeological evidence. She died in there,' Neil said quietly, thinking of the skeleton he'd unearthed.

A smug smile appeared on Annabel's face. 'Did

she, though? I came across this. It's a letter from Sir Nicholas. It seems he took pity on Elena. There was another young woman, a nun from a local convent, who had a real vocation and was yearning to be an anchoress; to die to this wicked world and spend her life in solitary prayer and contemplation. He asked for permission from the bishop to release Elena from her vow so that this Sister Hawise could take her place.'

'And was this agreed?'

'There's no trace of the reply, but in the records of St Leonard's a few years later, there's mention of the anchoress, Sister Hawise, who is a goodly and holy woman. Apparently she even requested that the entrance they'd broken into to release Elena should be sealed again, and she insisted on digging her own grave in preparation for her death.'

'I can't believe anyone would do that.'

'There are records of it happening elsewhere. They were different times — a strange landscape to our modern minds. I think it's Hawise you found. Elena got away.'

'Got away with murder, you mean,' said Neil. 'And that ring we found — *Lord have mercy on a sinner* — was just a pious request.'

A secretive smile appeared on Annabel's lips, as though she was nursing a delicious secret. 'Fancy a drink tonight?' There was a pause — the type of hesitation that could be full of meaning. 'Unless Lucy's back, of course.'

'What about your husband?'

'He's away,' she said. 'Eight o'clock at that place near the cathedral? I'll tell you all about it then.'

Neil felt he couldn't say no.

★ ★ ★

Tel saw Neil Watson talking to the posh woman with the long brown hair, seemingly entranced by what she was telling him. He'd had enough of emptying heavy buckets of soil into the huge sieve and watching while the archaeology students sorted through what was left, sometimes exclaiming with excitement over some fragment of pottery that looked to Tel like a filthy pebble.

He took out the phone, the one he kept for the special calls. He'd heard nothing for a couple of days, and he was starting to worry. She'd sworn to make contact every day, so she'd broken her promise, and he didn't like people who broke their promises. His mum had done that, and he hated her for it.

There was only one thing for it. If she wouldn't call him, he'd go and find her. It was only right. He'd take one of the archaeologists' cars; most of them were old bangers and easy to nick. And he'd take the thing from his rucksack and put it in his pocket; the object that made him feel all-powerful. Like a king. Like a god.

58

It had seemed like a good idea at the time, but now that Tel was navigating his way slowly up the rhododendron-lined drive, he realised that he didn't know exactly where to find her. He was to have been given detailed instructions, just as he had been with the couple and the old man. But they hadn't come, so he was on his own.

He fingered the gun he'd slipped into his pocket earlier. He'd imagined it would be simple; that he'd find her room, do the job and get out of the place before anyone realised what had happened. But now he realised that it wouldn't be that straightforward. There'd be loads of old ladies in there. Professor Nilsen — Ursula — was only one among many, so finding her would be like trying to find one sheep in a flock.

But it was what Pixie had told him to do, and he wouldn't be paid until he'd completed his mission. The rain had stopped and the sun had come out. He pulled onto a wide grass verge out of sight of the building. He'd come this far now, so he might as well try. And he was the one with the gun. The one with power over life and death.

He emerged from the car, blinking in the sunlight, and as he slammed the car door, his other hand felt for the weapon in his pocket. His talisman.

He began to circle the building, looking for a way in. He'd thought there'd be more staff and visitors coming and going, but the place was like the grave, which was good. He walked on tiptoe, bending as he passed each downstairs window, and at the back of the building, he felt a glow of satisfaction when he saw a door standing ajar. He pushed it with a tentative finger and it opened to reveal a kitchen filled with stainless-steel equipment. Pans bubbled on a large stove, and the unmistakable aroma of shepherd's pie and cabbage — the same sort of fare Tel had eaten in the children's home — filled the warm air, conjuring a feeling of desolation.

The kitchen door opened onto a spacious hall with a sweeping staircase, thickly carpeted so nobody would hear his footsteps. He could hear the babble of a TV behind the door to his right, and muted voices. Maybe she was in there.

The door began to open, and he froze, suddenly face to face with a stern-looking woman in a nurse's uniform. This wasn't in the plan.

'Can I help you?'

Tel knew that the real meaning behind the words was 'What the hell are you doing here? Shove off before I call the police.' He felt in his pocket again, and this time he drew out the gun. The woman took a step back, her expression completely calm. Tel had hoped for terror.

'Where's Ursula Nilsen?'

'There's nobody of that name here.'

The bitch was lying. He repeated the question, aware that his hand had begun to shake.

She didn't reply. He hadn't expected her to be so cool. The others had been terrified; especially the woman in the barn conversion when he'd backed her into the corner before pulling the trigger. He'd almost smelled her fear, and he'd enjoyed it.

Without warning, the front door opened to his left, and when he turned his head, he saw two men standing there. The black detective from Tradmouth who'd asked him all those questions about Nathan, and an older, fatter man. They stood quite still as he turned the gun on them, more nervous now.

'Pixie's been arrested and Rosemary's in custody. It's over, Tel. We know everything.'

The younger detective's dark brown eyes were staring into his, willing him to obey. But all Tel's senses were screaming not to give up. He raised the gun a little, pointing it at the detective's head and stood there paralysed by indecision.

'Put the gun down, Tel. Place it on the floor and step back.'

He didn't expect the sudden movement to his right as the woman rushed forward and knocked the gun from his grasp, sending him off balance.

★ ★ ★

As Wesley kicked the gun away, Gerry hauled Tel to his feet and snapped the handcuffs on, pushing him down to sit on the bottom step of the staircase before turning to Mrs Wardle who was standing stiffly in her matron's uniform.

'Nice work, love.'

'I served as an army medic many years ago. When you've undergone training, some things become instinctive.'

'Well done anyway,' Wesley chipped in. 'You probably saved our lives.'

'I'm a nurse; that's been my job for years.' Mrs Wardle's stern face cracked into a smile.

While Gerry called for a patrol car to pick up their prisoner, and gingerly placed the gun inside an evidence bag, Wesley sat down on the stair beside Tel, who suddenly began to talk, gabbling fast, eyes wide, pleading to be believed.

'It wasn't my idea. It was Pixie. She told me to . . .'

Wesley already knew the truth, but he said nothing. This interview would be done by the book. It was too important to make mistakes.

'How's Professor Nilsen?' he whispered to Mrs Wardle as they were leaving.

'She's as well as you'd expect, but I'd rather she didn't know about this incident. I don't understand why a thug like that would come looking for the professor armed with a revolver.'

Wesley smiled. 'I'll explain everything another time,' he said. 'Look after the professor, won't you. And tell her we've found Teresa alive and well.'

★ ★ ★

When Rosemary was told about Tel's arrest, she put her head in her hands and cried. The tape was running. This was the time for explanations — if the woman was minded to co-operate.

Rachel had volunteered to conduct the interview with Wesley, but Gerry said he'd give her a break because she should be taking it easy in her condition. Wesley sensed her fury as soon as the words left Gerry's lips. The boss might be a dinosaur, but he was a dinosaur with a heart.

'Pixie's your daughter, isn't she?' Wesley began, watching Rosemary's face. 'You've been told she's under arrest?'

The answer was a nod.

'Teresa Nilsen's been found. She's in hospital. What was Pixie intending to do with her?'

After a long silence, Rosemary spoke. 'She wanted Ursula to know what it was like to lose a daughter. To have her taken away and never see her again. That was what Ursula helped them do to my mother.'

'We found a familial DNA match. Ursula Nilsen's your aunt, isn't she? Perdita Crane was your mother.'

Rosemary looked at him, and he noticed that her eyes were sunken and red, as though she'd been crying. 'Do you know what they did to her — to my mother? They locked her in that place and tortured her. Electrocuted her; threw her into a cell and turned a hose on her. A doctor there, Birtwhistle, operated on her brain; robbed her of her personality and intelligence, left her a hollow shell. And a cruel nurse called Gerdner went along with it all. My mother was called a moral degenerate just because she had me. They locked her up for it and she paid with her life.'

'Pixie wanted to take revenge on her grandmother's behalf, and you agreed.'

'If she couldn't get to the parent, she punished the child. It's the only way we could get justice for my mother — by visiting the sins of the fathers upon the next generation.'

'And Charlie Maddox?'

'Pixie worked in that escape room for a short time and she saw how easy it would be to kill someone there. He was the only surviving son of the man who got my mother pregnant and abandoned her. I discovered that Rupert Maddox was already dead, but his son was very much alive. He died in his father's place. An eye for an eye. Isn't that what they say?'

'Charlie Maddox was your half-brother.'

She ignored his words and carried on, in a world of her own. 'My mother wasn't the only one who suffered.

I did too. The couple who adopted me, the Maltrits . . . ' She swallowed hard, as though the memory was painful. 'When my so-called father died, my mother — I can hardly bear to call her that — taunted me, saying I was the daughter of a whore and I was born in an asylum. She beat me and hid me indoors so no one would see the bruises. In the end, someone reported her. They said she was ill, but that was just an excuse. She was evil. Her husband had done his best to keep her under control, but once he was dead, there was nobody to stop her. It should have been obvious she wasn't fit to bring up a child, but to Ursula and her parents, I was something to be got rid of. Like vermin.' She spat the words. 'Eventually the authorities took me away from her and put me with a succession of foster parents, but when I was older, I discovered the truth about my real family.'

'How?'

'Before the Maltrit woman died, I went to see her. I needed to know who I was. Even though she was old and frail, she took great pleasure in telling me the truth — everything. She told me who my mother was, and how Maddox got her pregnant and put her in Darkhole Grange, where I was born. I looked for my family, but by that time there was no trace of the Cranes at Bartonford Manor. The last of them had gone to America. Out of my reach.

'For years I managed to put it out of my mind and get on with my life. Then six months ago, I discovered that a client of mine used to work at Darkhole Grange.

She came to me for help because she'd been affected by what she'd witnessed there. She didn't stay there long, but she remembered Perdita and she told me what they did to her. She told me about Nurse Gerdner, who was a disgrace to her profession, and Dr Birtwhistle with his cruel experimental treatments. I found out about the horrors my real mother had been subjected to. I doubt if anyone could have survived what she went through.'

She fell silent for a few moments, and Wesley waited for her to continue.

'I discovered that a man called Gerdner had set up as a private detective in Morbay. It's not a common name, so I wondered if he was related to Nurse Gerdner. I made an appointment, and when I asked him, he admitted that she was his mother, almost as if he was proud of it. I told him I wanted him to trace some people for me: Ursula, my birth mother's sister, and Rupert Maddox's son — my half-brother. He discovered that Ursula had returned from the States to live here. He also managed to find Dr Birtwhistle, who was housebound but had a daughter who lived locally. Then he found out that Ursula's daughter was over here visiting her mother. She was staying in a hotel nearby and he established contact with her saying he was from a genealogy company and was trying to trace her relatives. It was so easy, and it gave Pixie and me the idea for the ultimate revenge. Gerdner did the work for me and never suspected a thing.'

She took a deep breath before she carried on, and Wesley glanced at the red light on the machine that was recording her confession for posterity.

'I asked him to send tour tickets to the people he'd traced,' she continued. 'I told him to do it anonymously because I wanted it to be a surprise. They needed to realise what had gone on there . . . what they'd put my mother through.'

'You set fire to Gerdner's office to destroy all evidence of your visit.'

'Can you imagine me committing arson? Really, Inspector, you have no proof.'

For a while, nobody spoke. Then Gerry broke the silence. 'Your daughter Pixie killed Charlie Maddox for you because she knew about the boiler, but I think you got Nathan and Tel to do the rest of your dirty work. They both came to you for therapy, so it wasn't hard to discover their weaknesses.'

She turned her head towards Wesley. 'Just like I learned about yours, Inspector.'

Wesley felt the blood rushing to his face.

'Nathan was good at keeping an eye on people, but he was no killer,' she said. 'It was Tel who was keen to do the job. He's always suffered from feelings of inadequacy — not surprising given his upbringing, which wasn't dissimilar to mine. He saw it as a chance to prove himself and please me at the same time. I offered to pay him and he fancied himself as a hit man. But to be honest, I think he'd have done it for nothing.'

'You controlled him. You told him a version of the truth and he saw himself as your avenger.'

'If that's what you want to think.'

'With the possible exception of Dr Birtwhistle, you murdered innocent people; people who'd never done your mother any harm.'

'You're wrong. Gerdner and Maddox paid for the sins of their parents. Ursula and her parents punished Perdita for being a free spirit. But I see her as a saint. A martyr to their warped notion of morality. I have no

359

regrets about what I did. It's just a shame that Ursula wasn't made to pay for her part in it all.'

She sat back and folded her arms. The interview was over.

12 November 1956

I must pay a dreadful price, although confinement is something I have ever feared. I will never again smell a flower or see the sun. I will be as a corpse. A corpse who still breathes and moves. And yet it is what I deserve.

Elena's story echoes my own, but in my case it wasn't my lover who died but that pasty-faced wife of his. I telephoned her saying I wanted to talk, and she agreed to meet me on the cliff path. She had her silly little dog with her, and it yapped and snarled at me as though it knew what I'd done with her husband. It was a horrible little thing, and at the time I wished it had fallen over the cliff with its mistress.

How was I to know that my sister had sneaked out after me to see where I was going? How was I to know that she saw me meet Heather Maddox and witnessed our quarrel?

There is already speculation in the village that there is something suspicious about Heather's death. My mother says that a lot of people know about me and Rupert, because I have made little effort to hide my love for him. I thought discretion was for prigs and fools, but now I realise that my openness and disregard for convention might have been my undoing.

My father says that if the police think Heather's death wasn't an accident, I could face the gallows. But he told me he's come to an arrangement with Constable Maltrit. I did not know what he meant at first. But I think I do now.

So this is to be my punishment. I am the moral delinquent. The bad girl. The murderess. And I must be punished.

59

It was over. Tel was charged with murder and Rosemary was charged with conspiracy, while Pixie faced charges of murder, kidnapping and false imprisonment. It had come out in the interview that Nathan Hardy had helped her take Teresa Nilsen from her hotel room, believing she was being kidnapped for money and he would get a cut of the proceeds. But once he'd realised there would be no reward and he saw the conditions Teresa was kept in, he lost his nerve and threatened to tell the police. This signed his death warrant — he couldn't be allowed to ruin the plan — and Rosemary had persuaded Tel to deal with him. The two men had never got on anyway, and Rosemary had used her influence over her vulnerable client to transform him from a petty criminal into a murderer. To Wesley this was hard to forgive.

Teresa was still in hospital and Wesley felt it was time they told Ursula Nilsen the whole story. Rachel was looking restless, resentful at being cooped up in the incident room dealing with paperwork while her colleagues conducted the interviews, so he decided to take her with him.

'It's nice to be delivering good news at last,' she said. 'There's been too much of the other sort. How long do you think they'll keep Teresa in hospital?'

'They'll check her over and she'll probably stay in tonight. Then we can take her to see her mum.'

'Thank God it's all over,' said Rachel. 'Families, eh.' The words were said with a bitterness that surprised Wesley.

'You're lucky if you get a good one,' he replied, hoping there wasn't a hidden meaning behind her words. From what he'd seen of Nigel, he seemed a gentle, straightforward man. But you never knew what went on in other people's marriages.

'Is everything OK?' he asked, trying to sound casual.

Her hand travelled down to her bump and rested there protectively. 'I suppose I'm just feeling restless, that's all.'

'Pam was like that when she was expecting.' He watched her expression, hoping he hadn't said the wrong thing. But she gave a small smile and hauled herself out of her seat, eager to leave.

★ ★ ★

When they arrived at Woodtarn House, the place was quiet, with no sign of the earlier excitement. Wesley went in search of Mrs Wardle, while Rachel waited in the entrance hall. After a few moments, he returned.

'We're to go straight up. She's expecting us.'

When they entered Professor Nilsen's room, she was sitting in the chair by the window, as though she hadn't moved since their last visit.

'They told me Teresa had been taken to hospital.'

'She's had a check-up and they're keeping her in overnight,' said Rachel reassuringly. 'It's routine.'

'I realise that,' the old woman said sharply.

'Of course,' said Wesley. 'Did you know what had become of Perdita's daughter?'

'I lied before. I knew it was the village policeman who'd adopted her, and I imagine pressure was put on him to move out of the area. My parents wouldn't have wanted the child there as a constant reminder.'

She must have seen the look of disapproval on Rachel's face, because she leaned forward and pointed an accusing finger. 'And before you judge them, there are things about the affair you don't know; things that have never been spoken of but it's about time they came out into the open.'

Wesley shifted forward in his chair, wondering what was coming. A glance at Rachel told him she too was listening expectantly, breath held.

'You've been thinking of my parents as villains who locked their wayward younger daughter in a terrible institution because she disgraced the family by becoming pregnant with a married man. Am I right?'

Wesley caught Rachel's eye, but neither of them answered.

'I can see their actions would be regarded as evil, particularly in this day and age, but there are two sides to every story.' There was a lengthy pause. 'My parents committed Perdy to that place to put her beyond the reach of the law.'

'You're saying she did something illegal?' said Rachel.

'The most illegal thing of all, Detective Sergeant. She was suspected of murdering an innocent woman.'

The picture was starting to become clearer in Wesley's mind. 'Rupert Maddox's wife was alleged to have died in an accident. But Perdita killed her?'

The professor bowed her head. 'I was worried about her that day, so I followed her. She had no idea I was there. When it happened, I didn't know what to do, so I rushed back to the Manor to tell my parents. They wielded enough power in that village back in the 1950s to make sure the business was covered up.

They knew that the village policeman and his wife were desperate for a child of their own. They'd been refused by several agencies due to Mrs Maltrit's mental health problems. Perdita's child was a reward for the constable's silence.'

The professor sat quietly for a while before she spoke again. 'To my parents, the choice was simple — hospital or the gallows. The hospital provided the perfect opportunity to conceal Perdita's pregnancy so that no questions would be asked about the father and therefore there was no reason to suspect her of killing Rupert's wife. Rupert promised them that it was a good place where she'd be taken care of. As far as they were concerned, she was locked away safely for her own protection and that was all that mattered. They genuinely believed they were doing the right thing.'

'You told us Perdita died in Darkhole Grange, but we haven't been able to find any record of her death.'

Ursula took a deep breath. 'That's because I lied, Inspector. My sister's still alive — if you can call it that.'

Wesley waited for her to continue.

'When Darkhole Grange closed, Perdy was about to be thrown out into the community with no way of dealing with everyday life. What they did to her in that place had destroyed her mind, so I found her a place here and paid a lawyer to make sure everything was OK while I was in the States.'

'Her daughter came to see you here.'

The professor raised her thin grey eyebrows in surprise. 'Was that her? The Ms Crane Mrs Wardle told me about? Crane was my maiden name, but I never suspected she was a relative. It's not an uncommon name.' She took a deep breath. 'I've always been careful to protect my sister. I still fear retribution for what happened, but now I feel I can't lie any longer.'

There was another lengthy silence, and Wesley watched her face as he waited.

'Would you like to see her? Her room's just down the corridor.'

Wesley stared at her, lost for words. For so long he'd been led to believe that Perdita Crane had met her death within the oppressive walls of Darkhole Grange. One thing he hadn't expected was that she'd been nearby all along. Rachel looked equally stunned as she fetched the professor's walking frame before helping her to her feet. She hovered beside the old lady as she made her way slowly to the door, which Wesley leapt forward to open for her, feeling unusually nervous.

Ursula led them down the gloomy passageway. The door at the end was closed, and she reached out to turn the handle. They let her enter the room first, and heard her speaking softly, words of reassurance that they couldn't quite make out. After a brief interval, she beckoned them in.

A frail-looking woman with thinning snow-white hair lay in the large bed, like a tiny bird against the pillows and so thin that Wesley could make out the bones beneath her parchment skin. Her head turned towards him slightly, as though attracted by the movement. Her eyes, so like the professor's, stared blankly, devoid of curiosity; devoid of everything.

'I moved her here under the name Pauline Carter,' Ursula said, almost in a whisper. 'And when I returned to Devon for good, I came to live here with her. She's my sister. I wanted to do my best for her.'

A pair of claw-like hands grasped the sheet as the professor sat on the bed and murmured reassurance into her sister's ear.

After a while, she led them outside, out of Perdita's earshot. Then she looked at Wesley. 'I trust you won't arrest her.'

Wesley saw Rachel watching him, awaiting his reply. After a brief hesitation, he shook his head. 'I don't see what good it would do. She's done her time.'

'Do you think her daughter should be told where she is?' Ursula asked. For the first time, she sounded unsure of herself.

Wesley considered her question for a few moments before he replied. 'Don't forget Rosemary was convinced that you and your parents as good as killed Perdita. She was obsessed with her own version of her mother — your sister. She arranged for your daughter to be kidnapped.'

Ursula nodded. 'And if she'd been able to get to me here, I would have died too, is that right?'

Mrs Wardle obviously hadn't told her about the incident with Tel — which was probably a good thing. There was no point in causing her more worry and pain.

'I assure you I knew nothing of the kind of home Perdy's baby was going to. Neither did my parents. We thought the village policeman was a good man.'

'I think he was. But unfortunately, he died, and his wife . . . '

'I'm a wealthy woman, Inspector, and Rosemary's my niece. I'd like her to have the best lawyers.'

'That's kind of you.'

'Not really. She's family.'

368

60

Rosemary pleaded guilty to conspiracy to murder and Pixie to kidnapping, false imprisonment and to the murder of Charles Maddox. On trial with them was Tel — or Terrance Arbel, to give him his full name. He'd pleaded guilty to murder, but Gerry suspected that his defence barrister would insist that he was vulnerable and under the influence of his manipulative therapist.

After the dramatic events of May, Wesley and Gerry were looking forward to a summer of routine crime: thefts from boats, burglaries of holiday cottages and disputes between late-night revellers that had got out of hand.

Rachel confided that she wasn't looking forward to starting her maternity leave in late July, and Wesley knew he was going to miss her. Only time would tell how much.

He was longing for more time at home after the early starts and late finishes of the past few weeks. Michael was feeling better, and his bout of illness seemed to have tamed his teenage moodiness for the time being. But Wesley wanted things back to normal. It was all most people wanted.

A few weeks after the arrests, he was preparing to go home after a busy Friday afternoon when he received a call from Neil. He'd been so preoccupied with wrapping up the case that he hadn't seen his friend for a while, and he was pleased to see his name on the caller display.

'We're having an open day at the dig tomorrow,' Neil began. 'Just thought I'd let you know. Bring the family. We've got things for the kids.' The line went dead, and Wesley was left staring at the phone. 'Things for the kids' were hardly likely to appeal to Michael — or Amelia for that matter. But Neil, being childless, couldn't understand the subtleties of early adolescence.

However, to his surprise, when he reached home and told Michael, the boy's eyes lit up at the mention of the open day. Wesley suspected he'd always regarded his 'Uncle' Neil as a dashing Indiana Jones type figure, and he had no wish to disillusion him. At least archaeology was a healthy pursuit for a teenage boy.

Pam's mother, Della, had threatened to visit on Saturday morning, which meant the whole family set off for Long Bartonford earlier than they normally would have done in order to avoid her. Della was in the habit of entering the Peterson household like a whirlwind, which was something Wesley and Pam couldn't face after a long week at work.

Della had told Wesley how much he had upset her friend Susan Elwood by revealing the truth about her late father's time at Darkhole Grange. Susan claimed he'd been young, and with the arrogance of youth he might have made a few mistakes, which had been more than made up for by the rest of his blameless medical career. She was sure the police had twisted the facts. Wesley hadn't bothered to argue with Della. From experience, he knew it wasn't worth it.

When they arrived at the dig, they found a lot of people standing around: archaeologists chatting to locals, pointing out features in the trenches, all fenced off in accordance with health-and-safety regulations. Neil was standing beside the ruined wall of the old church, waving his arms enthusiastically as he explained something to an elderly couple.

Once the couple had wandered off and Michael had taken his bored-looking sister to examine the remains of a longhouse, Wesley and Pam headed for the church. As soon as Neil saw them, he raised his arm in greeting.

'Haven't seen you for a while,' he said as soon as they were within earshot.

'I've been busy wrapping up the case.'

'I still can't believe what Tel did. I thought he had a real interest in what we were doing here.' He looked disappointed, as though the betrayal of trust was personal. Then his face brightened. 'Annabel's been a great help. She found the final piece of the jigsaw.'

'You mean about the skeleton — Elena de Judhael?'

'It's not Elena. It's someone called Sister Hawise. A nun. Elena escaped. She was lucky . . . considering. But I suppose if you're the daughter of the lord of the manor, you can get away with murder.'

'Murder?' Pam sounded interested.

'Elena murdered her lover during a quarrel, but her family put it about that he'd been attacked by a local thug. The local powers-that-be knew she was responsible, though, and told her that if she agreed to become an anchoress and shut herself away from the world, no more would be said. It seemed like a neat solution for everyone. Scandal averted. Justice done — in a way. But she couldn't deal with the life, and kept running away, so the parish priest took pity on her and found a willing volunteer from the local convent to take her place. There's no record of what

371

became of Elena.' He paused. 'Or so I thought until yesterday.'

He took a clear plastic bag from his pocket. 'We were leaving the excavation of the main churchyard for the next phase of the dig because we expect to find a lot of human remains, but we did come across some remains buried outside the boundaries of the churchyard. There were several bodies, some with broken necks, buried haphazardly, not what you'd normally find in a Christian graveyard. I think we inadvertently came across a patch of unhallowed ground where felons and suicides were interred.' He paused. 'One of the bodies was female, and she had this ring on her finger.'

Wesley took the bag and examined its contents. A small gold ring set with a blue cabochon stone.

'There's an inscription inside. I examined it with a magnifying glass and it says *Elena et Denyes. Amor vincit omnia* – love conquers all. I think Elena ended up buried in unhallowed ground. Perhaps justice caught up with her eventually — or she hadn't been able to live with what she'd done.'

Wesley handed the bag back to Neil.

'I'd like to do a facial reconstruction — see what she looked like.'

Wesley smiled. He knew what murderers looked like. They looked exactly like everyone else.

★ ★ ★

Professor Ursula Nilsen sat by her sister's bed, holding her frail brown-spotted hand.

Perdita's eyes flickered open and Ursula gave her an uncertain smile.

'I'm sorry, Perdy,' she whispered. 'I never knew what they were going to do to you, I swear. If I had, I would have told the truth. Please forgive me.'

She brought Perdy's parchment hand to her lips and kissed it, remembering how she'd followed her sister to the cliff path, where she'd found her arguing with Heather Maddox, the annoying little dog yapping, joining in the quarrel.

She'd shouted, 'Leave my sister alone,' and lunged forward to stop Rupert's furious wife from attacking Perdita with outstretched fingernails. But as she shoved Heather away, the woman lost her footing and tumbled to the rocks below. Ursula would never forget that moment of frozen, horrified silence when even the dog stopped barking.

Perdita had yelled at Ursula to run. And she had, not stopping until she reached Bartonford Manor, where she'd locked herself in her room for the rest of the afternoon.

Her presence at the scene of the tragedy was never mentioned again. She'd returned to Oxford, and Perdita had never betrayed her part in Heather's death. Perdita's claims that it had been an accident had been greeted with disbelief, but still she'd kept quiet. Ursula had had a brilliant future ahead of her, with everything to lose, so she'd said nothing. She'd made a judgement, and now she feared it was too late for redemption.

As she bent her grey head over her sister's fragile hand, tears in her eyes, she was startled to hear Perdita speak, in a faint, gasping voice that sounded like the rustle of dry leaves. 'Don't cry, Ursy. It's all right. You're my clever sister – and I'm the bad girl.'

Ten minutes later, Ursula dried her tears and shuffled from the room to find Teresa waiting for her in the corridor. Smiling.

Author's Note

According to L. P. Hartley, 'The past is a foreign country; they do things differently there.' This is true in so many ways, and things once considered quite normal would horrify us today.

The initial idea for *The Stone Chamber* came to me while I was attending a writers' conference in Norwich. While I was there, I visited the cell of St Julian, an anchoress born in the fourteenth century who was isolated from the world in a small cell, where she stayed for life. Renowned for her spiritual wisdom, she was the first woman known to have written a book. St Julian was clearly a remarkable woman, but she was far from being the only one who followed this particular calling.

Anchoresses and anchorites were part of the spiritual landscape of the Middle Ages, and many embraced the solitary calling willingly. This is something we'd probably find hard to understand today. We might also find it shocking to learn that they actually had to witness their own funeral mass before being led to a stone cell (usually attached to a parish church), after which a Latin command from the priest or bishop was given and the candidate was sealed into their voluntary prison, never to be seen alive again. Surprisingly, there was no shortage of volunteers, and making the commitment was seen as an honour. Such an existence would not only bring them closer to God, but their prayers were thought to protect the community.

An anchorite's cell still exists in Chester-le-Street

in County Durham; however, my plans to visit it were thwarted by the COVID virus lockdown (something that seemed uncannily appropriate). A folk song about the Chester-le-Street anchorite describes how when the wall of the cell was breached to retrieve his body after his death, he was found in a shallow grave he had dug for himself in the dirt floor. It was indeed customary to bury an anchorite or anchoress inside the cell where they had lived and died.

However, not everyone could endure the life. In fourteenth-century Surrey, an anchoress called Christina Carpenter had a change of heart and was found outside her cell. She not only received penance for her disobedience, but letters exist ordering that she should be 'kept more securely', and the only small doorway into her cell was replaced by a solid wall.

There were anchoresses and anchorites all over the country, and several are recorded in Devon. One recluse lived in a cell at Axminster; Alice Bernard was enclosed in a cell at St Leonard's in Exeter in 1397; while another Alice was based at Pilton near Barnstaple. In the mid fifteenth century, Margaret Holt was an anchoress at Dodbrooke, Kingsbridge.

But it isn't only the historical aspect of a story that needs to be researched. When I began examining more recent events, I made some disturbing discoveries about the horrifying way in which some women were put away in asylums for the 'crime' of getting pregnant out of wedlock. I'd known that this happened during the Victorian period, when lunatic asylums were often used to get rid of inconvenient family members, but I was shocked to discover that the 1913 Mental Deficiency Act allowed unmarried mothers to be categorised as 'moral imbeciles' and confined in asylums. The act wasn't repealed till as late as 1959. Tragically, some of these women were still found to be incarcerated when the asylums closed in the late twentieth century.

Researching this book has taken me to some surprising places, but one thing I didn't need to research was Wesley's fear of confined spaces, because this is something I've shared with him for as long as I can remember. To look on the bright side, at least my avoidance of lifts has meant that I've had plenty of exercise going up and down stairs over the years. However, my claustrophobia means that if I'd lived in the Middle Ages, I certainly wouldn't have been one of those who volunteered for life as an anchoress!

THE HOUSE OF THE HANGED WOMAN

Kate Ellis

Derbyshire, 1921. When an MP goes missing in a Derbyshire village, Scotland Yard detective Albert Lincoln is sent to investigate. A grim discovery has been made in a cave next to an ancient stone circle: the naked body of a middle-aged man mutilated beyond recognition. The local police assume it is the missing politician but when Albert arrives in Wenfield he begins to have doubts. Two years earlier he conducted another traumatic murder investigation in the same village and he finds reminders of a particularly personal tragedy as he tries to help a vicar's widow who claims her husband was murdered. Then there is another murder in Wenfield. Could there be a link between all of Albert's cases?

THE BOY WHO LIVED WITH THE DEAD

Kate Ellis

It is 1920 and DI Albert Lincoln is still reeling from the disturbing events of the previous year. Before the War, he'd investigated the murder of a child in a Cheshire village, and now a woman has been murdered there and another child is missing. With the help of the village schoolmistress, Albert closes in on the original pre-war killer. He soon realises the only witness is in grave danger, possibly from somebody he calls 'the Shadow Man'. And as he discovers more about the victims he finds information that might bring him a step closer to solving a mystery of his own — the whereabouts of his son.

THE BURIAL CIRCLE

Kate Ellis

On a stormy night in December, a tree is blown down on an isolated Devon farm. A rucksack is found caught amongst the roots — and next to it is a human skeleton. The discoveries revive memories for DI Wesley Peterson: a young hitchhiker who went missing twelve years ago was last seen carrying a similar backpack. Suddenly a half-forgotten cold case has turned into a murder investigation. Meanwhile, in the nearby village of Petherham, a famous TV psychic is found dead in suspicious circumstances whilst staying at a local guesthouse. Could a string of mysterious deaths in Petherham over a hundred years ago be connected to the recent killings? As Wesley digs deeper, it seems the dark whisperings of a Burial Circle in the village might not be merely legend after all . . .